La Vyne

May you be inspired and
entertained!

Glen Classen
May 25/15

EVANSING

Heart Of The Irish Kingdom

CHAPTER I

In the late 11th century there lived in Ireland a young man who started life in a very difficult environment. He was living in a district in what is now County Meath in the Kingdom of Elfereth. This kingdom existed in a constant state of war with the neighboring Kingdom of Tissus. The young fellow was known as Edwin the Younger. His namesake was an uncle named Edwin who had had a reputation as a hard man full of revenge and great bitterness. This had unfortunate ramifications for the younger Edwin. The elder Edwin had now been dead for several years, having suffered the inevitable ending to his life. His final showdown was when he led a raiding party to a village just across the border in Tissus. The locals captured him and being well aware of his reputation as a ruthless raider, dealt with him in a most brutal, vengeful manner. They pulled his arms out of their sockets by putting him between two horses. They then stabbed him to death with a red hot poker. His screams were a most blood curdling pitch that gave the children in the village nightmares for months to come.

The reputation of the elder Edwin was so acrimonious it left a perpetual pall around Edwin wherever he went. This caused people to treat him with a combination of fear and disdain. At first this resulted in him responding with an unfriendly and even harsh way with people. This tended to create even more negative events for him because now he was creating his own history of conflict with people, which further deepened their perceptions of him being like his uncle. The association with his uncle was closer than normal because Edwin's own parents had died in a raid from Tissus when he was an infant. Edwin's mother was his uncle's youngest sister and so the elder Edwin took on the responsibility of raising his sister's child.

While the younger Edwin was grateful for being adopted by his uncle it was a mixed blessing. The elder Edwin was as you would guess a hard task-master. Love and affection were in short supply in his household. His aunt died of a broken heart when Edwin was only four years old. With no other children in the home and just his uncle it made for meager pickings as far as family presence. The other relatives of his mother and those of his father lived almost a two hour walk away, as his uncle wanted his own space. The only times Edwin saw his relatives was when his uncle went away on raiding parties. The rest of the time he was frequently alone. When he turned eight his uncle considered him old enough to stay by himself for up to a number of days at a time. Sometimes he would walk the several miles to his relatives or to other neighbors just to break the painful loneliness. He had trouble connecting because he just didn't fit in. So it wasn't always pleasant to try and be relational with the other kids and adults. This led to Edwin being more and more a loner and becoming more and more self-reliant in his day to day life. When he turned fourteen, his uncle took him on his first raiding party. He was given a sword, some rudimentary training in its use, and told to go at it. Raiding and war seemed to agree with the younger Edwin as it became an outlet for expressing his pain of life.

Edwin's prime means of survival and providing for himself was from booty from the raids. He had little inclination to engage in other activities such as farming or some sort of enterprise which created value for the community. He did hunt however and it became another area where he could excel and provide for himself. By the time Edwin was sixteen he had become in many ways like his uncle. Shortly later his uncle died. Now at age twenty Edwin started to get nightmares of what his future was going to be if he continued on his present path. He would wake up with cold sweats as he experienced the desperation of a life dominated by pain, and the desire to get revenge because of the pain.

One morning after a particularly fitful night's sleep and almost non-stop nightmares, Edwin decided he needed to do something different. As hard as it was to imagine life being any different or somehow better than now, he determined he had to at least try.

Edwin then recalled, not only were there nightmares but also pleasant dreams. But he couldn't remember any details. As he considered this, the thought came to him to go to the local monastery. He didn't have any connection with the monks or the people of the Church as his uncle had said it was a waste of time. However, something inside said he had a chance for change by going to the monastery and asking for help. He knew the priests were called Father and deep inside he wanted a father. Someone who would nurture and nourish the little boy inside him. He desperately wanted to be loved and even celebrated just for being alive. These thoughts and feelings were very strange for Edwin; he didn't know where they came from. But he decided to go with them and see what happened. It couldn't be any worse than where he was now, which felt desperate and painful. He knew there had to be something better than this. His only other option was to keep going on more and more dangerous raiding parties until he got killed or captured. The latter would probably end up with him suffering an ignominious death like his uncle.

As Edwin lay on his bed of straw contemplating these things, a Grey thrush with brown specks on its body came into his hut. The bird seemed not to be afraid at all of Edwin but rather curious and even friendly in his demeanor. Fascinated, Edwin watched the bird and threw it some bread crumbs. The bird pecked away at the bread and chirped in gratitude. Something in Edwin switched on as he experienced warmth in his heart he had not felt for a long, long time. An emotional shift occurred inside him as he realized his act of kindness toward the bird had done something in him as well. He threw the bird some more crumbs and again the bird chirped a happy song of gratitude. The warmth in Edwin's heart became more intense. It startled him for it was so foreign. Then the bird came closer to Edwin. As Edwin slowly extended out his right forefinger to the bird, the bird stopped and watched in silence. Then it hopped several times and landed on the outstretched symbol of friendship. Edwin had made a friend, his first true friend in many years. Edwin noticed hot tears rolling down his cheeks. This was strange, for warriors do not cry and Edwin was in many ways a consummate warrior. The bird remained on his finger with his head bent up looking into Edwin's eyes. He seemed to relax and quite enjoyed being on this unusual perch. Then something unexpected happened. The bird spoke. Or at least it seemed he spoke. Edwin started to get thoughts in his head as though the bird was indeed communicating with his mind. Now in that time of Irish history there were often tales of spirits inhabiting animals and communicating to people. This was different though; this bird was ''talking'' to Edwin not to someone else. It didn't seem to be a spirit and certainly not a malevolent spirit.

"How would he know the difference?" Edwin thought to himself.

He didn't except he had this inner knowing.

The bird was telling him his thoughts of going to the monastery were good and he was to ask for a particular monk called Percival. As Edwin pondered what was going on he started to experience something else he had not felt before. He believed it must be what is known as hope.

As he considered this new hope growing in him, the bird seemed to say goodbye and flitted away through the opening in the door. At first Edwin felt a twinge of regret about the abrupt departure. However, he knew what had happened was good, indeed very good.

Edwin gathered his paltry belongings, for raiding never seemed to bring enough after divvying up with everybody in the party. The chieftains got the lion's share even when they didn't accompany the raid. Edwin walked out of his hut without looking back and with a sense he wouldn't be coming back. Something inside Edwin had changed and he wasn't going to live the old life anymore. He had a growing sense of anticipation of a new life of love and adventure. Not that raiding wasn't an adventure, but a newly awakened part of him craved new adventures which didn't always require killing people. Not to say Edwin was now a pacifist. The Ireland he lived in required its men to be warriors. There was no other way to be a man except for those strange monks and priests, which now Edwin was going to visit. The nearest monastery was almost fifteen miles away. He went with a spring in his step and an expectancy of something very different but good awaiting for him there.

Edwin started on his way with the wind behind him and the sun in his face. It was one of those rare Irish mornings which had more sun than cloud. It seemed to Edwin like even the weather was cheering him on in his decision to change his life. After walking for four miles he came by the house of one of his mother's brothers. Two of his cousins saw him and yelled at him to stay away because he wasn't wanted. Edwin grinned at them and kept walking. A couple of miles later he came by the home of a man who'd had a bitter feud with Edwin's uncle. He swore at Edwin and told him he'd kill him if he had the chance. Uncharacteristically Edwin wished him a top'o the morning and briskly kept walking.

Edwin thought to himself, "What has happened to me?"

It all seemed so strange. Yesterday he would have been enraged towards his cousins and at the least would have yelled some disparaging words back. And with the man who threatened to kill him, if that had happened yesterday he would have challenged him to sword play with the full intent of killing him.

Edwin took out his sword and looked at it. This was his symbol of manhood and sense of self-value. He had become renowned for his ability to handle a sword with deadly results. He put it back in his scabbard wondering when he might use it again.

Up ahead he could see two men standing by the side of the road. They looked menacing. One of them stepped in front of Edwin and asked him if he had some change to spare. Edwin reached into his bag and brought out a couple of coins. The man then grabbed for the bag while the other man pulled out a knife and lunged at Edwin. Dropping the bag, Edwin grabbed the first man and pulled him around in time for the robber to be stabbed in the back by his accomplice. Down he went. Then Edwin pulled out his sword and skewered the second man through his heart. Both men lay at his feet dead or dying. Spinning around, Edwin looked to see if there were any other robber accomplices. None sprang forth. This surprised him because it was uncommon for only two men to take on one armed man, especially someone known as a mighty warrior like Edwin. Neither of them looked familiar so they weren't locals who would have known of his reputation. While picking up his money bag he noticed the first man had a tattoo on his arm showing him to be from Tissus. Edwin mulled this over and came to the one conclusion which could be made. These men must have been scouting for a raiding party, probably only minutes away. Unfortunately for them they must have believed their own lies that the men of Elfereth couldn't fight. The nearest clump of huts was about three quarters of a mile away. It was just north of the road he'd come on. Some of the people there were kinsmen. He needed to warn them and get the men assembled for battle.

Running with all his might he cut through a small forest following a well-worn path used by the women of the area to fetch water from the nearby stream. When he was almost to the huts he met one of the young ladies on her way to the stream. He stopped her, telling her of the danger and taking her hand continued to run toward the huts. Upon his arrival at the village, he informed the chieftain and his two sons what had transpired. The two sons went out to the fields to bring the rest of the people in for assembly. In the meantime other men in the camp also came to where Edwin and the chieftain were standing. Even though he was kin to some of them, the people of this camp were not too friendly with Edwin. They did have a grudging respect for his abilities as a warrior which they appreciated when he saved their lives on raids. Funny people, you would think that would win them over, but the people in these parts were strange, quick to hate and slow to forgive. However, one person did ask how it came to be that Edwin was in these parts in the first place. Edwin wasn't sure at first how to respond. They would never understand why he would want to go to a monastery. So he said he felt like walking on such a beautiful day and had walked an extra long distance.

This seemed to satisfy the questioner, but he looked at Edwin with a look of not knowing for sure whether to believe him. The man did not press the issue for now the more important matter was to get organized for the defense of their camp. First the discussion was whether to stay there in the camp or whether to leave en masse leaving only a few men behind. It was decided the wisest course would be to abandon the camp and have the women, children and several of the men, including the oldest, go to a nearby hilltop surrounded by a thick wood. Then the rest of the men would head back to the road and see if they could pick up the trail of the men from Tissus.

The chieftain did a surprising thing, which was not without controversy, but his word was law. He appointed Edwin as his second in command. This was a position traditionally held by one of his sons or some other valiant experienced warrior in the camp. This both surprised and pleased Edwin at this acknowledgment of his skill and bravery as a warrior. As they walked forward Edwin and the chieftain started to discuss strategy. They decided the force should stay together. Also they determined the most likely trail to be used by the men of Tissus. The path lay not more than fifty yards from the stream which was their chief water supply. Just prior to the road the men stopped to listen for sounds of a raiding party. They could see where the men were killed by Edwin had lain, but the bodies themselves were gone. This created alarm because it meant the raiding party must be quite close or else had moved on down the road further west. Two of the best scouts went out and found signs indicating the party was a large one and headed west.

Edwin realized they were proceeding in the direction from where he had come and the people he had seen earlier were now likely in great danger. There was also another assembly of huts south of the road several miles away.

The chieftain started to talk over with some of the clan's leaders whether it was wise to risk their lives for people down the road. They would be against a party far superior to them in size. Edwin interrupted them and said it was the only right thing to do. He encouraged them to consider that next time it may be their turn to have the people down the road help them. Several of the men told Edwin to mind his own business. The chieftain said his first priority was the safety of his village. He did not think it wise to endanger his people when the odds were so against them. Edwin argued the party could be aware of their little settlement and come for them on the way back. The chieftain said they would prepare a defense along the path toward the huts. There existed an ideal spot for them to ambush the invaders. They could hold a spirited defense even against a vastly superior force. Further imploring was useless. Edwin decided he could not stay with them. He left choosing to take a path through the forest, which ran more or less parallel to the road headed west.

At first Edwin couldn't hear anything, but after about two hundred yards he started to hear the rearguard of the Tissus party. The raiders were unusually loud, which indicated they must be extremely confident, even to the point of being overconfident. Was it because they had an extra-large number of men or was it because of something else which gave them an advantage?

As he continued along, the sounds became more distinct even to the point of hearing the conversation between the warriors. He repeatedly heard the name, Alwyn, mentioned with a sense of: we have them now.

Edwin thought to himself, "Alwyn, hmm, isn't that the Druid priest from the Kingdom of Randar? What would he be doing with the men from Tissus?"

The reputation of Alwyn was bigger than life because the renown of his power as a purveyor of evil Druid magic was widespread. In predominantly Christian Ireland of the eleventh century, there were few people still carrying on Druid magic and practices. Alwyn however was a big exception. Fiercely defiant of the Church he practiced magic on behalf of whoever would hire him. Though few people would openly acknowledge their belief in Druid magic, Alwyn had a steady demand for his services. The people of Ireland still had a profound respect for the old ways. Much of their spirituality consisted of a mixture of Christendom and the old ways, including Druidism.

Edwin continued to gain ground and wondered how he could make a difference with such a large force. A thought came to him. He had his bow and a full quiver of arrows with him. With one arrow he could take out Alwyn and the whole Tissus base of confidence would be gone. With this insight he started moving faster and faster until he got alongside the mid part of the war party. He inched along the ground until he could see the group passing by him about fifty yards away. There he noticed the one who must be Alwyn for he was all done up in Druid fashion and looked very confident.

He would have to get ahead of him and find a place for a clear shot. Ideally it would also enable him to make his escape for there would be a horde of Tissus warriors looking for him. Another forty yards ahead Edwin found the place which looked like it would fit both requirements. Again he inched himself along for a clear sight line of Alwyn. Here he came looking sure of himself. With great care and self-assurance Edwin drew back his bow and aimed at Alwyn's heart. Then with deadly accuracy the arrow went straight into Alwyn's heart. He looked stunned and even had a look of disbelief, but nonetheless he went down and stayed down, very still.

The Tissus party around Alwyn stopped abruptly and stared at the demise of their hopes to rout the people of Elfereth. Then a release of wild rage went out among the warriors as they started to look around for who could have done this.

CHAPTER 2

Edwin stayed low along the ground until he was sure he could get up without being seen. Then he ran as fast as the thick terrain of bush would let him, not totally certain where he was heading. The Tissus were more or less south of him and he wanted to make as much distance north of them. Their tracking dogs barking sounded close behind him. They probably had caught his scent for they were getting more and more excited.

A sudden shadow came upon Edwin. Then a huge black bird swooped down and picked him up and flew away. Resisting the initial urge to panic, Edwin decided to calmly go with being a passenger in the talons of this massive bird. The bird had been careful to hold Edwin in a way which did not injure him. Indeed he felt rather comfortable.

Gliding along was actually quite refreshing. He decided this was a good thing and therefore he would enjoy the experience. In the distance was a castle on a hill. Bathed in the sunlight the castle looked a fiery red. He had no idea whose it was or what it was called, for he was now in territory quite foreign to him. He knew he was some distance south of where he had been. He had been able to see the Tissus below him scurrying around looking for him. He chuckled to himself that they were looking in the wrong place. He thought some of them would surely see him for this bird could not be missed. In the distance he had also seen the huts of the people who wouldn't help. He noticed a large contingent of the Tissus headed that way. It looked like fortune had dictated they were going to experience the fruit of their cowardice and self-concern.

The bird started to drop in height as it came to the castle on the hill. When it was over the walls it gently dropped to the ground letting Edwin touch the earth once again. Then as though a flash of light had occurred, the once huge bird with wings at least twenty feet across was now of normal size.

Edwin thought, "Uh oh I must have fallen into the hands of someone with powerful magic. Maybe it's going to be retribution for me killing Alwyn."

A beautiful young girl of around eighteen came out into the courtyard. She wore a green robe richly brocaded with gold designs indicating she was of noble birth. She had long blondish red hair with brilliant blue eyes which seemed to sparkle in the sun. He had never seen such brightness in a pair of eyes.

As the young girl looked at Edwin for the first time, she saw a young man who radiated energy and quickness. He was tall, medium build with reddish brown hair. Being the warrior he had some visible scars. The most noticeable one appeared about two inches on his left cheek. As she discovered later this was the reminder of being grazed with a sword tip. She also noticed his green eyes had a hardness about them. Fortunately she would see them soften over the next several weeks.

She looked at him kindly and asked if he had had a pleasant journey.

He looked at her with some incredulity as she asked him the question as though he had come the usual way. He became aware of feeling a little shy of this most noble creature who seemed to have such an easy way about her.

"Yes, it was a most enjoyable albeit somewhat unexpected means of transport. Now can you tell me why I am here? And if I choose can I leave? And oh by the way where am I?"

She replied, "You are at the castle of my father, King Erith, in the Kingdom of Evansing. You are here because we have need of you. And can you leave? That is something my father will decide."

As he considered her response the gates at the south end of the courtyard opened and in came a man who must be her father the King. He was surrounded by several of his men and he looked rather serious as he walked toward Edwin.

He brightened as he came within ten feet and extended his arms in greeting. He clasped Edwin's hands and said he was happy that he had made it safely to his castle. He stated he knew it must seem confusing to him right now, but things would soon become clear.

Then Edwin asked him, "Why have you brought me here?"

"Notice of you came to us that you were a great warrior and by you coming to our kingdom we would be able to enhance our warrior capacity. You are a most unusual young man to the degree you have demonstrated personal courage and resolve. Now that you have experienced a personal shift in your desire to grow and be a person of nobility, we have need of your influence. You can create a class of noble warriors in my kingdom."

"Can I leave if I want to?"

The King narrowed his eyes, paused for a moment and then thoughtfully said to him, "When you realize all the good things I have planned for you, I am sure you will want to stay."

"You may well have many potential pleasantries. However, I am on a mission to go to the monastery nearest my home and inquire of the monk called Percival."

"What if we bring Percival to you here?"

Edwin looked at him sort of surprised but not totally. He was starting to believe almost anything was possible for this king, and yet he wanted Edwin's assistance. It seemed so strange. He pondered the possibility of getting whatever rewards had been planned for him and fulfilling a deep desire to connect with Percival. The latter desire surprised him with how deep it was. He knew it would be the only way he would stay.

"Ok if you can bring Percival to me I will stay."

The King smiled and said, "Good you will not be disappointed with your choice."

"So what will be done for me to stay here and help you?"

"Oh so that is not of total disinterest to you young man"

"Well let's see where do we begin? First you will have your own fine home within the castle walls. It is a suite of four spacious rooms overlooking the south wall, which gives you exposure to the sun and a rich view of the countryside. You will have a servant assigned to you to look after whatever chores you need attending. You will eat at my table so you will not lack for good quality food. I will give you one piece of gold for every fortnight you stay with us. Also as a special incentive if you should stay with us for at least three months, I will give you my daughter's hand in marriage."

Edwin quickly looked at the girl who had greeted him. She looked back at him with a smile. "Is this the daughter you are referring to?"

"Yes," said the King noting how Edwin's eyes lit up as he looked at his daughter.

Edwin looked back at the daughter and asked her what her name was.

"My name is Greer," she replied demurely.

"Is this something you would feel good about agreeing to even though you do not know me?"

"When I heard about you I knew you were the kind of man I could love. Since I have seen you here it has only strengthened my original thoughts about you. My heart says yes."

"How can any of you know already the changes that went on this morning? Who would have told you even about my being a warrior let alone a noble one?"

Greer responded in a bubbly tone, "My father has friends throughout Ireland and some of them have rather unusual abilities and powers. The bird which brought you here, is a small example of what is available to my father."

"Then why would you still need my assistance?"

"You are special. You bring an element which enables everything else to run at a much higher level of authority and power. Consequently you are a missing ingredient in my father's desire to affect much good through-out Ireland."

"What do you mean affect much good?"

"My father has a vision to see Ireland united and prosperous filled with noble warriors doing great exploits that transform our Isle."

Edwin looked at her with great surprise.

He thought to himself, "This is very strange, I have never heard of such a plan before."

Turning to the King he asked him, "Why do you want to do this? What ever inspired you to want to do this? Is it not for plunder and to obtain captives that you would want to do such a thing?"

The King looked at him with a serious look, but a smile started to creep up on his face.

"Let's discuss it over dinner. You must be hungry and I know I am."

The King led the way to the dining hall. Edwin walked with Greer at the back of the procession. Edwin was starting to think he had died and gone to heaven for this Greer was indeed a most delightful young lady. He recalled where he started from this morning to where he was now. It was a huge increase far exceeding anything he could ever have imagined possible. He knew he could do it. In other words he knew he could transform the King's men into an indomitable force of valiant warriors. First he had to make sure he wasn't actually helping someone who would be a tyrant over all of Ireland. Having that concern was foreign to Edwin. It wouldn't even have dawned on him yesterday that it would be an issue for concern. The only thing he could figure is something changed in him in the course of having those dreams last night. He noted how Greer radiated such warmth toward him and even pleasure at his behavior with her and her father. She obviously appreciated this new nobler side of him.

At the hall the King had Edwin sit at his right hand and Greer sat next to Edwin. The King had only one child and was a recent widower. He had a sadness, which still came up periodically in his eyes, as he had been very close to his wife. The more Edwin observed the King the less concerned he became about his intentions concerning Ireland. The King radiated sincerity and a good heartedness, which could not be feigned.

The King broached the subject himself about why he wanted to unite Ireland into one nation, which would together prosper and live in peace.

"Presently we have a land which spends much of its time and resources in incessant fighting leading to nothing except more warfare. We need a land where people feel safe and secure. If they don't there will be no opportunity to develop the land and its people to the level possible. No one will ever think in terms of achieving things which will impact multiple generations after them. As it stands now all anyone is concerned with is survival day by day or month by month. It is time to advance our land into a people of nobility who can build a civilization we will all be proud of."

"For this to work there must be a growing sense of identity that we are no longer citizens of this kingdom or that kingdom. Rather we are all citizens of the great nation of Ireland. We all share a common Celtic heritage and by the Grace of God we can start to live together in cooperation and peace. There will be growing trade and commerce amongst the various communities of Ireland, which will benefit us all."

Edwin ventured a question, "So how do you intend to accomplish this?"

"It will require negotiating with each kingdom the merits of working in harmony. I am going to start with our immediate neighbors. If they resist then we will have to use force. This is where you come in."

Edwin looked at the King for a moment and then said, "When do you start with your negotiations?"

"Next week I go to see the King of Nerland. It is about a one and one-half days journey from here. I would like you to come along for I believe it will help you comprehend what this is all about. Besides I want you to understand and contribute to all the parts necessary to make this a success. I have high expectations about your ability and the giftings you have been given."

"Giftings?" Edwin answered quizzically.

"Yes, in the course of your dreams last night you were massively gifted with qualities you don't even realize yet, but they are going to be increasingly evident and realized over these next few weeks. They are especially tailored for the very things I need for this pursuit of Irish unity."

"How did you know about my dreams last night?"

"Oh there are many things you will learn about my powers and resources. If all I had to work with was the normal physical realm then I wouldn't even bother. It would be too hard and probably impossible without tremendous bloodshed. My objective is to minimize the bloodshed and destruction, which will inevitably be a part of the process."

The King continued, "As a result of being under my protection you will begin to experience new things from the spiritual realm. New enablements will come to you when you need them and in the way you need them."

"Edwin, let me be frank with you; I want to groom you to be king."

Edwin looked at him dumbfounded.

He started to pinch his arms to make sure he was awake and then looked at the King, "Sire, this is a most unexpected turn of events. This morning all I knew was I needed to see Percival and now you say you want to groom me to be king. I can't even read."

"Not a problem. I'm sure one of the things Percival will do is teach you to read."

"Was Percival your idea?" asked Edwin as a new realization started to come upon him.

"Yes, it was. The bird which spoke to you, was sent by me. Percival is a most noble man who will change your life."

Edwin's head started swimming with a jumble of thoughts.

"Am I really awake? Is this really happening? How could this be? How could I wake up a destitute societal pariah and now this very night be accorded blessings people would kill for?"

The King and Greer looked at Edwin with concern for he had a most pained expression on his face.

Greer asked, "Are you alright? What is ailing you?"

Edwin looked at her and then to the King he said, "May I go to my quarters? I need to gather my thoughts because there is too much going on. I need some time alone and I am also very tired."

The King responded, "But of course."

Then he signaled to one of the servants to bring Edwin to the quarters designated for him.

Edwin expressed his parting thanks for the meal and wished the King and his daughter a pleasant rest. As he followed the servant he wondered where the new gentility about wishing them a pleasant rest came from. Ohhh! It was all so strange and yet all so delightful. As this latter thought came to him Edwin started to whistle and even skip a little for things were very good. Or at least they appeared to be. That thought sobered him up a bit.

"Hmmm," he said to himself, "there has to be more to this than what I am seeing."

Then he thought about the daunting challenge to unite Ireland. At first this caused him some fear. This greatly distressed him because Edwin did not like to experience fear. Then he felt an excitement about being part of greatness. The plan to unite Ireland was indeed a plan worthy of his life. This thought startled him because it was another idea so foreign to the old Edwin.

He shook his head and muttered to himself, "It is all so strange, so strange."

The servant stopped and opened a door to the suite Edwin was to occupy. Edwin was aghast at how richly appointed and spacious the room was. Then he went into the other rooms and they were all like the first in being spacious and richly furnished and decorated. He had never seen such living quarters in his life. Of course he had never been in a king's castle before. Even so Edwin had a strong feeling this was not typical for the average king in Ireland. King Erith was a rather unusual individual with great wealth.

Edwin came out of his thoughts when he noticed the servant standing there. He looked at him and thanked him for bringing him to his quarters. The servant gave him a look half of surprise and half of shock that he would be thanked for doing what was simply his duty.

"You are welcome, sir. There is no need to thank me for I am being assigned to you as your personal servant. My name is Jaffa. I will be staying in the room the next door down the hall on this side. I will be available to you at anytime and anywhere."

"What will I get you to do?"

"That, sir, is for you to decide. Breakfast is an hour after sunrise. Would it be right for me to come at sunrise and help you dress?"

"Help me dress??? Certainly I know how to dress by this time in my life."

"Yes, sir, I'm sure you do, but there are new clothes for you to wear. I have been instructed to make you familiar with them and assist in whatever way I can."

"Okay sure why not," replied Edwin as he wanted Jaffa to leave. "I would like to be alone now please."

Jaffa replied, "Of course, sir. Have a pleasant evening and sleep well."

"Thank you, Jaffa, may you as well."

Both were surprised by the degree of civility between the two of them. For Edwin this was because this kind of behavior was so foreign to him. The nature of the interaction was new for Jaffa because people don't typically talk that way to servants. Although he did recall Greer always had a gracious way with the servants and as far as that goes so did the King. Most of the people for whom he performed duties were not so gracious. He would like working with this pleasant young man who appeared to have great favor with the King and the Princess.

Alone in his new quarters Edwin sat down and mulled over the day's events.

Everything had been a test; it had started when he decided to respond to the bird and go seek Percival. Also the decision he had made to help the villagers and his subsequent determination to head off the men from Tissus. As well Edwin recalled his way of responding to the King and his daughter, and even how he responded to the servant. Everything had been a test. As far as he could tell he had passed. The curious thing was that what enabled him to pass had not been a part of who he was the day before. Again, Edwin had this feeling of being almost overwhelmed at the prospect of what had happened today.

"How could it be?" he thought to himself.

The stress of all the day's events became evident as he felt rather weary. He walked to his new bed undressing as he went and crawled between the covers. It felt so good.

"I could get used to this new life," he thought as he fell asleep.

CHAPTER 3

Right after sunrise there was a knock on the door. It didn't wake Edwin for he had already been roused by the rooster, which crowed at the breaking of dawn. He arose, put on his pants and went to the door to let in Jaffa.

"Good morning, Jaffa."

"Good morning, sir. Did you sleep well?"

"Yes, I did. I slept well. It is a comfortable bed and I was very tired."

"Did you sleep well, Jaffa?"

"Yes, I did, sir. Thank you for asking."

Jaffa then went to a closet full of clothes and started to pull out several different sets of clothing for Edwin to consider this day.

Edwin looked closely at what was being presented to him. He noted the material was exceptionally fine. Indeed any one of these outfits would be grand. He settled on a bright green outfit because for him it was a day of new life and green seemed the only way to celebrate it.

Before he could start dressing, Jaffa asked if he could wash his upper body.

Edwin looked at him with a blank look.

"Wash my upper body? Whatever for?"

"Well, sir, if you will pardon my frankness, you stink."

Edwin laughed at this admission. "Well then I have stunk for a long time and never realized it. So did all the people I knew back in Elfereth."

Jaffa asked Edwin if he would come with him to the room, which had a large bucket of water in it. He told him the bucket was for washing. He grabbed a cloth and rubbed in it some sweet smelling herbs and started to wash down Edwin's body. After five minutes he was done. Edwin smelled himself and was amazed at the difference. Jaffa told him it would be good for him to wash the rest of himself later on when he had the chance.

Then Edwin put on the green outfit he had selected and they walked out to the dining hall. The King and Greer were already seated and breakfast was about to be served.

"Good morning, Sire! Good morning, Your Highness!"

"Good morning, Edwin," they both chimed in.

They exchanged pleasantries and enquiries about each others rest. Edwin sat down between the King and Greer. He was feeling WELL!

The first course of roasted lamb and potatoes came out. Edwin looked wide-eye at having such a scrumptious course first thing in the morning. For him to have lamb was a treat. A servant also came by and poured a glass of mead for Edwin. Today there were about thirty people dining with the King. These were members of the royal family, his various government administrators, and his senior military men. There was also a person Edwin much wanted to meet.

"Edwin," the King said while motioning to the man next to him, "please meet a very good friend of mine and soon to be a very good friend of yours. This is Percival."

Edwin stood up and came to greet Percival. The two men warmly embraced as though they had known each other for years and had now met each other again after a long absence. Then they stood back and looked at each other.

Percival was a man of graying hair in his early fifties, with several warts on his right cheek, which made him look distinguished rather than ugly.

Edwin said, "When do we start?"

"Today after breakfast."

"I can't wait," replied Edwin.

Greer laughed and said, "Surely you have met before." Both men said no they hadn't, but they knew they were kindred spirits. Even though

Percival was thirty years or so Edwin's senior, they had this sense of uncanny connection.

During breakfast Greer primarily talked with Edwin, and the King mainly talked with Percival.

Greer, looking with admiration at Edwin, said he could call her Greer when they were one on one. However, she appreciated his addressing her in accordance with protocol when he had arrived this morning for breakfast.

Then she said with a mischievous grin, "Oh you smell so nice this morning, and you look dashing and full of life in your new outfit."

In turn Edwin replied, "Yes, Jaffa was a great help to me. You know, sometimes you don't know what you don't know until someone opens your eyes and nose," he said with a hearty laugh.

"Wow did I laugh like that? I never laugh like that. Truly there are amazing things happening to me. I must say I like them."

Greer with an admiring look said, "I much like them as well," ending with a most delightful smile.

Edwin could feel himself starting to feel things he had never felt before. This girl was indeed someone he was looking forward to getting to know a lot better.

Edwin was advised after he had spent the morning with Percival he would be having a private lunch with the King, Percival, some of the King's relatives, and several of the chief government and military men. The purpose was to get acquainted and to start planning specific strategy and tactics for the meeting with the King of Nerland.

Edwin and Percival left together to go to Edwin's quarters. As they walked they talked about Edwin's experiences the day before. Percival had already been briefed on a lot of it and had been expecting Edwin's arrival at the monastery. The arrival of the Tissus and the unexpected turn of events involving Edwin had necessitated drastic last minute decisions to ensure his safety and arrival at Evansing castle.

The original plan was for Percival and Edwin to stay at the monastery for a month or so and then come to this castle. As it turned out this was a far better turn of events. It would accelerate the education of Edwin in the new affairs of state, as he would now be in on the ground floor with the first round of negotiations.

Percival already knew a lot of Edwin's history, but he did ask questions about different parts of Edwin's childhood, his parents and of course about his uncle.

As Edwin responded to the questions certain things started to create emotional responses, which caused him great discomfort. Some of it even threatened to make him cry. This would never do because any warrior worth his salt never cried no matter how painful things were. It was most disturbing to Edwin. He had not felt these sorts of feelings nor recalled these sorts of memories for many years, or at least many for a young man of only twenty. After his aunt died, something inside him also died, for she had been his one respite of kindness. Unbeknownst to him a shell over his heart had been formed and locked firmly in place. All of this Percival had had some awareness and confirmed it in the course of their conversation.

Percival was the epitome of grace in the way he related to Edwin. He had a comforting fatherly way about him, which nurtured the soul and spirit of Edwin. It was as though Edwin had been waiting for someone like Percival all his life. He was glad he now had the opportunity to connect with someone of the caliber of Percival. Not only did they talk about Edwin, but also Edwin was able to ask Percival about himself and why he became a monk.

Percival as it turns out was quite a roustabout in his early years. He had been a warrior with a notorious chieftain in the west of Ireland. The chieftain was known for being cruel and ruthless in his conquests. Percival had been his commanding officer and had initiated many atrocities in his own right. One night twelve years ago, he got separated from his men and was on the wrong end of a chase. Over twenty men were howling for revenge as they chased the man who had brought them much pain during the past three years.

A man on a white horse appeared just in front of him. He motioned to Percival to jump on. The horse leaped to an effortless gallop through a torturous terrain while Percival hung on for dear life. After about an hour they had traveled about thirty miles and were now several miles inside friendly territory. This was of course impossible by normal horse travel.

The rider said this was as far as he would take him. After landing on the ground the horse and rider rode away without a further word. Percival knew he would never again conduct war the way he had done it before. After a while he was known for his generosity with the enemy. This led to disputes with his chieftain and other commanders who preferred the previous way of warring. One night undetected he left his army camp and headed east until he came to the monastery. There he had spent the past ten years.

Edwin drank all this in and then said to Percival, "How did you feel when you were on the horse?"

"Serenity unlike any I had ever experienced before. Indeed I kept thinking over and over about how I felt so much peace. It stayed with me for months and then started to wane. Finally I JUST KNEW I had to leave everything and find that peace.

Jaffa came to the door to let the two men know it was now time for the lunch with the King and others. Both men were surprised to realize the time had flown by. In some ways it seemed like they had only spoken for moments and had only touched the surface on a few things. On the other hand they knew they had created new links of friendship, which would benefit them both. Percival sensed that in Edwin there was a sensitive soul waiting to be accepted and loved.

Instead of eating in the dining hall they now were meeting in a much smaller side room. There were three tables moved together to form a triangle. Each table had a particular group sitting together, the King and the royal family members, government leaders and military commanders.

Right after the arrival of Percival and Edwin, the King announced the seating arrangement was not right. He asked the two people on the ends of each table to move to the table on their right. With looks of chagrin in some cases and surprise in others, the men did as requested.

Edwin was now sitting between two government ministers he had barely noticed before in the big dining hall. Soon however in the course of eating and interacting with one another he felt a degree of connection and warmth with these two gentlemen. Prior to this they would not have been of the type to socialize with the likes of Edwin nor him with them. He thought to himself again how strange to be able to connect so quickly with people with whom in many ways he had nothing in common. Then he realized they now all did have something very important in common. They were all together in the uniting of Ireland in one grand benevolent kingdom.

After a half-hour the King decided to start the business at hand while the eating was still continuing, albeit winding down. He had changed his original intention of beginning right away with the affairs of state. After switching the table partners, he decided it would be best to give people who seldom interacted an opportunity to get to know each other. He realized in order to bring unity and camaraderie for a common purpose throughout Ireland; it had to be first established in his own leadership.

"As you know next week we meet with the King of Nerland for the purpose of creating a new level of cooperation between us. We all have to be singing the same tune. There is a need for us to be completely convinced of the rightness of this initiative which has as its end objective the uniting of all Ireland. We must all be willing to invest our bodies and souls into achieving this goal. There has to be unanimous conviction that achieving greatness of purpose is more important than our personal comfort or safety."

"Does anyone want to express their opposition to the overall goal of uniting Ireland?"

Silence.

"Come, come if there is anyone who is unsure of this mission then speak up now because it will become obvious as the heat grows. And there will be heat. This is not an easy task. All of you know I am a just and fair king. I will not abuse those whose heart is not in this. You will need to be reassigned, but you will be looked after. All I ask is that you not be in active opposition. That of course will not be tolerated. I can understand some people will at best be neutral. But I cannot allow anyone promoting dissent, even if it is only in discussions with others."

One of the government ministers ventured to speak up saying, "Sire, I must admit I have struggled with the rightness and the difficulty of the task before us. For us to impose our will on the rest of Ireland for their benefit is indeed going to be an arduous task. Is it right for us to be committed to forcing our will on peoples that want nothing to do with us? I am troubled thinking many of those people don't know us nor are even interested in getting to know us. For us and the different peoples across this Isle, the only things we have in common are a Celtic heritage expressed in a myriad of ways and we share the same island."

The King looked intently and then replied, "Fenwick do you have any suggestions as to how we could proceed which would engage your heart in this pursuit of Irish unity?"

"No, Sire, because I am not convinced about the fundamental rightness of the cause."

"Okay then do I have your word you will not try to in any way interfere with this goal?"

"Yes, Sire, you have my word on it. My loyalty is not at stake here. I will support you in whatever way I can. I would never oppose you or work to undermine you."

"Okay then I believe you, Fenwick, and you are dismissed for now. I will reassign you to a less strategic role in the government."

Fenwick arose and left without further comment.

The King then asked again if anyone else was having wavering thoughts about Irish unity and the rightness of their cause to pursue it.

Again, silence.

The meeting continued on into the late afternoon until the King was satisfied with the initial work accomplished.

Greer came to the doorway of the room saying, "Father, something dreadful has happened. Fenwick was found hanging from his window over the northwest wall, an apparent suicide."

The King's face became dark with grief and horror. Fenwick had been a long-time faithful and competent government minister. The King even considered him a friend to the extent a king can consider a non-royal a friend.

This sudden turn of events was unfortunate. It could be considered by some as a possible murder by the King's men. There were men who thought the King should not brook those who could not give wholehearted support. This was a ticklish matter for the King as he did not want to be a tyrant over his people. The idea of imposing his kingdom and its allies' will on non-cooperative parts of Ireland was a challenged his sense of what was right. After much wrestling he had come to the conclusion the overall good to be gained was sufficient to justify the inevitable loss of life and property. As well it justified the imposition of the will of a united Ireland where necessary. He had settled it and he would not re-visit it.

The whole idea had come to the King in a dream. A dream so vivid and so wild in its emotional impact the King was unable to eat for three days. All he did was mull the dream over and over to the point his family and courtiers became concerned. Much of the Kingdom's business was put on hold as some major decisions needed to be made. During this point in time the King decided he must pursue the dream. He was convinced he had been given a call so massive he had no idea how he would accomplish it. All he knew was he needed to do something about it. When he snapped out of the time of mulling over the dream it was obvious this was no longer the same king as before the dream. The matters which seemed so important before now seemed inconsequential and even pointless. He now looked at how these decisions would impact the attainment of this dream. He started to discuss this goal with men he knew were like-minded. These were men who thought beyond their personal comfort and yet were not simply ambitious for the sake of personal gain. They were hard to find. After two years of diligent effort he had developed a network of men he figured were on the same page with him. Yet one of them could not in the end wholeheartedly support him.

On one hand it was good to flush out Fenwick and yet on the other hand it had been so hard on Fenwick that he killed himself. As it turned out Fenwick had left a note explaining his actions. He had been bitterly disappointed with his self-perceived lack of loyalty to his king in this most important of times. Yet he could not reconcile himself to this grand plan of uniting Ireland. Therefore he did as he wrote, "The only honorable act left to me is to remove myself from this life."

The funeral was held two days later with a crowd of over four hundred attending. He had a wife, several adult children and numerous grandchildren. He had been well liked and well respected. There was great mourning and there was of course the Catholic concern for his soul. The priests of the Kingdom said it was not right to give burial rites to a suicide. Percival was the one who officiated and ensured a proper burial send off.

The next day at breakfast the King announced they would resume their planning and strategy meetings at noon with another working lunch session. He had also sent a messenger to the King of Nerland requesting a two week delay. The messenger was expected back in a few days.

After breakfast, as had become their daily custom, Edwin and Percival went to Edwin's quarters and talked non-stop for hours. It seemed to Edwin he could share anything with Percival and be accepted. As he did so he felt lighter on the inside. Being a truly noble and excellent man became Edwin's number one objective. Nothing else seemed to matter. He also had this driving consuming desire to be an amazing husband for Greer. He figured the more excellent and noble he became the better he would be for her. Percival found this most endearing and indeed was determined to help Edwin achieve this objective. Of course this had been one of the overall objectives in the first place. The King dearly loved his daughter and was not about to entrust her happiness to an oaf who did not know how to be genteel with her.

Percival had been married only briefly, as his wife had died in childbirth with their first child. Losing both his wife and child propelled him on a path of cruelty to lash out against the world in revenge. During his two year marriage he came to greatly cherish his wife. It was that experience and the several months of courting, which helped Percival to input into Edwin what was needed to help with the process of preparing him for Greer. As well, he had the past twelve years gentling of his personhood and refinement of his faith connection. This gave him a pool to draw upon in order to provide valuable input for Edwin. Of course this was not only for his future marriage with Greer, but also for all the challenges which lay before him.

CHAPTER 4

The messenger came back from Nerland. He had welcome news. Two weeks would be acceptable and the King of Nerland looked forward to seeing his good friend King Erith of Evansing.

The King turned to Percival and asked him about the process of turning Edwin into a nobleman.

"Sire, the lad in spite of his rough background and in some ways rough manners has at his core a noble heart. Great progress is being made in making this fine young man into an excellent nobleman fit to serve the King. I would like to take the credit, but most of it goes to Edwin himself. In two weeks he will be ready to start working with the troops instilling the qualities you want. What he lacks in actual experience he will make up with heart."

Edwin felt a little embarrassed that he a mere twenty year old was looked to as the one with the key qualities needed for their army.

These men of the King's Council were much his senior and yet they perceived there existed something different about this young man.

Edwin still didn't know how he would accomplish the assignment before him in such a short time. The King wanted to get on the move with his initiative. Diplomacy would be the initial way to create alliances, but at some point the military would be required to deal with resistance. An intensive ten day training course with the officers began emerging in his thoughts. He started dictating them to Jaffa who also acted as his scribe.

At the end of the meeting Greer awaited Edwin outside the room. She asked if he would go on a walk with her outside the castle toward the lake several miles away. They would of course be accompanied by a dozen of the Royal Guards who would walk a discreet distance before them and behind them.

Edwin's face lit up at the prospect and looking in her eyes, "Greer, you know I would love to…" He stopped embarrassed about getting emotional. He steeled himself knowing the men from the meeting were nearby. Then he said in a soft voice, "Let's go."

After they had gone almost half way to the lake, Edwin, hesitating at first, boldly intertwined his arm around her arm and held her hand. Greer, with a surprised smile, looked up at him with obvious delight. The soldiers behind them also looked surprised and perhaps even a little shocked. This overt expression of public affection was not the custom in Evansing. They were shocked this newcomer and a commoner at that would be so forward with their Princess in such a short time. People tended to be discreet with their affections. Indeed too discreet. The Evansing people were non-expressive of their emotions when compared to their Celtic cousins.

The root of this began several generations earlier. A king had lost his dear wife and children and several other beloved family members in a raid from a nearby kingdom. The king in his distraught grieving state ordained it improper to express affection in public and should be restricted as much as possible even in private. His expressed reason being that God was a solemn God and therefore soberness at all times pleased Him most. The clergymen of the day also adapted this mindset and started to teach the people accordingly. It became so ingrained in the people that they passed it on to each successive generation right down to the present time.

As Greer and Edwin were walking along, she after the initial flush of delight started to consider their breach of societal norms. It violated the ancient Royal Ordinance still in effect. On one hand she struggled with what she had been taught and on the other hand it felt so right. This man Edwin represented everything she had dreamt a man should be. To think in less than three months they would be married. Edwin turned to her with a dreamy smile his eyes bright with love. Greer decided to cast aside all concerns about it being proper. She determined that if Edwin thought it acceptable then it was okay. Her Father highly regarded him and had chosen him to be her husband. She would obey him now as though he were already her husband.

"Oh oh," thought Greer as up ahead coming in the opposite direction one of the leading clerics in the Kingdom, Father Meurthin. As they got closer to him she could tell his face expressed displeasure at what he saw. He would tell her father. Oh well she didn't care. Her father had to realize this stupid rule needed to be changed. She and Edwin would spearhead the change. It would be a revolution.

"Good day, Your Highness," said Meurthin courteously with a tinge of disapproval he tried to conceal, but his tone and his face made his true feelings obvious.

"Good day," responded Greer and Edwin in unison.

Meurthin had been traveling some weeks into the surrounding districts and had not yet met Edwin.

"May I have the pleasure of being introduced to this young man?"

"Father Meurthin, I present Edwin of Elfereth who has been brought here by the King as a special advisor to the military. Edwin, I present Father Meurthin who is one of the Church leaders in the south district of our kingdom."

Meurthin looked at Edwin with surprise.

"To advise our military? How can such a young man be able to advise our military?"

Greer replied, "Don't let his youth disguise the wisdom that dwells in his heart. He has demonstrated wisdom beyond his years."

As she replied she gripped Edwin's hand tighter and also reached over with her other hand and gripped Edwin's arm in a spontaneous act of defiance. If she would have to answer to her father for something then let it be something of some consequence.

The act of defiance had its effect as the Father quickly tipped his head in respect to the Princess and begged his leave.

Edwin quite unaware of the reason for the negative undercurrent between Greer and the Father knew there existed something amiss.

After they had walked some further distance Edwin asked, "Why the bad blood between you and the priest?"

"Bad blood? You must be mistaken. There exists no malice between us. After all I am a Princess. How could he dare to have contention with me?"

Edwin stopped, disengaged his arm and hand from Greer and said to her, "Greer, I know what I heard, felt and saw. There was an edge to your meeting with that man. Now please tell me the truth, Your Highness."

Greer blushed as she realized she was found out.

"Edwin, I should tell you what you and I were doing by holding hands in public breached the custom of the land. Father Meurthin will tell my father and there may be ramifications for having done so. I decided not to be cowed by him."

A dawn of realization came upon Edwin as she told him.

"This explains the sense I had sometimes of thinking something was strange. No one ever showed any affection. Not even between parents and children or between husbands and wives. I don't remember consciously grabbing that thought, but it stayed in the back of my mind as something amiss."

"Amiss? Obviously by the way you took my hand you never thought it inappropriate for you to do so. By the way you describe our kingdom you make it sound like there must be something wrong with this attitude of no show of public affection."

"Wrong? Of course it's wrong. Affection is one of the staples of life. I haven't been one contemplating too much about what God is like. But I have to believe He likes affection and it pleases Him. So why a man of the Church would object seems to me to be a perversion of what God intended. I believe it to be an inherent part of the natural order of things."

Greer looked astonished at Edwin's reply. It expressed such a radical thought for her to hear. However, it resonated with the deep down part of her that thought the Royal Ordinance flawed and wrong. This must be why Edwin taking her hand delighted her, and she decided to accept his gesture.

"So what do you think your father will do?"

"I don't know. It's not a formal law with prescribed penalties. It's more an ingrained form of behavior which has a unique status of being officially enshrined by a Royal Ordinance. Only a few Royal Ordinances still exist.

These laws have no formal sanctions. They do however carry tremendous weight and can result in people imposing their own sanctions on people caught violating them. In addition, the Church has put its full support behind it and has incorporated it in its teaching. Most people respect the Church's view and respond in obedience."

"Oh well let's not let it interfere with our walk and our enjoyment of one another," answered Edwin as he again encircled Greer's arm and held her hand.

Greer looked up into Edwin's face with delight. Her admiration for Edwin increased another notch as she delighted in his boldness, his sense of purpose and his sense of rightness.

As they continued their walk Greer felt as though being bathed in light from Edwin's spirit. She had never experienced this before. She could tell he really liked her. She sensed herself being immersed by his pleasure in her. She had no doubt of his sincerity. Her spirit just knew it.

The lake which appeared before them was one of the largest in all of Ireland. Lake O'Meara measured almost ten miles long and over four miles wide. The sun shone in the distance above the horizon. Within two hours it would be dark. It would soon be time to go back. But there was no way Edwin would turn back before he had at least gone into the lake for a quick swim. So without any warning he let go of Greer's hand and started to run toward the lake, removed his shirt as he went, took off his shoes and socks at the water's edge, and then ran through the shallows, and dove into the deeper waters. A good thirty seconds later his head popped out of the water, much to the relief of Greer who had never seen such behavior before. Not that the men of her kingdom didn't go swimming but not in front of royalty. Other members of the Royal Family were too dignified to go swimming in such an undignified manner, assuming they could even swim. Swimming did not rate high on the desired skills list for Royals.

After ten minutes of swimming and playing in the water Edwin came out and one of the guards brought him an extra tunic.

"I'll bet you wish you could come running into the lake instead of being concerned about what the guards would think?"

"Really? What makes you think I wanted to do that?"

"You're like me. You want to play and enjoy all life has to offer."

Greer looked at him and laughed.

"Well I couldn't take my top off like you did. It would create quite a stir. I've never gone swimming. I've only walked along the beach and put my toes in the water as a little girl."

"When we get back to the castle I am going to talk to Jaffa about arranging for a change of clothes you can go swimming in. Ideally it would be a pair of breeches, but that might be considered too daring for a woman to wear."

"Might be considered too daring? More like a major moral outrage. I would be considered immoral and a disgrace to my sex. Before you go too far with deciding what I should wear keep in mind it must also be stylish. My seamstress will work with Jaffa on coming up with a design. Then I will need to approve of it first before it's made."

"Okay okay. I figured as much. It must be something that has less bulk and a bit shorter otherwise you will sink like a rock and that would never do. The objective is for you to learn how to swim and have fun in the water."

"Thank you kind sir for your concern. I must say you did look like you were having more fun than it looked right for anyone to have. How did you ever learn to swim?"

"I used to go hunting alone and one of my favorite places had a good sized pond, which was refreshing to dive into in the summer. I had seen people swim and I sort of taught myself. In my otherwise oft dreary life, being able to play in the water became a tremendous source of pleasure."

"Okay you ask Jaffa to see if something can be designed for me. When we go we will tell the guards to stay further back and I will have two of my maids with me. Also I will need to use the fisherman's hut to change."

"It's a deal. I am going to get a briefer set of breeches. To wear full pants like I did today noticeably dragged on me. Typically I would take everything off because there would be no one else around."

"I'm glad you remembered etiquette in the presence of someone else with you today. We've already created enough of a stir without further bending the rules of what our society considers proper. Of course I would have looked the other way." And then with a mischievous smile said, "Mind you I may have stole a peek or two."

Edwin smiled at her and laughed. This girl had started to become so much a part of him. It seemed beyond belief less than a week ago he never even knew she existed.

The party arrived back behind castle walls shortly after dark.

As was expected, there was a servant waiting to advise them that the King wanted to see them immediately.

They looked at each other, breathed deeply and followed the servant to meet with the King.

CHAPTER 5

The King looked somber when they arrived. He asked the servant to leave.

The King didn't say anything for a moment. He looked at the two offenders seriously, very seriously.

Then he laughed and laughed. Greer looked wide-eyed at her father. She had never heard her father express amusement so loud and so full. Since her mother died she hadn't heard her father even chuckle.

The King laughed loud and boisterously for so long he actually had tears in his eyes.

When he stopped he stood up. He looked at the two young people and motioned to them to come to him. He wrapped his arms around them and gave them both a great big long hug.

When he let go, Greer asked, "Are you alright father?"

"Yes, my dear, I am alright, in fact I have never been better."

"So what caused all this mirth and this hug?"

"After Father Meurthin told me about you two I was furious. I thought how could you Greer disgrace yourself in front one of the leading clergy-man of our Kingdom? Then as I thought about it more and more, I realized it had to have been Edwin's idea, and you went along with it. I also thought about why I had Edwin brought here. It was for that reason I wanted him here. I wanted him to infuse new life and new ways into our land and people. It's not just the military that needs inspiration it's our whole land that needs to know life is meant to be enjoyed. I have revoked the old Royal Ordinance. The more I thought about it the sillier and more wrong it became. I have also called for a meeting tomorrow with the senior church people, for the express purpose of this false teaching being rescinded. From hereon appropriate public displays of affection are not only acceptable they are desirable for a healthy happy populace."

Edwin and Greer were of course relieved to hear what the King had to say.

Edwin though was also thinking to himself, "How or why would he think I would be able to infuse new life and new ways somebody would want?"

He then expressed his thoughts to the King.

King Erith replied, "There are many things about the spiritual realm you need to learn. It doesn't work the way our visible world does. Insights into people's hearts and destinies are available which would never be possible otherwise. You have been observed by Percival for sometime. At his monastery miles away from where you lived he was discerning the true Edwin. Even though the outer Edwin looked unattractive in many ways there was an essence of nobleness and call on your life he knew would lead to greatness."

"The prospect of having you as my son-in-law pleases me greatly. I know even though it has only been a few days you have made a deep impression on Greer and she is very pleased at the prospect of you being her husband. I can't think of a better man so totally suited for her temperament. You two fit like a hand in a glove. You two, will continue to spark each other to new levels of fulfillment and love, of that I have no doubt."

"To ensure nobleness of intent and character is maintained I must insist you have at least one other person present whenever you are together. Your passion for one another is good and true, but passion is a two edged sword which can also damage. So for your sake and for the Kingdom's sake, I must insist on this rule. Take heart it will only be for a few months before you are married. Assuming of course Edwin stays for the agreed three months."

"Nothing could make me leave before then and I don't see why I would ever want to leave except to carry out Your Majesty's mission in other parts of Ireland."

"Good. Now, Edwin, good night to you and I will see you at breakfast tomorrow morning. Greer, I want you stay for a while as I have some things to talk to you about."

Edwin said good night to Greer and the King and returned directly to his room.

When he arrived back in his room, Jaffa had a plate of cold meat and a glass of mead. This was a welcome sight, for Edwin was famished and thirsty.

"Jaffa, could you please ask Percival if he would like to come to my room. I want to continue with my lessons."

A short time later as Edwin was finishing his meal, Jaffa returned with Percival.

Percival gave Edwin a big grin and a warm greeting and then exclaimed, "I hear, my young man, that you have had yourself a rather interesting and enjoyable day tweaking societal norms."

"Yes, indeed, but it was unintentional I assure you."

"Today has motivated me to want to learn all I can as quickly as possible. About spiritual things, about noble things, about all manner of useful things so I can live up to what you, the King, and of course Greer are expecting of me."

Percival laughed and replied, "Yes, you shall all in good time. However, there is a prescribed way of learning, so that it isn't only a head thing, but it becomes a heart thing. It must be so ingrained in you to do the excellent way every time. The only thing that is primarily intellectual is your reading and writing. We will begin tomorrow morning and will continue on for three mornings a week until you are literate enough to function as a member of the ruling class of Ireland."

"Tonight I think it is most important for you to express to me more about the pain of growing up alone much of the time and being rejected by other members of your community. Let's separate the rejection that came first because of your uncle's reputation and then secondly what came because of your own behavior."

"How can that get me where I want to go and be? We've talked about it already. Let's talk about new things, important things."

"Those are very important things. Unless they are resolved and healed it will forever taint your motives and aspirations. You will operate out of a need to prove and approve of yourself instead of knowing you are proved and approved."

Edwin looked at him a little frustrated and said, "Okay let's do it your way."

CHAPTER 6

The next morning before Jaffa came to get him up, Edwin had already been laying awake for awhile. He hurt inside and yet felt freer than before. The prior evening before had led to deeper self-exploration and it hadn't been easy. Even though he didn't like the process he decided he would trust Percival, and set aside his personal inclinations to get onto the "good stuff" as he described it. Then he realized the only way to make it more enjoyable and less frustrating was to see this process as part of getting to the good stuff. In fact it is part of the good stuff. He hadn't realized it before.

Rousing himself out of bed he stood by the water bowl ready to wash himself when Jaffa came in.

"Sir, did you sleep well?" asked Jaffa.

"Yes and no," replied Edwin in true Irish fashion. "In some ways I slept extremely well, but I woke rather early and wasn't able to get back to sleep."

"Something ailing you, sir?"

"Nothing that won't get resolved, Jaffa. It's some work on my past that Percival is determined to help me resolve."

"The past is the past. What is the point of trying to resolve it? Personally if I don't feel so good because of my past I get drunk. It works every time. In the morning I don't remember what I was depressed about."

"Well, Jaffa, I guess that is one way of dealing with your past. Wouldn't you like to resolve it once and for all, so you didn't have to keep getting drunk in order to keep it at bay?"

"I like to get drunk. It's good to have a reason to get drunk. That way I can feel like I'm doing something productive while I am getting drunk."

"Okay, Jaffa, if that suits you, so be it. If you want to consider another way then I think it would be great for you to speak to Percival. He probably would give you some great insights about yourself, in even a few minutes."

"Percival? Why would he want to help me? I am a servant. No one like him would care about me and whether I'm happy or not."

"Percival isn't like any other person. He has a genuine heart for people and a desire to see them be all they can be. That is why he is spending time with me."

"Well if I may be so bold as to say, sir, the King handpicked you and it is fitting Percival would be interested in helping you. You've got a very important position and it is imperative that you be properly trained and prepared. As for me all anyone cares is I keep my nose to the grindstone and I'm polite to all the nobles. Although I must say, sir, you do treat me rather well. You don't treat me like I'm a servant. I do appreciate your kindness."

"You're very welcome, Jaffa. How about I have you spend a half hour with Percival this morning right after breakfast, before I start my reading and writing lessons with him today?"

"As you wish, sir"

"No, Jaffa. I'm not making you do it. You can say no. I'm saying it's available, and I think it would be good for you."

Jaffa thought for a moment then responded, "Okay, sir, I will do it."

"Wonderful," replied Edwin, "You won't regret it and I know Percival will love the opportunity to talk to you."

During breakfast, Edwin chatted amiably with Greer. They frequently laughed at each others cutisms. What is a cutism? Simply put it's when two people are in love and they laugh at almost anything their beloved says because it's cute.

Edwin took a brief leave from Greer to ask Percival if it would be okay for him to meet privately for half an hour with Jaffa.

"But of course I could. I would love to talk with him. I have noticed that underneath that stoic exterior there seems to be a melancholic air about him. You and I have much to do so there won't be much time to set aside for Jaffa for some time to come. However, I am sure we can fit in a little time now and then. I will look for opportunities to do so. Edwin it is a fine gesture in your offering me to talk to Jaffa. That is the way true nobility should think about their servants. You are treating him as a fellow creature created by God. May you never lose your sense of connection with the common people."

"Thank you, Percival, I appreciate your kind comments. It's not hard. After all it was only a week ago I was a very common person myself."

He rejoined Greer and immediately they laughed at another cutism.

Tomorrow, he would leave for Nerland.

CHAPTER 7

Edwin woke up excited for today they traveled to Nerland. They were to begin the first round of discussions that would lead to working together in uniting the kingdoms of Ireland.

Edwin would divide his time between observing the kings' discussions and being part of the Evansing military contingent building camaraderie with their Nerland counterparts.

At the dining hall the atmosphere had a great buzz due to the anticipation of leaving on the trip to Nerland. Back in the late 11th century of Ireland traveling any distance beyond ten miles was considered extraordinary by most people. The upper crust of society did do it more than occasionally, but even for them it created a cause for excitement.

Edwin took his customary seat beside Greer except this morning she hadn't yet arrived. This was most unusual for she always arrived there before Edwin. He was not the morning person she was. As he considered this, one of Greer's ladies-in-waiting came to him and said Greer was quite ill and remaining in her suite.

He got up and said he wanted to go see her. The lady didn't know at first what to say as it was not considered proper that any man other than the King should visit the Princess in her bedchamber. She shrugged and motioned to Edwin to follow her.

When they got to the Princess' suite there was already a gaggle of concerned people outside her door. They were primarily Greer's royal relatives, but also several household servants concerned about her health.

The royal physician had ordered that everyone except two of her maids and the King were to be kept outside as he diagnosed her. In spite of this order Edwin opened the door and went inside. One of the maids heard the door open and went out into the entryway. Upon seeing Edwin she indicated to him to be quiet. In response Edwin motioned her to come to him. He whispered in her ear that she should ask the King if he could come into the bedchamber. She left and came back in a few moments. The King had said yes. Edwin followed her into the bedchamber where before him lay a very pale Greer. Her breathing was erratic and forced. The physician had a worried furrow on his brow and looked puzzled. When Greer looked up to see who had arrived she brightened at the sight of Edwin.

She whispered to Edwin to give her his hand. He placed his hand into hers. She took it and placed it on her forehead. Instantly she changed for the better in her appearance. The color started to come back into her face and her breathing began to get easier and easier. The people standing around the bed looked with astonishment as to what they had witnessed. The physician confessed that in all his days he had never seen such a sudden change for the better in a patient. Within a half hour Greer sat up and looked as healthy as she ever had.

The King asked her if she knew Edwin's hand would bring her healing. She said something inside her told her his hand had what she needed.

"Well Edwin you have not disappointed us," said the King, "you have turned out to be much better than we expected. Indeed Percival says there are no limits to what is possible with you. This morning you have shown us something we didn't know you had in you."

"Well I didn't know I had it in me either. I am as surprised as anyone. I must say though it couldn't have happened at a better time."

"I'm hungry," piped up Greer.

The crowd outside her suite brightened at the sight of Greer coming out and looking her usual perky self. Several relatives gave her hugs and kisses. As they discovered what had caused the sudden change in her condition, they looked at Edwin with a new sense of respect and even a bit of awe. Opinion had been divided about the wisdom of the King bringing this strange young man to Evansing. And even more controversy got stirred up at the prospect of him being given Greer in marriage. However, Edwin had conducted himself well and more and more he won the approval of the royals. He demonstrated he had rare qualities that could benefit the Kingdom. Even the prospect of him being King some day no longer created the same kind of passionate resistance. People were beginning to see in Edwin the qualities of a leader they knew they would need to maintain the unity of Ireland beyond King Erith. This being accomplished by someone with Edwin's background was remarkable. Having it accomplished in a few weeks was a miracle.

As breakfast drew to a close, Edwin looked at Greer with tears in his eyes and said, "Wow I am so glad you recovered. I have had enough tests in my life without having someone like you be snatched away. I've been thinking about stories my aunt said about how relatives on my mother's side had been known as healers. I never saw any kind of healing and so I dismissed it as exaggerated tales. I guess there must have been something to it after all."

Greer with her beautiful blue eyes looked intently into his eyes and said, "You are a mighty prince and you are greater than you think."

Then the King's chief steward announced everyone going to Nerland must meet in the courtyard and be ready to leave in half an hour.

They both walked out to the courtyard to be greeted by a typical Irish day. Overcast and threatening to rain. They chatted about all manner of things until the order came to mount up. Then Greer grabbed both of Edwin's hands, squeezed them and wished him God speed and great success on this trip. They both wanted to hug, but the time and place was not yet proper for that.

Edwin mounted his dark brown mare, and then he and the others were off. He looked back several times to wave to Greer standing by the gateway. He noticed she waved more vigorously than what you would expect a royal to wave. He smiled at her willingness to be at least little bit undignified in her expression of affection for him.

Like everyone else in the party of thirty or so representatives from Evansing he was excited to go to Nerland. He also struggled with self-doubts about his ability to impact the Nerland military. Then he remembered what Greer had said about him being a mighty prince. He mulled it over and over until after awhile the self-doubts had gone and indeed he felt like a mighty prince.

In spite of the overcast sky it turned out to be quite a pleasant day for an extended ride. The mood of the entourage stayed buoyant and expectations were high for a productive time with their Nerland counterparts. Relationships between Evansing and Nerland had been close and friendly for many years. Indeed no one alive could remember when they weren't friendly. Much intermarriage had occurred between the two royal families. If Greer hadn't been promised to Edwin, she may well have married one of the Princes of Nerland. Rumor had it that the Crown Prince of Nerland had been rather disappointed to find out Greer was no longer his possible bride. He had met her some two years earlier and had been quite struck by her beauty and her bold ways.

Accompanying the party were 100 warriors. Their presence being a matter of protocol as security concerns were not high. However, it remained prudent to have adequate protection for the King of Evansing and his family.

Edwin chose to ride up front with the chief scouts to keep an eye out for anything suspicious. A half mile or so down the road Edwin noticed an unusual sight. Crows were sitting in the trees about a hundred yards on either side of where their entourage was going, but none appeared to be sitting in the area directly ahead near the road. He mentioned this to the chief scout who dismissed it as being the way it was sometimes. To him no possibility existed of there being a serious threat along this path. Edwin, however, had the advantage of not being lulled by the familiar. He knew for crows to do that must mean something or someone waited ahead. His experience as a hunter as well as a warrior had sharpened his senses to the unnatural. He mentioned his concerns again to the chief scout and said he felt it important to stop the procession and check out what lay ahead. The chief scout, sensing the urgency and also considering the respect Edwin held as a warrior, decided he would do as advised. He and Edwin and the other scouts rode back to the party some seventy-five yards behind them and advised the King they had some concerns. They felt they should be investigated before continuing further. The King rather impatient to get going was tempted to dismiss it as being too cautious. However, he had high regard for Edwin's judgment so he agreed to stop the journey and have fifty or so troops go on and check it out.

Edwin decided forty would continue on the road and the other ten would continue on foot taking a side path some hundred yards or so from the road. They would leave ten minutes earlier with the objective of coming in from the east side of the road. They would be in a position to come in from behind if an enemy force awaited them. Edwin would lead this group of ten. They would also signal any sightings by a distinctive bird call given three times. This was a call Edwin had perfected. A call distinctive enough but not so as to tip off the other side that something was amiss.

The first part of the path appeared quite clear, but as they progressed it became apparent the path had not been much used in recent months, for it started to be overgrown with under brush. As they progressed they noticed it was very quiet ahead. Motioning to the men with him Edwin indicated to be silent. He took a couple of the men with him and told the others to remain within visual contact but to follow a few minutes behind. Edwin progressed ahead holding his battle axe at the ready. The axe Edwin held had a two foot handle with a large head on it. This axe made larger than a hatchet but smaller than a regular battle axe, was a favorite weapon, for what could be close hand to hand battle. Up front he noticed some movement and heard two men talking quietly. He stopped and crawled as close as he dared so as to hear what they were saying.

"Eldreth has said if Erith has his way it will change our lives for the worse and he must be stopped."

"How did he ever find out about it?"

"One of the household servants has been very cooperative in sharing information."

Edwin thought to himself, "Eldreth is the Crown Prince of Nerland."

The two men were notified by a third man that riders were approaching and they were to move closer to the road.

After they moved out of sight of him, Edwin gave his distinctive bird call three times. The men on the road heard the call and started to slow down ever so progressively and also go into a defensive shell. In the meantime the rest of the ten men were now reunited. They were all to proceed into the direction of where they saw the three men walk.

The Nerland men with Eldreth were confused at what they were seeing on the road. There was no king and it looked like the Evansing men were expecting trouble. Eldreth decided to not give the signal to attack.

Since these were Nerland men Edwin decided it would be wisest to let the Nerland men attack first. This ensured no mistaking their intentions. If they were attacked by Edwin's group it could be argued they were actually attacked by the men of Evansing.

It started to appear the Nerland men were going to let the contingent of forty men pass by. All of a sudden arrows flew from two of the Nerland archers who did not realize the signal to attack had not been given and that there had been a change of plans. This resulted in two Evansing riders going down. Edwin's group responded by attacking the middle part of the Nerland force composed of twenty or so men. The Nerland men had a numerical advantage of about two to one, but they no longer had the element of surprise and strategic position they had counted on. Quickly they lost a number of prized warriors in this fierce hand to hand battle. Edwin was challenged by two Nerland warriors one to his left and another to his right. One of the soldiers thrust forward with his sword, as he did so Edwin sliced down hard with his axe cutting off the man's forearm. The man howled in pain and fell to the ground. The other man swung at Edwin's left side but struck the handle of Edwin's sword hanging from his waist. With a sweeping back handed motion Edwin's axe came across and struck the man full on in his rib cage. There sounded the crunch of breaking bones and then the man fell dead at Edwin's feet. Edwin swung around in time to deflect a blow from a person who had the Nerland's Royal House insignia on his tunic. "This must be Eldreth," Edwin thought to himself. Edwin pulled out his sword. He felt it would be nobler to fight a prince with the sword than an axe. The two clanged away at each other with vigorous sword play. Both were strong and skilled swordsman. Then Edwin with two handed slashes against Eldreth started to surge forward and created an advantage in the momentum. This resulted in his last over handed slash knocking Eldreth's sword out of his hand. Eldreth yielded as Edwin held his sword point to his throat. His arms were bound with rope behind his back. After ten minutes of battle the Nerland group started to retreat, leaving sixteen dead behind and another twelve captured, several of which were seriously wounded.

The other contingent had started to come when they heard the commotion ahead. The King was most distressed when he realized the Crown Prince of Nerland had been captured and identified as the leader of the plot. As he considered the implication of this it certainly complicated things with Nerland. How would his dear friend Keltic the King of Nerland respond to what had happened? Would he believe his own son was behind the attack?

As he pondered this there arrived a new contingent of Nerland men, but this group was headed by their King and carrying a flag of peace before them. As they got closer they could see Keltic was looking very distressed. Indeed as they got within hailing distance the King of Nerland called out to Erith and asked if he remained well.

Erith responded he was and in turn asked Keltic if he remained well.

To this Keltic replied, "I am well physically, but I am greatly distressed in my heart at what has happened."

Certain men had heard what had been conspired by Eldreth and had informed their King.

King Keltic had already decided in his heart what needed to be done. To violate many years of friendship with Evansing in such an act of betrayal was unforgivable. He walked up to his eldest son, drew his sword and stabbed him in the heart. Eldreth had a look of unbelief as fell to the ground with blood spewing from his chest. There arose a hush at the sight of what had transpired. He then commanded his men to kill the other Nerland captives. No one who had participated in this betrayal would be allowed to live. To one of his commanders he gave the order to hunt down the others which had fled.

Keltic then walked up to Erith and apologized profusely for what had happened. He invited him to continue on to Nerland and proceed with the original plan of relationship building and discussing how the two kingdoms were to cooperate more closely in commerce military and political matters. Erith felt surprise at how coolly Keltic could consider business as usual after killing his own son. There existed one big difference between him and Keltic. The latter had a more cold-blooded approach to life. This manifested in some of the brutal ways he dealt with opposition and lawbreakers in general. The two continued on to Nerland riding side by side. The conversation stayed subdued understandable given what had happened. They discussed about what the next several days would entail. Erith started to fill in some of the gaps of what he had told Keltic about earlier. It was important they cooperate one to one as kingdoms. They needed to work together in bringing unity to all of Ireland. This was not a total surprise to Keltic as this was something he and Erith had discussed at some length years earlier. Both of them had at that time expressed an affinity to the idea of Irish unity. It seemed so out of reach they both dismissed the idea as impossible. Now it was coming up again and this time Erith was determined to make it reality. Keltic could feel Erith's conviction so strongly he started to get very excited at the prospect. Here was an opportunity for them both to pursue something bigger than themselves. Bigger than trying to keep peace in the land and live a good life. It would be difficult, but these were Irish warriors who had iron in their souls. They had stuff of legends. Now here lay an opportunity to create folklore. Only these would be true stories that would leave a multi-generational impact on all of Ireland. No longer would their focus be only on extending a little bit of territory here and there and taking a little bit of booty. They would now start to focus on being benefactors for all of Ireland and all of her citizens. Kings don't typically think like that. But true kings do. True kings know they are given positions of power and influence to benefit people, not simply to enjoy advantageous situations for themselves.

In the distance they could see the gray moss covered walls of Nerland castle. News had gotten to the general populace about the aborted attack and there already arose sorrow at the lives lost and the ones soon to be lost as the word went out that all the ones who participated were to be executed on sight. Although the response could be considered harsh it was in fact the only way to respond to this betrayal. Eldreth had been the Crown Prince and therefore expected to be first to support whatever policies his father saw fit to implement.

Right now the task existed to keep everybody calm and maintain order. Keltic knew almost all of his nobles and military were in favor of closer ties with Evansing. Moving them to a level of cooperation required for working toward Irish unity would be a challenging task. Deep in his heart he knew he needed to do it. With his son's blood he had already invested a huge price. Although Erith hadn't come out and said it, Keltic knew Erith expected to lead. It wouldn't be in a demanding way that would demean Keltic or Nerland, but nevertheless there wouldn't be any doubt as to who was the leader. He knew Erith had resources beyond the mere visible to ensure whatever he put his hand to would be successful. No matter what the odds against him, Erith had a conviction victory was his.

CHAPTER 8

The first evening in Nerland was spent supping together in a lavish affair that had all the trappings of a good time but remained subdued. The members of the Nerland royal family were mourning the loss of Eldreth. And yet there existed general acknowledgement that what had happened was necessary. Eldreth had dishonored the tradition of safe conduct granted from one king to another. As well, many Nerland royals, nobles and commoners had close blood ties with Evansing. The whole affair had created quite an ambivalence of emotions.

Edwin sat with several of the leading military men of Nerland. They were indeed surprised at the youth of this protégé of Erith. They were generally in their mid-thirties or older, but yet they knew this was not an ordinary youth. He had a wisdom and way of being beyond his years. They had also heard how he had led the capture of Eldreth and had bravely led his men against a group of Nerland warriors, even though outnumbered two to one. This of course didn't come from Edwin. Rather the nobles of Evansing had shared it with their Nerland counterparts and then it spread from there. Edwin said nothing of the battle and given the sensitivity of the topic no one asked him about it. It seemed almost like it didn't happen.

Edwin, in the meantime enjoyed being the mighty prince he was. His internalization of Greer's words bore much fruit for he felt quite comfortable with these leading Nerland men. He didn't feel at all like he didn't fit in or measure up. Some people at the banquet of course did not feel quite so amiable toward Edwin. They were either mourning the loss of a loved one or they were feeling the humiliation of losing a battle to Evansing.

The evening ended well with Edwin making some new acquaintances and perhaps at least one new friend. The new friend was the third ranking military man in Nerland. He was not much older than Edwin being only in his mid-twenties. Like Edwin he had demonstrated amazing leadership and courage. They both seemed to click with one another as soon as they had met. Within minutes they were sharing rather personal details about their lives. The Nerland commander's name was Glynn. He had recently married and was quite intrigued by the news that Princess Greer was destined to marry Edwin. They parted at the end of the evening with pledges to continue where they had left off.

The next morning the day started an hour before the common breakfast meal with a closed meeting of the entire Evansing contingent. King Erith gave instructions to everyone for the duration of their visit they were to maintain a low profile while in public and not go anywhere alone. The mood in Nerland remained pretty raw and was expected to stay that way for at least the week they were there. The plans were to continue connecting and building relationships with their Nerland counterparts and generally circulate. If there were certain key relationships that were going deeper then it was appropriate to invest extra time on those. As Edwin gladly thought about being able to spend more time with Glynn the King did an adjustment in the groups. The King assigned Edwin to the royal contingent with the express objective of building relationship with the new Crown Prince Gondar. Initially Edwin was disappointed as it meant less time with Glynn, but he knew a key goal was to befriend the new Nerland heir. As he considered this he realized the reason for the assignment was obvious. He himself was being groomed to be the Crown Prince of Evansing. For a moment he considered the total impossibility of it, but he had heard it with his own ears from the King's mouth.

"This life is very strange," he thought to himself. "How can I have gone from living by myself in a rundown thatched hut to heir apparent of Evansing and perhaps of all Ireland?"

At the initial meeting with Gondar the tone was quite the opposite of his meeting with Glynn. Gondar struggled with the conflict between what his emotions and what his head were telling him. On one hand he had lost his brother and Edwin had played a big role in his capture. On the other hand he had been commanded by his father to get over it and start building relationship. King Keltic was above all pragmatic and did not want to lose time with the unfortunate series of events which had occurred. Whether this would sow seeds of discontent among the Nerlanders or between Evansing and Nerland was yet to be determined. It wasn't ideal to plough ahead in such a strained environment. Erith considered these matters along with the two key deaths already transpired in the pursuit of this Irish vision. When he considered these matters he always came back to the resolute conviction that it had to be the right thing to do. Such fierce opposition only came when an idea's time had come. Nothing great ever came without attack. It seemed to him the life environment supported the status quo and would block whoever and whatever to maintain it.

After spending the morning in attempting to build some sort of connection with Gondar, Edwin decided he would like a break in the afternoon to spend time with Glynn. Erith agreed as long as he re-joined the royals in the evening.

Glynn and Erith decided to go riding accompanied by a small contingent of both Evansing and Nerland troops. The plan remained for the two armies to start doing maneuvers together. The objective at this stage was to give each army a taste of working together.

The two young commanders raced along the Nerland countryside enjoying being young and free to do something very few of the populace could participate in. Both had come from poor backgrounds and both by fortuitous interventions had found themselves in enviable positions. At the end of their ride the two had bonded to a new level. Having fun together has a mystical capacity to create more glue in relationships.

"So what can you tell me about Gondar?" asked Edwin.

"He is a hard one to figure out. He tends to be quieter and less inclined to socialize than his elder brother. He had a fairly close relationship with Eldreth. He isn't too fond about being the Crown Prince. He was content with being a Prince with minimal expectations upon him. So besides the loss of his brother he is also struggling with his new future and the weight of being heir apparent."

"This is good to know. I will try to adjust my way of relating to him so I can empathize with where he is at. Anything else you can tell me?"

Glynn hesitated for a minute, and then added, "Yes, there is one thing you need to know. One of my field officers told me he overheard the Prince say to his younger sister that he would never try to like you no matter how much his father wanted it. He would only pretend to go along with it."

Edwin laughed and said, "Well this morning he didn't try very hard to pretend. Unless his feelings are so strong he felt like he was in which case we have a serious relational challenge. I will treat it as a personal test to win him over. I am determined to like him and get him to like me. The mission demands it."

"What is the mission?"

Edwin a little surprised Glynn didn't know was uncertain as to the suitability to share details. But Glynn had already demonstrated a willingness to share privileged information so to do less in return would be an affront.

"The ultimate mission isn't simply to build greater cooperation between Nerland and Evansing; it is to establish a united Ireland."

Glynn was only partially surprised for he had heard rumors about this being the true objective of this meeting with Evansing. Nevertheless to hear it from the purported future King of Evansing made it sink in a lot deeper. Before it was a rumor, now it is a truth, a rather astonishing truth. He thought to himself, "How could they ever achieve such an undertaking?"

"I had heard rumors about it and I'm glad you told me. You and I are developing a strong friendship very quickly. Indeed I can't remember ever getting so close so rapidly with someone before."

"Nor I," replied Edwin, "I am glad you and I met. I have never felt as open to any male before except Percival. But he is more like a father than a good friend, although he is that too. You are a buddy and a soul mate, someone I can trust and be myself with.

At the closed Evansing meeting before the evening's events, Erith asked Edwin how things were progressing with Gondar.

"They are strained, but Gondar is civil toward me. I think it is a challenge for him to be so. I believe the added element of me not being a born royal makes him feel like he has to lower himself to connect with me. But undoubtedly other events have contributed as well."

"Well I am sure you are up to the challenge, Edwin. You may not win him on this trip but at least try to gain some foothold of friendship with him. I will again restrict your times to him tomorrow to twice a day and even then you will always have other members of the group with you. Tonight should be a fairly light evening as we will dine together and view entertainment from the musicians and dancers of Nerland. The need to interact will be minimal. Enjoy yourself tonight. This objective will take time."

That night Edwin did just that he enjoyed himself. Indeed he had more fun than he had ever expected. In the course of doing so he had some enjoyable interactions with the royals from Nerland. His only relating with Gondar involved greeting him and later saying good night. Edwin decided the indirect approach would be the most effective way. He had such confidence in his ability to radiate a positive environment that he felt in due time it would thaw out Gondar's attitude. Besides, connecting with other high level royals who were blood relatives of Gondar couldn't hurt.

As he went to sleep Edwin thought about Greer. Oh how he missed her. She had become such a big part of his life.

"Oh well it won't be long before I see her again."

Then he drifted asleep.

* * *

When Edwin woke he had a splitting headache and knew something was wrong. The plush room he went to sleep in had been replaced with a dingy room and he lay sleeping on a pile of straw. The air hung heavy and smelled of urine and human excrement.

"Ooh, where am I? What happened to me?" he moaned.

In what must have been the cell next door he heard a reply, "They brought you last night looking like a crumpled rag."

"Who are you and where am I?"

"My name is Daro and you are in the dungeon of the King of Merethath."

"King of Merethath! What quarrel could he have with me?"

"I don't know, but he had a reason to put you in here. Who are you?"

"Edwin of Elfereth, but of late I have been of Evansing. I was in Nerland when I was taken."

"You do get around don't you?"

"What do you do to move around from place to place?"

"I'm a simple guy who likes to move around."

"Yeah right that's why you're here. It sounds like they must have exerted quite an effort to bring you here. You would think they would just kill you if you represented a threat to them. You must be of noble rank and have something they want in order to bring you here alive."

Edwin said nothing.

As he sat there pondering what next, a squad of six men came to his cell door. The one with the keys opened the door and told him to get up because the King wanted to see him.

They tied his arms behind his back. A guard grabbed each arm and they walked away with him. They went through several dimly lit corridors and up a steep set of stairs. At the top they made a sharp left turn jerking him sharply he winced in pain embarrassed he gave away that it hurt. Then they came to a large room and at the opposite end sat a man on a large chair, not a throne but distinctive. Here sat the King, a burly man with bushy eyebrows and a malevolent stare. When they got to within ten feet of the King they pushed Edwin down to his knees.

"Welcome Edwin to Merethath. I am King Taryn. I am your host during your stay with us. Hopefully for your sake it will be a brief one. I have already contacted King Erith that you are in my custody."

Edwin remained silent.

King Taryn continued, "It has come to my attention that you are an integral part of King Erith's mad plan to takeover Ireland. I don't intend to be a part of it. You may wonder why I didn't kill you. I've decided there may be a better way. If I kill you that will only slow Erith down, but he's bent on this objective and it won't stop him. So I've decided I am going to use you as a bargaining chip to create a treaty to keep Merethath out of this Evansing/Nerland union. I want nothing to do with something that will take away our right to rule as we see fit. I know Erith is an honorable man and even if he is forced to make an agreement because I have you as hostage he will not break his word. Ha! What a fool! His so called honorable way is a weakness which can be easily exploited."

"So what have you to say about that?"

"I don't have anything to say, Sire." replied Edwin.

"What! A feisty young man like you has nothing to say?"

"Have I been misled as to who you are? Are you not this great warrior who is supposed to lead King Erith and his lackeys into victory?"

Edwin remained silent.

One of the guards struck Edwin over the side of the head and barked, "Answer the King!"

Edwin partly knocked over straightened himself up and replied, "Sire, in Elfereth I have experienced some success in battle."

"I understand you have had some recent success on your trip to Nerland. Perhaps I should keep you and see what you could teach us. I suspect though we wouldn't get your best. No, I will for now use you to get favorable terms with Erith. In the meantime behave yourself and you will stay healthy and fit to be returned. I have already arranged to have my ambassador meet with Erith in Nerland. He will present my terms to him next week. For your sake I trust he will agree quickly. If he doesn't I will send you back to him piece by piece."

Looking at the guards, he ordered Edwin to be taken back to his cell. "Ensure there are six men outside his cell at all times."

Once back in his cell they untied him and the cell slammed shut.

Lying on the dirty straw he thought to himself, "What do we do now? Can Percival and Erith somehow get me out of here?"

He gazed back at the six men standing outside his cell. They looked bored but also curious about this young man so prized by two kingdoms. One of the guards started taunting Edwin, "You don't look like much now do you? You may think you're big stuff, but here you're just another piece of crap."

Edwin looked away to the wall and started to remember the last time he saw Greer. He would remember her and not let these thugs have the satisfaction of distressing him. In fact he decided he would be happy regardless of where he was. This represented another opportunity for personal growth and greater freedom. He would choose to think and act like a mighty prince.

He started to smile to himself at the prospect of using this time as an opportunity to gain the strength of character Percival intended to do through discussions and reflection. This increased the pressure and forced the process to speed along more rapidly. Good, he was getting a vision for how this could be a good thing. After all, Erith would make a deal for him and he would be out of here probably in a week or two at the most.

CHAPTER 9

Ten days later Edwin was summoned to see the King of Merethath. Edwin expected good news, but by the look on the King's face that may not be the case.

"Your lord and master has seen fit to belabor the negotiations. I have told him if he doesn't come to terms I will send you back to him piece by piece."

Edwin stiffened but said nothing.

"Erith has indicated unless you are returned immediately safe and sound he will invade our kingdom and burn it to the ground. I know that is true and with his Nerland allies they outnumber us by a vast amount. The only saving factor here is he has promised to grant us an exemption from having to supply soldiers for the ongoing pursuit of Irish unity. He is still insisting that we cooperate commercially, politically and provide food and weapons as required. I could be stubborn and still send him pieces of you, but what would it accomplish?"

"You are to be taken back at once. A troop is waiting outside to escort you to the Nerland frontier. There you will be met by your countrymen."

Edwin let out a cheer. Smiling he thanked the King and left to join his escort troop.

As Edwin rode along he thought to himself what an astonishing turn of events, "Who would have thought the King of Merethath would all of a sudden be so amenable to letting me go even when he didn't get what he wanted?"

He thought further, "The extra forces Erith counts on to help him must be working because there is no other explanation. People like the King of Merethath don't do reasonable. Some kings would stage fierce resistance even if vastly outnumbered. Indeed the King of Merethath didn't seem to be himself. In fact he seemed down right pleasant. It was a side Edwin hadn't seen before and as far as he had heard not too many other people had either."

At the Nerland border Glynn and a dozen of Evansing's troops greeted Edwin. To help with the integration process and as recognition of Glynn's friendship with Edwin he had been put in charge of this escort detail.

As Edwin and Glynn rode together they started to chat about what had happened when it was discovered he had been kidnapped

"It was easy to discover you had been taken. There was a note left specifying all of Merethath's demands together with threats to your person if they weren't met."

"You are going to have a most delightful welcome at the Nerland castle. Not only will the two kings welcome you, but Greer herself insisted on coming to Nerland to wait out your return. She was most distressed. You are very fortunate to have a woman like that in your life."

"Yes, I know. Remembering her beauty and our times together helped me to maintain a positive outlook on things while in Merethath's dungeon. It was not a pleasant place I can assure you."

Edwin then switched the conversation, "Glynn are things melding together between the two armies and the royal families? And how about the government people, are they making progress? And is Nerland coming to terms over the death of their prince and the other men?"

"It is difficult to see accurately because of course the King is adamant about his people supporting this initiative of King Erith. He has indeed announced this to his lords as a co-initiative between him and Erith. From what I have observed so far there seems to be general approval of this unity quest. The parties are working together to make it happen. For most part I would say it is with a genuine desire to make it work. There are pockets of Nerlanders who are still quite concerned about what will happen to their kingdom's ability to govern itself. Also the thought of their men going to war for the pursuit of Irish unity is not easy for some of them to accept.

Keltic is keeping a tight hold on the front of unity between Nerland and Evansing. People in Nerland have tremendous respect for Keltic. Even if their private views differ, most would still remain loyal to their king."

They arrived at the outskirts of the castle and were about to cross over the moat when they heard an excited squeal from the top of the walls.

"Edwin! Edwin!"

They both looked up to see Greer waving her blue handkerchief in greeting. She beamed with joy and willingness to be undignified in her expression of it. Princesses were not known to do public displays of emotion.

The two men walked their horses over to the nearest stairwell on the castle wall and awaited Greer's descent. In a few minutes a breathless Greer came down the stairs and gave Edwin a warm hug. They embraced for a moment or two before they realized decorum required they cease what they would rather do which was to stay in embrace.

Greer looked into Edwin's eyes and started to cry, "I was so worried I would never see you again. My father told me not to worry that it would all work out, but I couldn't seem to believe him. Now I realize he did know what he was talking about and I worried for nothing."

"Remembering you is what I used to keep up my spirits while in that Merethath dungeon. I would remember our times together and see your face in my mind's eye. It is so good to see you again. Here is a good and true friend, Glynn of the Nerland army."

"Pleasure to meet you Glynn. Thank you so much for bringing him back safe and sound."

"Well I can't claim that. He was already safe and sound and I got to ride along with him."

"Well thanks then for keeping him company. I'm sure he appreciated seeing your friendly face after that ordeal. It must have been dreadful to be kept in a smelly dungeon."

Edwin responded, "It wasn't easy that's true, but now it's over and let us go on to new things, much pleasanter things."

Greer replied, "Yes, that's true let us go to the dining hall where the two kings are discussing affairs of state and also waiting to celebrate your return.

When Erith saw Edwin enter the dining hall he excused himself from Keltic and hurried over to greet Edwin.

"Welcome back young man it is good see you look fit and healthy. King Taryn must not be quite the scoundrel I always he thought he was."

"Thank you, Sire, it is good to be back. King Taryn is every bit a scoundrel, but he's not totally stupid. His good senses were able to rule and decide letting me go was preferable to his kingdom being burned down. He was quite upset about your unwillingness to cooperate with his demands."

"Well I am glad for his good senses because I must admit I would have been very sorry to have lost you or to see you suffer mutilation as he threatened. But I couldn't allow a precedent for blackmail to succeed no matter what the cost."

He continued, "King Keltic and I have had some fruitful discussions and he is on side with us as far as how we are going to work together."

"So what have you agreed to?" Edwin asked.

"Nerland and Evansing will both put armies in the field together under Evansing overall command, but there will be Nerland commanders in the combined forces. We have eliminated all barriers to trading between our two kingdoms. King Keltic will rule over Nerland as before except now there will be the King of Evansing over him in matters regarding the two kingdoms as part of a greater whole, namely a united Ireland."

"Enough of that, let's celebrate your return," said Keltic.

"Yes, let's bring out the entertainment you talked about," replied Erith.

"Bring out the dancers and the food and drink," commanded Keltic.

The evening progressed pleasantly for Edwin and Greer. The only sour note for the evening was when he discovered Jaffa had been the servant who had informed Nerland's Crown Prince about the affairs of state at Evansing. He had been implicated by some documents found in his possession and had confessed to betraying state secrets. The penalty of course was death, but it had been stayed until Edwin returned to Evansing. King Erith decided since Jaffa was Edwin's servant he should have final say in his fate.

Edwin was distressed at hearing what had occurred. He was fond of Jaffa and had a heart to help him advance in life. He did not relish the fact Jaffa's ultimate fate would now depend on him. However, he knew he was being trained to rule and decisions of this type were what kings encountered all the time. While deciding whether a person would live or die should never be easy, it had to be done. It had to be done in a way which resulted in a wise and just outcome and minimized the personal anguish. Edwin would not return for at least another week. He decided in the morning he would send a messenger to Percival with a request that he talk to Jaffa. His objective was to do an assessment of Jaffa's character and ascertain the motivations of why he committed an act of treason. As he thought about what had transpired and how it had been characterized as a dreadful act of treason, he couldn't see how there could be any other outcome other than death for Jaffa. Of course there was the possibility Jaffa had been unjustly accused and wrongly implicated. Yes, he would ask Percival to do a thorough investigation in the evidence against Jaffa.

"How was the confession obtained?" he wondered.

He knew even in Evansing that coercive methods could be used to encourage confessions.

Greer would sometimes notice Edwin deep in thought and at first she ignored it, but after a while she became irritated.

"Are you bored with me, Edwin?" She asked during one of those moments of deep thought about Jaffa.

"No, no, of course not, I'm finding myself thinking about Jaffa and how I have to come up with a wise and just solution. I'm sorry I have been distracted. How could you ever even remotely entertain the thought that I or anyone would be bored with you? You are a Princess of Evansing and I am deeply in love with you."

Her eyes brightened at him saying he was deeply in love with her.

Then she replied, "It's true I am a princess, but maybe the dark side of that is I sometimes think it's all about me, so I expect people to be always focused on me. After all, most of the people around me are focused on me. You are not like those people. Sometimes this challenges the dark side, but I know it's good that you can be real with me. Besides I know you connect with me as Greer the person not just Greer the Princess."

"So do you know what are you going to do about Jaffa?"

He filled her in about the instructions he would send to Percival. He also told her how he was glad Percival wanted to stay back in Evansing because now he could get him to do some initial investigative work on Jaffa.

Greer looked at him giving her rapt attention. She admired the desire he had to be wise and just, even with a servant. This was not a common concern for nobles. Servants were treated as little more than chattels which legally they were. She found herself sometimes thinking that way as well. It was easy to do when you were in a position of privilege and power. Yet she had been trained by her father to have at least a somewhat benign and benevolent attitude toward their servants. Under the influence of Edwin she was becoming even more concerned about the well being of the servants in her charge.

She had decided she would be kinder with her servants and more involved in trying to help alleviate their personal concerns. Yes, that is what she would do. For her to see how heartfelt the distress Edwin had over Jaffa was deeply convicting for she realized she did not yet have that same level of concern for even her closest personal attendants. Some of them had been with her since she was a little girl and yet she had never bothered to inquire to any degree about their lives.

After Edwin finished discussing his thoughts about Jaffa he lowered his voice and looking more intently into Greer's eyes said, "Enough of that. I am here to be your returning Hero and you are my welcoming Beauty. You do deserve my undivided attention and I promise I now will give it to you."

Greer blushed at her self-centeredness but only for a second; after all she was a princess of the Realm of Evansing. Being self-centered was her normal state.

"But no," she thought to herself, "a true princess focuses on her subjects and the concerns of those around her. Oh this is a challenge!"

King Erith came by and said to Greer he would like to escort her to her room for the night. She would be placed in the suite next to his with a small army of guards. Then he turned to Edwin and told him his quarters were to be on the other side of the King's quarters with extra guards for him as well. Then taking Greer's arm he began toward her quarters. Greer looked back at Edwin with a mournful look indicating she did not want to go, but she didn't say anything to her father.

Edwin regretted to see her go, but then he noticed Glynn and walked over to his table and sat down.

CHAPTER 10

In the morning Edwin woke up with a troubled sense something was not right about the charges against Jaffa. He'd had a dream about the accusations. In the dream he saw a member of his community back in Elfereth on the witness stand saying all kinds of damaging things about Jaffa. They sounded sure to convince the judge of Jaffa's guilt. What troubled Edwin was that the person in question was a well known liar. In his dispatch to Percival he would mention this dream as well and ask for his input as to its meaning.

Today was meant to be a fierce day of training. After breakfast Edwin went to the open field being used for maneuvers. There Edwin worked with the officers in basic training activities designed to create a new level of camaraderie and higher performance on the battlefield. Soon they would work with the lower ranks, but it was important for the officers to assimilate these new attitudes and ways of being. It related to treating their troops with respect. This didn't mean there wasn't the usual military discipline, but officers were to treat their men as though they had value. This was unusual during this particular time in history. Warriors in the ranks were treated as though they were expendable and dealt with harshly for the slightest infraction. Edwin knew the latter was another issue that needed to be reviewed and reconsidered as to what warranted serious punishment.

In spite of a number of officers giving encouraging responses, Edwin could sense about a third of them were not enthralled with the idea of changing their ways. This concerned Edwin, but he had a back-up plan he hoped would change at least most of them to the new regime. A key aspect of it entailed them receiving specially designed training maneuvers.

At the end of the day Edwin could sense some progress being made with the reluctant third of the officers. With the other two-thirds Edwin was surprised at how quickly they were adapting to the new ways. To ensure it stuck they would do it again tomorrow.

That evening in the dining hall the officers from both armies celebrated a successful first day of learning new leadership skills. Beer and ale flowed freely and as the evening progressed the officers became more and more boisterous. New levels of camaraderie were being formed between the two armies until one of the Nerland officers took offense at what an Evansing officer said to him. It was one of those jesting remarks which had a twist of meanness to it. Having been fueled by too much drink the Nerland officer pulled his dagger and challenged the other to battle to the death. The atmosphere changed from festive to tense as the two men started to position themselves for hand to hand combat. Edwin had to quickly assess whether to let it go on or whether to intervene. He decided the best approach would be to let them go for it. If he intervened it may be construed as weakness by Evansing. Before he could consider it further the Evansing officer also drew out his dagger and the two started to circle around looking for an opening. The Evansing officer, named Terrence, lunged for his opponent's chest. His opponent backed up in time and came around with his dagger to catch Terrence's left shoulder. There came a yelp of pain and blood started to ooze out of the wounded shoulder. Before the Nerlander could strike again, Terrence grabbed his adversary's dagger arm and tried to drive his dagger into the Nerlander's chest. However, his own dagger arm was grabbed as well so now both men were clutching each other's arms and wrestling to get free for a blow. Terrence's shoulder wound took its toll as he weakened his grip on the other man. Thus freeing his dagger arm the Nerlander drove a blow deep into Terrence's chest narrowly missing his heart. The blow was grievous enough that Terrence dropped to the floor and stayed there, not moving.

The hall became silent as the onlookers considered what had happened. The two kings meeting in an adjacent room had been notified a fight was in progress and they arrived just before it ended. Both looked displeased and distressed by what had occurred.

Erith's personal physician pronounced Terrence dead.

Erith came over to Edwin and asked him why such a thing was allowed to occur. Edwin told him he felt it best that the dispute be resolved between the two men as they had decided.

Erith looked at Edwin a bit troubled saying, "Sometimes I think you like blood too much." Then he walked away and the two kings resumed their meeting.

Soldiers from Evansing removed Terrence's body from the hall and would transport it back to his wife in the morning. Nothing further was mentioned of the incident as it was decided to treat it as a personal issue of the two combatants and not an issue between Nerland and Evansing.

Shortly after, Edwin excused himself from the hall so he could seek out Greer. They had arranged earlier to meet at a much smaller meeting hall near the main one. She was attended by two of her maids plus there were six guards providing security. The two maids were waved away to remove themselves to the other side of the hall and the guards were also asked to withdraw some distance away. This allowed them to have some level of privacy. The two young lovers still had lots of chaperones in the same room. This occurred during a time when no proper lady would be alone in private with a male other than an immediate family member. Edwin came to Greer with the smell of beer and ale to which she playfully turned up her nose to act like she didn't like it. Edwin had been moderate in his imbibing, but he'd had a few to be sociable and he did like to drink a little bit now and then. He wasn't into getting drunk because he didn't like the feeling of being out of control.

Greer was happy to see Edwin even if he did smell of drink. She had been busy during the day getting acquainted with Nerland royals. Her father decided to incorporate her help in building bridges between the two royal families. She had enjoyed it, but now she only wanted to hang out with her favorite guy. Usually there was a steady flow of chatter between the two. At times they could also be quiet and enjoy sitting in silence wrapped in each other's spirit. Tonight they chatted for both wanted each other to share all about their day.

Greer had created new friendships with several of the Nerland young ladies. She considered inviting them to Evansing for a couple of weeks of socializing with the Evansing royals. She was betwixt as to whether to invite all four of those young ladies at the same time or whether to split them up into groups of two. The first option would avoid the other two being disappointed or slighted by not being invited first, but it may be more difficult to give sufficient individual attention to them all. The latter option of course had the problem noted above, but at least it would be easier to get to know them. As she shared these concerns, Edwin of course wanted to share his advice, but something inside him told him, "NO!" Rather he listened intently giving his full undivided attention and was genuinely interested.

After she had shared her day and her concerns about the invitations, she asked Edwin how it went with the training. Edwin expressed pleasure at the favorable reception and rapid progress already made. He shared some specific aspects of it but gave a fairly high level review of the day's events. This of course was not acceptable to Greer. He did not gloss over the combat incident in the dining hall. That he went into some detail describing. However, he did not share what Erith had said to him. Greer seemed rather intrigued about the battle which had occurred and expressed some distress at the death of Terrence.

After finishing with the combat she expressed her view to Edwin that he could share greater details about the maneuvers and more of his conversations with the Nerland officers. She hungered to know whatever there was to know.

So he revisited some of the previous conversations by adding more details which at first he hadn't thought would be interesting for her. But as he noticed how engrossed Greer was with what he shared he started to expand more and more.

At midnight Edwin escorted her to her suite, gave her a moderate embrace and went to his own quarters.

The next day came rather early for Edwin and also for the rest of the officers especially those who had been drinking heavily. At the dining hall the officers were straggling in and many were looking rather hung over.

As Edwin observed them he realized it was going to be a slow start this morning. No one mentioned the combat the night before.

During breakfast, news came of raiding marauders in the west end of Nerland which had attacked and burnt several villages. Upward of fifty people were reported kidnapped along with at least a dozen killed. Initial reports indicated they were a renegade group who did not belong to any particular kingdom. However, kings sometimes disguised their troops as renegades. This avoided retribution for expeditions designed to capture slaves and take away other available booty.

This would change things because there needed to be a response. In the west part of Nerland the forces were quite thin. They would need to be reinforced if they were to defend other villages and also pursue the perpetrators. Of course if they were no longer in Nerland there would be the complication of considering crossing into a neighboring kingdom. This could provoke a military response and strain relations. King Keltic commanded that a force would leave by noon today. At least half the troops at the Nerland capital would be sent to restore order.

Erith saw this raid as an opportunity for Evansing to demonstrate at least some measure of benefit to Nerland for their new alliance. He asked King Keltic if all ninety-nine of the remaining Evansing troops could accompany the Nerland army. This would also include Edwin. Keltic happily accepted the offer.

When Greer heard Edwin would be leaving within the hour she struggled with her disappointment. The two lovers were able to spend ten minutes or so saying good-bye.

Edwin ended it by looking her in the eyes and said to her, "Promise me you will not worry while I am gone. After all you know with the plan to unite Ireland I will be gone much of the time. You can't be worrying all the time. Pray I will be safe. That will be a better use of your time instead of worrying."

Greer returned his intense gaze with an intense gaze of her own. She remained silent for a moment and then nodded, "Yes, you are right. Worrying is a foolish waste of time. I will trust you will be protected and will come back to me."

They hugged deeply and shared a lingering good-bye kiss. Neither cared about propriety. It was their first kiss and it felt good. It ended when Glynn entered the officers' quarters they were in. He was there to inform Edwin it was time to leave. With reluctance the two ended their kiss and embrace. With a final look Edwin turned to leave with Glynn. Of the three only Glynn felt embarrassed.

Four hours later the Nerland and Evansing troops entered their first village that had been attacked. The villagers still there were in a state of bewilderment at the destruction of their homes and fields. Almost everyone had had a family member either killed or kidnapped. Several troops were assigned to start gathering information on the identity of the raiders. They were to also find out where they may be now.

Glynn, leading this particular force with Edwin his second in command, decided after about twenty minutes no useful information was going to come out of that village. Glynn gave the order to move on to the next village. One hour further west, they entered another village. It had the same look of destruction as the previous one. Again, no useful information was discovered. Since darkness approached with the next village being at least an hour away; Glynn decided to camp the night among the ruins of this village. Indications from the villagers were that the raiders had left at least ten hours earlier.

That night around the campfire Glynn, Edwin and several other officers conferred about what their thoughts were as to strategy the next day. A couple of officers thought it would be better to split their force to cover more territory. Glynn and Edwin and several others decided dividing their force would make them vulnerable to being outnumbered. They would err on the side of prudence rather than risk losing a substantial part of their force.

CHAPTER 11

The next morning there hung a heavy mist. As the troops were rousing from their sleep, almost two hundred raiders came out of the mists overpowering the sentries and charging on to the main force. Edwin instinctively grabbed his sword and stood up in time to repel a battle axe aimed for his skull. The force of the blow almost knocked his sword out of his hand. Edwin grabbed his sword with both hands and gave a furious slash against the neck of his attacker that neatly sliced off his head. As Edwin twirled around another raider came after him with a sword. The two clashed against each other. Both deftly defended each others thrusts and slashes. Edwin lost his footing and fell backwards. His attacker leaped forward to press his advantage for the kill. As he was about to thrust his sword into Edwin's throat an Evansing archer found his mark and the raider fell forward dead falling onto Edwin.

Edwin rolled the dead man off of him and once again was in the midst of sword play with another foe. The attacker lunged at him with his sword headed for his heart. Just a last second cross over by Edwin saved his life. His opponent, a large man, yet quick on his feet swung hard.

Edwin thought to himself, "This won't be easy, but it's doable."

The raider came in swinging and for a time both men were slashing away at one another. Edwin thought he had an opening and made a lunge of his own, but it was stopped by a brilliant comeback. The two men stood back a moment catching their breath. Then the raider again came in swinging his sword determined to end this battle once and for all. Initially this caught Edwin a little unprepared for the ferocity of the assault and he took several steps back. Then he stood his ground refusing to budge another inch. He started to tire as the man continued to rain down blows on him. At this point, Edwin executed one of his patented favorite moves. He hit low on a backhand cutting deeply into the side of his opponent. Blood spurted out. The man continued to fight, but after another moment or so he collapsed. Edwin left him there to die, which he did a few minutes later.

The raiders decided their advantage of surprise was not enough to give them victory. So they sounded a retreat and disappeared back into the mists. Edwin took a group of one hundred and fifty men with him in pursuit of a group headed east. Glynn took another two hundred or so and headed after those headed north. Almost a hundred others were left behind to look after the sixty or so wounded, dying or dead.

The pursuit into the mists required stout hearts because they could easily be ambushed, but they were willing to risk it. It would be unconscionable to let them escape.

Sure enough a sizeable contingent of the enemy forces decided to set up an ambush position not more than fifty yards from the village. They were very lethal in their initial assault, but they had underestimated the fighting capacity of the Nerland/Evansing troops under the command of Edwin. Again, the raiders found themselves at a disadvantage and they turned to flee. This time they were fairly easy targets to be struck down by Evansing archers and other troops rushing them with their swords. When at last the chase stopped only a handful of the swiftest raiders got away. The Nerland/Evansing troops gathered their wounded and dead and returned to camp. They also had eleven captives.

Shortly later Glynn and his group returned with another twenty-one captives. Now they could find out where they came from. Of course it may require some persuasion. Being persuasive was something these troops would not have any trouble demonstrating. As it was, the talk was that all the captives should be executed in some fitting way. After all they weren't regular troops. They were just kidnappers and murderers. Back in that time even regular troops were often mistreated and executed when captured. However, in this case they were first going to get the captives to tell who commanded them to raid villages in Nerland.

The interrogation of the prisoners began gently, relatively speaking. As they maintained their resistance to tell where they came from, and who ordered them to raid the villages, firmer measures were implemented. One of the prisoners was tied to a post. An Evansing soldier took a burning poker and jabbed it into each of his eyes. As he screamed the others were advised that one by one they would suffer the same fate unless they started to disclose everything their captors wanted to know. After the screaming became intolerable one of the Nerland troops put him to death with a quick stab to his heart.

What the men told was most disturbing. They were from a confederation of kingdoms bordering Nerland and beyond, who had decided to try and distract the move to unite Ireland.

What to do with these men? According to them most were members of the standing armies of their kingdoms. Inquiries were made as to whether any of them had a measure of wealth, or wealthy family members who would be willing to ransom them. None of them seemed worthwhile to try and ransom. So as an act of expedience and revenge they were summarily executed by the sword. Their bodies were left for the villagers to bury.

The troops then set out for the next village. There they discovered villagers more progressed with rebuilding and getting back to relative normalcy. This village had been able to defend itself to a significant extent. Consequently it suffered minor destruction and loss. Edwin interviewed the head man of the village. His name was Jaather. This man in his late 40s had a no nonsense way about him. The troops did not in the slightest intimidate him. Nor did he seem like he would be intimidated by anyone. He had trained the men of his village to fight back in case of attack. Looking at some of his more fit men showed they shared the qualities of their leader. Here stood a true leader of men. He knew how to impart what he had. Edwin wondered how they could utilize his unusual and yet highly desirable qualities. He would not likely be willing to leave the village. Of course financial incentives may help. That and promises to provide help for his fields. As a last resort he could always be forced to leave. But that would be undesirable.

Edwin shared his thoughts with Glynn. The latter agreed here was a consummate leader of men. But he couldn't be certain as to whether they had a place to utilize him in the regular army or some related service.

Edwin approached the village leader.

"Jaather, how would you like to leave this village and see new sights across Ireland?"

"Well, young man, that idea has crossed my mind. My wife died last year. My kids are grown and I've been thinking I would like to do something else."

This came as a surprising answer from an older village person. Almost all of them by his age just wanted to keep doing what they had always been doing. But he wasn't your typical villager. His answer further confirmed for Edwin that Jaather could mold a group of fifty or so soldiers into a very special unit. A unit of fearless men who would take on outrageous assignments no one else would consider possible.

As Edwin shared his thoughts with Jaather the latter's eyes lit up at the prospect of training men in doing the seemingly impossible.

Jaather responded, "I will do it for I have been made for more than this," motioning towards the village.

"Alright, does it matter to you if you work with Evansing or Nerland troops?"

"No, not at all. We all bleed when we're cut."

"Good because I'd like you to work with the Evansing men."

The troops delayed for one hour their departure for the next village. This gave Jaather a chance to say goodbye and allocate his land and possessions to his children and gather a few things. He turned over charge of the village to his closest friend, who Edwin had noticed earlier as one of those most fit men.

Many of the villagers wept as they saw Jaather leave. To many he had been like a father. Edwin smiled to himself. Jaather would be the perfect one to train and lead the group of troops he had been envisioning. It would be interesting to see how this would turn out.

The last village they were assigned to visit required almost two hours of travel. Upon their arrival they were greeted with a sight of total devastation. The raiders burned or carried away everything. The stench of unburied human and animal corpses hung heavily over the remains of the village.

Glynn decided since there were no villagers around that the troops would be assigned to bury the dead.

The army spent the night just outside the village. There were double the sentries than had been posted the night before.

The night passed uneventful and so did the morning as the troops turned east towards the Nerland capital. If they kept up a steady pace they should get back around dusk.

Edwin thought to himself about what this news of kingdoms conspiring against them would mean. One solution came to him. This would be the ideal time to use a small select group like the one he wanted Jaather to train. The objective would be to kidnap and/or assassinate the top leaders in each of the kingdoms opposing them.

"Jaather, I've been thinking about your first assignment, or at least the first assignment of the men you will be training. What do you think about training men to be consummate kidnappers and assassins? Men who would go behind enemy lines and either bring out leaders or kill leaders. The select few I want eliminated are the ones behind the attacks on your village and other villages."

"Sounds like a worthy objective. I can do it and I will do it," replied Jaather.

"Where did you learn to fight and how to train others to fight?" asked Edwin.

"You probably think I've never been out of my village before. At your age I had already been fighting on the Continent for three years. I had left my home in search of adventure. I found plenty of it in battle. After about eight years of fighting for various lords I returned home. I was forever changed, too many battles and too much blood. However, I knew I had a gift for battle. Not just certain types of combat, but all types of warfare. When you mentioned training assassins and kidnappers you're talking about something I specialized in for two years. Sometimes I brought back their head and sometimes I brought them back with their head still on their shoulders alive and well. It depended on whether my master loved the ransom money more than he hated the man."

Edwin experienced pleasant surprise at what he was hearing although in his heart he wasn't all that surprised. Something told him no one who had spent his whole life in a remote Irish village could fight and lead the way this man could.

"Good to know. It makes my decision to hire you look just that much more like genius."

"Tonight I would like you to start considering who you want in your group and what is the best way to proceed further. To make it easier you can watch the drill we will have tomorrow. It will be the first time the officers have worked with their troops."

Shortly after arriving in the Nerland capital, a servant informed Greer of her sweetheart's return. She went to where Edwin and the troops were dismounted and unpacking their gear. Edwin introduced his new friend Jaather to Greer. They exchanged pleasantries and then Edwin left his horse with Jaather to take into the stable. Edwin would walk on with Greer. Their faces beamed with delight while holding hands, which was another advancement in their willingness to give public display to their affection. They walked down the street together. After about two hours of walking around, they decided to go to the dining hall. There the two Kings would be awaiting news and deciding strategy. When they arrived they received a rather curt response from Erith who had expected Edwin to show up forthwith. But he got over it quickly enough when he realized Greer had been the main reason for the delay. Erith found it hard to get upset and stay upset with his daughter.

The Kings together with their officers were starting to consider what course of action to pursue.

Edwin asked if he could propose an option.

He continued, "I have with me a man who is qualified to train a special troop of assassins and kidnappers. This troop would go on covert missions behind enemy lines. Their purpose is to either assassinate or kidnap key enemy leaders or other individuals we have targeted. I propose we allow one month for their training.

Even though it means our waiting a month to respond, the advantage is the avoidance of assigning large numbers of troops for extended battle. This would entail huge expense and also large numbers of troops killed or wounded. To unite Ireland will require all the resources we have. It is imperative to avoid unnecessary expenditures so early in this quest. By taking out the key leaders in these three kingdoms we can send a very clear signal that opposition will not be tolerated. The investment required for these objectives to be achieved will be minimal compared to the alternative. I suggest the officers now review their men and determine which ones qualify as having extraordinary physical and mental prowess. These men should also have a desire to be assigned to this special unit."

After several minutes of conferring between themselves, the two Kings said the idea had merit and they gave orders to the officers to start the selection process. They were to report tomorrow evening with their fifty men selected. The Kings also indicated that tomorrow morning they wanted to meet the man selected to do the training.

The next morning Jaather looked forward with great anticipation to the opportunity to meet the kings. Each king met him warmly and he competently handled their questions and concerns. He assured them that one month would be adequate time to pull off this kind of assignment. He also advised them he had briefed the officers as to the type of qualities most fitting for this type of troop. He would also have the final say as to which soldiers would be selected for his troop. The Kings were impressed by this man who feared no one. He conducted himself very naturally in front of them.

The Kings thought to themselves, "How could this man remain hidden in a remote village for so many years?"

After Jaather left the presence of the Kings he went straightway to where the officers were staging their selections. Jaather determined to be as useful as possible and also cull out the wrong selections as early as possible.

Edwin, Glynn and a couple of officers known for personal heroism were also going to help Jaather in the training. Edwin almost volunteered himself as part of the special force, but he knew his duties precluded him from participating in such a troop.

That evening the final selections were introduced to the Kings. Some of them were queried by one or both of the monarchs. This was mainly a formality, but the Kings were interested in knowing what kind of man would be most suited for this type of assignment.

The Kings were satisfied with the selections. From even a very cursory examination by them they realized these men were unique and exceptional. They each had a fearless confidence about themselves, which lent them to exude an air of invincibility, the very quality Jaather wanted. Training would begin tomorrow morning. It would be intense and it would be difficult. Jaather already had about 90% of the training plan worked out in his head. The man had a mind like a steel trap. Nothing escaped him and he seemed to be able to recall anything from previous events in his life. Whether a conversation from three days earlier or from his days as a warrior; he could recall detailed facts of a situation. Edwin mused to himself what an amazing find this Jaather had turned out to be.

Edwin looked across the room to where Greer sat. Even though women wouldn't normally be permitted to attend this kind of meeting; Greer had managed to gain entrance along with her four new friends from Nerland. She and Edwin weren't sitting together because he and she both knew the temptation would be too great to distract one another. Oh well in a few minutes they would be able to distract one another freely without concern about whether they missed something important.

The Kings decided that tomorrow, Erith and the contingent from Evansing plus Jaather and the fifty man special troop would return to Evansing's capital. The special troop had thirty-nine men from Nerland and the balance from Evansing. Things had progressed quickly from where they started. They were considered part of a united Ireland force, but for now they were in effect part of the Evansing army.

When Greer and Edwin had a chance to get one on one again they had great excitement knowing they would be going back to Evansing the next day. The only troubling thing concerned dealing with Jaffa. As soon as he got back he would have to ask Percival for his assessment of Jaffa's character. He needed to know whether there existed any chance of the evidence being false or the confession being obtained under duress. Enough of that decided Edwin, now was a time to give his girl the undivided attention she deserved. So with a quick about face from the serious to the hilarious he became totally fascinated and captivated by Greer. Of course that was the state Greer loved her guy to be in. Perhaps that is a state that most women like their man to be in. She told him how she had decided which two of her Nerland friends she would bring first to Evansing. She had decided to tell all four of them her predicament and let them decide amongst themselves which two would go first.

After telling Edwin this, she looked him straight in the eye and said, "Wasn't that clever of me?"

He looked back at her and laughed and said, "Of course it was clever, you are a very clever, young lady."

CHAPTER 12

The next day the Evansing contingent arose before dawn to get an early start. Shortly after sunrise with a quick breakfast, they were on the road back to Evansing. A Nerland force of two hundred men accompanied them on the way back. King Keltic rode with Erith for the first ten miles or so discussing future plans and to give his farewell.

Greer rode with her two Nerland friends, while Edwin rode up ahead with the scouts looking for anything amiss. The convoy travelled to Evansing without incident.

As they entered the Evansing castle they were greeted by Percival. Edwin felt a relief and joy at seeing his mentor. He hadn't realized how much he had missed his meetings with Percival. Getting off his horse he ran up to Percival and gave him a big hug. Indeed a joyous reunion.

"Edwin, you have had quite the adventures in your absence and yet you don't look any worse for wear."

"Yes, Percival, I have been very fortunate."

"Well I'm sure your Divine Protector had something to do with that."

"Yes, you are probably right. I never thought about it that way."

Edwin's face got serious all at once as he recalled Jaffa.

"Percival, what have you to tell me about Jaffa? I need to make a decision soon."

"Yes, I know and I think I have some information which will be useful. My discussions with Jaffa and others have made me conclude it is unlikely he is guilty."

"What makes you say that?"

"First is the character of Jaffa. From talking to him and those that have known him well it is hard to believe he would do something so disloyal as to share state secrets. He has been known as a servant with a history of exemplary service. Second, I have discovered the interrogators applied torture during the questioning. I have examined marks on Jaffa's torso and legs and they are recent wounds consistent with torture. The initial accusations came from an anonymous note left in the dining hall. No one has come forward to acknowledge they had evidence as to why they suspected Jaffa."

"So what do you think should be my next course of action?"

"If I were you I would talk to Jaffa yourself and try to form your own opinion. If you are also satisfied he is innocent or at least there is sufficient doubt as to his guilt, then you will be able to convincingly talk to the King. I'm sure Erith will not be happy with torture being applied in the interrogation. Mind you he has authorized it in the past so it's not like it's never been done. But I think his thoughts are moving from promoting that kind of tactic. He is becoming a gentler monarch as time goes on. His personal beliefs are shifting and it is creating for him a different perspective as to what is permissible and what is best in ruling. Yours and Greer's willingness to flout the rules of public displays of affection have caused a veritable domino effect in him of re-examining a lot of beliefs he held to be true. He has realized many things he thought to be true have indeed only had the appearance of truth. Consequently, as he has delved deeper into the basis of why he has believed certain things, he has concluded they are at least flawed and in many cases totally false. Therefore when you talk to him, I am sure he will agree that a confession obtained under torture is somewhat suspect."

Edwin considered what he had heard and then shared his intention to go straight away to visit Jaffa.

"Jaffa, my good friend I have to come to visit and discuss with you what has happened during my absence."

Jaffa looked up at the source of the cheery voice. He smiled at seeing Edwin.

He stood up and came to the bars with a hopeful smile on his face, "Sir, I am so glad to see you. The jailer told me if it wasn't for the fact I was your servant, my head would already be resting on the west gate of the castle."

"Well hopefully your head will stay on your shoulders for many years to come. Why don't you tell me what has happened."

"Well sir the news came back about how there had been an ambush on your party. The next day someone discovered a note which accused me of being the informant. It was a total shock that anyone would accuse me of such disloyalty. What would I have to gain from doing such a dastardly deed? My life as your servant has been the best I have ever had. I would have to be a total dolt to do anything to prejudice that let alone commit high treason. It didn't matter to the authorities that I denied any knowledge about what they were accusing me about. Then they found some letters which connected me to previous secrets being passed along to the Nerland Crown Prince. I have no knowledge of how those letters got in my room. It would not be hard for someone to put them there as I seldom lock my room. What do I have that's worth stealing? I'm only a servant. If you look at the so called documents incriminating me; you will notice those purported to be written by me don't even remotely look like my handwriting. I am sure someone has examples of my handwriting. Compare them and you will be able to tell right off it's not my writing. The officers would not even consider comparing my writing on other things I have written. They just looked at the name signed at the bottom of the page and said it was my name, so it must be me who wrote the letter. There were also incriminating letters addressed to me. I can only assume the person who would do such a thing must be the person who is the actual informant."

"Is there someone who holds a grievous grudge against you so that they would decide to target you?"

"No one I can readily think of." But then a strange look came upon his face.

Edwin noticed the look and asked, "What are you recalling?"

"Well there is one person who has been rather sore at me for several years."

"Who is that and why?"

"I must admit I am embarrassed to share why. I let my baser instincts get the best of me and I, I got into an affair with this fellow's wife. He discovered us in bed one morning when we had expected him to not be back until that evening. As it turned out he had had his suspicions about us and he decided to check it out. Fortunately, I fought him off. I got my clothes and ran out. I never saw the lady again, or shall I say at least not in the way that I used to. I discovered later he had expressed an oath vowing to get me someday, one way or the other."

"Does he strike you as someone who could set you up like this, and also be the informant? For he would have to be both. He must have prepared the incriminating letters sometime in advance. There wouldn't have been enough time for him to do it in a day. He must have known it was going to happen. The only way he would know is if he was the one doing the informing."

"Well he can read and write. His name is Alfred and he is a merchant in the town square. You know the recent changes in the relations with Nerland must have cut into his business. I know he has benefited from having trade barriers with Nerland. He has charged premiums based on the difficulty of getting goods from other kingdoms. With easier trading he has no basis for charging extra."

"Good, tomorrow morning I am going to pay a visit to his shop and see what I can discover. In the meantime sleep well. Is there anything I can get for you before I leave?"

"Yes, sir, I would like my pillow if it isn't too much difficulty"

"No, of course not, I will arrange for my interim servant to bring it down to you. Don't worry your position is secure with me. As soon as we get you out of here you will resume your previous duties. Good night."

CHAPTER 13

The next morning after breakfast, Edwin and Glynn made their way down to the square and entered Alfred's shop. The pungent odor of sweat hung in the air like a moldy rag. Consequently it surprised them to note the shop carried a wide variety of quality merchandise. They are of the sort which commanded a profitable margin. Edwin recognized some products from his home area. They were priced three to four times what they would be back in Elfereth. Some of it undoubtedly due to the transportation and customs duties required to bring them to Evansing. However, Edwin estimated at least half the excess was profit. A man in his early 40s approached them and as he did so the disagreeable smell became even stronger.

"Edwin, sir, what brings a distinguished personage like yourself into my humble shop?"

Then turning to Glynn he greeted him with a good morning. Glynn just nodded.

Even though Edwin did not recall ever meeting Alfred or ever seeing him around before, something tweaked him when Alfred recognized him. Edwin knew he was well known in Evansing's capital, but he had the sense Alfred had a greater familiarity with him than what should be appropriate for someone of the general public. He didn't know why he had that sense but he did.

"And what is your name, sir?"

"My name is Alfred, but surely you must already know that."

"No, I didn't know that. I have never laid eyes on you before, or at least to the best of my knowledge I haven't.

Alfred straightened up a bit at the brusqueness in Edwin's voice.

"How can I help you, sir?"

The inappropriate familiarity of only a moment earlier had disappeared.

"I want to purchase this very ornate drinking cup. It's from Elfereth, right?"

"That's correct, sir, from one of the finest craftsman in all of Ireland."

"I would like you to write up a bill of sale for me please."

"Of course, sir, I would be happy to write up a bill for you."

In a few moments Edwin had his cup and bill of sale. He and Glynn headed straight to the Sheriff's office to examine the documents being kept as evidence in the case against Jaffa.

At the office of the Sherriff they were greeted by a clerk, "Sirs, how I can help you?"

"We need to look at the documents being held in connection with the case against Jaffa."

The clerk went to a storage bin in the back and pulled out several parchments.

"Here are the parchments you are wanting."

Edwin and Glynn spread them out on a table off to the side. Then he unrolled his bill of sale and laid it beside the incriminating letters. Glynn compared the handwriting and he could instantly see the striking resemblance between the alphabet letters r, e, and p in the bill of sale and the letters. He pointed out to Edwin the similarities. Edwin agreed there was a basis for believing the same man wrote both the letters and the bill of sale.

Edwin asked the clerk if the Sheriff was in his office. The clerk told him no, as he remained in the courts that morning but would be back after mid day. He asked the clerk to send a messenger to him in the castle as soon as the Sheriff was back, for he wanted to see him as soon as possible.

Later in the day while he and Percival were having another one of their learning sessions, someone knocked on the door. Edwin opened it and greeted the clerk from the Sheriff's office.

"Sir, the Sheriff will see you this afternoon."

"Ok, I will see him shortly."

Looking at Percival, Edwin asked, "Would you like to accompany me to the Sheriff's office? I would appreciate it if you would."

"Yes, of course," replied Percival, "I would like that very much. Let's leave now and ensure enough time with the Sheriff."

At the Sheriff's office both men were warmly greeted by the Sheriff and ushered into his office. The Sheriff knew he was hosting two of the most influential men in the kingdom. He took pains to show great courtesies to them both.

"I already have on that table the documents you examined this morning, Edwin."

Edwin unfolded his bill of sale and started to point out to the Sheriff and Percival the letters he and Glynn had noticed that morning as being strikingly the same.

"Hmmm," the Sheriff said as he pondered this new development. "I must say you are right in saying they are much the same. What are your thoughts on the matter, Percival?"

"Yes, I would say the alphabet characters Edwin has pointed out are very similar. Indeed to the point where it could be said they are written by the same person. Also notice how the writing is imprinted fairly deep in the parchment. Deeper than I would say most people write. The bill of sale reflects the same imprinting."

"Okay, gentlemen, do you want to swear out a warrant for the arrest of this merchant, Alfred?"

"Do you think our evidence is sufficiently weighty to prove his guilt?" replied Edwin.

"No, Edwin, I don't believe it would be."

"Well then we need to come up with some additional evidence. At least we have something, so I can justify to the King why nothing has been resolved on Jaffa."

The two thanked the Sheriff for his cooperation and started to leave when they were stopped by the clerk.

"Sirs I have something which may be of value to you."

"Oh really? What is that?" asked Edwin.

"I have a friend who lives next door to Alfred the merchant. One evening a couple of days before Jaffa was arrested, my friend heard Alfred screaming at his wife. He said he would teach Jaffa a lesson he would never forget."

"Why didn't you bring this up before?"

"Neither my friend or I thought it anything but an idle threat. He had heard Alfred scream threats before to his wife about Jaffa. When I overheard you mention the similarity of the handwriting on the letter with Alfred's bill of sale; I realized you have suspicions about him."

"Can you take us to your friend so we may talk to him?"

"Yes, of course," the clerk replied.

He looked to his master the Sheriff for his response.

The Sheriff nodded his agreement for his clerk to take Edwin and Percival to visit his friend.

At the clerk's friend's house they were able to question him about what else he may know regarding Alfred's actions and people he associated with.

When Percival and Edwin left to return to the castle they went to the quarters of one of the servants to the King's chief administrator. A middle aged man with a pock marked face answered the door and was surprised to see Edwin and Percival.

"Sirs, this is a most unexpected pleasure. How may I help you?"

"Yaworth we would like to ask you some questions. May we come in?" asked Edwin.

"Yes, of course, sir," answered Yaworth, "Please come in."

"Yaworth, we would like to know the nature of your relationship with Alfred the merchant down on the square."

Yaworth looked shaken by the question, but he tried his best to recover so no one would notice.

"I have only had cause to see him once in awhile in connection with trade."

"Really? What kind of trade?"

"Oh you know just things I thought might be of interest to my master."

"Did you buy anything for your master?"

"No. I did not"

"We have been told you have been seeing Alfred at times well after his shop closed. And that you have seen him at least a dozen times in the past two months. We have also been told that almost every time you have been seen to carry a parchment."

"A parchment? A dozen times? That's a lie! Who has been telling you such things?"

"Who is not important. Have you or have you not been carrying messages to Alfred?"

"Me? No, of course not, I know nothing about such messages."

While Edwin questioned Yaworth, Percival quietly moved around the room and noticed a parchment under the bed. Unnoticed he took the parchment and started to read it: "The King is about to order new supplies of weaponry. The expectation is he will order a march on the kingdoms west of Nerland in no later than two months."

Percival brought over the parchment and presented it to Yaworth.

"Perhaps you would like to explain why you have been writing this message regarding secret plans of the Kingdom. Yaworth looked at him with a look of extreme discomfort.

"I'm making notes to myself. It's like a journal."

"A journal of Kingdom secrets? Hmm, a strange expression of ones thoughts," replied Percival.

Edwin and Percival both looked at one another. Then they looked at Yaworth.

"We request you accompany us for further questioning."

"Why? What do you mean further questioning? I've done nothing wrong."

"Then you have nothing to fear. Bring what you want to wear and come with us now."

"As Yaworth reached for a brightly colored tunic to put on, he suddenly swung around with a knife and made a thrust for Edwin's heart. The latter deflected the knife with his wrist receiving a mild cut in the process. With the other arm he delivered a heavy punch to the side of Yaworth's head. Yaworth went down like he had been hit with an axe.

Percival asked Edwin if he was alright. Edwin nodded and replied it was nothing serious.

They looked down at Yaworth, now starting to come back to consciousness.

"Percival, would you please get a couple of guards to come here and I will watch over our friend here."

In a few minutes there were four guards at the door ready to escort Yaworth to the castle dungeon. Being late at night, Edwin decided they would question him further in the morning.

Edwin also gave instructions to the Captain of the Guard to send out a detachment to arrest Alfred and his wife and bring them to the castle. In addition he wanted men posted around Alfred's shop to arrest any of the traders who regularly visited Alfred with goods.

The next morning, Edwin and Percival were present with the King's chief interrogator, Maello, to question Yaworth. Edwin had already made it plain he didn't want to use torture since its results were suspect. People could be forced to say anything with the right amount of pain. After a couple of hours of questioning though, little headway had been made. Yaworth turned out to be an unusually recalcitrant individual, unwilling to acknowledge anything. Even to the question of why he tried to kill Edwin, his only response was silence. Edwin started wondering to himself whether some physical pressure would be necessary. As he thought about his views on torture and physical abuse he realized what a shift had happened since he came to Evansing. Back in Elfereth, doing whatever necessary to secure what he wanted from a person was Edwin's normal operating procedure. Once, to obtain information on an enemy army's whereabouts, he used a dull knife to cut off the fingers one by one of an enemy prisoner. After four fingers the prisoner talked. Edwin cut off the last finger on that hand just for spite. To Edwin that experience and others like it seemed surreal as though it had been another person. What caused this change in him? He wondered if he was getting too soft.

Well there was a point where toughness was necessary. He indicated to one of the guards stationed at the interrogation cell to do his role of roughing up the prisoner without inflicting undue damage. The guard smiled and came up to Yaworth and proceeded to punch and kick him several times before Edwin told him to stop.

Edwin then reminded Yaworth he already faced death as a result of his attempted murder.

"You can make it easier on yourself by helping us uncover the spy ring working in Evansing."

Yaworth looked as defiant and resistant as ever. Edwin thought to himself whatever would make a man so determined to protect people who were involved in something evil. Perhaps Yaworth believed he and his co-conspirators were involved in something noble and worth defending. Either that or he was simply one of those who will not give in. Edwin recalled the time a boy much smaller than himself kept attacking him. No matter how many times he threw the smaller boy to the ground the smaller boy would not quit. Finally the boy's mother came and pulled him away and took him home kicking and screaming. Nobody seemed to be aware that Edwin hadn't wanted to hurt the boy, all seemed to believe he was being the neighborhood bully. That hurt, especially since it wasn't true. Of course, it could also be that Yaworth resisted because there existed something more fearful to him than what Edwin and the King's representatives could inflict upon him.

Edwin conferred with Percival and Maello and they decided to return Yaworth to his cell. They had Alfred in a cell and after lunch it would be his turn to be questioned.

During lunch, Greer and Edwin had a chance to catch up as they hadn't seen each other for a couple of days. Edwin shared with Greer concerning the recent events. She in turn shared how she and her Nerland friends had been having a splendid time together.

After lunch, Percival and Edwin returned to the castle dungeon to begin the task of questioning Alfred. They went to the interrogation room where Alfred awaited his turn to be questioned. To Edwin and Percival's surprise Alfred looked as defiant as Yaworth. Maello also thought it strange a servant and a merchant could be capable of such defiance. Normally people would be full of fear in these circumstances. In this case, it seemed like something had risen up in these two men to give them backbones of steel. At this point, Edwin who already disliked Alfred from his initial meeting decided he didn't want to pussyfoot around. He walked up to

Alfred and kicked him in the face and grabbed him by the throat and gave him a vicious right across the side of his head.

As it turned out it didn't encourage Alfred to talk, but Edwin felt good doing it. It released this internal rage bottled up inside him. It surprised and even disturbed him a little, but it felt good. Alfred continued to stonewall his interrogators in spite of being subjected to several beatings by the guards. After an hour and a half Edwin decided to return him to his cell. They would take a break and discuss strategy with how to question and deal with Alfred's wife.

The three men took refreshments and considered initial impressions about Alfred's wife, Lanya. The report from Maello and the arresting officers was that unlike her husband she was very upset and fearful. They decided they would ask Lanya about which regular visitors to her husband struck her as being different from the norm. Also what behavior of her husband struck her as being odd? Subsequent to the arrest of Alfred, the merchant's shop had been thoroughly searched. The records of who traded with him had been seized and reviewed as to the traders who most frequently appeared in his records of transactions.

Lanya appeared much more amenable to talk than either Alfred or Yaworth. After an hour little of use had been gleaned from her. Either she was a consummate liar or else her husband cleverly kept her in the dark about his goings on. Neither Edwin nor Percival felt there existed much to be gained by pressuring her further so they returned her to her cell.

Now what to do? New strategy had to be developed in dealing with Alfred and Yaworth. They had found no direct evidence against Alfred. True they had evidence of sorts with respect to the handwriting and because of Yaworth's response to being questioned about Alfred. But they had nothing to convict him with, yet.

In spite of being warned to always have a detachment of guards with her, Greer sometimes liked to go alone around the capital with only one or two of her ladies in waiting. As they were enjoying a walk around the market area they decided to take a shortcut down a narrow back lane. Halfway down this lane, four men leaped out of a doorway. They grabbed both Greer and her two ladies in waiting and pulled them inside.

CHAPTER 14

After a couple of hours, the castle guard raised the alarm that Greer and her ladies in waiting had gone missing. Edwin, along with Percival and Maello were considering their next steps in questioning their prisoners, when a courier delivered to them the message about Greer's disappearance. Edwin and Percival dashed out to the King's command center. When they arrived they saw the King looking very ashen. The realization of his pride and joy having gone missing was slowly sinking in.

Erith looked up at Edwin. They both embraced.

Edwin stepped back and said, "We will find her, never fear."

The decisive confidence with which he said it surprised both him and the King. For some reason even though he too had a major cause for concern, he had a total rest in his being that things would work out. But first he wanted to get the latest update on where she had last been seen and whatever other details may be available. The King informed him it was now almost three hours since Greer and her ladies were last seen going into a narrow back lane. All the residences along the lane had been searched as well as the immediate surrounding area. As they shared this with Edwin, the thought came to him the Princess and her ladies were no longer in the city.

"I need the bird which brought me here, quick now!"

The King looked to Percival.

"Okay." Percival replied, "Go out to the courtyard in ten minutes and it will be waiting for you."

Edwin looked at him strangely. Then an insight came to him and he looked at Percival with a new measure of wonder.

Percival excused himself on the grounds he needed to summon the bird.

Ten minutes later Edwin stood out in the courtyard and so did the same bird which brought him to Evansing.

He walked up to it and said, "Hi, Percival."

The bird looked like it smiled. Edwin hopped on and away they went.

The first time the bird held Edwin in its talons. This time he held for dear life onto the neck of the bird while sitting on its back. After a few minutes in the air he started to relax. It became more like riding on the back of a horse, only somewhat more stimulating riding up in the air two hundred feet above the ground.

He spoke to Percival, "I see a covered coach over to the northwest. Let's check it out."

The bird turned in the direction indicated. The closer they got, the more definite Edwin felt in his heart that here they would find the three ladies. He could tell there were four men with the coach. Two were riding on horses alongside and two in the front of the coach. They were headed for the frontier with the Kingdom of Dagarath. That kingdom was known to be troublesome. They were only fifteen or so miles from the border. What could he do to stop them? He decided he needed the bird's direct involvement in the attack. He asked Percival to come up behind the coach and try to take out all four men with his talons, beak and wings as he swooped over them. At the same time Edwin would land on top of the coach and take out whoever remained. He would then take control of the team of horses who would undoubtedly be spooked by a giant bird swooping over them.

They started to descend and they came in behind the coach. Both men on horseback and one of the ones on the coach went down. Edwin landed heavily on the coach behind the fourth man. He quickly recovered and pulled out his knife and went after the remaining man. The man turned around and caught Edwin's wrist thus averting being stabbed in the neck.

The two men struggled on the coach as the horses started to run faster and faster. The man on the coach was exceedingly strong, indeed much stronger than the average man. Edwin was being sorely pressed to try to overcome or prevent being overcome himself. The man fought like a man possessed and would not quit. He also pulled out a knife and caught Edwin in his left arm. Blood spurted out profusely, but Edwin would not stop. Both men fought each other with what seemed like supernatural strength and energy, and narrowly avoided falling off the wagon. As the road started to narrow, the horses started to slow down perceptibly, but the men fought each other with no let up. They were relentless. Neither would grant each other quarter and both sustained wounds. Both were covered in blood. Finally Edwin pulled off a rather acrobatic move, which threw his adversary off the coach. The man fell with a thud on his neck breaking it and killing him instantly. Recovering, Edwin tried to stop the team of horses, but the reins had fallen to the ground making their recovery difficult. The only other option was for him to jump on their backs and slow them down. This he did and after a brief distance they eventually came to a halt. Exhausted from the exertion and weakened from the loss of blood, Edwin managed to dismount. He stumbled to the wagon. He opened the door and inside he found his prize. Greer and her ladies were tied up, gagged and blindfolded. Edwin untied them and then after he freed the last lady, he became dizzy and collapsed at their feet. Greer and her two ladies desperately ripped up parts of their dresses to provide bandages to stop the bleeding. A few moments later, Percival showed up on the scene and also ran to give assistance. He had with him a special herbal potion, which he promptly administered to Edwin. Shortly after, Edwin's pulse started to pick up as it had gotten dangerously faint. Percival, along with the three ladies, picked up Edwin and gently placed him inside the coach. Greer and her two ladies tended Edwin as Percival assumed control of the coach, turned it around and headed toward Evansing's capital.

Percival got the horses to pick up speed as they got nearer where the three men were knocked off. He didn't know if one of them was still a threat. For though he had killed one of them with his bill and had crushed another in his talons; the third had been simply knocked off his horse by the bird's wings.

As they got closer to where the initial attack had occurred, Percival became ever more vigilant for the possibility of encountering the third attacker. Sure enough, up ahead he saw a man on a horse. Percival considered his options. As the team and wagon got closer and closer they started to lift off the ground. Percival had changed back to his bird form and had lifted the entire team and coach up into the air, fifty feet over the shocked man sitting on his horse in the road. They continued on for almost two miles before Percival gently lowered the team and coach. It was a delicate maneuver to land without injuring the horses, but one by one they got landed on their feet and remained steady. The ladies who were inside could not look outside for the coach's doors were covered. However, they had noticed something was different. For they heard no road noise and neither did they feel the normal rocking and being shook about by the roughness of the road.

Shortly after returning back to normal, Percival and the coach met a troop on horseback, which had been sent from Evansing. Their commander and his soldiers looked at Percival rather strangely. They most certainly would have seen the bird and the coach and horses in the air.

Percival chose to ignore their looks of bewilderment and told them Greer and her ladies along with Edwin were in the coach.

Back in the castle its residents expressed great rejoicing at the return of Greer and her maids. The King did not even say anything about her going out without a guard. He was so glad to have his little girl back. Of course the celebration was a little subdued because of Edwin's wounds. They required him to stay in the castle infirmary and receive constant medical attention. Greer stayed most of the time by his bed helping to keep him comfortable and just to be with him.

After three days, Edwin left the infirmary and showed up for breakfast at the dining hall. He received a standing ovation as the people loved Greer and were becoming increasingly fond of this most unusual young man.

After a few more days of taking it easy, Edwin determined to get back to the task of questioning the prisoners. Further investigation gave strong support they were behind the kidnapping of Greer. This gave Edwin even greater incentive to gain their cooperation. During Edwin's recuperation, both male prisoners had been subjected to vigorous examination. This involved techniques that certainly would be described as torture nowadays but were considered mild back in 11ᵗʰ century Ireland. In spite of this both men were still uncooperative, revealing little of any substance. This further convinced Edwin there was something more at work here than what they were seeing with their physical eyes. Edwin started to think again there had to be some and maybe lots of Druid magic involved to enable these men to withstand the pain that they had been subject to. Oh well he would sort that out later. First he wanted to go and kick the crap out of both of them just for the satisfaction of revenge. They had caused him and others a lot of trouble. So with Maello and Percival present, Edwin proceeded to afflict some of his own pain on Yaworth and Alfred. He kicked them in their ribs several times and a little harder than he would normally if he wanted to preserve their already weakened lives for questioning. But something in Edwin started to not really care if they talked. He may decide to kill them. The thought started to become rather appealing to him. With both men it was Percival who pulled on Edwin's arm to get him to stop. However, Percival did not indicate any disapproval. This surprised Edwin, given Percival's position as a spiritual advisor and long-time resident of a monastery.

With both men Edwin did not bother questioning them after kicking them. He simply turned around and left. All three men went back to Maello's office to discuss the next move.

On the walk to Maello's office, Edwin thought to himself about the power and influence he had gained in Evansing. He knew he had been given carte blanche authority to do as he saw fit to Alfred, Yaworth and Lanya. Edwin had become a law unto himself with only the King having more authority. Edwin did not carry a formal authority, other than as a military officer. However, his influence with the King, Greer, Percival and more and more of the royal family and military had created for him a most powerful informal authority. As he thought about it, it almost seemed like a rush of adrenaline went through him. It felt good and yet in some ways it troubled him for he knew he was not in this position just to express his baser instincts. In other words to simply kill the prisoners would not be the best expression of his authority, even if he could get away with it. He could not allow himself to become unjust, even with people who looked like they deserved it. Yet the thought of killing them seemed like it would satisfy an inner yearning.

"Curious," he said to himself as he considered that he had these internal parts debating such diametrically opposite views.

His head and part of his heart wanted to be noble, just and merciful, but most of his heart wanted to be vengeful and have its full of blood.

At Maello's office the men sat down and started to consider their options. Edwin introduced the idea that a powerful Druid influence had to be at work. Either a spell so strong on these prisoners it prevented them from talking, or else they had a strong fear of reprisals against them if they did talk. Either tactic was typical of how Druids would influence people. Invisible magical influence or brute fear instilled at such a core level that it masked as courage. There weren't many Druid priests around anymore, but the ones that were could be very powerful and difficult to deal with. They had to be to survive as they had few followers and much opposition amongst the general populace.

"Percival, what do you think about the possibility of Druid influence?"

"I would think it is almost guaranteed. I have several friends back at the monastery who are familiar with some of the leading Druids in this area. Two of these friends are former Druid priests themselves and they still have connections which keep them informed about the goings on in the Druid community. I will send out a messenger this afternoon to ask them to make inquiries."

Edwin asked, "What about breaking off the influence on them? Could you do that? After all you obviously have an understanding of the spiritual realm."

"True," Percival responded, "I do have some understanding of that realm. I can ask God for more. I will also ask my friends for their input."

Edwin responded further, "In the meantime I don't think there is much point to continuing our present course of questioning. They will probably die in the course of our persuasion or tell us lies. I believe Lanya knows more than what she has let on, but I think she too has been endued with something which keeps her from sharing what she knows."

"Maello, what are your thoughts on all this?"

"I believe the idea of Druid magic is probable, for I have not had such responses from men before. There has to be something powerful at work on them."

"We have been easy on Lanya. We could up the degree of cooperating influence on her considerably. At least we could give it a try and see what she shares. We don't have a lot of experience with women prisoners, but we could deal with her in ways which would be more specific to her gender. I understand she is extremely proud of her long flowing hair, which one of her neighbors said is Lanya's most precious possession. We could cut it off bit by bit as she is asked to reveal more and more. If she doesn't share what we believe she knows, we will shave her head bald."

"Interesting approach, it just may work," replied Edwin. "You are quite right in saying we have been easy on her. Sure why don't you look after that. I'm not interested in spending my time with questioning her. I give you authority to do what you need to do in order to get satisfaction that she has shared what she knows. My only restrictions are no sexual assault, and no techniques beyond what the men have experienced."

"As you wish, Edwin. I have no desire to be harsh with the woman. Even though getting people to cooperate can be a nasty business, it's not like I necessarily want to afflict pain on people. Gee, did I say that? Where did that come from? Actually I love hurting people, it's one of my favorite things. That's why I love my job. But I can truly say I'm not into hurting women, so I will be gentle, in a manner of speaking, with Lanya."

Edwin smiled at Maello, "I'm sure you will Maello."

Edwin continued, "We have a strategic strike force being readied for a series of kidnappings and assassinations. I believe there may also be an opportunity to utilize some of them for uncovering more about the identity of who Alfred and Yaworth are working with. They must have an extensive communication network for it didn't take them long to put together the kidnapping of Greer. Our spies in Dagarath have told us that three of Alfred's most frequent traders have been discovered to be part of the inner circle of the King of Dagarath. The men were headed to Dagarath with Greer and her ladies. I am going to assign our strike force to kidnap those three so called traders."

With that Edwin stood up and he and Percival left to go visit the head trainer of the strike force. They went to inform him of the new assignment that they would be undertaking. The King of Dagarath had been placed on the list as a target for assassination. He hadn't been linked directly to the problems in Nerland. But he was an all-round troublesome man always stirring up problems with Evansing. The king of Dagarath was also known to be one of the few kings openly sympathetic to Druids.

"Jaather, how have you been keeping?"

"Edwin, it's been grand. I haven't had so much fun since I killed Teutons almost twenty years ago. Training men to kill well in difficult circumstances is very satisfying."

"I have a new assignment for you. I need three men associated with the King of Dagarath to be captured and brought back for questioning. If you are a little short of manpower then we could postpone one of the other assignments. This one is top priority."

Something rose up in Edwin as he added, "In fact Jaather I wouldn't mind joining the force assigned to go after those three men."

Both Jaather and Percival looked in surprise at Edwin. Actually Edwin was a little surprised at his offer, but he liked the idea and decided to go with it. It wasn't the most sensible thing for him to expose himself to this kind of risk. Greer may not like it. However, in their conversations she let it be known that she knew Edwin was a warrior, and warriors fight. That was one of the reasons she loved him. She would live with the discomfort any time he left to go to battle knowing it may be the last time she saw him.

"Of course I should also join your training for that mission. Treat me like one of your trainees. I will share with you what details I have received about these men and their whereabouts."

The next day Edwin joined the strike force assigned to kidnap the three 'traders'. They would be traveling with the force assigned to assassinate the King of Dagarath, until just prior to the border with Dagarath. They would rejoin after their respective missions were completed and travel together back to Evansing's capital. Extra forces of the regular army would be assigned to be posted near the Dagarath border, to protect against any pursuit from Dagarath. It had also been decided the assassins, a group of five men, would try to kill as many members of Dagarath's royal family as possible. They wanted to eliminate his two sons and three daughters. They had on their side the element of surprise and superior strategies and abilities. Therefore they believed they could overcome a vastly superior force protecting Dagarath's king.

A total of fifteen men, five per captive, were assigned to kidnap the three men in question. They were known to be in the King of Dagarath's castle. However, there were occasions when they traveled to an unknown place some distance from the castle. Every fortnight they would leave early in the morning and return late at night the same day. Jaather and Edwin decided that was the best time to take them. The assassins would coordinate their mission with the kidnappers.

CHAPTER 15

On the morning of the departure for Dagarath, Jaffa came in to help Edwin prepare for the trip. All Jaffa knew was that Edwin would be going out of town, but he didn't have any idea about his purpose or destination. Even though Alfred, Yaworth and Lanya hadn't been convicted there had been sufficient evidence to free Jaffa. Attempts were still being made to unlock whatever Druid influences they were under, but so far all attempts had been unsuccessful.

Greer and Edwin had spent the previous evening being together. They enjoyed laughter and light hearted banter, but there also existed a noticeable underlying air of tension at the prospect of Edwin going away on a dangerous mission. Greer had decided she would be at peace no matter what the danger her young man would find himself in. She decided not to stress herself over it. After all it would give her lines on her face and it wouldn't help Edwin.

At the base outside the Evansing capital, the fifteen kidnappers and the five assassins were being given their final briefings. The remaining seven strike force members were leaving the next day for a kingdom on the north side of Evansing, the Kingdom of Tara.

They were assigned to kidnap the Crown Prince of that kingdom and bring him back for ransom.

En route to Dagarath the rain clouds hung overhead with a steady drizzle. Not a pleasant start, but a normal day in Ireland. Near the Dagarath border, the groups split up into separate parties. The assassins were heading for the King's castle in the Dagarath capital. The kidnappers headed in the same general direction but chose to travel separately to lessen the likelihood of their detection. They carried on to the road east of the Dagarath capital to intercept the three targeted individuals.

Continuing on across fields and through unmarked forests, the group Edwin led came across a patrol of the Dagarath army. There were about twelve of them. All of the strike force members laid low in the grass. The patrol passed by, unaware the enemy they were searching for lie hidden only a short stone's throw away. After about fifteen minutes of continuing to lay low, Edwin looked up and saw the patrol had travelled about one hundred yards. He resolved that the next time they were outnumbered no more than two to one he would give the order to attack.

The group continued on its way. They should be beside the road in question by around 7:00 that evening. The targets would be coming by about 8:00 the next morning. The men prepared for a night of being quiet and aware of their surroundings. The other two teams joined them shortly after 8:00 that evening.

The next day it again drizzled. Oh well it would give extra cover in the early morning. Breakfast consisted of a quick unheated piece of mutton and a potato, a medieval version of army rations. The night before the three groups discussed further how they would handle their assignments. They needed to consider the nature of the flat terrain and the expected escort of almost twenty men. There would be a barrage of arrows to take out as many of the escort as possible. The targeted men, according to intelligence reports were dressed as gentlemen and should be easy to pick out. All three were known to be excellent swordsmen.

They intended to get at least two of the men alive. These men were expected to be a valuable source of knowledge. Hopefully they hadn't been endued with all kinds of Druid influence. That would make their cooperation difficult, if not almost impossible.

The next morning, the strike force lay awaiting their prey. A low whistle sounded indicating the lookout had sighted the procession coming their way. As previously reported to them there were twenty or so soldiers, but no gentlemen, at least none were distinguished by their attire. Quickly, Edwin passed the word to hold fire. As he watched the group of what appeared to be all soldiers, he noticed one man who had a large feather sticking out of his hat. The man next to him had a gold chain and next to that man rode a man with green breeches when everyone else had blue breeches. They were in the centre of the procession. Edwin passed the word to his right side that the archers were to take out the first eight. Then he passed to his left side that those archers were to take out the last eight. The remaining soldiers and gentlemen were to have their horses shot from underneath them.

Edwin gave the signal to release the hail of arrows. They found their mark as twelve of the escort fell off their horses. Then another volley and another four men hit the ground. With the second volley the horses were downed that were carrying the gentlemen and remaining soldiers. Upon the downing of the horses, Edwin and all the accompanying men charged toward the men struggling to get up from their mounts. Edwin yelled orders to take the gentlemen alive, pointing to the specific men so as to avoid confusion. As expected the gentlemen were not going to give up without a fight. Edwin came up against the one with the feather in his hat. They thrusted and parried at one another fiercely, Edwin leaned back in time to avoid a slash toward his throat. After several minutes, Edwin sensed the gentleman starting to tire. Edwin pressed his growing advantage in carrying the fight to his adversary. Finally he struck the sword of the gentleman and it flew out of his hands. Then the man pulled out a twelve inch dagger. The man seemed to know his attackers wanted him alive so he obviously felt he had an advantage as to what his options were. Edwin threw down his sword and pulled out his own dagger. They both started to dance around looking for an opening. Then it ended. One of the strike force members came up behind the gentleman and struck him with his fist on the back of the head and at the same time grabbed his arm holding the dagger. The gentleman lay on the ground groaning semi-consciously.

As Edwin looked around he could see the strike force had secured their objectives. All three gentlemen had been taken alive except one had been severely cut. His bleeding would need to be stopped if he were to remain alive. The man received treatment from the medic accompanying the group. The medic's face bore a grave look. He glanced at Edwin in a manner which indicated this man's life force was rapidly dissipating.

Edwin put his hand on the man's forehead and said "No!"

With that command something dramatic happened to the wounded gentleman. Where he had only a moment before been pale and white, his color came back. His previously closed eyes now were wide open looking alive. The medic looked up at Edwin, astonished.

The mission had been a success. The strike force had dispatched all of the escorting soldiers while only suffering a couple casualties with minor wounds Their horses were brought out including three extra for the prisoners. The prisoners' hands were securely bound in the front of them and they were fastened to their horses by their legs.

Now for the dash home to safety. The clouds were gathering overhead and rain started to pour down. The strike force split up into their original three groups and took their predetermined routes.

After almost four hours Edwin's band neared the frontier with Evansing. Off to the right they could see a squad of Dagarath soldiers headed towards them. They must have been part of a regular patrol, which just happened to come across Edwin's troop.

In the rain and the mud the footing had turned treacherous, yet the band picked up the pace and maintained the distance between them and the patrol. Several of the patrol started to catch up. As they got close to Evansing they noticed a contingent of Evansing soldiers who realized what was happening. This guard had been designated to meet them. The Evansing patrol ventured across the frontier to confront the Dagarath troops. They outnumbered the latter by almost half again. The Dagarath soldiers started to slow down and decided the odds were no longer in their favor. When the two groups were within a hundred yards of one another, the Dagarath troop turned around and sounded retreat.

Once on the Evansing side, the strike force gave a tremendous whoop of celebration. They were soon joined by the Evansing troops who escorted them back to Evansing's capital.

All the strike force members returned successfully from the kidnappings. The members of the assassins group had not yet returned and there was no news of their mission.

Meanwhile, in the Dagarath capital the assassins had encountered some unexpected difficulty. The closely guarded whereabouts of the King had been changed from where they had originally expected to find him. The Evansing spies were unable to provide the necessary information. Getting into the castle had turned out to be a greater challenge than expected, as the guards were carefully screening everyone and checking for weapons. Consequently the force hid out in a nearby forest awaiting definite word of the King's hiding place.

Unbeknownst to them the astonishing revelation came that the King of Dagarath was indeed the gentleman with the feather. This discovery made when they searched his person and found the Dagarath signet ring. To verify their suspicions, a man from Dagarath now in the employ of Evansing, came to examine the captives.

His face lit up as he exclaimed, "This is the King!"

One of the guards advised King Erith of this news who then immediately went down to the castle dungeon. He questioned his Dagarath counterpart. Now he had the interesting problem of deciding what to do with the very much alive King of Dagarath. He could still decide to interrogate him as originally planned as if he were a regular gentleman. That would still be the course of action to take. After that it would have to be decided as to whether to kill him or consider a ransom. Or keep him as an indefinite prisoner.

"Hmmm, interesting," King Erith said to himself. A thought came to him, "Perhaps, just perhaps the King of Dagarath could be won to our cause. That would be an interesting challenge."

A courier dispatched word to the assassins to come back as their quarry was in Evansing. The secondary objective of killing the king's family did not warrant risking loss of the force.

In the meantime, Greer and Edwin were starting to make plans for their wedding. Edwin had had little time to contemplate it. But Greer had been increasingly preoccupied by the prospect of becoming a bride in the midst of great pomp and celebration. She had pulled out her mother's wedding dress and had decided she would like to wear it in memory and honor of her mother. This most elegant gown fit almost perfectly as mother and daughter were much the same body size and shape. There were a couple of minor modifications to be done around the shoulders. Greer also decided to add a couple of lace adornments, which appealed to her. So now Edwin had to get his head around this most agreeable prospect of being married to Greer. At the same time getting answers from the prisoners also preoccupied his attention. He decided he could not do justice to everything at the same time. So he decided to off load his responsibilities to obtain answers from the prisoners to those trained in interrogations. Besides the wedding plans, he also wanted to maintain his ongoing meetings with Percival. He needed to continue his education and personal development. A big bright spot was the rapidity with which Edwin learned to read and write. Edwin started having dreams at night about reading and writing, which would give him a surge in his vocabulary of new words.

One thing he decided he must ask Percival, "What was it like to live with a woman?" Percival had been married and it sounded like he had had a very loving relationship with her. It had been only for a few years and many years ago. Even so he must have something he could share with Edwin for his future with Greer.

The next time the two men met, Edwin asked, "Percival, as you know I am soon to wed the loveliest of creatures, Greer, my beloved."

He said this with a twinkle in his eye and extra expression. He enjoyed expressing it in a savoring fun sort of way, ending with a bit of a laugh.

Percival cut in and said, "And you want me to give you three easy ways to be happy in marriage, right?"

Edwin looked at him a little sheepish. "Are there three easy ways to be happy in marriage?"

"No, as a matter of fact there aren't. However, there are principles which will increase your likelihood for success."

"Tell me Edwin what is your experience with women and what do you know that would likely keep Greer happy?"

Edwin replied, "My experience has been rather limited prior to Greer. I lived an isolated life with only a woman in the house for the first few years of my life. My experiences with females have been limited to sometimes playing with cousins and neighboring girls when young. When I got older I occasionally would try to create some kind of connection with a girl. But it never went anywhere because I felt completely inadequate to connect with them. As a warrior I felt totally confident. As a friend, let alone as a lover of a woman, I felt lost. Sometimes there were raids that involved raping of village women we had conquered. I never did that though. I couldn't feel good about forcing myself on a helpless woman. I remember seeing the look of horror on the faces of those women, who had been raped. I think it is something they never got over."

He continued, "For me to get along so well and so comfortably with Greer has been a major miracle. I don't understand how it happened and how it became possible for us to be so close so soon. I realize though it is one thing to court and get along. It is another thing to live with a woman day in and day out."

"You are quite right, Edwin. It is another matter altogether to maintain domestic felicity in the midst of daily pressures and challenges. It is possibly the greatest adventure anyone can embark on. To explore the fullness of a woman is fraught with dangers and pleasures requiring willingness to risk. However, the risks are a type that requires a willingness to expose ones inner being to another human. Unlike a warrior whose risks are external the risks in marriage can go to the core of ones being. The consequences can be great pain or great pleasure. At times it seems the only way to get to the pleasure is to do the pain. The pain which remains deep down tends to deaden ones capacity for pleasure. To expose those painful areas to a woman is extremely vulnerable. Way scarier than taking on ten enemy soldiers by yourself. I remember when my wife and I had our first heart to heart conversation after we were married. She expressed dissatisfaction with my approach, which mirrored how almost all the other men in the village related to their wives. In other words treating them like a sex object complete with cooking and housekeeping services. No, my woman wasn't about to settle for that. She made it very plain. So began the painful and I do mean painful process of becoming a real person with my wife. We used to spend hours in discussing how we wanted our life to look. She had all these ideas about how we would do life together. I tended to live day-to-day from one battle to the next. She forced me to consider life with her as mutually exploring and developing ourselves as individuals and as a couple."

"I think it is great you would ask me about your future with Greer. She is a most amazing young lady and not just because she is a princess.

She has more than a surface nobility. She is nobility deep down. I guarantee she will want all of you. She will not be satisfied with the typical status quo marriage at court."

"Great! Now how do we successfully accomplish this great adventure?" replied Edwin.

"Well first of all we need to continue working out some of your heart issues. For if you do not have a heart capable of loving a woman or another human, then rules will only be a source of frustration."

For the next three hours the men started to do a deeper work with some of those hurts of abandonment and abuse. When they were done, Edwin felt like a limp rag. He had just relived and processed some major pain and had shed many tears. He felt sheepish for this non Irish warrior behavior. Percival, unfazed by all the tears joked that he still respected Edwin.

Percival went to tell him that perhaps the most important principle in marriage was to value the relationship. He needed to consistently direct his attention to his mate in a way which would demonstrate value of her and the relationship.

They decided that they would meet again the next day and continue where they had left off.

On their way to the dining hall for lunch they were met by the King. He joined them in the walk and brought up the topic of the upcoming wedding.

All of a sudden he stopped and whispered in Edwin's ear, "What is distressing you? Your eyes are all red like you have been crying."

Edwin blushed at this revelation. Percival smiled and took the King's arm and gently led him away. He shared that there had still been no news on the pursuit of the Druid connection with their prisoners. His friends were still making inquiries. The King quickly forgot his question of Edwin. Rather he got quite engrossed in discussing what further possibilities were available to them.

Greer, at the dining hall awaiting Edwin began to wonder what had happened to him. She lit up when she saw him come in. Edwin felt like he had been running uphill all morning. But seeing Greer and her beaming face he decided to crank up his ability to relate in an animated way with her. She, however, picked up that he was not his normal self. At first she wanted to be a little miffed since he wasn't oohing and gushing over seeing her again. Then she decided she could do better than that. Instead she decided to caringly ask him if he was feeling alright. Edwin tried to assure her he was just tired, but it didn't ring true for Greer.

"Edwin, as you know we are going to get married in just over a month. If we are going to have a great marriage then we need to be honest with one another. Edwin winced when she used the "H" word.

"Oh drat," he said to himself. "She is always trying to get me to be honest. Why is it such a challenge for me?"

He liked it when he did it, but it never seemed to be any easier the next time.

"Okay, Miss Honesty. This is the deal. Percival and I delved into my deep heart issues and I have been crying like a woman all morning. There! You have it!" Edwin responded, feeling a little testy in the process.

Greer felt relieved when he shared what had happened and she overlooked the testiness and the gender comment. She knew it must be a challenge for him to share that. She also knew what Percival did with him would be good for her future with Edwin. Greer would not settle for the shallow existence that many of the people in her acquaintance shared with their mates. Since many of those people were relatives, she knew that her nanny made the difference. Her nanny had raised her during the ages of four to twelve. That woman had an extraordinary degree of influence on Greer. The nanny had a large heart and spirit who radiated bliss and well-being. Greer loved being with her. She would drink up the lessons of life that that dear sweet woman poured into her. As much as Greer loved and respected her mother, she had been lacking in her capacity to deeply nurture and nourish Greer. The nanny filled in those gaps. As a result, Greer herself became a large hearted, large spirited woman who had an incredible appetite and capacity for a full love relationship.

"Edwin, I am so glad you shared that with me. I know that you and I are going to be so happy together. These meetings with Percival will ensure that the real you will be out in the open instead of hidden deep down. I am so excited to see you become all that you were intended to be."

Edwin looked at her a little surprised and certainly pleased. He remained in a state of almost continual amazement that somehow he had connected with this most wondrous creature. "Where did she get such wisdom?" he thought to himself.

CHAPTER 16

The next morning Percival and Edwin got right back at it to sort out some more heart issues.

Percival went for the jugular and asked, "So Edwin what is your greatest fear about marrying Greer?"

"Her becoming disappointed with me."

"Why?"

"I'm not sure, but it is something I have pondered more than once. It is something I have struggled with ever since I was a little boy."

"My uncle definitely expressed disappointment with me. It is probably where it got started. He didn't cover up the fact he did not want to look after me when my parents died. He continually communicated I was a burden and I should be different than who I was.

"So now you're concerned Greer will think the same way?"

"No, I'm not concerned. I'm terrified she will think the same way."

"Did you know your uncle planted a lie into you, which you have believed must be true?"

"What do you mean?"

"Simply put, as a young boy you believed what your uncle communicated to you must be true. After all he fulfilled the role of adult authority figure in your life. As a young boy you were unable to differentiate between what he said was legitimate and what was simply his own hurting self. From what you have told me, your uncle demonstrated the qualities of a much damaged man incapable of fulfilling the responsibility of fathering a young boy."

"Okay so what do we do about it?"

"Two things come to mind. First you must quit holding any resentment towards your uncle. You must forgive him."

"Forgive him? You must be kidding. Why would I forgive him for being such a mean hearted bastard?"

"What's more important to you? Staying angry with your dead uncle or being a wonderful husband to Greer?"

"What does my forgiving my uncle have anything to do with Greer?"

"Everything. Poison in one part of your life will inevitably affect all of the other parts of your life. For example how do you think you will relate to Greer if you are constantly terrified about her being disappointed in you?"

"What does this have to do with forgiving my uncle?"

"The fear of being a disappointment is directly tied in to your attitude towards your uncle. Unforgiveness keeps it locked in place. More will need to be done to get you totally freed from this fear of being a disappointment. Without forgiveness first we can't even consider the next step."

Edwin considered the need to forgive his uncle. This stirred up his emotions, especially anger. His uncle did not deserve forgiveness. But Percival, who seemed to be wise in these matters, told him he needed to do this. He certainly didn't feel like forgiving. If he did it, it wouldn't be with his heart.

"Okay, Percival, if I do this forgiving my uncle for being such a knot head how do I do it if I don't have a heart sense of doing it. The expressing of forgiveness would just be words."

Percival replied, "Words are good as a start. Better to start the process and it is a process, by at least expressing forgiveness. Then I will bless you to be healed and set free from the wounds in your heart associated with feeling like a disappointment."

"Okay so how do I do this forgiving thing?"

"Say after me: I forgive you uncle for treating me like a disappointment."

Edwin repeated those words after Percival. He didn't feel anything while saying it, but he did have a sense what he did was a good thing.

After Edwin expressed forgiveness, Percival responded, "Congratulations Edwin. You took a big step towards your happiness with Greer. Now I bless you with healing in your heart and freedom from the wounds of being treated as a disappointment."

Edwin could feel a curious response inside him while Percival blessed him. This response continued for sometime. It felt strange and good all at the same time.

After a few minutes, Edwin brightened and said, "Thanks, Percival. It felt good. Something definitely happened and I feel better."

The two men then turned their attention to teaching Edwin how to read and other areas of his education.

In the afternoon Edwin continued to work with training the Evansing troops. A major component of this training involved strengthening and enlarging the spirits of the soldiers. Percival added his insight and input to this area. There seemed to be natural warrior strength to Edwin's spirit, but it had gotten bigger and more dynamic from the sessions with Percival. These new insights were things Percival tried to incorporate in a way which would not be perceived as unmanly to the soldiers. This could be tricky to pull off. But he was able to embed this strengthening in certain exercises which were useful for toughening their resolve to fight even in the midst of overwhelming odds.

Another dimension of the training involved creating soldiers who could think strategically as well as tactically. There were maneuvers developed which forced the troops to think quickly in ways typical of an officer. The officers still developed strategies as a starting point in war given a certain set of circumstances and objectives. They also developed the tactics considered most appropriate to go with the strategies. They desired to create soldiers who could develop their own strategies and tactics in the event of a major shift from what originally had been expected and planned for. This stretched Edwin and the other officers, but they progressively saw a new dimension of fighting spirit and confidence among the men. The men seemed to see themselves beyond just someone to swing a sword or axe at someone. They began to see themselves in a new light as if they too were officers. The respectful treatment of the enlisted men without compromising discipline and unquestioned obedience produced the best of both worlds. The soldiers were not only disciplined, but they could also operate at a high level of fighting intelligence.

At supper the King shared with Edwin that he looked forward to him becoming his son-in-law. The objectives he had in bringing Edwin had been exceeded in their attainment beyond his expectations. He had never anticipated Edwin becoming such a noble and competent individual so quickly. He enjoyed the added bonus of his daughter becoming so in love with Edwin; as though they had been tailor made for one another.

The King's comments encouraged Edwin, for the dealing with emotional issues had made Edwin feel a little tenderer inside. It felt good to receive some positive nurturing comments from an authority figure like the King.

Although the relationship between the King and Edwin had been friendly and the former had accorded much leeway and authority to Edwin, it had lacked in real emotional connection. Perhaps this typified kings, as they had to be careful in their relationships. However, Edwin hoped for something more with his future father-in-law. He decided he would talk to Percival about this desire. If anyone could facilitate an emotional shift in the King it would be Percival. He had the most influence of anyone as a confidante and respected friend of the King. Even the King's closest family members did not have the same degree of connection as did Percival.

The next day the mood of the breakfast was rather somber. News had come back indicating the mission to Tara had failed. All except two of the men sent had been captured or killed.

CHAPTER 17

The news of the failed Tara mission hit a great blow to the whole strike force. Not only to the force itself but also to the momentum building for achieving Irish unity.

After breakfast in a closed meeting, the King, Edwin, Glynn, Percival, Jaather, several senior military officers and the two escaped soldiers met to discuss what had gone wrong. Details at this point were quite sketchy. Apparently they had been ambushed just outside of Tara Castle. This disturbing news once again pointed to the possibility of there being a breach of security. As the two soldiers shared it, they were not aware of being observed prior to the ambush. Everything seemed to be going okay right up until they were attacked. To listen to them it seemed extraordinary these two had escaped. At first it appeared to be rather fortuitous, but something in Edwin's gut did not sit well with him about their story. Upon his later discussion with Percival he discovered they both shared some of the same concerns with what the soldiers had shared. There existed something about the degree of good fortune they experienced in escaping. That part of Tara was flat and barren containing little cover. The Tara military were known to have some of the finest tracking dogs in all of Ireland. Even at night there would have been a relentless pursuit. Nerland spies reported the Tara troops, even before the ambush, were mobilized to a greater level of alertness and numbers. Unfortunately the mobilization occurred just before the strike force arrived and did not allow enough time to warn them. It also noted the mobilization happened off the route originally designed for the strike force. After the force passed by, the Tara military closed behind them. The precision of their movements made advance awareness of the strike force's route an almost definite certainty. The fact they had blocked escape for the force and yet these two had escaped, added additional fuel to the possibility they were in collusion with the Kingdom of Tara. Edwin ordered an investigation into the backgrounds of both men to determine whether any connection existed with Tara or other enemies to Evansing and Nerland.

In the meantime the two soldiers were given leave from their normal duties. They weren't informed about being under suspicion. The reason for the leave was because the operations of the strike force were being suspended for a period of one week, so as to allow a review of what went wrong. Also during this time the leadership made a review of the new missions planned to be executed over the next couple of months. Certainly the brevity of time allowed for training and preparation had to be considered. The King, though eager to get going knew this had to be balanced with what made for successful outcomes. Adequate preparation remained essential even if you had highly gifted and able warriors to work with.

In a couple of days the investigation had uncovered one of the men had roots to Tara on his mother's side. This now gave a little more evidence of possible betrayal, but it wasn't adequate. The other man did not appear to have any background which would indicate sympathies with their enemies. Edwin decided a new consideration for prospective strike force members must also include a thorough investigation of their background, including their family origins.

The next morning when Percival knocked on Edwin's door, it awoke Edwin with a start. He had been dreaming and the theme of the dream consisted of, "What is truth?"

Percival entered with a look of slight bewilderment on his face.

"You know," he said upon entering, "I had this morning's game plan all mapped out and while I walked over here it just popped into my head, 'what is truth?' I believe we are to talk about truth this morning."

Edwin laughed.

"Yes, I think it's right. In fact I know it's right. I just had a dream with the same theme. Your knock on the door woke me from the middle of it."

124

"That is wonderful. I pondered whether it would appeal to you. What are your thoughts on what is truth? Share your dream if it's okay with you."

"Well, Greer and I were walking in the town square. She kept pointing out all these people and commenting on their beautiful white robes. I would look closely at the same people and all I saw were black rags. I tried to explain to her she must be color blind because they weren't white or beautiful. They were black rags."

"No matter how much I tried to convince her otherwise she still insisted they were beautiful white robes. Finally I went up to one couple she said had white robes and I asked them, 'I need to know what color you would call your robes?' They looked at me blankly, and said they didn't know. I looked at them, amazed they didn't know what they were wearing. I said to them, 'This isn't a hard question. What color are the clothes you are wearing?' They again looked blankly and even looked a little frightened because of the aggressiveness in my questioning."

"Then I woke up."

Thoughtfully, Percival considered the dream which had been shared.

"You know," Percival began, "truth is having an accurate picture of reality. The problem is no one has a totally accurate picture of reality. We all have a skewing of truth. Of course in each part of our lives there is a different type of truth. Your dream seemed to reveal your perception of people. I say revealed because dreams often demonstrate truths about us the conscious mind is incapable of acknowledging. Dreams also tend to have an extreme element about them so as to make a point. Greer, the most wondrous of creatures and I say that with utmost sincerity, has naturally a way of seeing the best in people. Yet she is not naive about people and is not incapable or unwilling to see the not so beautiful aspects of people. The thing which sets her off from most people is her first bent to look for and expect to find the best in people. Consequently, though they may have lots of defects she will emphasize their strengths and areas of beauty. This explains her ability to connect so strongly with you right at the beginning, even though there were some rough spots in your manner. She overlooked those and concentrated on those key areas where she found great beauty."

"Beauty? Percival, I'm a guy, why are you using beauty in connection with me?"

"Beauty is a non-gender word even though we "Celtic warrior types" think of it in terms of a beautiful woman."

"So are you saying then I have a bent to seeing the things wrong with people?"

"What do you think?"

"You know I believe I do. I considered it being wise about people. But now I am starting to think I have not been nearly as wise as I thought I was. I have often compromised the degree of connection with someone by deciding about them before I even knew them. Often I have discovered the error of my initial impression. I think most people do make snap judgments about people, thinking they are insightful. However, I know of a couple of men, one in Elfereth and yourself who seem to make consistently accurate assessments in a very quick manner. What is your secret?"

"It is true I have had great success in making rapid evaluations about people. I would say my success with people really took off when I increased my ability to stop having preconceived ideas about people. Those areas of bias based on how they look, where they come from, how they dress etc. etc. It hasn't been easy because of course we all have biases or prejudices for one reason or another. I haven't won the battle totally and I suspect it will always be there as something to conquer. But to the degree we can conquer it; we will be more successful in our ability to accurately assess people.

Edwin this time decided to interject, "Percival, what can we do to maintain hope and assist others to maintain hope?"

Percival looked a little surprised at the question. "Why with all you are enjoying and anticipating would you ask me that?"

"I know I have many things to be positive and happy about, but I still have those times when I wonder 'what is the point?' and it makes me feel a sense of hopelessness."

"That's those deep down hurts still trying to express themselves. When it happens ask yourself why you are feeling that way and what is the root cause. Those emotions are opportunities for freedom. When you can identify the specific causal issue you can take steps to get healed and freed."

They then commenced to get into certain deep hurts resonating with Edwin. It felt good to Edwin to have a father figure like Percival bring his nurture into those areas so raw. Edwin felt totally safe and secure with Percival.

"I wish I'd had a father like you," Edwin blurted out to Percival.

"Yes, I know. Anyone who has had no fathering or poor fathering has a yearning for the right fathering. In fact I think it is the number one longing many people have. In most cases they don't realize it. It gets disguised as a desire for a romantic relationship, more goods, bigger house, faster horse or any number of other things. I'm willing to bet if you dug a little deeper you would find the hurt they are trying to soothe, or if you like, the itch they are trying to scratch, is actually a lack of good fathering. It's the most important relationship we experience. It's imperative we fill in some of the lack before your wedding. If we don't, there will be parts of you looking to Greer to fill in those parts missing. You will frustrate her because instead of being the man you will act like a boy. Conversely, because King Erith was probably a better than average nurturing father, you will have a fairly minimal degree of father related conflict with Greer, at least as far as her issues. This is because she won't be looking to you to be a father to her. Given Erith's own father, who was distant and remote, I can only attribute to divine good fortune his bent to consistently demonstrate proper fathering love to Greer. In fact I think in some ways he actually loved her more than his wife. Mind you King Erith and his wife were still very close, and he greatly misses her, but I noticed a certain lack in their relationship. They both had rather poor fathering, and that prevented the extra dimension of connection which otherwise would have been available to them. It is good for you to be aware of those times where it seems like she is looking to you to provide something a father should have provided. You will need to be okay about that and make a shift from husband to father. Likewise you need to be aware of those times you are looking to her to fill the parental gaps. It would be wise for you to avoid that and instead come and talk to me about it."

"Whooo, we are so complicated," said Edwin. "I can't handle anymore of this stuff. Let's go for lunch."

As the two men walked to the dining hall, a messenger met Percival with a letter from his associate searching for the Druid connections. Percival thanked the courier and quickly opened up the envelope to read the letter.

They both read the letter as follows:

Dear Percival,

I have both exciting and ominous news for you. We have discovered the main force behind the Druidry working against Evansing. He is a master sorcerer, perhaps the most powerful of all. His name is Brydon and he is a close kinsman of Alwyn. The suspicion is he was amenable to help because of Edwin being the suspected killer of Alwyn. In addition he has been rewarded handsomely by those kingdoms opposed to the uniting of Ireland. Randar and Tara are known to have contributed to those funds.

The thorniest part of trying to stop Brydon is gaining access to him, for he is currently staying in a remote castle known as Grange. It is well fortified and situated in Randar some twenty five miles south of its capital. It is located on top of a hill thickly forested with one narrow road leading to its front door. The back of the castle has a sheer drop of a cliff so treacherous it makes it unassailable. He has a comprehensive network of associates carrying out his commands. In addition he has been known to change into animal forms so as to move around the country undetected. His favorite is as a type of bird so as to rapidly transport himself to carry out his evil purposes. He is ruthless and indeed one of my associates paid with his life for some of the key information in this letter. At this time I have ceased my efforts to try and gain any more information, as my associates have indicated they will not pursue this matter further.

Regards,

Grabree

Both men were silent for a moment as they tried to digest what they had read.

Edwin spoke first, "Erith will be disappointed to find out Randar and their King Jaspeth are actively working against him. His connection with them has been quite limited, but he had considered them to be potential allies. They have played it very close for none of our spies have given us any suspicions they were so strongly against us."

Percival replied, "It is indeed ominous to discover we have such an adversary as Brydon. Before we move ahead with our plans he must be stopped. Otherwise he will plague us with breaches in our supply and communication lines and compromise the security of our leadership. We will need to discuss this with the King right away."

At the dining hall they saw the King already in a meeting with several of his key advisors. They decided they would wait until after lunch and approach Erith at that time.

Greer and Edwin had a chance to re-connect as they hadn't had much time for one another in the last couple of days. Greer continued to visit with her friends from Nerland and enjoyed them so much. In fact she had considered asking them to stay another week. As they sat beside each other they sat really close together. This represented a new development for they typically sat close together but not that close together. They were actually sort of doing a sideway hug with one another as they enjoyed the contact. The King glanced over and had a bemused look as he saw the two take their public display of affection to another level.

"Edwin, I have now finished designing my wedding dress and my seamstress has already started. I shouldn't have left it so late, but she assures me she will get it done. Of course you won't be able to see it until our wedding day. Have you selected your outfit yet?"

"Uhh no, as a matter of fact I haven't."

"Edwin! You are going to have to focus more time on the wedding preparations. I have done most of it already, but there are some things you and I need to discuss. Besides I want it to be us deciding not just me. We can decide together on your outfit. What are you doing this afternoon?"

"Well I had this afternoon free, but Percival and I have just received some news about the Druid we've been looking for. We need to meet with your father and discuss a plan of action."

"Hmm, it figures. You know sometimes you have to put us first."

"Greer, this is a matter of top state security. What would your father think if I were to miss this meeting to go check out a wedding outfit?"

"I don't care what he would think. There will always be something which has to be attended to. This wedding has to hit the top of your priority list or else there won't be a wedding."

At this point she started to sob and being embarrassed she rushed out of the hall.

Edwin looked after her dumbfounded not knowing what to make of it. He looked around him and people quickly averted their eyes away from him. One pair of eyes didn't and that was the King. Erith came over to where Edwin sat very much alone.

"So did you have a little lover's quarrel?" Erith asked.

"I guess you could call it a quarrel, but it happened so quickly I didn't realize it was a quarrel until she walked out."

Erith chuckled, "Welcome to the world of women."

"Sire, may I ask a favor?"

"Sure go ahead."

"Percival and I have received news about the Druid we have been looking for. Would it be alright if I miss the meeting we planned to have with you now so I can attend to wedding plans with Greer? After all Percival can share with you what we know at this point."

At first Erith's face hardened slightly at the thought Edwin would even consider asking to be excused from something so vital. But then he realized his darling little girl needed some attention.

"Sure, you attend to Greer and get back to me and Percival when you can."

With a big smile on his face and already leaving the hall, Edwin thanked the King profusely for being so understanding.

Edwin caught up with Greer in her chamber where she still felt upset. One of Greer's maids came to the entrance. She asked Edwin to remain outside as she closed the door and went to tell her lady he was there.

After ten minutes, Edwin still waited outside the door and started to get concerned about whether a mortal wound had been suffered in the relationship. At that moment the maid came back and said he could now enter. She brought him into the antechamber of Greer's suite. There she asked him to wait. Now he waited another twenty minutes. Edwin decided he would be patient. A part of him wanted to get up and leave after ten minutes. But his better judgment decided he could wait and would wait as long as he needed to wait.

Then Greer appeared. She looked totally delightful with a bit of a mischievous grin on her face. She asked what had brought him to her suite when he needed to attend to pressing state business.

"I decided we are more pressing and the King agreed with me. I could tell at first he didn't like it, but he must have had a quick internal dialogue and changed his mind. I think it's because he likes you. Can't imagine why," he said with a smile.

She batted him playfully on his chest and feigned chagrin at his response, but she couldn't resist a smile which betrayed her true feelings for Edwin.

"So what pressing matter did you want to attend to with me?"

"I want to check out the suit I am to wear on our wedding day."

"Oh goodie," she replied, "we can go over to my seamstress right now and see what she has for suggestions. I don't think she will have time to make yours, but I know she has some assistants who could make it with her oversight."

They then left arm in arm.

CHAPTER 18

G reer and Edwin had spent all afternoon and evening looking after wedding details. The next morning he wanted to attend to other details of life. Such as the further investigation of this Druid who had been identified as a serious opponent to Evansing and the whole Irish initiative.

Attending the morning meeting with the King were Percival, Edwin and several other key military advisors. The discussion centered on what the various options were as to how this Druid could be captured or killed. The general consensus concluded a military action by the regular army would be too costly and unlikely to succeed. The preferred action would be to use the special strike force in this matter.

Edwin got a strong sense this represented the perfect mission for him and Percival to team up in their own inimical way.

"Sire, may Percival and I undertake a special assignment to accomplish this objective?"

The King looked back and gave an interested look. Then he responded to Edwin and Percival, "Yes, I think it would be an excellent idea. I had given it a fleeting thought, but I dismissed it because it is going to be a rather risky mission."

Percival had a bemused look on his face. He of course had thought about the possibility of him and Edwin doing this operation, but they had not actually discussed it. He decided to go along with the idea and made no comment.

"Well," continued the King, "I think this is about all we need to spend on this matter unless there is something someone has to add." No one said anything. The King addressed Edwin and Percival, "I imagine you two will want to discuss your plans further. Let me know whatever you need for resources and of course discuss with me your plans before you leave."

Percival and Edwin went to Percival's suite to discuss their strategy. When they got there Edwin started to discuss his ideas first. In mid sentence Percival stopped him.

"Please wait a moment until I do something first. He went over to a small table and took a clay jar of what looked like water. He then started to take out small amounts and throw drops of it around the room and especially on the walls.

Edwin looked at him incredulously and then said, "What are you doing with the water?"

"This is not just water; this is special blessed holy water."

"So what is it supposed to accomplish?"

"Not supposed to accomplish, but what it will and did accomplish."

"Okay, then what did it accomplish?"

"We are dealing with a very powerful Druid priest who has powers far beyond the normal physical material world. It would be a small matter for him to sit in on our meetings and hear what we are talking about."

"What about our meeting this morning with the King and the others?"

"Before the meeting started and before anyone arrived I took out a little pouch of water. Then I did what I just did with this water now. The purpose of this is to block all capacity of our Druid friend or his accomplices to use their powers to listen into what we are saying."

Edwin looked at him amazed, but he had too much respect for Percival to question what he had been told.

When Percival had put back the jar he looked at Edwin and said, "Now tell me, Edwin, about this plan you and I have of taking out Brydon."

Sheepishly, Edwin began, "I'm sorry if I volunteered you for a mission I never discussed with you, but it just happened and I figured you would be amenable to do it with me."

Percival responded, "Of course I would say yes to this sort of thing. I understand how it happened. Next time though it may be better to say you wanted to discuss with me the possibility of us doing the assignment."

"Yes, you are right I should have done it that way. I tend to be a bit on the impulsive side and sometimes I make assumptions I shouldn't make. O wise leader, please forgive me and help me to be a more excellent man."

Percival laughed and said, "Yes, I forgive you and by the Grace of God I will help you to be a more excellent man, indeed a most excellent man."

"Great! Thanks, Percival. Now for my plan, mind you I haven't really thought about it in any great detail. I haven't thought about it in any detail other than this: You turn into a big bird, I jump on your back, we fly to Grange and we take out the bad guy."

"That's about how detailed I thought your plan would be. Hmm, I think we need to consider some additional thoughts on the matter. One matter is how we approach Grange without being detected. Brydon is sure to have ways of picking up any movements towards him."

"Why don't we go under the cover of darkness?"

Percival responded, "Brydon sees as clearly in the darkness as we see in the noon day sun. No, we will have to consider other factors besides darkness as a potential covering."

"What about the altitude we fly at? Do you know if his power gets weaker if we go higher than normal?" asked Edwin.

"Good question. Let me ponder it and see what comes to me. Another matter is how are we going to enter the castle? Do we enter on foot or fly over the castle walls? Both have pros and cons. That is something else I will ponder.

You would be best to ponder it as well. Ponder both of these matters. Do you ever make much use of dreams?"

"Not really. Normally the only dreams I used to get were nightmares and I didn't do anything with them."

"What about now?"

"I don't get nightmares anymore and other than that dream we talked about the other day, I haven't had any dreams I can recall. Oh, there were those dreams I had just before I came to Evansing, but I can't remember any details."

"Before you go to bed say to yourself you would like to get dreams tonight that will give you solutions to these two key problems."

"Okay if you say so, I will do it," said Edwin

"Good, tomorrow morning we will compare what ideas come to us."

That night when Edwin went to bed he said to himself he would like dreams that would solve the problems they were considering.

Edwin flew on Percival at approximately 800 feet, at four o'clock in the afternoon and they were coming in the back of a castle. They landed behind a thick clump of trees. Between the tree line and the rock wall up to the castle rose almost 300 feet of bare ground. There only appeared to be one sentry on that wall. Then a most strange thing happened. He saw himself pull out a small leather pouch and before he drank its contents he said, "With this sacred wine I now become invisible." Then he disappeared.

Edwin woke with a start and pondered what he had experienced. It seemed all so real and yet it was a dream. Utilizing his still basic writing skills he made some notes on what he had seen in the dream.

The next morning Edwin excitedly shared what he had dreamed the night before.

Realizing the dining hall to not be a safe place to share his dream he waited until he and Percival were back at Percival's suite.

"Are you going to do your little procedure with the water again?"

"Yes, Edwin, as a matter of fact I am."

After Percival had finished with the water, he then looked at Edwin and said, "So what did you dream?"

Edwin shared with him his dream. When he finished it, he summed up what he understood to be the strategy, fly at 800 feet and come to the castle around the back about 4:00 in the afternoon. Then he stopped, "But I don't know what to do with the part where I disappear."

Percival looked pleased with what he had heard.

"Congratulations! You have embarked on a new dimension of your life which you will find to be powerful and useful. I got the same strategies. It makes sense. At 700 feet or higher the Druid senses are incapable to pick up our movements. Also, around 4:00 in the afternoon is when Druids typically have their lowest level of power and sensitivity. By the way I should tell you even though you can see me in my bird form when you are riding me; there is actually an optical illusion over us. Therefore to anyone more than thirty feet way I look only slightly larger than a normal bird and you are essentially indiscernible from my body. Of course it didn't work so well when flying with the wagon and horses. They were too big."

"I wondered why people on the ground didn't seem to take notice. Yet I never thought to ask you. It acted like a cloak on my mind."

Percival replied, "Well actually there was. It is another aspect of keeping things hidden. Your mind had been blocked from further investigation."

"Okay so we are in agreement with what altitude and time to fly and where to land. The part which has me baffled, is my disappearing act. What's that all about?"

"It's time to go see Erith and get introduced to one of those powers he alluded to when you first met him."

"You mean I can actually become invisible?"

"Yes, for a limited time, normally around twelve hours."

"But how can this be? Isn't that using dark powers?"

"Certainly they could be, but we don't tap into that source. We tap into the Divine Power available to us as believers in the Christ. Scripture records he disappeared into thin air or reappeared out of thin air. It is unfortunate the extreme supernatural is often assumed to be from the dark side."

"Before we go to see Erith let us discuss what you do after you turn invisible. Being invisible will eliminate concern about getting over the flat ground unseen. The next problem of course is how to scale the wall."

"If I can truly become invisible why don't I go through the front door?"

"Druids can detect invisibility because it is something they practice themselves. The reason the dream told you to go to the back of the castle is because there it is less likely you will be detected by Brydon or his fellow Druids. He probably has at least several key practicing Druids working with him. The same thing came to me in the dream I had. In fact my dream and your dream were almost identical. There is a solution to the scaling the wall part. First, have you had much experience in scaling rock walls?"

Edwin replied, "Minimal experience. It is not something I have had cause to do."

"Okay, let's just sit here in silence for half an hour and see what comes to us."

A half hour later, Percival broke the silence and asked Edwin what came to him.

Edwin looked rather amazed as he shared what he had seen. He had a clear view of the cliff face and the wall. Along the southwest corner he could see a series of handholds and footholds which had been chiseled into the cliff face and the wall, and went all the way up to the top of the wall. They were invisible unless you got up real close. The top of the wall must be about sixty feet from the ground. The wall itself only measures about twelve feet with the rest being the cliff face. It would be a challenge, but Edwin felt confident he could do it. After all he had strength and agility.

Percival remained silent for a moment.

Then he responded, "Okay so after you get to the top what do you do then?"

"I would think the most sensible approach is to simply find Brydon and kill him. To try and kidnap him makes no sense. He is too dangerous alive."

"I agree with you, but how are you going to find him in the castle?"

"I know, why don't I tell myself to have a dream about it tonight and see if I can get a detailed plan for where he is in the castle?"

"Now you're getting it Edwin. You are a quick learner. Let's see if we can meet with Erith and have him explain the invisibility part to you."

They came to the King's chambers and announced to the guards outside that they desired to see the King. Fortunately he was readily available.

"Sire, we have an important matter to talk to you about. Before we do, did you do your water thing over your chambers?"

"Yes, of course," the King replied, "I have been doing it daily. There is no point in taking chances on letting our Druid friends know what we are about."

Edwin had a quick thought, "What do you do if you are outside?"

Percival answered, "Simply sprinkle the sacred water around you and whoever you are with in the area."

Then he turned to the King and began, "Sire, we are here to talk to you about our plans for Brydon. They include invisibility."

The King looked pleased at the statement.

"Good, when might we start to use more of those extra powers? How did you come to know the possibility of being invisible?"

Edwin explained to the King his dream and his subsequent discussion with Percival.

Then he asked, "So where do I get the contents in the pouch which made me invisible?"

Without immediately answering, the King walked over to a shelf took a key and then went to an adjoining room. After a few minutes he returned with a leather pouch in his hand.

"It looks like the pouch I saw in my dream," exclaimed Edwin.

The King smiled, "Yes, this is the pouch. It has a special divine wine, the recipe given to me in a vision."

He handed it to Edwin.

Edwin took it and looked at it with a sense of bewilderment.

"So you've actually become invisible yourself with this wine?"

"Yes," replied Erith, "Several times."

"Hmm, most amazing. This is going to be interesting, a new experience. Oh well why not. If I've flown a bird and about to become the future husband of a beautiful princess, anything can happen."

The King inquired, "Do you need any other resources?"

Percival answered, "Yes, we need special climbing shoes for Edwin as he will be climbing around sixty feet to the top of the castle wall."

"You are indeed fortunate, for I have earlier today blessed and anointed a pair of shoes so that they will facilitate its wearer a special divine energy for climbing. When you told me you were interested in this mission, I thought these shoes would be useful for Edwin, so they should fit him. I had the Royal household shoemaker work yesterday late into the night making them."

Edwin tried them on and his head nodded approvingly at the fit.

He looked to the King, "So what exactly does this anointing on these shoes mean to me?"

"It means you will be both protected and given new ability in your climbing up that wall and cliff face."

"Could I still fall off?"

"Yes, of course. You will still need to apply your wisdom and pay attention, but unless you are rather foolish during your climb you should have no problem making it. You are strong and athletic, which will certainly help as well."

"I see. I better not fall off for I will be thought of as playing the fool if I do."

The King and Percival laughed. Then soberly the King said to Edwin, "Expect to do it and you will."

The men thanked the King for his resources and left the King's chambers. They went their separate ways as Edwin had a training session with the army that afternoon. They agreed to meet again the next morning.

The afternoon session was most unusual for one of the officers challenged Edwin to a trial by combat. Apparently he had felt he had been insulted by Edwin the day before. This challenge put Edwin in a most uncomfortable position for obviously the officer had misunderstood what Edwin communicated to him. Yet in this environment for Edwin to try to soothe it over with words would make him appear to lack the courage to battle. This would not normally be the case with someone of Edwin's demonstrated courage. However, there still existed a measure of resentment about Edwin, a young outsider being given so much authority in the army. Edwin decided this officer would have to be sacrificed for the overall maintenance of his authority and discipline in the army. He had internally wrestled for a moment as to whether he should fight with the intention of killing him or only wounding him. He decided unless the officer was in a position of being disarmed and helpless to defend himself, he would fight with the intent of killing him. Anything lesser would cause a potentially lethal result for Edwin. When one fought in a combat of this nature, one must always go for the jugular. Anything less created a hesitancy which made one vulnerable.

CHAPTER 19

The two men prepared themselves for combat and started to walk toward one another with their swords. They both had large broadswords, which they held with both hands and high in front of them. The officer swung first at Edwin's head with the latter deflecting the blow with a quick slice to his left. Quickly recovering Edwin endeavored to catch the officer with a back hand swing against the midsection of the officer. The officer also managed to get his sword across in time to stop the blow. The two men then backed up a few steps to reassess their opponent. Edwin led with his sword a little lower this time pointing to his opponent's head. The officer did likewise toward Edwin's head. Suddenly he dropped down and did a quick thrust at Edwin's stomach. Edwin brought his sword down hard on the officer's sword, stepped forward and did an upward slash to his right aiming for his opponent's throat. The officer managed to lean back and away, missed by mere inches. He regained his balance and slashed back a vicious right against Edwin's sword. The suddenness and the force of the blow almost took the sword out of Edwin's hand. Edwin, surprised by the recovery stepped back and the officer aggressively followed up his blow and his advantage with more blows.

Edwin managed to recover from the disadvantage and started to press the battle to his advantage. He did an unexpected sharp movement to his left and at the same time swung his sword to his right catching the officer hard in the side. The officer led out a yell. Blood started to spurt out. Edwin then quickly repositioned his sword and swung to his left catching the officer in his rib cage. There was the sickening sound of rib bones being smashed. The officer went down.

Edwin stopped and put his sword down. Sweat poured down his face as the battle had been a very vigorous affair. He looked down at the officer and said nothing. He looked up and said someone should fetch the physician. However, the officer appeared to be beyond the help of any physician. His loss of blood was profuse and most likely some vital organs had been severely damaged.

Edwin announced the day's training over and would be resumed at a time to be announced later. Then he left the field and returned to his quarters. He cleaned up and considered what had happened. He told himself he had been justified in the way he had dealt with the officer. Yet there remained a lingering regret about the whole incident. After about a half hour of pondering, he decided it had been partly inevitable and surprising it hadn't happened before. Still he wondered why it happened now. It would be important to determine whether something not readily apparent had spurred this confrontation. He as any officer tended to bark out orders, which would not normally be expected to offend someone to the point of wanting to fight their superior over it. In this case even though Edwin did not hold the position of commander over the army, he was the commander on the training field. So it had to be an extra measure of offense for this officer to challenge in effect his commanding officer and accuse him of insulting him. He thought back over the interactions he'd had with this officer. Nothing unusual came to mind. He decided to talk to Glynn and get his feedback on the matter. Also he would call a meeting of the top six officers and see what they could tell him. Then Edwin resolved he had spent enough time thinking about it. It happened and it couldn't be changed. He now determined to realize what could be learned from it.

He looked forward to seeing Greer at supper and that is what filled his thoughts as he walked toward the dining hall.

When he arrived, a sudden silence fell as people looked furtively at him and then away.

"Hmm," he thought to himself, "I must be the main course tonight. The King, Greer and Percival all looked at him with concerned looks.

Instead of simply sitting beside Greer as he normally would, he went over to the King and Percival.

"Greetings, Sire and Percival, I assume you have heard of the unfortunate events on the training field today."

The King responded, "Yes, Edwin, we heard and you probably don't realize the officer you killed was a nephew of the King of Aldred, the next kingdom with whom I hoped to establish a close relationship. At this point it is too soon to determine what the ramifications are. I have instructed messengers to be dispatched to King Barris and express our great sorrow at his loss."

The news surprised Edwin. "I had no idea that is who he was. If I had known that I may not have killed him. His accusations were threatening discipline and my authority. It's a mystery to me as to what would spark his response to me. I am thinking there must be something more than what initially appears to be the case. "

The forthrightness and unwavering resolve in Edwin's voice both surprised and pleased the King and Percival. It indicated Edwin's maturity growing at an astounding rate.

Erith replied, "Well I am sure you did what you believed you had to do. It was a most difficult position to be in. It's a difficult situation to totally win and it certainly was possible to lose big if you lost the respect of your men, or if you had gotten killed."

Percival interjected, "As Edwin had earlier indicated, there may have been some hidden influences at work. I think Edwin and I need to move quickly with the plans we discussed with you earlier. Tonight Edwin will get the final specific strategies he needs for this mission."

Edwin looked at Percival, and chuckled, "You certainly don't lack for confidence. You say it as though it's for sure."

Percival replied, "That's because it is. You will see."

"Okay I believe you and I also expect it to come to me tonight."

The King looked a little bit quizzically for a second or two and then it dawned on him what they were talking about.

"Yes, I also use dreams as a tremendous source of insight and means of resolving problems. I'm glad to hear you are starting to use them yourself Edwin."

"Anyway leave this King Barris issue to me and you focus on your mission, which is way more important right now. We will try to put the best spin as possible on the events. Barris is a just man and when he realizes it was in a fair combat his nephew initiated, he probably will respond in an understanding way. The major problem will probably be with his family members. Some of them may well react from emotion rather than from the truth of the matter."

Edwin excused himself and walked over to Greer and sat down beside her.

Greer had relaxed after seeing the positive interaction Edwin had had with her father and Percival.

She began, "So from the looks of it my father and Percival aren't as upset with you as it first appeared."

"Oh you mean they were upset with me? Why?"

"It happened at a most unfortunate time when my father planned to talk to King Barris. I think he had a bit of a knee jerk reaction and thought perhaps you could have handled it less directly."

"Really? I didn't get that impression from him. Was it his perception or was it your perception?"

Greer looked at him a bit surprised and a bit annoyed at his question.

"Well I guess when you put it that way, perhaps it's more my thoughts on the matter. Sometimes I think you are a little too ruthless in your approach to dealing with obstacles in your path, especially when those obstacles are living breathing people."

"Really? How do you call this killing a rebel in honorable combat ruthless? Where have I been ruthless in dealing with people since you have known me?"

"Couldn't there have been the opportunity to at least discuss the differences with this officer?"

"Actually, no. The whole situation with my coming here as a foreigner and as a young man is fraught with underlying resistance. If I had shown any weakness in dealing with this officer all the credibility I have been building could have unraveled in a single afternoon."

"Okay and what about your treatment of Alfred?"

"What do you mean?"

"I heard you punched and kicked him."

"I don't call that ruthless. Believe me I am capable or at least I used to be capable of much worse. I know you are a gentle, wonderful creature who would like everything in life to be beautiful. The truth of the matter is it's not. Consequently life on occasion requires tough responses. Just because something is seemingly ruthless does not necessarily make it wrong. To ensure I would fight this officer with the necessary intensity required to win, I needed to fight with the objective of killing him. If you call battling to win ruthless, then yes, I was ruthless. I make no apologies for it."

"As far as Alfred, I must admit my personally hitting him stemmed from frustration. I did also order the guard to rough him up. It's part of getting cooperation from a very uncooperative prisoner, pretty standard operating procedure. Indeed our treatment of Alfred and the others with him have been extremely gentle in relation to what normally would be the case. You might say it's a gentler, kinder ruthlessness."

Greer didn't quite know what to make of that. "Well, I certainly don't want to let this spoil anything between us. I don't fully understand your approach, but I do know you are a good man."

They then continued on to the much pleasanter topic of ironing out the details of their upcoming wedding.

That night when Edwin slept he found himself taken to Grange. He had just climbed to the top of the wall. To the left he could see the one guard assigned to the wall. He stepped out onto the walkway. The guard looked right at him. At first Edwin felt alarmed because he had been spotted. But the guard only glanced over and then looked away and started to walk in the opposite direction. Edwin realized the guard couldn't see him. He noticed a tiny beam of light on the ground ten feet in front of him. It moved down the stairway to the next floor. Edwin followed after the light. The light turned right at the bottom of the stairs and then a quick left down a hallway. Edwin made a mental note of the directions taken. At the end of the hallway there was another stairway and the light continued on down it to the next floor. At the bottom of the stairs there were two guards standing blocking access to the floor. He considered his options for a moment. Then he did a very juvenile thing. He tapped one of the guards on the shoulder and the guard turned enough to allow Edwin to squeeze by him. After passing by them he continued on down the hallway to a door where the light stopped. There was a guard on either side of this door. Edwin paused considering what to do next.

He felt quite amused by his ability to stand right in front of the guards and not be seen. Then he realized he had to keep his focus. He walked right through the door.

Edwin woke with a start. "What was that?"

CHAPTER 20

He got up and wrote down his recollection of the dream. The next morning in Percival's suite he shared his dream. "I've got a new trick to come up with. How's walking through a door sound?"

Percival looked at him and smiled. "Interesting, we do have something for that, but it only works once in a four hour period."

"So I get in, but I may not get out."

Percival considered the predicament.

He replied, "If you open the door to get out and even if you walk past the guards, they may notice their master is dead. That could lose hours of advantage in facilitating your getaway."

Edwin replied, "The only way out of this is to kill the guards and drag them inside the room, and hope nobody notices for a while the guards aren't at their post."

"Okay sounds reasonable. The other option is for you to fly like a bird out of his window, but I don't think you are ready for that yet."

"Are you serious? Is that a possibility?"

"Yes," replied Percival. "Eventually."

"Well in the mean time I guess I kill the guards."

"What do I need to go through the door?"

"I have a friend a day's ride from here who has a special power to do this. He can also impart it to others so they can do it for up to ten days after the impartation."

"When do we leave?"

Percival replied "Why not in the hour? Time is of the essence. Arrange to get a squadron of twenty men to accompany us. Let's meet at the court-yard."

"Okay let's do it."

By supper time Percival and Edwin pulled up to the small farm house of Percival's friend.

A tall man with a long white beard came out and gave a loud shout of greeting when he saw Percival.

"Hey, Percy, how've you been? It has been over a year since I last saw you."

"Hi, Jackie, it's good to see you too," replied Percival. He did wince a bit at being called Percy in front of his companions, but he quickly brushed it off.

"I'd like to think you made this special trip to see me and share old times, but I suspect given your escort there must be some official reason for you being here."

"Yes, Jackie, there is a reason besides seeing your beautiful face."

Motioning to Edwin he introduced his friend, "Edwin, this is Jackie and Jackie, this is Edwin. This young man is the reason we are here. We need to talk to you in your house."

Inside the house, Percival asked Jackie if he had sealed his house against eavesdropping. After a positive response, Percival continued with why they were there. "Edwin needs your special impartation for him to go through a door or a wall."

Jackie looked at Edwin. "I should tell you there is a one in three chance that it won't work for you."

Edwin replied, "Isn't there a way of checking it out before you need it?"

"Even if you tried it out now it wouldn't mean it would work later and vice versa. Therefore you take your chances."

"We're here now so if you could please do your impartation I would appreciate it."

Jackie came over and put his hands on Edwin's head and muttered some words unrecognizable to Edwin. Then after a moment he stopped.

Edwin looked up and said, "That's it?"

"Yes, that's it," replied Jackie.

Then he turned to Percival and they chatted amiably for about twenty minutes before Percival cut it short and said they needed to start back. They would stop for overnight in a couple of hours, but it would make for a shorter return tomorrow.

As they pulled out of the farmyard Edwin asked Percival if it went according to his expectations. Edwin had almost called him Percy, but he decided if Percival liked being called Percy he would have heard people call him by that name before.

"Not totally, as I was not aware of there being such a high failure rate of it working. We'll just have to expect it to work as per your dream."

Late the next morning the party arrived back in Evansing. Percival and Edwin had both decided they would leave shortly before 3:00 that afternoon, with an expected arrival time in Grange of around 4:00.

CHAPTER 21

At 700 plus feet in the air Edwin hung for dear life onto Percival the giant bird. This riding on the back of a giant bird was always an exhilarating affair. The Irish landscape below appeared breathtaking from this prospect. Edwin thought to himself how only a very few people in all of Ireland would see their country from this perspective. All of a sudden Edwin felt incredibly privileged to be one of those few.

Eventually they saw a castle in the distance which fit the description and location of Grange. As planned they started circling behind it while still miles away. They landed hidden by the thick forest behind the castle which was about a mile away. After a moment or two on the ground, Percival changed back into his human self. Edwin watched fascinated as he saw the metamorphosis happen before his eyes for the first time.

"Wow!" said Edwin, "What a strange thing to behold."

Percival replied, "You should be the one experiencing the transformation. Now that is a rush."

"You said eventually I could change into a bird as well. I can't wait."

"All in good time my young man. You are being so accelerated. If I give you too many new experiences your system will seize up from overload."

"Hey I'm into overload."

"No, I'm not going to do that to you. On top of all this you are getting married. That is going to be a big adjustment for you as well. I want to make sure you are fully there for Greer. Those first nights, weeks and months in a marriage are key for the rest of your time together."

Edwin gave Percival an affectionate hug and said, "Thanks for protecting me from myself."

Edwin took out his pouch and drank it. After a few minutes Percival told him he had become totally invisible. Then he left on his trek through the forest toward the castle.

At the edge of the forest where the clearing began, he took a deep breath. Then he boldly stepped out and walked toward the rock face situated under the southwest corner of the castle wall. He could see the sentry patrolling the wall and even looking in his direction. But he obviously could not see Edwin, for he neither sounded an alarm nor issued a challenge to Edwin.

At the rock wall, Edwin located the footholds carved into it just like his dream. Edwin thought to himself, "Who would have thought I could see something in a dream so true and precise?"

For a brief moment Edwin considered how there was so much more to life than what he had previously believed. In a matter of months he came from not believing in anything beyond his five senses to believing in a realm of invisibility at least as real as the visible.

Edwin started his climb. After almost ten feet he realized this was going to be a challenge. Fortunately he was strong and athletic, but it began pushing him to his limits. At the halfway point he stopped for a moment to rest briefly and gave his aching arms and legs a moment's respite. He had to hang on tight so he didn't have much of a rest.

When he hit the actual wall part, the footholds weren't quite as deep and he almost slipped at one point. After recovering his grip he hung on for a moment. Then he recalled in the dream he had gotten to the top. "There," he thought to himself, "it's done." After that fresh infusion of confidence he made it to the top.

At the top he dragged himself over the wall. The sentry stood some thirty feet away and looked right at Edwin but made no sign of seeing him. Edwin continued on down the stairs following the directions in his dream. Two guards came around a corner and almost ran into Edwin. He managed to squeeze himself against the wall and one of the guards barely grazed him. The guard could tell he had touched something and he did glance back over his shoulder, but he couldn't see anything so he carried on, most likely thinking he must have touched the wall. By the time he got to the door of Brydon's room where the two sentries were standing, Edwin felt very excited. This was an adventure extraordinaire. It seemed as though all his senses were bristling with stimuli. Even though invisible to others, he could see himself as he always did. This created extra challenges to his sense of reality and stretched his faith in being truly invisible to others.

As in his dream, Edwin walked right through the door. In the room he looked to the right and there sat Brydon. He must have sensed something because he looked up in Edwin's direction in a concerned angry way. However, before he could fully move to the realization Edwin was there; he was dead, as Edwin had made his way across the room and sank his dagger into Brydon's heart. Edwin, the consummate assassin had been well-schooled in the manly art of killing his fellow man.

Standing over Brydon, who had been the object of their scheming, Edwin savored for a moment his victory. He studied the facial features of Brydon. He rather looked like someone's kindly grandfather. Probably was. Certainly didn't look the role of the sinister deadly Druid priest who had caused King Erith and his kingdom so much grief. Then he turned his attention to dealing with the two guards. He opened the door, the guards undoubtedly thinking it must be Brydon, came to attention with their eyes straight ahead.

Edwin plunged his dagger into the heart of the guard to his right and then with a back handed motion stabbed the heart of the other guard. Looking down the hall and not seeing any one he then dragged the guards inside the room, closed the door and started his escape.

As he came up the stairs to the top of the wall, he encountered two Druid priests who had intense expressions on their faces. He killed them both with thrusts to their hearts. "Two less potential successors to Brydon," he muttered to himself.

The descent down the wall and rock face was physically easier than the ascent but emotionally more challenging. This was because Edwin's adrenaline pumped wildly after killing Brydon. He could hear an uproar as bodies were being discovered.

Even though invisible, Edwin kept expecting an arrow in his back as he ran across the open field into the forest. When Edwin reached Percival he was exhausted but still flush with victory. He gave Percival a look that only a successful hardcore warrior can give another human. Of course since he remained invisible the look was lost on Percival. Mind you Percival had seen that look many times in his years as a warrior, and had experienced that look himself.

"The deed is done, Percival!"

"Congratulations, Edwin! Give me a moment to make my change and you can tell me all about it on the way back."

After sharing about the exploits in the castle, Edwin asked Percival something he had wanted to ask ever since yesterday. "Why didn't we fly down to see your friend instead of riding?"

"There is a certain amount of stress and strain to do the transformations. I could not have done that trip and then this one without at least a week in between. Besides it is good to limit the exposure of this type of mystery."

When they arrived back in a wood just outside the Evansing castle walls, it was dark. Edwin continued to be invisible. He still had a few more hours before the invisibility wore off. "Gee, Percival, I hope this stuff wears off like it's supposed to. It would be a bugger if I stayed invisible. Greer would not be impressed."

"I'm sure if Erith gave it to you, you'll be alright."

"So what am I going to do now while I am waiting for it to wear off?"

"We'll wait in my suite and we can do reading lessons."

"Percival, you must have forgotten what it is like after you've killed five men. To kill someone always gives me a rush. And given all the various other dynamics involved in this mission I am pumped. There is no way I can settle down and do reading now. Let's go for a brisk walk or something. I need to release some of this energy swirling around in me." The pair walked and talked around the Evansing capital for three hours before Edwin started to reappear. This created a rather curious sight, as Edwin appeared to be a ghost, for he hadn't yet materialized into full physical form. Since it was dark and late no one noticed or at least no one they were aware of noticed. It was a bit reckless of the two to risk being sighted during that time of transition.

The next morning at breakfast the King expressed excitement at seeing the two men back and wanted to talk to them in his chambers later.

In the meantime, Edwin sat down with Greer. She knew about the mission and of course was excited to see her future groom back safe and sound. He said he would tell all the details later in more secure surroundings. Then he decided to invite her to the King's chambers. He, the King and Percival had decided sometime earlier it would be okay for him to share whatever he felt was appropriate to share with Greer. She, the King's daughter was in effect part of the inner circle. Greer had the character of someone who could keep secrets and was not prone to just chat about whatever came to her mind. The invitation to join the men in the King's chambers was, however, another step higher than what had ever been accorded a woman before. When he invited her she looked at him rather bemused.

"What's the matter?" he asked.

"Do you realize what you are saying?"

"Yes, I think so. I invited you to join us in the King's chambers."

"Yes, but do you realize that is never done? Women do not join the men in the King's chambers to discuss affairs of state."

"Well, why not? I can't see any reason why your father should object."

She laughed. "You don't have any sense of no or can't when it comes to rules and protocol do you? I mean that of course in a good way. I love that about you. I just plain love it. You look at all these societal rules and say why? Yet you aren't lawless either. You seem to have an innate sense of what is just and appropriate.

"So how are you going to broach the subject of me going to the meeting?"

"You are going to accompany me on my arm and we will assume this is the way it is done all the time."

"Oh really? I don't know about that. I think you will stretch the sensibilities of the King if you take him by surprise like that. I think you should go over and ask him if it is okay."

"No, let's live a little dangerously. Let us be willing to incur the wrath of the King. Let's stretch him."

"Oh, Edwin, you are such a brat. Remember my father is the King. Not someone you can fool around with."

"He's also going to be my father-in-law and I want some kind of real relationship with him. I don't want to be just another subject with special status because I am married to his daughter. I know it is a bit risky to spring this on him. But I believe if we play dumb about these rules you're talking about, he will come around like he did about us holding hands and walking arm in arm in public. It will also create another relational connection. Conflict has the potential to deepen or destroy relationships. I believe this will deepen the relationship I have with him. I believe it will also do that for you with him."

"You think my relationship with my father needs to be deepened?"

"Yes, I do. Even though he dotes on you and loves you very much, there is still a need for greater emotional intimacy between you and him."

"Where did you ever get such wisdom?"

"I think it must be from all the time spent with Percival. I've been getting new insights about all kinds of areas of life, even those I haven't specifically discussed with him. All of a sudden I have started thinking differently, very strange and yet very delightful. I am gaining an appreciation and even a fascination for truth and ideas. So leave it to me, let's give it a go and see what happens. I know it may be a bit cheeky, but not so that we are going to create great offense. Besides if he insists you not attend then I guess you won't attend. But I am willing to bet he will let you in. Be sure to have on your most disarming smile. It is a winner every time. Who can resist your smile? If he still looks hesitant, then give him a hug and kiss and tell him, 'I love you Daddy.' If he still resists, then the man must have a stone for a heart."

"Edwin, you are being a schemer. Let's do it."

After breakfast the pair walked over to the King and Percival to accompany them to the King's chambers. Instead of doing the expected thing of Greer saying good bye and walking away, she walked into the chambers on the arm of Edwin.

"What are you doing, Greer? You know better than to come in here when I am in session on state matters. I am having a private meeting with Percival and Edwin."

She smiled at him.

The King was not impressed. "What are you smiling at me for?"

Feeling the encouraging squeeze from Edwin she walked over to her father and hugged and kissed him and said, "I love you Daddy!"

He looked at her not knowing whether to be exasperated or pleased. Finally the pleased part won. "Oh I guess you can stay this time but don't expect to make it a habit."

Then looking at Edwin, "I suppose you were the one who put her up to it." He tried to give Edwin a stern look and initially it did look rather stern but soon after his face softened.

"Yes!" thought Edwin, as he did a high five to himself, "Another breakthrough in relating to this man in a more personal way. Even kings need to be real people."

In the meeting, Percival and Edwin shared with the King and Greer all which had transpired. Their audience had their rapt attention for it certainly was an extreme adventure of the most unusual kind. Flying bird, invisibility, walk through door, powerful Druid killed and a successful escape. They looked in amazement at what had transpired and how it transpired.

The King also shared some rather amazing news, which definitely proved the connection with the uncooperative prisoners and Brydon. For late yesterday afternoon, around the time Brydon died, the prisoners all started to share information about their contacts. Officers were being dispatched to round up all those available in Evansing and Nerland. A number of the contacts were in other kingdoms and the special strike team was being organized and made ready for these new assignments. They also shared information, which proved beyond doubt the two soldiers under suspicion for the failed Tara mission were guilty of betrayal. They were both promptly arrested.

Edwin relieved at the news, said now he could more fully focus on the preparation of the wedding, only a few weeks away.

The King also shared that the initial response from King Barris had been favorable. Some of his nobles, especially those close to the slain nephew of the King wanted to take some form of retaliation, even if simply to refuse cooperation with Evansing. Barris determined to maintain cooperation with Evansing, but in order to soothe them he had decided to at least postpone further discussion for one month. He would evaluate the atmosphere at that time. Erith decided it was just as well because then there would be no interference with his daughter's wedding. The young couple could spend uninterrupted time together. Ireland could wait.

CHAPTER 22

It was the morning of the wedding. Both of the main participants were nervous and excited and eager for everything to go well. Greer of course was more concerned about the details going according to plan. Edwin, like most guys, was more relaxed about all the details. For most part all he concerned himself with was that he would be married by the end of the day. If every little carefully planned orchestration didn't quite work out, he probably wouldn't notice or would shrug it off.

Percival would be co-officiating and he was actually feeling a little nervous. There had been some discussion with the Church officials as to whether Percival qualified to marry the couple. Strictly speaking he wasn't a full-fledged priest even though he often fulfilled much of the priestly duties as a monk in the monastery. The King resolved the controversy by asking the bishop who would normally perform a royal wedding, to do the official exchange of vows part.

Percival would do part of the service, including a special blessing over the wedding couple. He had put great thought and care and love into crafting a blessing, which would have great significance and leave a deposit in the spirits of the two young people. He did not see this blessing as simply some nice words to add to the ceremony. He saw them as something that would help ensure the future happiness and success of the marriage.

Edwin waited with Glynn his best man for the wedding to start at 2:00 PM. A couple of Greer's royal cousins also attended him. Greer was attended by two of her cousins and decided to choose her dearest Nerland friend, Athandra, of the Nerland Royal House to be her Maid of Honor.

A knock at the door indicated Edwin and his attendants should now proceed to the chapel to await Greer and her attendants. They came by the side door into the chapel already packed with people. Attending were several of the kings of the surrounding areas and their immediate family members. The Evansing royal family was in full attendance. In addition, the key leading men of Evansing and their families were there.

Edwin waited nervously and excitedly for Greer to show up. Glynn gave him a reassuring smile and patted his arm, just like a best man should. Then there she appeared, in all her glory, his bride to be. Of course she looked radiant as a bride should. She and her attendants slowly made their way from the back to the front. All the while she had her gaze fixed on Edwin and his on her. As she got closer he felt more and more relaxed. This was going to be good. He decided to savor this experience.

The bishop led them in the exchange of the vows and exchange of rings. They kissed.

They signed the register and Percival presented them to the people in attendance as husband and wife.

Then came Percival's time to bless the new couple. He began, "In the name of the Father, Son and Holy Spirit I bless you Edwin and Greer with the endurance to stay the course and withstand the pressures life will bring your way. May your thoughts as individuals and as a couple be continually and only filled with what is true, noble, pure, lovely, admirable, excellent and praiseworthy. May your life together consistently manifest the fruit of the Spirit, love, joy, peace, patience, kindness, goodness, faithfulness, gentleness, and self-control. May you both wake up each morning with the excited anticipation of celebrating life together. May your lives be characterized by superior wisdom in all matters and especially in your relationships with God and one another. May you live together preferring one another and desiring and finding ways to demonstrate your value of each other and your relationship. May the Lord bless you and keep you. May the Lord make His face to shine upon you and be gracious to you. May the Lord give you peace and life continually."

Percival experienced some emotion in the course of delivering the blessing. His heart so full with desire to see this couple excel and enjoy life together. Even the King looked like he was getting emotional. This of course was a major struggle for Erith because he didn't do real well with those kinds of expressions. Celtic warriors don't cry and certainly not kings. Many of the people in attendance, however, had no problem with tears of emotion, especially Greer's aunts and female cousins.

Now the time for celebration in the dining hall; where much food and drink and music were ready to be enjoyed.

The beaming new couple sat in the place of honor and were thoroughly enjoying themselves. Numerous toasts were offered up and many people shared their favorite stories of Greer, while Percival and Glynn and several others shared stories about Edwin.

When the dance part began the wedding couple was the first on the floor and then joined by other couples. The dancing went on well into the night. The couple excused themselves around 10:00 PM. The quarters of the Princess had been renovated and enlarged somewhat in preparation as the residence of the new couple. They now made their way to their new home together. The crowd cheered in sending them off on their new life together.

At their new quarters, the young lovers looked at each other both a little nervous and also excited with anticipation of their first night together. Edwin brought out a necklace encrusted with emeralds. He knew Greer adored emeralds. She oohed and awed over it and gave him a big kiss. The kiss lingered and lingered and got more passionate. After a moment she pulled back and said, "Wait I want to give you your gift, but first put on the necklace."

He placed on her necklace with him kissing her hair and back of her neck as he did so.

Then she presented her gift, a brilliant blue tunic, which she wanted him to wear tomorrow when they went to the lake. They wanted to recreate that memorable time when they went the first time. If pleasant enough weather they may even go swimming.

Their honeymoon time was to last for two weeks during which time Edwin would not have any responsibilities, except to be with his new wife. Due to security concerns they would remain in the capital except for occasional day-time trips to nearby attractions like the lake. When they were out and about they were to be given an extra measure of space to be together as they so chose.

Edwin tried on the new tunic. Both he and Greer were pleased with the fit and he expressed his gratitude for it.

Then they resumed their embrace and progressively worked their way to the bedroom. The last thing to come off was the new tunic.

The next morning the young lovers woke side by side enjoying the feel of flesh upon flesh. They looked dreamily into one another's eyes and resumed where they had left off the night before.

Early afternoon the young couple emerged from their suite. They went in a cavalcade headed by twenty troops with another twenty coming behind them. They were on their way to the nearby lake.

CHAPTER 23

The two weeks flew by far too quickly for the two young people enjoying the fruits of their love for one another. The first two weeks together had been an incredible time of further cementing their relationship. Edwin had displayed remarkable sensitivity to Greer and she had been captivated by his acts of devotion to her.

King Barris of Aldred had indicated his family had cooled down sufficiently to resume discussions with Evansing on how to work together in a more cooperative manner.

Edwin was slated to accompany the Evansing contingent leaving for Aldred. The planned departure date would be in three days. In the meantime meetings were being held as to how to best persuade the Kingdom of Aldred to work in close harmony with Evansing. Ideally they would come on board like Nerland. Initial intelligence had indicated the Crown Prince of Aldred had grown fairly warm toward the idea of close ties with Evansing. At this time no mention had been made of the plan to incorporate them in the quest for uniting Ireland. However, it was an open secret so undoubtedly they knew it would be part of the agenda.

The Crown Prince of Aldred, Kerris, avidly participated in hunting. Therefore, Edwin had been assigned to connect with Kerris and engage him in a hunting expedition.

Kerris had a beautiful younger sister named Chandra. Therefore, Carson, a good looking and charming nephew of Erith had been chosen to come along with the express objective of facilitating a marriage between the two kingdoms. Kerris was known to love his sister and they had a close sibling relationship. Percival and Edwin were to spend time with Carson over the next few days to help prepare him for the role of suitor. He was known to be a bit of a ladies man and Erith did not want any inappropriate behavior by him with Chandra.

Carson did not seem all that interested in the idea of playing suitor. He had doubts about whether Chandra was as desirable as the reports indicated. He had a current relationship not sanctioned by his family which involved the daughter of a local merchant. While he liked the girl he did not love her. She was fun and willing and for a young man like Carson of only nineteen she was quite adequate for his current aims and needs in life. Those aims and needs were focused on having fun with little concern for weightier matters. However, his father and his uncle, the King, had had some discussions with him about his responsibility to Evansing. Some of his indolent orientation needed to be eliminated. Carson's natural good looks and charm had resulted in him being somewhat indulged while growing up. To now create a young man of character would indeed be a challenge. Percival and Edwin were discussing this matter and how to motivate Carson to make a rapid shift.

Percival had a gleam in his eye.

"Edwin, this problem is impossible. Therefore it requires an impossible solution."

Edwin looked at him wondering what rabbit he would pull out of his hat now.

Percival continued, "The only way we will be able to get Carson up and running to at least a reasonable level of the required character is through a dramatic night vision experience."

"Okay, so how do we or rather I should say how do you do that?"

"This is something I have been thinking about doing with you soon to accelerate your learning process. I haven't done it yet because it has been important that you and I build relationship in the course of your lessons. We don't have sufficient time to spend with Carson before we leave. In some ways it might be smarter to leave him behind and try this connecting with Chandra at a later date. However, there have been some overtures from another kingdom about Chandra as a possible wife for one of their royals. We have no one else eligible, as good looking and charming as Carson who is also about the same age as Chandra. We also know that a man's good looks and charm are extremely important to her. King Barris takes her preferences seriously."

"Tonight I am going to appear to him in his dreams."

"What? You are going to do what?"

"I am going to appear in Carson's dreams tonight and the next two nights. I will bring him special messages, which will impact his subconscious to the point where he will shift and mature in time for our departure."

"So how can you do that?"

"Tonight at bedtime I will first take the Eucharist. I will then ask Holy Spirit to take me into Carson's dreams even while I sleep. The first night I will create a shift in his perspective on life, so he is open to the next two nights of maturing him."

"Do you know what specific message you are going to use to get him to shift?"

"No, but it will come to me when I am in his dreams."

"Percival, you are making my head tilt. But I don't know why because my whole life has been on tilt the past three months. Oh well I should soon become unimpressed by anything you tell me. No, I take that back. I don't ever want to stop being amazed at the new wonders you introduce me to."

That night Percival did what he told Edwin he would do. After taking the Eucharist he lay down and asked Holy Spirit to take him into Carson's dreams. Nothing happened for some time because Carson had been out partying late with friends.

"Percival, what are you doing in my dream?"

"I'm here to create a shift from the self-absorbed little boy that you are into the man you need to be in order to be a true prince of Evansing."

"Maybe I don't want to shift."

Percival ignored his petulant little boy response. He then started to share about who Carson had been created to be. He started to share how Carson was called to be much bigger than someone who simply took up space and wasted his time in self-indulgence. He had a purpose for being here, a purpose for greatness, a calling to be someone who could make a difference for good wherever he went. He would have a role in building the Kingdom of Evansing.

The next morning when Percival and Edwin met with Carson they could tell something had indeed shifted in Carson. First they noticed Carson looked at Percival with a look as if he didn't know if he was awake or still sleeping. Also there appeared a newness in his bearing like he'd had a revelation about his life purpose.

Finally Carson blurted out, "How did you do that?"

"How did I do what?"

"How did you appear in my dream?"

"Oh did I?"

"Yes, Percival, I know you are into some pretty powerful stuff. Nobody has ever actually told me that. But I have always thought you are someone who marches to a different tune, and not just because you're a monk."

"Okay I confess I did go into your dream."

"Why would you do something so extreme?"

"Time is of the essence and the only way you are going to be the kind of man we need you to be, is if you are shifted in your perspective on your life. By the way, tonight I would appreciate it if you would go to bed earlier as I really didn't like laying awake waiting for you to get to sleep. The way this works is I can't fall asleep until you are asleep and ready for the dream state, which is sometime after you fall asleep."

"What? You are planning on doing this again? Isn't this an invasion of my privacy or something? I mean you getting into my dreams. This is so bizarre. And I will go to bed whenever...."

Then he stopped. He started to get this bewildered look on his face as he must have been pondering something. "You know," Carson began, "This is very strange. I'm getting these new thought patterns which say I should do what you say and get to bed early tonight. These thoughts in me are saying my life here is for something more than hanging out in self-indulgence. Hmm, I don't get thoughts like that. Percival, what did you do to me?"

"I brought some enlightenment to your darkened soul."

"What? I don't have a darkened soul. I don't need any….." Again he went into silence with a perplexed look on his face. "Now my thoughts are telling me I do need enlightenment. Have you taken over my mind, Percival?"

"No, Carson, I haven't taken over your mind. Rather I have freed your mind. Or at least I have begun the process of freeing your mind."

"Freeing or possessing my mind?"

"Freeing your mind! You must be enjoying a new sense of purpose to your being here on this earth."

Carson looked at him for a moment in a way which demonstrated a new capacity for depth of thought not previously there.

"I hate to admit it, but I guess there is a part of me which appreciates this new thinking coming alive in me. Wow did I say that? This is so weird. I'm not sure who is me and who is someone else in me."

"Carson, what is happening is perfectly natural for someone who has had a major shift in such a short time. You may feel a little confused and disoriented today. Relax and enjoy the process."

By this time the fight had left Carson and he didn't know how to respond. He obviously had an internal conflict going on inside. "So what would you like to talk to me about now?"

Edwin and Percival then proceeded to deposit more seeds of true nobility and character. These would be watered and accelerated to a greater maturity during the subsequent night time visits.

On the day the entourage readied to leave for Aldred, the change in Carson had become so remarkable Erith couldn't help but notice. He took Edwin and Percival aside and said what had transpired in Carson was nothing short of a miracle. His highest expectation for Carson was hoping he wouldn't screw up by doing something reckless with Chandra. Now having seen the way Carson conducted himself and from having conversation with him, he could tell he was a man on a mission for the Kingdom of Evansing.

The journey to Aldred took the better part of a day. En route the only notable occurrence involved Carson engaged in conversation with Percival and Edwin. He treated them like dear friends. Whereas a few days ago he tended to be rather sullen and quiet around them, he now chatted amiably with them on topics of state and the prospects of him delighting Chandra.

By the time they arrived in Aldred it was almost dark and everyone was glad to be there. King Barris came out to meet them with his officials and members of his family. The entourage included Chandra. Erith had mentioned in a dispatch to Barris about the possibilities of a match up between his nephew and Chandra. Barris had indicated he would assist them meeting and see what transpired. He would not force his daughter to marry someone simply to strengthen an alliance. In this way he thought like Erith, both men gave their daughters tremendous leeway in determining their own life choices. Both men wanted their daughters to be happy. This contradicted the norm of how kings thought of their daughters. In most cases daughters were considered items available for trade to facilitate advantage of one form or another. Not that they wouldn't intervene in the case of something really silly contemplated by their daughters. Fortunately for both men their daughters had good heads on their shoulders and a strong sense of what it meant to be a princess of the realm.

The initial meeting between Chandra and Carson went better than expected. Chandra had of course been advised of his purpose for being there, as had her brother the Crown Prince. Carson proved adept in engaging the Crown Prince in matters which created a positive impression. Edwin also had a positive initial meeting with Kerris and they lost no time in making plans to go hunting the next day.

Percival later that night said to Edwin that Carson was indeed a quick study, as he had progressed well beyond his highest expectations in such a short time. It's like someone had removed a veil from Carson's eyes and now he began seeing life in a way previously unavailable to him.

The next day during breakfast the seating had been arranged so that Carson could sit with Chandra, Edwin and Kerris at the same table. Percival joined Barris and Erith and others at the head table. Even though the first four would normally sit at the head table, for the sake of relationship they would be at their own table set a little off to the side for greater privacy.

In the afternoon Edwin and Kerris, together with a number of royals and nobles from both kingdoms went stag hunting. The afternoon went well as the party got three kills. Even more incredible, the degree of connection created between the two. They found they had similar outlooks on life and temperaments, which meshed well together. Kerris was curious about Edwin adapting to married life. Indeed he was quite keen to find a bride himself, but something inside him seemed to block his ability to press the issue. Being already twenty three and the eldest he was expected to marry in a way appropriate to his status. For the one he married would one day be queen.

He loved to engage Edwin in sharing about his courtship with Greer. At times it seemed he found that more fascinating than the hunt. He had become more interested in another type of hunt, the hunt for a soul mate. Edwin's sharing of his relationship with Greer convinced him he could not simply marry someone for political expediency or because she would be ideal as a queen. He would like those of course and needed to consider them, but she must also be his soul mate.

A party of young royals and nobles from both kingdoms had had a day of mingling and getting to know one another. Only males came from Evansing, but Chandra had been joined by a number of young women as well as men from Aldred. Chandra's attentiveness to everything Carson said and his attentiveness to her, clearly demonstrated they liked each other.

The four young people again sat at the same table and this time the conversation became louder and more animated than in the morning. Everyone started to feel more comfortable as a result of fun interactions during the day. This time Chandra asked Edwin some questions about getting married and what it was like courting Greer. She expressed how wonderful it would have been if Greer had come along. Edwin noted this and decided either Greer would come next time or else they would invite Chandra to Evansing. Upon further reflection he decided Greer coming to Aldred would be the best. Barris would probably feel better about that, plus Edwin knew Greer enjoyed traveling and would love coming to Aldred.

Chandra and Carson continued to engage each other in animated conversation. They tended to both be very dramatic and loved to talk when they were with people who could appreciate what they had to say.

Edwin and Kerris continued a conversation which mingled affairs of state with hunting and finding your soul-mate. "I was just plain fortunate in meeting Greer. I can take no credit for arranging the meeting. It happened beyond my control. In the morning I'm alone and friendless and before the same day is out I am standing before this wondrous creature. She and I seemed to hit it off and it progressed from there. There is one young lady which comes to mind that I think could be a good match for you. She is of the Nerland royal family, one of King Keltic's nieces. Quite possibly she is his favorite. In many ways she is the mirror image of Greer. She was Greer's Maid of Honor. Her name is Athandra. Hey, it rhymes with Chandra, it must be fate," he laughed.

Edwin's suggestion intrigued Kerris. He knew Edwin wouldn't throw something like that out there just for conversation. In such a short time he felt he knew Edwin well enough by now to know him to be a man of substance. He also had profound respect for Edwin's judgment in the area of women. He felt if anyone could win the heart of someone like Greer then he had to be an expert in the area of women and love.

"Edwin, would you be willing to act as a go-between to initiate the overture for me with Athandra?"

"I would be delighted to act as your go-between. I am going to do something more. I am going to give you a first hand opportunity to meet Greer so you can have some idea of the qualities Athandra possesses. Plus Greer will have a chance to share with you those things she feels you will need to be aware of in order to successfully woo Athandra. I would not suggest Athandra to you as a prospect if I did not believe you were of sufficient quality to meet Greer's standards as a future mate for her friend. Of course I will first get Erith's okay since he loves his precious Greer."

Erith was pleased at the prospect of bringing Greer along to help create connections with Aldred. The fact that it had a double connection by also involving Nerland struck him as pure genius.

"Edwin, you are diplomatically astute."

"Well, Sire, I would like to take credit for the diplomacy aspect, but I was more concerned about creating a love match for Kerris. Mind you I knew an opportunity existed to further the relationships between the kingdoms involved.

Barris responded with delight when he became aware of his son's desire to meet with the King of Nerland's niece as a prospective mate. There had been little connection with Nerland as they had no common border and had never pursued much in the way of relationship with one another. Given the growing connection with Evansing it made sense to try and cement closer ties with Evansing's closest ally. Edwin's offer to facilitate the match greatly touched Barris. As well, he considered it a great honor that Edwin wanted to bring Greer to meet his son to help with the process. He insisted a troop of Aldred men would be waiting at the border with Evansing to add to the escort for Greer to Aldred.

Erith sent a courier with a message asking Greer to join them. The official dispatch also included a separate sealed envelope, whereby with the help of Percival, Edwin expressed his love for Greer and how he missed her sooo… much. He also filled in extra details on what he had been doing in Aldred. He knew she would like details. He also told her what sparked the official reasons for her coming to Aldred.

The dispatch brought great joy to Greer. She had been a little miffed at not being asked to come along. But it was not the norm to bring women when traveling on official business to other kingdoms. She had so missed her cuddling time with Edwin and she was looking forward to resuming where they had left off.

Early the next day after receiving the message from Aldred, Greer embarked with a troop of two hundred men. Two of her maids accompanied her. As promised by Barris they were met by a troop from Aldred at the border. When they were an hour from Aldred Castle, Greer experienced pleasant surprise at seeing Edwin on the horizon riding toward her with a troop of people. Several of whom she recognized as being the young nobles and royals from Evansing.

Greer speeded up to join her husband. The two kissed and warmly embraced while on horseback. For several moments everyone else disappeared and it was just them as they shared how they missed each other.

In the meantime all the others around them maintained a discrete distance and let the two re-connect undisturbed. Then all of a sudden the two realized they weren't alone and there were others standing around waiting on them. They blushed slightly, smiled and waved at the others.

The first order of business involved introducing Greer to Kerris and Chandra. Pleased and so proud he looked like he would pop his buttons, Edwin began the introductions:

"Greer, this is Kerris, Crown Prince of Aldred and his sister Princess Chandra of Aldred. Kerris and Chandra this is my wife, Princess Greer of Evansing."

Kerris and Chandra both ooohed and awed how splendid it was to meet Greer after having heard all the wonderful things Edwin had shared about her.

Greer laughed. "Well that's good because he should be my greatest fan. I know I am his greatest fan," looking at Edwin adoringly.

Both Kerris and Chandra were so struck by the depth of connection that existed between the two. They had seen newlywed couples before, but this looked different. This couple had something special. They could tell it transcended the mere physical and emotional. This couple had a spirit to spirit relationship so strong you could almost touch it. It created in them both a yearning for the same thing in their lives.

"Hello Carson how is my darling cousin?" said Greer.

"Very well, Greer. You have created quite a stir by coming to Aldred."

"Surely you are exaggerating."

"No, I'm serious. Ever since we've heard you were coming that is all anybody talks about. I don't understand it." Carson said with a wry smile.

Greer laughed. "Well of course I'm just your cousin." Then she looked at the party surrounding her and said, "I do hope I meet your expectations." Kerris then introduced her to the other Aldred royals and nobles. As well she greeted and re-connected with the other young Evansing royals and nobles who had come along for the ride. Greer, renowned for her graciousness in relationships, made an effort to acknowledge and interact with even those she saw regularly back home.

Erith beamed with great joy at the sight of his daughter. It gave him much pleasure to introduce her to Barris and other Aldred personages who were meeting together with their Evansing counterparts. Barris felt pleased at the honor of Greer coming to visit his kingdom and help Kerris connect with Athandra.

At supper the group of four now became the group of five with the addition of Greer. Both Kerris and Chandra were enthralled with the opportunity to talk to Greer. Edwin and Carson sat there and once in awhile smiled at one another in amusement. Edwin of course being hopelessly in love with Greer could understand their reaction to Greer. It challenged Carson to understand why all the fuss, but he did appreciate his cousin was rather exceptional.

The next day while the group of young royals and nobles rode to a nearby lake, Greer had a chance to chat a little more one on one with Kerris as they separated themselves some distance from the rest of the group. She asked him about those internal blocks he referred to in connecting with the right woman. Kerris hesitated for a moment and then he shared that he had concerns about not feeling sufficiently passionate with the woman of his future. He liked women and he liked the idea of being married. However, something seemed to be missing as far as his ability to get passionate about the idea of being married.

Greer asked him, "Why do you think that is?"

"I'm not certain, but I think it may be partly because I noticed my parents seemed to have a rather lukewarm approach to their relationship."

Greer replied, "So how did it make you feel?"

"When younger I of course didn't know anything different. As I got older I realized there was something missing in my emotional makeup. For some reason Chandra has a more passionate way of being. I've always loved that part of her personality. For me hunting has been the one area of passion. Now it is starting to wane and I realize I want more passion in my life than just hunting. Talking to Edwin about his relationship with you and I realized he was experiencing already what I wanted to experience. He has so much passion when he talks about you. Indeed he has passion about a lot of things. I can't think of too many areas we have talked about where he didn't have passion. What do you think I can do to break out and be the man I want to be, a man of passion?"

"Focus"

"Focus?" he asked.

"Yes, the only way a person can be passionate about anything, is when he or she is focused on a particular person or activity. Think about when you are engaged in hunting. You are focused and consequently you feel passionate about it. Why don't you spend a moment seeing yourself hunting until you feel that passion? Then transfer that passion to something involving your duties as Crown Prince."

Kerris had this look on his face which indicated a growing passion while envisioning hunting. Then it looked like it sort of disappeared, but then it came back. He looked at her and smiled.

"I felt a passion for some of my least favorite administrative duties. That is remarkable. Of course I will have to see how well it works when I am actually doing it. So how about my view of women? I want more than a passion based on physical drive if I may be so bold as to express it that way."

"No problem, I appreciate your frankness. So tell me what makes you think you would be good for Athandra? I need to tell you right now she has a zest for life, which could shake your world. She is a rather unusual girl in the degree and wide range of things, which she feels passionate about. So if you want to connect with her you will need to grow in your capacity to be passionate, first and foremost about her and also about life. She loves life. Even though life can be difficult, there needs to be a mindset of embracing difficulties as times of growth. They force out or at least if we allow them to do so, force out to the surface the true self existing deep within us. Passion requires our true self to be visible and engaged with the world."

Kerris looked amazed at this young woman not much more than a girl who shared this truth he knew to be great wisdom. "Wow if I can tap into being consistently passionate there is nothing I can't do and I know that my life will shift from being a bore to being a joy. So how do I get there? How do I become this focused lover of life?"

"Well it is a process. It won't be accomplished in a few days. One person I would recommend you spend some time with is Percival. He has done wonders for Edwin. He also did some great things with Carson so he would, shall we say be more appropriate for Chandra."

"So Percival is a gifted man when it comes to relationships?"

"Yes, I would say so. I know he has also done marvelous things with my father. My father and I have a much warmer relationship over the last several years and I would say it is largely due to the influence of Percival. Ask Edwin to take you to him."

A little later Kerris came alongside Edwin.

"I can see why you are so excited about Greer. If Athandra is half as wise and pleasant I will be a blessed man."

Edwin beamed at what he heard. He loved to hear good things about Greer.

"Greer said it would be good to have you take me to Percival and see if he could help me with some of those internal blocks I told you about."

"Sure I can do that. Percival loves to help people to be all they can be. He is very good at it."

At supper that night, Edwin brought Kerris over to Percival. "Percival, the word has gotten out you are a genius in helping people in relationships. Therefore my good friend Kerris would like to spend some time with you. He wants to increase his ability to enjoy relationships, especially that special relationship he would like to enjoy with Athandra."

Percival smiled at Kerris and said he would be pleased to help him in any way he could.

That evening in Kerris' quarters the two men talked about various things Kerris remembered from his childhood. They seemed to have an adverse effect on his capacity to enjoy relationships and life in general. One of the things which seemed to come up as a big issue concerned the matter of performance. All his life Kerris had been rated on the basis of how he did things. Seldom did he feel like anyone celebrated him for being Kerris, beautiful just for being here and alive. He felt like being the perfect Crown Prince was all that mattered to people.

Percival replied, "Welcome to the adventure of personal transformation. You are going to start experiencing life at a higher plane." With that Percival began to work with Kerris in ways similar to how he worked with Edwin. They were releasing those things of the past that had left lies embedded in his understanding of life.

When they were through, Kerris sat exhausted in a state of good tiredness. Kerris began experiencing a new dimension and depth of peace and well-being he hadn't experienced before. That night he slept well.

Kerris walked along the muddy, straw strewn streets of Aldred. However, one major difference, he didn't hold the title of Crown Prince. He was just Kerris, regular guy walking along enjoying the sights and sounds around him. Nobody accorded him special favor or recognition. He wasn't a prince on the outside, but he knew deep down it didn't matter. He was a prince on the inside and to the core of his being he knew it.

Kerris woke up feeling stronger and more complete than he had ever felt before. As he pondered the dream, he realized it didn't matter if the only way the people related to him was as Crown Prince. He now accepted himself just for being Kerris, apart from his official position. "Wow! What a revelation!" He couldn't wait to see Percival and tell him the good news of his personal change. Also he wanted to share his new insights about himself and his new way of being with Greer and Edwin. He liked these people from Evansing. They had something special. At this point he thought Carson married to his younger sister Chandra would be an ideal match, not only for her, but also a way of solidifying his ongoing relationship with Edwin and Greer.

At the breakfast table, Erith decided to honor Barris and Aldred by officially installing Edwin as the Crown Prince of Evansing, while they were in Aldred. This answered the question before as to why Erith had made no mention of Edwin becoming the Crown Prince at the time he married Princess Greer. Barris and Kerris were both pleased at this special honor being bestowed upon them and their realm. Of course even more pleased were Edwin and Greer. They had had no warning of this happening. They had both been puzzled at the silence of Erith on the subject. It was one of those sudden things he sometimes sprang on people. Fortunately they tended to be pleasant surprises.

At the chapel in the castle, the royals, nobles and other key personages were assembled to witness the investiture of Edwin. In the short time he had been in Aldred, he had already won for himself great favor in the eyes of many people. He had become well-liked and the gracious Greer added to his popularity.

The ceremony started with the local Bishop proclaiming a blessing over the event. Barris received the privilege of handing a gold crown to

Erith, who then placed it on Edwin. This crown had twelve points on it with each point containing a bloodstone gem.

Erith intoned, "I now crown you Edwin, Crown Prince of Evansing. May you enjoy God's favor in all your dealings."

The crowd then cheered and moved on to the reception area next to the chapel for a time of celebration.

Greer came up to her husband with admiration glistening in her eyes. "My fine Crown Prince." She hugged him tightly.

At the celebration, Kerris could not wait any longer. He had to tell Greer and Edwin how his time with Percival had given him a whole new perspective about himself. He had a new sense of calmness of spirit and well-being that hadn't been there before. He also shared about the dream, and how he had never before been one to consider his dreams as a possible source of valuable information.

Edwin asked him, "Do you want to go see Percival again?"

"I don't know. I mean what else could there be to uncover? I feel the best I have felt in years. Maybe the best ever since I was old enough to remember."

Edwin replied, "Have you shared with Percival yet what you've told us?"

"No, I haven't had a chance. He has been busy with my father and Erith."

"When you do share it with Percival, ask him if he thinks it would be good to see him again. He may well have some other insights he thinks would be good for you to know."

"Alright I will do it," responded Kerris.

In the meantime Carson and Chandra were continuing to create a reservoir of mutual admiration and affection. At the celebration they danced and talked with great animation. At one point they even went outside onto the balcony alone to talk. Carson took hold of Chandra's hand and held it while looking into her eyes. Chandra smiled coyly and looked back at him with a bemused look on her face. She liked this fellow, but she didn't want to reveal the full extent of her feelings to him, just yet. Chandra tended to have a bit of a mischievous teasing side to her. Not maliciously, but perhaps as a bit of a defense against her heart being wounded in relationships. If you kept friends a little bit at bay, then there wouldn't be quite as much of yourself invested in them. However, she had noticed her level of satisfaction in her relationships wasn't as high as she would like.

Carson noticed the look back at him did not reflect the same level of ardor which he emanated toward her.

"Either she is not interested or else she is playing hard to get," he thought to himself.

Then he said it, "Oh come now Chandra be real with me. Invest yourself. Don't hold back."

CHAPTER 24

He surprised himself at what he had said. He wouldn't normally be so bold in challenging someone like Chandra, another kingdom's princess and about something so profound. He dismissed it as having to be another one of those changes in him resulting from his dreams and time with Percival.

Chandra looked surprised and a little bit uncertain how to respond to such a daring challenge to her. Her first impulse would have been to take away her hand and get in a huff. But something told her, "No, don't do that." She liked him holding her hand. She had looked away and then she looked back at him. She found now she had a new respect for Carson, which hadn't been there before. He was demonstrating a willingness to go beyond catering to her whims. He wasn't allowing her to be the princess who always got her way. He wanted something more. As she considered everything before her, she decided, "Yes." She did want something more than what she had had before. Something in her decided that no more did she want to play it safe with Carson. She would let her feelings be free to explore what this relationship could be.

Carson, in the interim is thinking, "Oh no, what did I say that for? Erith is going to be furious with me."

He did notice though she hadn't taken away her hand. Uncharacteristically she appeared to be thinking rather deeply. That was one thing in his new way of being which troubled him a bit about her. She didn't seem to have a lot of depth to her.

Then she replied with a smile, "You are right to challenge me Carson. I wasn't allowing myself to be fully engaged with you. I want more of me to be with you."

Carson was cheering inside as he heard her speak. It was almost beyond his belief that saying something so bold to her would get such a welcome response.

He replied with a big smile and a bit of a chuckle, "Do you know the way you bounce your head is so cute when you express yourself with great passion."

She was taken aback at his response. Chandra had expected something serious and profound. Instead she got a bantering kind of reaction. At first she didn't know whether to laugh or get mad. She decided she would laugh at his impetuous way. She flicked his ear as at least a mild way of expressing her chagrin at his not taking her seriously

"Take that for being so unimpressed with me pouring my heart out to you."

Carson turned on the charm and shared how he adored her and how it delighted him to hear her desire to be more available to him with her emotions. With that they returned to the hall and began to dance once more.

Kerris had noticed the young couple was out on the balcony for an extended time. He almost started getting concerned, at which time they returned. He didn't want any improprieties to spoil what looked like a promising alliance. Kerris saw that there appeared to be an extra measure of mutual delighting in one another in the way they looked at each other. On the dance floor they were having great fun together.

"Looks promising," he thought to himself as he watched them dance.

When Edwin and Greer had stopped dancing and had returned to their table, they were joined by Kerris.

"Would I be too bold to ask if you would approach Athandra on my behalf to see if she is interested in meeting me? I would be happy to make the journey there. Perhaps we could all make the journey together and make it an event."

Greer responded, "Oh that sounds like a magnificent idea. Do you think Edwin we could do that in the near future?"

"Well, we will have to get Erith's approval for I know he has plans for my involvement. First, you will have to get Athandra's, her father 's and her uncle's approval about Kerris coming to see her."

"I will write her while we are here. If necessary perhaps she could come to Evansing," added Greer.

"Yes, I think that might be more amenable to my schedule. Mind you I'm sure Erith will recognize the value of building relationships with and between allies," said Edwin.

CHAPTER 25

Four days later a messenger arrived from Nerland. Athandra, her father and her uncle, King Keltic had all agreed to at least have Kerris meet her. Since Evansing sat mid-point between Aldred and Nerland it had been agreed to meet in Evansing in fourteen days. The meetings in Aldred were expected to be done in less than a week so the timing was ideal before other junkets were planned to take place.

Kerris excitedly shared the good news with his family. Chandra asked if she could travel with them as well. Barris at first was a bit reluctant. But after cajoling from Kerris how Chandra would be safe with him and in the care of Edwin and Greer, he finally agreed.

Erith was also pleased to see how the relationship building had gone much better than his expectations. It seemed as though everything pointed to a strong union between the Evansing, Aldred and Nerland royal families, and their kingdoms. However, two prominent noble families in Aldred felt strongly that Aldred's role in any union should only to be to facilitate commercial trading. They did not want to offer military assistance other than allowing Evansing and her allies limited safe passage through Aldred territory. They wanted to limit where the troops could go and also keep the numbers to no more than five hundred at a time in their kingdom. This created great concern for Erith and Barris for they knew that wouldn't be enough to achieve the objective of Irish unity. Barris had decided to give his full support to the Irish Quest. It stirred up that part of him that sought to leave a legacy for his kingdom that would last generations.

The youngest son of one of the dissenting noble families, a seven year old named Josh, went missing two days before the meetings were scheduled to be over. Being a rather precocious boy, he would sometimes wander off into the woods by himself. Even though his parents told him about the wood elves getting him if he went in there, he did it anyway. Search parties were organized and many of the Evansing party volunteered their services.

News of this young boy missing especially touched Carson. He'd had a close call with his eight year old brother the year before. He remembered the torment his family went through when his brother had wandered into the forest. The searchers found him three days later in a very dehydrated condition. His little brother would not have lasted another day. The hunting dogs lost his scent as he had jumped on to the back of a straw wagon and rode for several miles before jumping off.

So with great resolve to make a difference, Carson first went to the parents to ask for some information regarding their son. They were ambivalent about talking to someone from Evansing, but their love for their son overcame their prejudices. Carson gleaned that their son liked to go into the nearby streams. Together they studied drawings of where the streams were located and a description of the terrain. They weren't deep or fast streams, but if Josh had gone into one he could lose the hunting dogs engaged in the search. It seemed as though Carson had a sixth sense about where Josh had gone, for he headed in a direction where nobody considered looking. It was a particularly forlorn area and difficult to enter. The entry though was a stream that wound its way through the middle of that area.

The trackers came up short, for at one of the streams the dogs lost the scent. That left them not sure where to look next.

Meanwhile back in the forlorn section of the forest, Carson waded along in the stream leading into it. After several hours he noted a hut ahead with smoke trailing out of its chimney. He walked quietly not knowing what he would find. The young man held his dagger close at hand and also had a short sword strapped to his waist. It was now twilight. Up ahead he thought he noticed some rustling in the trees. He stopped. Then he heard a young voice, "Let me go, let me go."

There was a gruff reply, "Shut up, kid, or I'll beat your hide."

The boy kept struggling, but he didn't say anything. Then the man, a broad shouldered, stout, rough looking individual gave the boy a cuff on his head. The boy let out a scream. Then the man grabbed him and yelled in his face to shut up. The boy Josh, now terrified started to scream. Before the oaf could strike him again, this time with a closed fist, he received an unexpected dagger in his back. He dropped like a dead man, for indeed he was a dead man. The dagger went right into his heart stopping it instantly.

Carson hadn't been a total lay about. He had been trained in how to fight with daggers and swords. The youth had proven very adept at it.

The boy, terror stricken looked up at Carson. He stared agog at the blood stained dagger held by his rescuer. Carson smiled at him and put the dagger down.

"Hi, Josh, I won't hurt you. I came looking for you when you were reported missing."

With that he gave Josh a hug as the little boy cried and cried in relief. As they walked back now in the dark, Josh explained what had happened. It's true that he had traveled a short distance into the forest. When he turned around to go back home, that man grabbed him and forced Josh to go with him.

After a couple of hours of walking back through the stream, the young boy was too exhausted to go further. They went out of the stream and found a little shelter and cuddled together to try and get some rest. The boy slept until dawn. Carson, however, had a rather fitful sleep. He worried that perhaps the dead man would be discovered and have a friend or relative who would want revenge.

Carson, relieved when Josh woke up, was eager to get going. They shared a couple of slices of bread before they started off. After almost three miles they were out of the roughest part of the forest. Fifteen minutes later they were met by a posse of five men involved in the search. The two exhausted individuals were given additional supplies and quenched their thirst with spring water in a canteen.

One of the searchers went ahead to inform the parents that their boy had been found. Before they had even gotten within a mile of Aldred they were greeted by the parents who had come on horseback. Their son shared about his daring rescue by Carson. Both parents showered profuse thanks and appreciation on Carson. By looking at the tatters that were now Carson's clothes and his state of physical exhaustion, they knew he had exerted great effort to get their boy. They had an extra horse for Carson to ride on the way back. Josh rode with his father. Neither parent even considered disciplining their little boy. He had been disciplined enough.

Back in Aldred the rewards of finding Josh were first and foremost the look of admiration and gushing adulation from Chandra. She couldn't seem to say enough good things about how selfless and brave Carson had been. Chandra, the dark haired beauty looked more beautiful to Carson with every gush. If there had been any doubt in Chandra about Carson, it had been utterly removed with his act of courage. She was now sure she could respect this man.

A most welcome bit of news came the day before the Evansing people were to return. The two dissenting noble families had now decided to support whatever arrangement Barris intended for Aldred with Evansing and its allies. This included providing military forces to the Irish cause.

The trip back to Evansing had a festive air about it for their time in Aldred had been a great success. They were added to their number by the Crown Prince of Aldred, Kerris and his sister Princess Chandra. Both were excited about the opportunity to see new territory geographically and heart-wise.

Over in Nerland, Athandra started making arrangements to travel back to Evansing.

Her cousin, Crown Prince Gondar told her he didn't think it such a good idea about her considering a potential marriage with someone from Aldred.

"Why? What is your basis for saying that? My father, your father, the King and my very good friend Greer, think otherwise."

Gondar looked at her and stated that he didn't want more entanglements with Evansing and its allies.

"Gondar, Nerland is already entangled about as much as we could be. If I marry the Crown Prince of Aldred it won't make that much difference to any great degree."

"It will to me," said Gondar. "I hoped you would be mine."

Athandra looked at him amazed. There had never been any hint of interest from him before. Besides, marriage between first cousins while not expressly prohibited tended to be discouraged.

She said, "This is a fine time to spring this on me. Kerris and his sister are already en route to Evansing. Why are you saying this to me? You have never given me more than the usual cousin attention before?"

Gondar tried to be sincere but being a rather poor liar replied, "Oh I have always had an ardent attraction towards you and now I realize it's more. I love you, Athandra."

"Gondar, you lie. You don't love me. You just want to continue with your reticence to embracing our Evansing allies and the Irish Quest. Get over it. If it is about Eldreth or whatever, get over it."

Gondar felt both ashamed at being found out and angry at his cousin's scolding.

He glared at her and then turned on his heel and left.

Athandra looked after him and shook her head. "Whew what an emotional roller coaster ride." Or at least she would have if they'd had them back then. Instead she said some 11th century Irish equivalent.

Two days later Athandra travelled on the road to Evansing with a couple of her cousins who were also friends with Greer. She had excitement at the prospect of meeting this man highly praised by Greer, the man who could become her husband. She may then eventually become the Queen of Aldred. Wow, such new possibilities when only a few days earlier she had no knowledge of them whatsoever. What appealed to her most of all was that Kerris sounded like someone she could love. And in turn, he sounded like he could love her. One did not typically marry someone of the position of Kerris for love but for position and power. To have those and love was the best of both worlds.

The walls of Evansing were glistening in the sunset as the contingent from Nerland approached. A troop of horses with two men and two women galloped towards them. They waved gaily at the Nerlanders. As they approached, Athandra and her cousins recognized Edwin and Greer. The other attractive people they didn't recognize. Athandra said to her cousins, "They must be the brother and sister from Aldred."

As Kerris got closer and closer he did not disappoint her. Kerris had those striking good looks with chiseled features, which any woman would love in a man.

Greer was first to greet and hug her Nerland friends. For a brief moment or so they got caught up with chatter amongst themselves. Then Greer politely stopped the conversation and introduced the two newcomers to Athandra and her cousins.

Kerris inquired after Athandra's trip and whether she felt tired after traveling from Nerland.

"We had a great trip and I am excited to be here. Let's go dancing," replied Athandra.

The robustness of her response pleasantly surprised and pleased Kerris.

"Greer told me you are a lover of life. Such zest, I will do my best to keep up with you."

And dance they did for a celebration party had been organized for the arrival of the royal parties from Aldred and Nerland.

Other than some of the usual awkwardness in a new boy-girl relationship, they were quickly becoming comfortable with being in each other's presence. Kerris thought to himself, "Boy, Greer wasn't kidding when she said that Athandra had an amazing love of life."

Athandra thought to herself, "He has just the right amount of life and yet he has a calming influence on me. If I had someone like me it would be an impossible relationship."

It had been planned that the Nerlanders and the Aldredites would spend a week in Evansing. Then they would assess how things were going and decide whether to stay longer.

Edwin, Erith and Percival were meeting to decide what to do about strengthening the relationship with Gondar. His cousin, Athandra shared how he had tried to keep her from going to Evansing.

Edwin first shared the obvious, "We of course need to come up with something that doesn't look like we are reacting to what Athandra told us.

I know, let's make our alliance with King Taryn work for us. Get him to kidnap Gondar and I will rescue him." He said this with such a straight face that at first Erith and Percival weren't sure if he was serious or not.

When Edwin realized they weren't sure how to respond, he started to smile.

Percival said, "Ahh, the joker in Edwin has arisen."

Erith chuckled, "I would normally have you lashed for that in such a serious meeting, but I will refrain this once."

Edwin thought how good to see Erith gradually loosen up in the time he had known him. The King had become more and more the kind of person that Edwin wanted for a father-in-law.

Erith continued, "You are quite correct, if we try to initiate something right away with Gondar he would probably be suspicious about why and it could be bad for his relationship with Athandra. I suggest we wait for our annual games coming in three months and ask him to come as part of the Nerland team. We will ask him to enter the spear throwing competition. He is a strong thrower and has won a number of competitions. Also, he loves horses and competing with them. I am putting up my chestnut mare, Meta as the prize to the winner of the overall horse jumping event. When Gondar came for Edwin and Greer's wedding, I could tell he was impressed by Meta."

"The next order of business is to leverage this games event with as many potential allies as possible. It's interesting, Edwin, that you mentioned King Taryn, for I am going to invite him and his two sons and three daughters and whoever else he wants to bring to be our guests. His two sons are avid wrestlers and so we will invite them to compete. What do you say about that?"

"Yeech, I can tell by my initial gut response that hearing Taryn's name with the prospect of seeing him again, is not one of my favorite things. For the sake of the Quest I will suck it up."

Percival interjected, "Not just for the sake of the Quest but also for you and Greer."

This brought up Edwin short as he at first was irritated by Percival's reminder. After all he and Percival had had several sessions on the issue of bitterness and unforgiveness.

"Okay, Percival, Mr. Perfect, I get it. I will need a little time with that though, but I promise I will make the effort. I am glad you brought him up. I didn't realize how much hard feelings I had towards him."

Erith smiled and continued with the next name on his list.

"I also want to invite King Jaspeth and whoever he wants to bring along from Randar."

Edwin smiled. He thought to himself, "Even if Jaspeth didn't accept, it indicated the hand of friendship had been extended to him from Erith."

Erith said, "I know the odds are low on Jaspeth accepting, but I thought to at least give it a go. I'd rather win him by friendship than by force."

"The list gets more interesting. I want to invite Crown Prince Evo of Dagarath. Maybe he will come so he can visit his father, King Nelwyn. I'm still mulling over what to do with Nelwyn. Perhaps if we meet with his son and other family members we will have a better idea."

"My final name is King Clarendon of Tara. It would be quite a coup if he accepted."

"That gives us a potential of seven kingdoms participating in the games this year. Besides ourselves, two allies, one ally forced by treaty, and three, Randar, Dagarath and Tara, fairly overt enemies. If they all accept it should make for rather interesting games. Of course the most interesting events will be happening off the games fields."

Percival spoke up, "We will need to get messengers out with invitations within the week. First we must finalize their wording. As I am sure you will both agree it would be important that each party know who is being invited."

Erith replied, "I had thought that ten weeks would be enough time, but I agree with you that we should get them out as soon as possible."

He called to a servant to bring in a scribe for he decided that they might as well get the invitations done now.

Over the next two hours they dictated the invitations to the scribe. They made minor modifications to each one to address certain conditions unique to the King or Crown Prince being invited.

Two weeks later the first response came back. To the surprise and pleasure of Erith, King Taryn, his sons and daughters would be coming. Also a number of leading lords and ladies of Merethath would be accompanying them. He even expressed thanks and gratitude at being invited. "Most peculiar," thought Edwin when he heard the news. "How could someone like Taryn do such a turnaround?"

CHAPTER 26

Edwin's writing skills had been coming along quite quickly, but he still needed a scribe to write a dictated message to his good friend Glynn.

"Glynn, I have just received news that Merethath's King Taryn has graciously accepted an invitation to come to our games in almost two months. He is bringing his children and other leading lights of that realm. It doesn't seem right that he would be that pleased about creating friendship with Evansing. Though he responded to Erith's demands regarding my release, he only did it because at that time he knew he would lose. What do you know about the status of Merethath's military preparedness and their alliances with other kingdoms known to be antagonistic towards us?"

(signed) Edwin

Percival was surprised to see Edwin at his door. He had been informed earlier that Edwin would be training the troops for the day. He could tell that Edwin had a look of urgency on his face.

"What's up Edwin?"

"Perciva,l I need to talk to you about Taryn and his unusually warm and prompt response. I know Erith is very pleased and is hoping that this will mark the start of much warmer and more cooperative relations with Merethath. For me something is not right. I have sent a dispatch to Glynn regarding Taryn as to what he knows and I wanted to talk to you about it. I even delegated the start of the training to one of my very capable captains."

For a moment both men stood there in silence.

"I think you are right to be concerned. There is a rather strange impression that I am getting when I consider Taryn wanting to be good friends with Evansing."

Just then, a knock on the door, it was one of Erith's personal messengers. The news he shared came almost as surprising as the one about Taryn. It concerned Jaspeth of Randar who had also accepted and indicated he would be coming with his family and leading nobles as well.

Both Percival's and Edwin's inner knowing started acting up now. There was something amiss. It seemed to both of them that there had to be a conspiracy. How could avowed enemies, even one bound by treaty, have such a 180 degree change in their attitude towards Evansing? There hadn't been any significant diplomatic activity with either one. The only recent movement with Randar involved the killing of Brydon. Given Jaspeth's sympathies with the Druid community in his kingdom, that particular act would not endear Evansing to him. That is if he even knew that Evansing did it. Of course, Jaspeth probably had strong suspicions of Evansing's involvement in Brydon's death. Yet there had been no response from Jaspeth in connection with that action. Intelligence had indicated that the Randarian Druid community had been devastated by the loss of Brydon. However, they were in the process of re-grouping and deciding upon a new leader. Jaspeth had been known to attend some of those meetings. There were strong suspicions that he may be a practicing Druid himself. This created all kinds of potential security problems with a whole kingdom possibly dominated by Druid magic and philosophy. All of which avowed opposition to Irish unity.

"What do you think about you and me going on a reconnaissance mission with respect to both these guys?" Edwin asked.

"Yes, I can see that that could be a good thing to pursue. We will need to consider the how, when, where, what, who and why of our objectives."

"Oh you mean we can't just use the planning standards according to Edwin?"

"No, I mean real planning standards, one with some details."

"Oooh details! Sounds boring. I like my standards of just going and unfolding the plans as we are doing it. Seriously though, after our Brydon exploit I do have a new respect for a certain amount of advanced planning. We are starting to undertake missions a lot more sophisticated than go in and bash some heads and grab some stuff."

Edwin continued, "I need to get to the training grounds. At least we are on the same page about our suspicions. Let's meet tomorrow morning. I would love to meet tonight, but Greer has plans for me to be with her and Athandra and her two cousins for a dinner in our suite. They return to Nerland tomorrow. Let's both see if we can have dreams tonight that will clue us in to where to start and also receive some confirmation about whether our suspicions are correct. You know, Percival, using dreams as a form of insight otherwise unavailable is one of the most marvelous things that you have taught me. Then again you have taught me so many wonderful things. I have gone from being an unsophisticated, callous and insensitive clod to becoming someone who can actually feel and act like royalty. You and Greer have been such huge forces for good in my life."

That evening in their suite Greer and Edwin entertained their three Nerland visitors.

Athandra said, "Kerris is such a dream. Thank you so much Greer for thinking that it would be good for us to meet. He is planning to come to Nerland in three weeks time so that we can pick up where we left off. At this point it looks promising. I am quite taken by him and he is quite taken by me."

Greer replied, "I knew that Kerris had the essentials to be good for you, including the motivation to take whatever steps were necessary to enhance his love of life. I knew you would not be happy with someone who lacked in passion for life."

"Yes, you know me well enough that I would leave someone like that in the dust. As it is I know Kerris was a little bit stretched in the beginning, but he picked it up to another level. As we progressed in our time together he became more and more comfortable at moving at greater intensity. I don't need him to be just like me nor do I want him to be. I find his being more laid back is the perfect complement for me."

Then Edwin joked, "Yes, this is all good, but of course we know that the most important thing is that it will cement the alliance between Aldred and Nerland."

Both women were sitting next to Edwin, who sat at the head of the table. They each punched him in the shoulder closest to them to show their contempt for his statement. All in good fun of course.

"That will only be considered as a bonus by me," replied Athandra. "I need to know that he is someone I can love and want to live with for the rest of my days. No amount of political advantage will ever sway me otherwise. Fortunately my father and uncle care about my feelings on this subject. Even though King Keltic may seem rather cold at times, he does have a soft spot for me. He respects my preferences."

That night Edwin asked to have dreams about Randar and Merethath. There sat King Taryn on his throne looking as malevolent as ever, when a messenger came to say that King Jaspeth of Randar had arrived. Taryn told him to bring Jaspeth in without further delay. The scene then switched to both kings looking at a map of Evansing.

"What are we going to do about this pestilence Evansing?" asked Taryn.

"We are going to lull it to sleep and then cut its throat," replied Jaspeth.

"How do we do that?" asked Taryn.

"By means of a rarely used Druid enchantment we are going to inspire Erith to invite us to Evansing's games later this year. We will respond so wholeheartedly to his invitations to us that he will believe we have a change of heart. Consequently his guard will be down. You will then have a clear route into Nerland and I will come up from Randar to invade Evansing."

Edwin woke with a start. "That settles the confirmation part."

That morning both Percival and Edwin were able to share dreams that were essentially the same.

"The troubling thing is to know that Jaspeth is involved in using Druid magic and somehow his reach is strong enough that he can impact Erith. We need to discover what has created this susceptibility in Erith to such enchantment. I believe its power is such that Erith won't believe us. Therefore we need to break its power over him."

"So how do we do that?"

"Well, Edwin, I am about to pull another trick out of my bag that I haven't told you about before."

"Prospero may we have your assistance please?"

With that, a being materialized out of thin air, a very glorious being. He looked like a young man of twenty-five or so with long blond hair. He stood well over six feet tall, well-built and his white robe shimmered.

Edwin froze with fear, not knowing what to do, so he didn't do anything except stand there looking in awe.

"Relax, Edwin, he is for us not against us."

"How can I help you, Percival?" asked Prospero.

"Our King Erith has an enchantment that has been put upon him. We need your help to break it off. Would you please do that for us?"

"Yes, I can help you with that. Would you also like to know how come he was vulnerable to receive it?"

"Yes," replied Percival.

"I know, I heard you talking about it before you asked me to help," replied Prospero. The angel continued, "Breaking it off will require bringing in some reinforcements, because Jaspeth invoked some rather high level dark spirits to enforce the spell. I can tell you that the reason for the spell's success is because Erith committed a rather heinous crime against a village called Rexnorth in south Evansing near Randar. The news of it got to Jaspeth and now he has pulled it out to use at a crucial time. We can break it off, but it will keep coming back. Plus this curse will interfere with Evansing's ability to battle Randar. It will also thwart Nerland's capacity to defend against Merethath. Only by Erith making restitution to the descendants of the villagers will the power of this curse remain broken."

Edwin stared in disbelief at what he had heard. Working up the courage, he asked, "How is it possible that Erith could commit a heinous crime?"

Prospero gave Edwin a piercing stare that seemed to go right through him. Then he answered, "The event in question occurred twelve years ago. At that time Erith was quite different than how you know him today. His views of reality and justice were not nearly as developed as they are now. If you read of the account in the official Chronicles of Evansing you will get a watered down view of what really happened. The truth is he overreacted to some perceived slights and resistance to his authority. Consequently he destroyed an entire village and its inhabitants."

Percival and Edwin stood there in stunned silence.

Percival offered that he had heard something about it, but that no one wanted to talk about it and it had been passed off as inconsequential. He hadn't tried to read the Chronicles scroll on the event.

Edwin, getting bolder with Prospero, asked, "Why hasn't Erith done whatever he needed to do to atone for this grievance?"

"He is incapable of recognizing it as wrong."

Edwin replied, "Incapable? How is that? Given what you have said it looks open and shut that it was wrong. How could he be incapable?"

"Lies, big lies, masquerading as truth," responded Prospero. "Until there is a shift he will remain convinced that he did the only thing that he could do."

"How do we create the needed shift?" asked Percival.

"You will have to find a way of presenting the situation to Erith in such a way that the veil will get removed. It will require an indirect approach that will facilitate your eventual direct approach."

With that he disappeared.

"Wow that was different. An angel, I don't think I really believed in them before."

"Any ideas on what he meant by an indirect approach?"

"Not yet, but I will come up with something. Probably some kind of story by which I can prime the pump and go for the jugular."

"Do angels always look like that?" asked Edwin.

"Like what?"

"What do you mean, like what? You saw him. He looked about twenty-five, over six feet tall with long blond hair, in glistening white robes."

"I saw him looking about thirty five, short black hair, around six feet and dressed like a regular guy you'd see in the town square," answered Percival.

"What! Are you serious? How could you see him look like that? You are kidding me, right?"

"No, Edwin, I'm not. I haven't figured it out yet. And when I ask an angel why the discrepancies, they look at me with a sort of mischievous smile and don't tell me. All I know is that it must be a combination of how people expect angels to look and how the angels choose to allow people see them."

"We will have to consider what needs to be done to shift Erith. In the meantime, let's go and read the official account of this event so we have some fuel for our spirits to process a solution."

The two men walked up to the clerk of the Chronicles of Evansing. They made their request. He looked at them strangely. After fifteen minutes, during which time they could hear some whispering in the backroom, he came back and said that that particular scroll could not to be found.

"How is that possible?" asked Edwin.

"I don't know your Highness. It just is."

"We would like to go in the back and look for ourselves."

"The King himself has told us that no one, but those he has specifically authorized can go back there in the room containing the Chronicles."

Crown Prince Edwin looked at the clerk wondering whether to brush him off.

Edwin took Percival aside, "What do you think we should do?"

"We go to Erith and ask him for permission to read about it."

The next morning the two men asked the King if they could access the scroll regarding the village of Rexnorth, which had been destroyed twelve years earlier. Erith's face darkened and his pleasantness abruptly turned to suspicious anger. "Why would you want to read about those rebels?"

"We have evidence that village is possibly being used by our enemies as a means of undermining our kingdom," replied Percival.

"Nonsense!! Who told you such rubbish?"

"A very reliable source."

"Does this so-called reliable source have a name?"

"Yes, he does. His name is Prospero."

This gave the King a start for he knew of Prospero and had met him twice while with Percival. He didn't know how to reply to that.

Then he issued a command to his attending servant to take a message to the clerk at the Chronicles room. He wrote a short message on a piece of parchment that he kept available for making notes and handed it to the servant.

An hour later Percival and Edwin re-visited the Chronicles room and this time lo and behold the previously missing scroll had been found. They took it into an adjoining room and started to read it. The scroll indicated that the village's inhabitants had been guilty of rebelling against the King. As a consequence the village had been punished. No specific details were provided.

"Not a lot of input for us to work with. It makes you wonder what the full story is if there is so much resistance to us even reading what is available," said Percival.

"Why wouldn't Prospero tell us what we need to know and save us all this bother?" replied Edwin.

"That my fine young man is one of those mysteries of life. Sometimes they will tell us everything we need to know. And sometimes they seem to relish in teasing us with tidbits that require us to search for more."

"I know from previous experience that trying to get the story out of people here is not going to work. We should take a little trip down to the village site and see if we can find clues. Perhaps people in the surrounding areas will talk."

The next morning, the two men and a troop of forty soldiers went down to the location of the village. They travelled over ten hours through rolling hills countryside. When they came to within about two hundred yards of where the village had once stood, the atmosphere noticeably cooled. Everyone felt it physically and in their spirit. As they rode right into what had been the village location, they noticed the stench of death which hung over the site. Considering the carnage had occurred twelve years earlier the men thought it most unusual that this stench would still be in the air. The place had an eerie silence and the men could feel death in their souls. Everyone in the party began experiencing a growing fear. Edwin gave the order to leave and dismount just beyond two hundred yards from the village boundary. Here they were not aware of any negative influences. Ten minutes were taken to rest and consider the next step. The men could see smoke trailing from the chimney of a nearby farmhouse.

Questioning its inhabitants seemed like a logical thing to do, so the men rode over to it.

A woman who looked to be in her early forties greeted the troop. She appeared to be quite amazed at seeing all these men in her front yard.

"Greetings," Edwin began, "We don't mean you any harm. We are in the King's service and we wanted to ask you some questions."

Edwin and Percival both indicated to her that they would like to talk to her inside her cottage. They did not want all the troops with them to hear the story.

"We have discovered that the Chronicles account of what happened to the nearby village is incomplete and perhaps even inaccurate. As a neighbor you must have been aware of what happened. Could we ask you some questions?"

The woman was not quite sure what to say. Finally she blurted out, "We were told not to talk about it upon pain of severe punishment. Please do not force me to endanger me and my family."

Edwin reassuringly, "We are authorized by Crown Prince Edwin. You have no need to fear any consequences in telling us what you know."

"The King himself, through his soldiers said we were to remain quiet on the matter. We don't even talk about it amongst ourselves."

"I give you my word as an officer in the King's army that you have nothing to fear."

Reluctantly at first and then with a profound sense of relief and release the woman started to share what had happened.

"A couple of days before the soldiers came; we got word that the villagers had been complaining about an extra tax now payable. They had been having a very difficult year because of poor crops. With the extra tax they were in a place of having to choose between paying the tax or eating. They decided they needed to eat more than they needed to pay the tax. A delegation was sent to the King to explain their situation. We found out all about this when we heard screaming from the village. A King's messenger had ridden by us twenty minutes earlier with a sack tied to his horse. Without a word he threw the sack into the village square and rode back our way. Before he had passed us on his way back we started hearing the screams. Of course we were curious as to what had happened so my husband and I walked down to the village. There we were met by people beside themselves with grief. The sack had contained the heads of the four member delegation that had gone to talk to the King."

"Two days later at night, we heard horses go by our house. Shortly thereafter we heard screams and flames shooting up into the night sky. In the morning we saw the King's troops ride past us returning to Evansing town. Three of them came by our house and warned us to not speak about anything that had happened that night. One of them suggested that they kill us, but the other two said no, there had been enough bloodshed. I feel like I have been allowed now to be a voice for the dead. That village had over two hundred people in it. The village had been burned to the ground and all the people had been killed and buried within its boundaries. We never go there. Nobody around here goes there. We all give it a wide berth."

The two men sat in silence when the woman had finished. They let sink in what they had heard. That Erith, whom they loved and respected, had ordered this was almost beyond their comprehension. Clearly the man had had gigantic shifts in his character since this massacre.

Percival asked, "Do you know of any descendants of those villagers that remain alive?"

"Yes, there had been one complete family of parents and their four children who were visiting a sick relative some miles away on that fateful night. The parents in that family lost their siblings and their own parents. They live five miles west of here on a small farm. Also I know of three children of the villagers that live around here. Of course by this time there are also some grandchildren."

"Good. We will be back to request your assistance in contacting them regarding this most unfortunate event. We expect that amends will be made."

The two men thanked the lady for her courage and assured her once more that she did not need to fear any reprisals.

"Prospero spoke the truth when he called this a rather heinous crime. I am going to have an interesting time talking to Erith. The presentation must enable him to see the truth of this event and avoid him putting me in irons or worse," Percival said and smiled as he spoke the latter part.

They didn't seriously think Erith would do such a thing, but given what they had heard they knew the man could be capable of extreme actions. They recalled his threat to King Taryn. He had made it clear to Taryn he would devastate his kingdom if necessary. That kind of will seemed like a good thing. To accomplish the task of uniting Ireland required someone willing to do what needed to be done. Even to do what seemed very distasteful.

Percival mulled over the matter regarding how to deal with Erith. He spent two days in considering the best approach. Finally he had what he believed he needed and made a point of bringing it up when he and the King would be alone in his chambers.

"Sire, I have a troubling situation which requires your input to ensure justice is achieved."

Erith looked eager to bring his intervention power to right a wrong.

"A landlord west of Evansing has recently doubled his rents to his tenants. This has now placed them in a place of choosing between paying the rents and starving or not paying the rents and eating. Needless to say eating is preferable to starving. The tenants appointed spokesmen to represent them to the landlord. However, the landlord had all four of the spokesmen killed with the sword. Now he has threatened to do likewise with all his remaining tenants."

When Erith heard this he got furious. "This landlord must die. Who is he and where is he? We must dispatch the Sheriff to arrest him and bring him to trial."

"That man, Sire, is you."

Silence.

The King was mortified and speechless.

"W-what do you mean, that person is me?"

"Remember Edwin and I asked you for permission to check on the Chronicles account of the destruction of Rexnorth?"

No sooner had the words left his mouth than they cut Erith to the quick in his heart and he started to sob uncontrollably.

Most men in Percival's position would have been embarrassed and uncomfortable sitting in the presence of their he-man King sobbing. For Percival this was the objective. And it looked like it had been achieved.

After several minutes, Erith started to collect himself and tried to regain his composure. He appeared at least a bit chagrined at having so lost it in front of one of his subjects. Although strictly speaking, Percival was not his subject but a visitor from another kingdom. He had a permanent invitation to remain in Evansing.

Erith looked at his friend and said, "Percival, you are very clever. I have never sobbed like that in front of anyone since I lost my favorite pony as a young boy. You played me like a lute. Even though a part of me is embarrassed, if I needed to do that, I can't think of anyone else I would rather have done it in front of."

"So what happened, Sire?"

"All the pain of that event burst past the lies guarding it and I had to finally acknowledge the truth of what I had done. I realize now I have had a major part of my emotional energy allocated to keeping the truth hidden and at bay."

"So how can I ever make restitution and atone for what I have done? It is so huge I can't comprehend anything being sufficient."

"Prospero indicated the curse's power could be broken through restitution to the descendants of those villagers. We have discovered someone who can help us find all the known descendants which live within several miles of the village. Since they have such fear of even talking about this event it will be a challenge to get them to come forward. They will find it difficult to believe you want to make amends and not harm them. However, we have established trust with a local lady who I am sure will help us in the persuasion process. As to what restitution, I believe we leave that to the descendants to decide. It is risky of course, but I believe Grace will abound."

The next day Edwin and Percival along with forty men, returned to the farmhouse of the lady they had talked to before. With her help over the next few days they met with all the descendants which could be identified as living in the area. It came to light that another known descendant now lived over the border in Randar. He may well have been the source for the information of the village massacre coming to the attention of Jaspeth. This created a challenge as to what to do about contacting him. The man's brother agreed to get him and have him included in the discussions as to what to ask for restitution.

The discussions for restitution were both subdued and heated. Some people's pain created a quiet almost helpless resignation effect on them. For others to re-open this old wound created tremendous anger and desire for revenge. They were informed the King would come down personally to confess this great wrong and award compensation.

After two days they reached a consensus whereby they wanted the following:

- Public apology from the King and it is entered fully in the Chronicles of Evansing.

- Tax exempt status for the next twenty years for them and their families.

- Ten fold restoration on whatever tax they had paid during the past twelve years.

For the man living in Randar they adjusted it to fit his particular situation. They wanted him granted an estimated equivalent in monetary and livestock compensation.

Then the King arrived. There was both awe in seeing the King so close up and a stirring up of emotion at finally seeing the source of their pain. Erith of course did not feel his normal self-assured kingly self. This proved an extremely difficult and painful time for him.

The moment came for him to address those who were present.

"With great sorrow and contrition in my soul I come before you not only as your King, but also as a man who has realized he has done a great wrong. When the slaughter of the villagers occurred, I considered it as the right and proper response to what I perceived to be rebellion. I realize now my perception and my response were totally wrong."

The King sank to his knees and with great emotion breaking up his voice asked these people for their forgiveness of this great evil which had been perpetrated against them.

Four members of the descendants had been selected to respond. Each one in turn expressed the pain and loss they had experienced. And each one ended by extending forgiveness to their King.

After the last descendant spoke, the King stood up and thanked the people for their graciousness.

"As has been indicated to you, restitution is being calculated as some way of restoring and compensating you. I realize nothing can ever truly repay you for your losses. To ensure your claims are dealt with justly and promptly I am appointing these two men who have been meeting with you to be your ombudsmen if necessary. Let me introduce them to you for I know they have remained anonymous to you. This young man is the Crown Prince Edwin and this other gentleman is Percival, who is my dear personal advisor and friend."

The lady who had been helping Edwin and Percival felt astonished when she realized she had been dealing with such high level personages in her own home. She loved to recount the story for years to come.

As the King returned to Evansing Castle the curse over him broke. All of a sudden he realized something amiss with the warmth of the responses from Taryn and Jaspeth. He started to discuss this with Edwin and Percival as they walked their horses beside each other. They decided since the two kings only had malevolent intent, the best action would be to retract the invitations. Orders went out for beefing up the troops along the Evansing border with Randar. King Erith sent a messenger to King Keltic advising him about what had transpired and recommending he bolster his border with Merethath.

CHAPTER 27

Both Taryn and Jaspeth were dumbfounded when the retractions were received. Shortly later they were also informed that new levels of troops were amassed on their borders. At first this created alarm and concern of an imminent invasion. However, after several days they realized it to be only a defensive maneuver. At this time Erith and Keltic had no intention of invasion. Recent revelations though certainly indicated invasions may be necessary in the future.

Erith and his council had decided no future military actions would be taken until after the games. They would first do an assessment of how relations were developing with the potentially troublesome kingdoms which had been invited to the games. Two weeks later, Crown Prince Evo of Dagarath expressed lukewarm acceptance. His tone of course was to be expected given the fact that he did not like Evansing.

Tara never did respond.

As the time for the games approached, Evansing town and castle were spruced up and prepared for the distinguished visitors from other kingdoms. The military assigned an extra regiment of soldiers to be on duty in and around the sites of the games. Most of the events would occur on the military training field.

The games would include for the first time a new sport called Gaelic football or "gah" for short. Due to its newness only three teams were entered for this competition. It involved kicking or punching a round ball toward goals at either end of a grass pitch.

The other team sport, with all kingdoms competing was hurling, which is played with sticks and a ball.

Also to appear at these games were the tried and true favorites of wrestling, spear throwing, archery, horse racing and horse jumping.

In addition as an aside, there were to be opportunities for musicians and dancers to demonstrate their skills, thus adding to a festival like atmosphere.

Edwin entered spear throwing, archery, horse jumping and tried for the "gah" team. He had quickness and his natural athletic ability working for him to make up for his inexperience in playing "gah". But then the experienced players had only started playing the year before. The people making the selections would find it hard to cut Edwin from the team, even though he assured them there would be no hard feelings. To their relief, Edwin performed well enough to not put them in that difficult position. He made the team by merit and not by the position he held.

Some members of the Royal family questioned the wisdom in the Crown Prince entering so many competitions. The King and Greer knew Edwin loved to compete. So even though it exposed him to ridicule if he did poorly, Erith and Greer were both willing to take that risk. And so was Edwin.

As the time got closer for the games, Edwin devoted more and more time to preparation and practice. His favorite fan, Greer, would frequently be an avid spectator cheering him on and congratulating him on every success.

Surprisingly the first visitors to arrive were from Dagarath; Evo had come to spend extra time with his father. King Nelwyn would be allowed, under heavy guard to watch his kingdom participate in the Games. Also for his visits with Evo and other family members, he could use a heavily guarded suite, which had been set aside for him.

The initial formalities of greeting the party from Dagarath were stiff as you might expect. Edwin managed to get a smile and even sort of a chuckle out of Evo. This did not go unnoticed by Erith. Inside he rejoiced at seeing Edwin turning into a skilled diplomat.

The next day, the contingents from Nerland and Aldred arrived to an exuberant reunion between old friends. The only dampening influence was Crown Prince Gondar. Several days before the Games he had fallen off his horse and injured his right shoulder. He would not be competing and as it turned out he tended to be sullen and unsociable for the duration of his time in Evansing. The Games created another opportunity for Athandra and Kerris to build their already warm relationship. Anticipation grew of an important announcement to be forthcoming, perhaps even at these games. The other couple had also been progressing, but not as well as their initial connection would have predicted. Something with Carson was amiss. Indeed the news got back to Erith and he asked Percival to meet with Carson and discover the problem.

The day before Chandra and the Aldred party were to arrive, Percival and Carson met in Percival's quarters.

"Is there something significant about Chandra that you don't like?"

"No, I can't say there is."

"Can you point to something affecting your feelings for her?"

"Yes, I don't feel comfortable making a commitment. If not for the changes you have helped to create in me, Percival, I wouldn't even have known of such a thing."

"Is there any reason why you don't feel comfortable?"

"You know I am only nineteen and I have had my share of flings with a variety of girls, all fun and no responsibility. Now I am facing the prospect of devoting myself to one woman for the rest of my natural days, and it includes responsibility. Even though you have done a tremendous shift in me from where I used to be, it would appear I need more shifting."

"Are you willing to be shifted?"

Silence.

"Put it this way Carson, would you be pleased as punch to have Chandra as your girlfriend?"

"Oh yes, of course. She's a doll. I have no reason to not want her. In fact I know a part of me desperately wants her forever and not just because Uncle Erith wants me to. She is special; there is no doubt about it. But another part of me is…is…scared. There I said it. Oh I hate admitting it, but it's true. A part of me is scared."

"Hmmm," Percival mused.

He placed his hand on Carson's chest and commanded the fear of commitment to go. He also spoke to the tearing down of any negative soul structures supporting it.

Carson's eyes got as large as saucers as he could feel a rhythmic sensation going through his body. Then after a moment it stopped.

He looked at Percival and asked, "What did I feel?"

"You felt freedom. You have now crossed over to a new place. A place where making a commitment to Chandra will seem as natural as breathing and as delightful as anything you have delighted in."

Carson closed his eyes. While he sat there he started to get a big smile on his face.

"I see myself with Chandra on our wedding day and I had absolutely no qualms about it. I could sense joy and anticipation of our life together."

"Percival, you are a marvelous man. Now I can't wait to see Chandra again. I know she will be glad to see the change. Last time we saw each other she could tell I didn't feel right. She told me if I had doubts about her that I should tell her. I didn't know what to say so I tried to brush it off as me not feeling so well. But I could tell she didn't buy it."

The next day when Chandra saw Carson she could tell something good had happened to him. He showed great pleasure at seeing her and gave her his total attenton.

"Wow, Carson, what happened to you? Last time I saw you I was began to think you had lost interest. If you hadn't perked up this time it would have been over between you and me. I must say I am very happy to see the change in you."

"I am very happy about the change too, Chandra. My favorite magician, Percival, worked his magic with me and eliminated some dorky feelings, which were affecting me. It had nothing to do with you, Chandra. All to do with my skewed way of being in this great adventure called relationship between man and woman."

"Amazing! This man Percival is making an impact on my family. He helped my brother Kerris in his ability to connect with Athandra and now he has helped you in your relationship with me. We must express our gratitude to him."

Chandra continued, "So, Carson, are you ready for the Games?"

"Yes, I have been practicing with our hurling team, and," while looking a little cocky and smiling at Chandra, "I have been appointed captain."

"Oh that's wonderful. You are obviously pleased about that. Good for you."

"Also I have my horse, Silver, primed for the racing events. I expect to be at least in the top three."

Early the next morning, Edwin set out for a walk. He wanted to think and be alone. When he turned a corner he was greeted by a young woman in armor sitting on a warhorse. This startled Edwin for women do not dress up as warriors. He had never seen such armor before.

"Edwin, you are highly favored."

In response, Edwin looked back at her, not knowing what to say.

"I have been sent to you by the Archangel Michael. My name is Joan. I come to you from hundreds of years in the future. Michael sent me to give you strategies for how to progress you forward in uniting Ireland."

Edwin is thinking to himself, "Hundreds of years in the future? Did I hear her right? Who or what is she? Is she an angel?"

Reading his thoughts, Joan replied, "Yes, you heard right and no I am not an angel. I am a human like you except my time frame on this earth is four hundred years later than yours. I live in the early 1400s in France. I will be known as the Deliverer of France.

Even though I am a young woman, I have the fierce heart of a warrior. By His Great Grace we are throwing out the English and re-establishing once again a united and free France. Which is why I have been sent. I come qualified to help you."

"How can I know what you tell me is true?"

At that moment a fierce angel appeared. The angel did not at all appear like Prospero. This angel stood at least eight feet tall, dressed in armor with scars on his body and dents in his armor. He had a fierce and determined visage.

"Edwin, this is Joan of Arc and what she tells you is true. Time travel is no problem for the spiritual realm and that includes moving humans around into different times. Listen to her for she has wisdom and insight to impart to you."

In the meantime, Edwin is hoping he hasn't embarrassed himself in front of this young woman.

Then as quickly as he appeared, the angel disappeared.

In the ensuing pause, Edwin tried to collect his composure.

He managed to whisper, "Who was that?"

"Michael, the Chief Warrior Angel. He is an archangel who carries great authority."

"I believe you. I knew he was not your run of the mill angel. Mind you I don't have a lot of experience with angels. I've only met one before. He wasn't nearly as fierce as Michael."

Edwin started thinking to himself, "What is going on here? I am talking to someone who says she is from hundreds of years in the future. It's like I'm making regular conversation with someone I know well."

"Don't worry, Edwin; it is natural for you to feel a bit strange about all this. After all, it is different than your normal regular life."

"So Joan, how does this relationship work? How do we work together?"

"Sometimes I will come when you ask me to come. I may not come immediately, but I will come unless it is a season when it is not the right time to do so. At other times I will show up unannounced as a messenger of strategies or to encourage you. The purpose of this initial meeting is to introduce myself to you."

With that she vanished from view.

Edwin stood there for a moment and then briskly walked back to his suite. His head swirled with what had happened. Should he share it with Greer? Would she think he was crazy? He recalled the first time he met her. She saw him arrive on a bird and she acted like it was no big deal. She also knew about the Brydon mission. She will probably think ho hum just another supernormal experience.

Greer appeared quite intrigued by what her husband shared. Yes, she had had angelic experiences and had been aware of many magical goings on. But she had never experienced a time traveler before.

"Was she attractive?" asked Greer.

Edwin looked at her and smiled. "Don't tell me you are jealous of this Joan?"

"Well she is young and she is a very exceptional woman. It wouldn't hurt to have some idea of who we are dealing with here, especially if you are going to have an ongoing relationship with her. Did she appear in a physical form like a regular person or did she seem other worldly?"

"Hard to say, on her horse and in that strange armor she certainly seemed bigger than life. I would say otherwise she could have passed for a regular person."

"Okay, was she attractive?"

"Greer, she is not my type. You are my type. You alone are my type."

"Was she attractive? I'm just curious."

"Well yes, I guess you could call her attractive. I wouldn't call her beautiful like you, Greer. She had a wholesomeness combined with a very purposeful gaze, which did give her a certain appeal."

"Wholesomeness combined with a very purposeful gaze," repeated Greer.

"Would you say I have wholesomeness and a very purposeful gaze, Edwin?"

Edwin thought to himself, "Oh no, I have fallen into a trap. I was too honest. I should have said she was ugly and have been done with it."

"Actually, Greer, she was incredibly ugly. That's the truth."

"Oh no, you don't, that might have worked before, but now it is too late."

"Do I have wholesomeness about me like she does?"

"Yes, Greer, only more so."

"Are you being honest? I want you to be honest."

Edwin in quick succession is thinking, "No, she may say she wants me to be honest, but she doesn't REALLY want me to be honest."

"Part of your great beauty, Greer is your amazing wholesomeness."

She looked at him not sure whether he sounded totally sincere, or whether he was telling her what she wanted to hear.

"How does my wholesomeness get expressed, Edwin?"

Edwin to himself, "Oh no, I am falling."

"You know, like wholesomeness gets expressed, like really whole."

"Edwin, that doesn't tell me anything. You must have some specific way of describing it."

"Greer, it's not something specific, it's a way of being. It's an aura, it's a sensing about someone. You and Joan both radiate this wholesomeness."

That seemed to satisfy Greer.

"Do I have a purposeful gaze?"

"Okay, Greer, let's be real. This Joan says she is the Deliverer of France. She gets sent from hundreds of years in the future and has a fierce warrior archangel backing her up. Do you have a purposeful gaze like she has? No. Neither are you just going through life with a blank look and no sense of purpose. You are a princess. This gives you a significant purpose most people don't have. It's reflected in your face."

With that, Greer gave her man a hug and told him she loved him.

CHAPTER 28

The day of the Games began with special opening ceremonies and a small parade of the participants. Each kingdom had dancers and musicians as part of their parade contingent.

The two young ladies, Athandra and Chandra were in the position of cheering against their countrymen in those events including their beaus. Kerris would be competing in the horse jumping and archery. Not unexpected given his interest in hunting. Carson as indicated earlier would be participating in the hurling and horse racing.

The two young ladies, along with their cousins and friends, sat together with Greer and her cousins and friends. They formed a massive hen party, spending more time chatting amongst themselves than paying attention to the competition. The exception came when a particular male or males were involved in something crucial. Those of course who were their husbands or beaus or brothers.

The first day saw Kerris and Edwin both succeed in advancing to the next round of archery and horse jumping. Tomorrow, Edwin would do spear throwing in the morning and the first "gah" game against Nerland. There were only three entrants for the "gah" competition due to its newness, the other team being Aldred.

Carson's team had beaten Dagarath in their first hurling match. Tomorrow he would be running in his first horse race.

In the evening of the first day of the Games the attendees did much feasting and drinking. The athletes were expected to exercise restraint, but there were no official proscriptions against excessive drinking and eating.

Edwin and Greer personally invited the Dagarath Crown Prince and his wife to join them at their table. To their pleasant surprise the Crown Prince accepted. The evening went well considering the state of affairs between the two kingdoms. A real connection got forged as the Evansing couple charmed and regaled Evo and his wife, Tamara. The person to person contact of laughing and having fun together seemed to transcend the political realities dividing them. Tamara was a real card and seemed indifferent to the politics. She liked to have fun. Even to the point where she probably stretched her more conservative husband. She and Greer laughed and laughed, and often got their men to join with them.

By the end of the evening it seemed as though they had broken down all the barriers. What the reality would be like in the cold light of day tomorrow remained to be seen. Right now they related like lifelong friends.

The next day, Edwin competed in spear throwing. He felt good. Really good! His first throw achieved one of his best ever. Each contestant had three throws. The best toss of each participant determined their final placement. Edwin ended third out of twenty competitors. He placed in the top ten and thus advanced to the second round. The next round would be played on day four of the Games.

In the afternoon, Edwin's team lost a close football game to Nerland. A bit disappointing, but he had fun. Whoever had the most wins after three games won. Since there were only three teams, they would toss dice to see who they would play in their third game.

Carson's horse, Silver, won handily its first race and advanced to the next round.

That night, Carson basked in the adulation of Chandra who rejoiced over the fact his team which he captained had won. She reveled over how he was one of the stars in the game. And now today his horse had won convincingly. They as a couple were looking more and more like they too would have an important announcement in the near future. Perhaps even at these games also. Chandra and Athandra were both exchanging inside information as to the possibilities of making special announcements.

Their men were talking about making the announcements this week. Any final approvals from parents and in the case of Athandra also her uncle the King, were expected to occur without a hitch. For indeed the relationship building would not have gone this far if they hadn't approved.

The third day started off with moderate rain and stayed overcast all morning. The Games were delayed several hours until the rain stopped. The prime concern as to the conditions related to the horse jumping, as muddy slick conditions would add to the danger of the event. The equestrian contest would take place as late as possible before it got dark, so as to allow the field to dry out.

The archery contest had Edwin and Kerris in a competition of ten men. The top five would advance to the final round. Kerris finished first in this competition.

Edwin experienced lack of success. He struggled that day. The normal confident air which he had displayed the first day seemed to be eluding him. He shot erratically. He placed in sixth place at the start of the final shooting. For a master marksman like Edwin this was unbelievable. Those watching him could tell something wasn't right.

Princess Greer yelled, "Edwin, remember who you are."

That seemed to shake Edwin out of a seeming stupor. The nobleman from Aldred who Edwin had to beat in order to at least get the fifth and final spot had struck a perfect bull's eye. Edwin took his turn. A hush settled with everyone's eyes on him. Most of the people figured Edwin would lose. After all how could he beat a perfect bull's eye?

Edwin coolly now and with calmness, looking like his normal self, pulled back on his bow and released the arrow. The shot sliced the other arrow in two and landed in the middle. A cheer went up from Evansing. Then everyone else cheered as well for regardless of their loyalties, they recognized a great shot. This event became so well-known it became incorporated in the legend of Robin Hood, over a hundred years later.

That afternoon, the games officials decided to carry on with the horse jumping even though conditions weren't ideal.

The first four riders completed the course without mishap. Then the fifth rider got thrown as his horse slipped at the third jump. The rider appeared shaken, but otherwise seemed to be okay. The competition halted as some of the more troublesome spots in the course were worked on, thus bringing them back to a level considered at least adequate.

Kerris went through the course in flawless form. He demonstrated he had spent many hours in the saddle.

Then came the ninth rider, Edwin. The initial part of the course started well and then his horse had trouble at the fifth jump. It looked like it had lost a bit of its footing just as it made the jump. The horse caught the top part of the barrier. Instead of landing cleanly one of its hooves did not get down in time with the other legs. The horse fell with Edwin thrown clear. It didn't look good. Both rider and horse lay there not moving. People ran onto the field to see whether Edwin was okay. Greer was beside herself with concern. But she had been learning not to worry about anything regarding Edwin. Though part of her was upset, another part remained calm and expected the best.

Edwin looked to be unconscious. The doctor and Percival both started to administer whatever assistance they could. The doctor didn't have a lot to work with, but Percival poured some sacred oil on Edwin's head. A few moments later he came to and a short time later he sat up. He felt the bruises, but otherwise he felt okay. When he stood up he winced with pain for he had a moderate sprain in his right ankle. Aides helped him off the field. The competition that day ended with Kerris advancing and Edwin being eliminated. His horse had broken a leg and had to be destroyed. Nobody faulted Edwin except Edwin himself who thought he could have guided the horse better. He also mourned the loss of his horse. He tended to get attached to his horses. Edwin had been a quick learner in horse riding. Prior to Evansing he had had little experience with actual riding of horses. For him to enter a horse jumping contest with little experience was unusual. He always dared to be remarkable. A discussion ensued which carried on into the evening about the wisdom of putting riders and horses at risk when conditions were wet. If necessary it should have been cancelled, or so some of the people thought.

That day Edwin withdrew from the football and the spear throwing contests. His leg would not mend for several days. He would still do the archery.

Carson continued to wow Chandra and the other onlookers with his on-field successes in hurling. He looked to be getting stronger and stronger as the Games progressed. Evansing led by Carson defeated the team from Nerland with a strong come from behind effort in the last ten minutes of their match.

As Edwin and Greer were ready to retire for the night, Erith came over to their table.

"You two have been cutting wide swathes into the hearts of the people from Dagarath. I have been getting good reports from Evo about how he and his family have felt so accepted and befriended by both of you."

With that he gave them both a big hug.

"Wow," Edwin thought to himself, "another hug from Erith," as he experienced the King's embrace. It felt so good, like getting a hug from a father. He experienced a warmth of healing going through his body.

Both of them enjoyed the extra attention and affection from Erith. It felt good to see him in a state different than his usual king mode.

The next day saw Carson finish second in the horse racing and therefore advance to the final round to be held on the last day of the Games.

Kerris and Athandra and Carson, and Chandra joined Edwin and Greer that night.

Both couples whispered as they told their hosts they would announce their engagements and upcoming wedding dates on the final night of the Games

Greer got so excited when she heard the news. She gave all four of them a big hug. She added a little extra chiding to Carson saying she would be keeping an eye on him to make sure he was a most excellent husband. Carson at first gave her a face in jest. But then got serious and gave her permission to tell him whatever he needed to know. Greer also felt excited about the prospect of having Chandra move to Evansing and become a dear friend.

The rest of the evening they spent in great spirits enjoying extra bowls of celebratory mead and wine.

The next morning started with unusually bright Irish sunshine and a great day for the archery finals. Kerris and Edwin were of course both competing. They also competed against an archer from each of the other kingdoms. Great interest existed in this competition as archery was one of the favorite events. Also, the two crown princes added to the excitement and appeal.

After the first five shots, Edwin and Kerris stood neck and neck in the lead. Now came the sixth and final deciding shot. Edwin fired first and made a fine shot. It was a great effort by most people's standards. It was only an okay shot for Edwin in such a key match. Now all eyes were focused on Kerris who was a fearsome competitor in archery. He shot and swoosh the arrow missed the mark. Edwin had won. Yeah for Edwin! The hometown fans erupted into cheers and did the wave. Kerris consoled himself that afternoon with winning the horse jumping. Athandra was much excited when her guy won. She walked toward Kerris, combining dignity and a speed acceptable for a princess in public. At the end, the speed overtook the dignity as she broke into a run and practically leaped into his outstretched arms.

The Evansing hurling team defeated the Aldred team. Romantic connections were stronger than blood and cultural relations as Chandra cheered on Carson's team. That was probably a more accurate way of how she saw it anyway. She cheered on Carson not Evansing.

The next day would be an extra grueling day for Carson as he would be riding in the horse race in the morning and playing hurling in the afternoon.

Carson and his horse Silver were among the three frontrunners heading into the final stretch, when all of a sudden Silver broke loose and won by an astonishing four lengths.

It looked like heartbreak on the hurling field when with less than five minutes (more or less given the limited accuracy of water clocks) the Aldred team pulled into a commanding lead. Then Carson led his team to break out of their end and with a swish here and a swish there they scored. Again Evansing got the ball; they shot and scored tying up the game. The home crowd went crazy, they congratulated each other and did high fives. Once more the hometown team got possession; time was running out. Carson got the ball, he was coming in, he had an open net and he fired it wide. Oh no, and time had run out. Drat!

The home team and their fans were shocked into silence. The Aldredians cheered and celebrated.

Carson hung his head in disgrace. All that glory right there and then it disappeared. His beloved raced up to him and hugged him and said she was proud of him.

He looked at her in disbelief, "But I blew it, I choked, I had an open net and I missed."

"Whatever! There will always be another time. You played your best. So you're not perfect. Welcome to the real world. You're my hero!"

At that point missing the shot stopped being a big deal to Carson.

That night the winners were presented their awards. Special medals of gold to the winners and silver to the first losers, I mean second place finishers. There were no recognitions for third place.

After all the medals had been given out and the congratulations expressed, the time came for special announcements. The open secret had been buzzing for the whole Games. Yes, Kerris and Athandra announced their engagement and their wedding date would be in Aldred some three months from now. Then came the next announcement, not as widely known or expected as the first one but neither wholly unexpected either. Carson and Chandra announced their engagement and their wedding in Evansing in four months time.

Fun, frivolity and relationship building were over. Now came time for war.

CHAPTER 29

The War Council of Evansing and Nerland was convened. Erith, Keltic, Edwin, Percival and the rest of the military commanders of both kingdoms were meeting. They discussed what target would be the most effective one to focus their resources on. They decided Randar would be the target. King Jaspeth and his Druid connections represented to them the greatest danger. Also Evansing and Nerland each shared a common border with Randar, thus facilitating logistics of the war.

They planned to be ready to assault in fourteen days. There would be two different thrusts from Evansing and one from Nerland. They would move in such a way as to create a pincer, which would come together at the Randar capital.

Later, by himself Edwin started thinking about his meeting with Joan.

"She said she would give me battle strategies. I need to ask. Okay Joan I need some strategies for Randar."

He waited, nothing happened and then a voice came to him very distinct.

"Here I am, Edwin. How can I help you?"

"Why can't I see you?"

"I won't always appear physically to you. The first time was to deepen the initial connection. Today I am just a voice to you, although I am in this room with you. I am choosing to remain invisible to your material world."

"Okay," as Edwin took a deep breath, "this otherworld stuff is all very strange.

Joan, we are planning to attack Randar in two weeks. My assignment is to lead the middle foray of the three that will be invading. At this point it's pretty straight forward. We go in and kill and destroy the Randarian army. As well we are compiling a list of Druid practitioners with orders to capture and execute them on the spot. In addition there are four key strongholds on my route to their capital. These are known to harbor strong Jaspeth sympathizers. The War Council decided the people in those strongholds are too recalcitrant to win to our cause. Therefore we will destroy those settlements and all the men will be executed. We will spare the women and males under sixteen. Assistance will be provided to resettle them in other parts of Randar and ensure they don't starve. Our assistance will be in the form of requiring people in other parts of Randar to look after them. They will have rights to approach us, if they are not being properly looked after."

"There is talk among the War Council members that Evansing and Nerland should annex Randar. Others say no, rather we should leave Randar as a separate kingdom and place someone on its throne who is reliable and sympathetic to our cause."

"Joan, what can you tell me would be the best way to go, given what I have told you?"

"I know your plans in detail. The biggest flaw is your plan to have two armies going from Evansing. The troops to the east will be going through an area where you will be subject to fierce guerilla warfare. That terrain provides them with much cover while your troops will be exposed and vulnerable. Expediency says to negotiate with the inhabitants in that section of Randar at a later date. It would be wisest to consolidate all the Evansing troops into one army and follow essentially the course you have already selected to take. The only change would be to include a fifth stronghold, to the east thirteen miles of your planned route. It's called Lakeland. This stronghold has a small but influential group of Druids. They are unknown to you for they are covert in their activities. However, they are in close relations with Jaspeth and could be damaging to you if left alone. It holds control of Mara Lake which makes its physical location key. The people are not strong supporters of Jaspeth. There is no need to devastate them. Eliminate the Druids. The other locals can be cultivated to be supporters of your cause. The other adjustment to your plans relates to the third stronghold, called Kerriwath. The people are not as recalcitrant as your reports have told you. You would be better to spare their lives and the community. Take captive or execute the top twenty leaders. I leave it to you to decide."

She continued, "Annexing Randar is not a good idea for future relations with other kingdoms. Evansing and Nerland will appear to be in an axis geared to territorial enrichment. To avoid that it would be advisable to place reliable people in power who will support you wholeheartedly. The man called Chafen, now in exile in Nerland, would be your best choice. He is widely respected among the people of Randar. Many thought it unjust what Jaspeth did in seizing his lands and killing several of his family members. Seek him out."

"So how do I get everyone to agree with these plans?"

No answer.

"Joan, oh, Joan, are you there?"

"I guess not. Percival would be the man to talk to about this. I will tell him about Joan and see what he says about her ideas."

In Percival's quarters, Edwin started to explain to Percival about Joan.

Percival listened and actually registered some surprise and slight bewilderment at what he heard. Even to him, a young girl warrior coming from the future to give strategies to Edwin sounded extraordinary.

His eventual response was, "The supernatural is the supernatural. It's beyond. It's beyond. We can't fully understand it, but we can work with it."

"We can tell Erith about your new informant. He is open to out of the box revelations about the supernormal. He is counting on it to make this Irish unity quest reality. To strengthen our case we need to gather some hard evidence we can supply to him and the Council. Why don't we get Jaather and his special strike force involved? Their objective would be to scurry across the border and check out some of this information. Ideally they would establish contact with our spies in Randar and gain whatever information will support what you were told. We may also need to postpone by a few days the initial attacks."

Edwin responded, "Let's give Erith a heads up then about what we know, so he can consider it in his communication with Keltic and the other Council members. The biggest change will be in integrating the command of the unit going to the east."

In Erith's chambers the two men shared what they had discussed earlier and the source of their new intelligence.

Erith raised his eyebrows at the mention of Joan and her origins.

"Hmmm. It stretches me gentlemen, but anything can happen when it comes to Divine intervention. I stopped trying to figure it out long ago. Go with the flow."

"In order to make a convincing argument to the Council members we will need more support. We will share this, not about Joan of course, but indicate to them consideration of these changes in our plans. We can share that certain intelligence sources have indicated these new developments to us. We can also point out we are taking steps to verify this new information. I agree the special strike force should be dispatched promptly to investigate further. Even though we can probably believe this Joan, I consider it prudent we take steps to verify what she has told you, Edwin."

"As for the maintaining of Randar as a separate state and placing this fellow Chafen as King, I will discuss this with Keltic. I have had my reservations about annexation for the same reasons put forward by Joan. There has been some mention of Chafen being considered. I will ask Keltic to do further investigation on his activities in Nerland. Also we can ask the strike force to make inquiries about him as well."

"You mean you believe me?"

"Yes, Edwin, I believe you. I have no reason to think you would tell me nonsense at a time like this. Remember how I told you I have a lot of unusual resources available to me? I should explain that one of those resources is that people who are aligned with me in heart and spirit will experience the extraordinary. You are one of those people. Therefore you could tell me just about anything and I would believe you. It's not in your character to be frivolous and foolish. Besides you have already demonstrated an amazing propensity for supernatural encounters."

That night Edwin and Greer were enjoying a quiet candlelight dinner together. Several glasses of wine later they were wrapped all over each other and enjoying being alone together and married.

The next morning, it was tough to get started for the training field, because once Edwin got Greer going she didn't want to stop. Finally Edwin extricated himself over the protests of his lover. Then he surrendered and returned to Greer. An hour later he left for the training field where the troops were waiting. His second in command expressed some impatience when he saw Edwin show up. Given his fifteen years age difference to Edwin, it galled him at having to take orders from someone so much younger. To be made to wait created an extra measure of challenge for him. Mind you this was only one of a few times Edwin kept them waiting. All of them occurring after Edwin's wedding. The men looked at each other knowingly when their commander showed up.

Edwin noticing their looks tried to avoid looking embarrassed and thought to himself, "We got to start these trainings later."

Several days later news from the strike force supported what Joan had revealed. The report said the original attack plan would have been a disaster. This created a new level of confidence in the integrity of what she had to share and would share in the future. Erith, Edwin and Percival all agreed her insights would be a valuable source of ongoing inside information.

The time of the attack rapidly approached, Edwin and the Evansing force were to leave today and be ready to cross the border in two days time. They had been joined by half of the forces in the northern part of Evansing. Erith and his top generals considered it prudent to leave a substantial force in the event of unexpected forces coming against them. Tara was the only one considered a possible threat and that is where most of them were situated.

Initial secret meetings with Chafen won his agreement to be the new King and to support the Irish unity quest.

Greer and Edwin said their tearful goodbyes. Carson would also be involved, holding rank of lieutenant. He would work with Edwin as his adjutant.

The time came to leave. What a glorious day to go off to war. The men were cheerful looking forward to the opportunity to earn their spurs. Many had never been to war, so for them this still represented glory. Erith and Percival were accompanying the troops. During actual battle they would be staying in the rear along with a couple of the top generals. They would be involved in assessing the situation as reports came in and give new direction as required. The Evansing troops had much optimism about their fighting ability. The officers had been indoctrinated with Edwin's military command methodology. Changes, significant changes, had been noted in the effectiveness of their men's ability to adapt to unexpected events and changes in the battlefield.

The first day went without a hitch. They spent it waving to cheering crowds, who didn't know what was up but were thrilled to see their military. It gave them a welcome break from their normal mundane activities. They knew something major must be about to happen.

The next day the air got a little more serious as they were getting close to the border. They would arrive near the border in the afternoon but not invade until early the next morning. The element of surprise would have dictated they attack immediately. However, the troops needed to rest. Reports indicated the Randarian forces seemed to be unaware of any imminent attack. At least no overt evidence existed they were aware. It would be surprising if they didn't have at least some consciousness of the force coming to take them away. They must have spies informing them of the troops moving down to the border. Even if they were aware they would be no match for what they would encounter with Evansing. At least that was the official line the Evansing troops were given. Randar's King Jaspeth wanted to be a political force in this part of Ireland. Evansing would change that. They would crush him. Part of the plan included Jaspeth and his family, both immediate and extended, being all eliminated. This would also apply to all the nobles known to be loyal to his policies.

The time had come, Evansing crossed over the border just before dawn.

CHAPTER 30

The border troops were nowhere to be seen. Obviously they knew something was going to happen. After an hour of being inside Randar the scouts came back. They reported that the Randar troops were massed at the top of a hill three miles ahead. The troops they referred to could be seen from where the Evansing troops were situated. This created a disadvantage for the troops under Edwin for they would be faced with an uphill battle. Edwin decided his troops would skirt the hill, being careful to stay out of range of the enemy's artillery and arrows. He decided it was preferable to face the prospect of Randar troops in front of them and behind them, rather than attempt an uphill attack. Instead, they would march ten miles down the road to the first stronghold and destroy it as planned. As they marched around the hill the Randarian force were incredulous. They hadn't expected this. Now they had to decide on a new strategy which entailed chasing after Evansing and fighting them on level open ground. Something they did not want to do. Not that the Randar troops weren't capable fighters, but they always wanted an advantage.

Now they had lost it. Edwin and his command had gone two miles past the hill when they could see dust behind them. The Randarians were coming after them. At this point no troops were in front of them. He gave the order to turn around and face the enemy. The archers were set and started to release volley after volley. Their projectiles hit the mark as many of the opposing army went down. And still they came on foot and on horseback. The infantry were sent in and started the grisly task of facing arrows and engaging in fierce hand-to-hand combat. Then the cavalry led by Edwin charged on the left flank coming as an onslaught moving through the opposing infantry. The Randar cavalry continued to remain in the rear. They appeared to be in a state of confusion as to what their role should be. Finally their leader gave the order and the enemy horsemen started to come toward the Evansing cavalry.

Edwin and Carson were fighting side by side demonstrating their swordsman skills. Edwin's horse took a mortal blow and went down. Edwin jumped off and avoided injury. He faced an infantryman who wielded an axe. Edwin ducked at the first blow aimed his way and fended off the second attempt against him with his sword. He then ran his sword through the man, who had left himself open after the last swing. The man's heart had just been missed and so he wasn't killed. He still had fight left and he swung again at Edwin, though more erratically and with less vigor. Then Edwin ran him through again, this time in the heart.

Carson had his own desperate struggle. Two infantry men with swords attacked him at the same time. His horse reared up and kicked one of the enemy soldiers in the head, killing him instantly. That left only one, which made things much easier. With a series of slashes to the opposing soldier's upper body, Carson subdued the enemy soldier.

Edwin managed to recover the horse of a fallen comrade. He could see the opposing cavalry closing in on them. The cavalry of both armies carried swords and small shields. He and Carson started to charge onward to meet them head to head. They each picked out a horseman and zeroed in on them. Slash, clang and bang. Edwin was thankful for his shield as it protected him from several blows. His opposing number looked to be a high level noble given his distinctive markings. He came in with an over-head slash, which forced Edwin to raise his sword high to stop. Then they both engaged in furious sword play. At this point something very strange happened to Edwin, all of a sudden everything slowed right down. The enemy's movements were so verrry slow. But then so were his own. He saw the thrust coming and it looked ridiculously slow, but his response was as slow or slower. He took the thrust deep. Everything went black.

He noticed the battlefield below as though he were levitating above it. A brilliant light beckoned him and he now stood in a room with a man who looked every inch a warrior king. Though small he had the fierce gaze of a warrior who had been in many battles. Edwin, confused, asked him where he was.

The man smiled and said he was in an antechamber of Heaven.

"And who are you?"

"My name is David, you may have heard of me in the Bible, known as King David."

"No, I haven't heard of you. But then I haven't read or heard too much of the Bible."

"If you keep fighting like you have been, you may want to up your reading a bit."

"Why am I here?"

"You died, but someone has put in a special dispensation for you. Your original lifeline was meant to expire today on that battlefield. Apparently Joan of Arc has been intervening for you. She likes you and wants to see you fulfill your assignment."

An angel came into the room and handed David a message. He read it and smiled.

"Yes, you have been given an extension on your earth life. Use it wisely."

Edwin looked up into the eyes of a weeping Carson. "Why are you crying, Carson?"

Carson jumped at the sound and sight of Edwin talking to him. He looked for the wound in Edwin's body and it couldn't be found. The battle had moved on and was a din in the distance. Carson had come back looking for Edwin. It was just the two of them surrounded by the dead and dying.

Carson helped his friend and commander stand up. "You know Edwin I realized today you are a friend and I really cared about you."

Edwin smiled wanly back.

"Thanks, Carson, I consider you a friend too."

"You know I could have sworn you were dead. That wound had a lot of blood come out of it and it looked as mortal as any wound I have ever seen. Now you are alive and the wound disappeared only leaving an ugly scar. Oh look there's a new scar on your back as well. You took a sword thrust right through your body. Did Percival do some of his magic while my eyes were covered with tears?"

"I don't know, Carson. It's a mystery." He explained what had happened while he laid dead.

"So you were dead and because of a woman liking you, you got to come back?"

"Yeah, something like that. I met a fellow called King David who talked to me. He said he's in the Bible. Have you heard of him?"

"King David, in the Bible? You mean he's a real person?"

"That's what he told me."

"Well that is interesting. I thought some priest imagined him so as to make a good story. The account of him killing Goliath certainly makes for an interesting tale to tell a kid at bedtime."

"Do you think you will be able to ride a horse?"

"I, I, think so, I am progressively feeling stronger. It does feel rather weird where I received that wound. It's like fire burning inside of me. No pain, mind you. Most peculiar."

Carson got on his horse and rode over to catch a stray mount bereft of its rider.

"Take this one, Edwin."

With the healing rapidly taking over his body, Edwin got on without assistance.

They rode on to join the fray, which had now turned into a route of the Randarian forces.

The day had been an overwhelming success for Evansing. They had suffered significant casualties themselves but had managed to overwhelm the Randar army, partly because they had a considerable numerical advantage. Also there seemed to be an extra measure of iron in the souls of the men from Evansing. They fought with a serious sense of mission, which would not be denied. The troops of Randar fought for an ignoble despot. That puts such men at a disadvantage against those in a noble cause.

At the camp that night, part of the discussion centered on the miraculous recovery of Edwin. A number of men had seen Edwin go down in what appeared to be a fatal blow. One officer had even seen the sword come out his back. Edwin was a bit reticent to share what had happened because it was so out there. He decided to share it from the perspective of what he recalled happening to him. If people wanted to believe he had been hallucinating or dreaming then that was their prerogative. One thing they could not explain away was the recovery from the nasty wound, which had left two very visible scars.

That night as Edwin slept, he had a dream. Joan came to visit him. She warned him of an ambush which had been set up just before the first stronghold they were to take. Specifically, there were archer assassins who had orders to kill him.

CHAPTER 31

Edwin woke with a start. Now that was a different way for Joan to visit him. She always had a new trick up her sleeve. He hadn't thought to thank her for her life giving intervention. He said, "Thanks, Joan, for the help now and in getting me back." He didn't hear a response, but he had a sense she heard him and acknowledged his gratitude. He had to share Joan's involvement with Greer. It would warm her attitude toward Joan. Greer still didn't know how to respond to the idea of another woman visiting her husband.

The strike force members accompanying the army were gathered together at a briefing with Edwin. He informed them that intelligence had come which indicated there were some archer assassins up ahead, just before the stronghold.

The strike force men got out maps of the area and assembled a plan of coming in behind where the enemy troops were expected to be situated. By noon they had left on their mission.

It was good to have a day of sorting out the wounded and chaos after the day of battle.

In keeping with custom and the original plan, almost all the prisoners had been executed, or were in the process of being executed. Only a handful of nobles were spared for now, to determine if any advantage existed in keeping them alive.

Edwin spent the day resting for he still felt a bit whacked by his experience. He decided to write a letter to Greer in which he explained what had happened. As well he again and again shared his heart of how much he missed her, adored her and loved her.

Late that afternoon the strike force returned. They had successfully eliminated the risk of ambush. The special force had had the element of surprise for the assassins weren't expecting someone to come from behind them. It had been a fairly easy battle, for they killed most of the enemy in the initial flurry of arrows while they were standing around their camp.

By late morning the troops were ready to march. The stronghold was a small walled village of approximately eight hundred people.

The troops pulled out the artillery to rain boulders and all manner of nasty things against the walls and over the walls. As well, the archers were out in full force launching arrows over the walls. The people in the stronghold did not want to surrender and they also kept up their firing of arrows. In addition they were throwing over the walls boiling oil or large boulders on top of the soldiers manning the battering ram against the gates.

At shortly after four o'clock water clock time, the gates were smashed and the bars of iron behind them were cut through. Many of the townspeople that survived had holed up in the tower of the church. Erith conferred with Edwin and his other officers. The majority wanted to burn it, thus killing everyone remaining inside. Edwin, prior to his death experience would have said sure. That would have been the most expedient way to deal with the problem. But now he didn't want to do that.

He asked the others to consider how the report would sound to other kingdoms, of them killing everyone by fire in a tower, including women and children. There would be the pro of scaring into submission everyone who heard the story. The con, and a big con, would be that it would make Evansing seem like bloodthirsty monsters.

Erith agreed with Edwin and decided he would offer the occupants the option to let the women and children go to their freedom. This included boys under sixteen. He promised they would not be harmed.

The people in the tower refused to let anybody leave. The men inside reasoned they would be safer if the women and children stayed.

Erith needed to move quickly. He hated to lose men taking the tower if its occupants could simply be burned out.

There were almost two hundred people inside the tower. Two-thirds were thought to be women and children. Erith decided he would leave a force of three hundred men to wait it out. After several days the conditions would be unbearable in the tower. No food and water and crowded filthy conditions.

The officers didn't like the decision. But Erith was the one in charge. He, Edwin and his two senior officers all agreed they needed to create an optimal balance of toughness to encourage cooperation, with mercy to curry favor.

The army continued on the way to Randar's capital. There were no sightings of the Randar army prior to the next stronghold, very peculiar. Surely they had more fight than that. When they arrived at the fortified settlement, it had an eerie silence. No one stood on the walls. When a squad was sent to check the gates they could be pushed open. No one was inside. For some reason they did not want to stay and defend it. Erith ordered the stronghold to be destroyed.

As the men were moving in to destroy the settlement, a scout arrived with the news of a massive army coming toward them. Somewhat larger, perhaps forty per cent larger than the one they had already fought. This meant they were almost as large as the Evansing force. The destruction of the fortified settlement would wait. All troops were to assemble and be ready for battle. The enemy force was only five miles away. Erith counseled with his officers and they formulated a plan. It was all very disconcerting because somehow their scouts hadn't picked up earlier that their opponents were so close. This time the Evansing leaders decided the cavalry would charge up the middle to divide the Randar army. This would be preceded by a huge assault of arrows against the middle, so as to substantially thin it out for the cavalry to run through. The horsemen would then divide into two and come up from behind against each Randarian flank.

Edwin and Carson were riding at the front of the mounted force with the other cavalry officers. They would be taking the left side of the charge. Up ahead they could see the banners of their enemy. Edwin had a sense this battle would make or break the campaign. A severe thrashing of Randar at this point should break their back. King Jaspeth was reported to be leading this army coming against them. Whether he led their charge or whether he sent orders from the rear was not known.

The two armies were barely within range of each other's arrows when Evansing's archers started to rain down a carpet of arrows on the middle part of Randar's troops. The arrows achieved as expected. A major part of their men in that area went down creating an opening for the Evansing cavalry. Their warhorses were snorting and eager to join the fray. The charge went better than expected as Edwin's section ran over whatever troops were in their way. They then encircled behind the Randarians. A portion of Randar's mounted troops came against them.

Edwin noticed a general of the opposing side. He set his sights on doing battle with him. Carson rode alongside and intended to go after the officer accompanying the general.

The general could see he had been targeted and he started to come straight toward Edwin. Likewise his fellow officer came directly towards Carson. Both Randarians carried short lances. This would create a challenge for the two Evansing officers who only carried a sword with a small shield. They would need to knock out the lances which could be aimed at their horses. They intended to force their Randarian foes to fight with swords.

Edwin readied as he could see the general pointing his lance at Edwin's horse. At the last possible moment Edwin swung his horse out of the line to allow him to use his sword against the oncoming lance. His hard downward slice broke the lance in two. The general fended off Edwin's follow-up swing with what remained of his lance. The two men turned their horses around and faced each other. They now both held their swords and started to race toward one another. Their swords were extended outward towards their opposition. Clang, clash as they engaged each other. Edwin took a glancing blow on his left shoulder; he grimaced as he pressed his counterpart and delivered a deep slash to the other's horse. The general's horse stumbled from the blow to its neck, almost fatal but not quite. The Randar officer swung hard a sideways blow which Edwin deflected down and away, coming back with a thrust which narrowly missed the enemy's head. They were now apart, facing each other. Edwin kicked his horse to jump forward. The sudden movement startled the general's horse already slowing down from its wound. It reared up on its legs throwing its rider off. The man hit the ground hard but managed to gather his wits in time to partially avoid Edwin's slash against his back. The man yelped in pain as he still received a substantial blow to his right shoulder blade.

Edwin turned his horse hard and came right back at the fallen officer knocking the man's sword out of his hand. Our hero then held his sword at the man's throat.

"Surrender or you die."

The man looking very angry acted like he might pull out his dagger or try to grab his sword. Edwin was about to run him through when the man thought the better of it and raised his hands in surrender.

As Edwin looked at his captive more closely he noticed royal insignia. This man must be part of the royal family of Randar.

"Identify yourself."

"I am Jaspeth."

Edwin's eyes widened as he considered the possibility that this was the King of Randar.

"Do you mean King Jaspeth?"

"Yes, and I claim the right to be treated as my rank entitles me to."

Edwin thought to himself, "Obviously he doesn't realize his rank entitles him to death."

Carson managed to extricate himself from the one on one contest he had with the King's assistant. After much back and forth battling he had killed his opponent with a slash across the throat, which almost completely severed his head. Jaspeth appeared visibly shaken when he discovered the death of his son, for that is who he had as his adjutant.

Edwin introduced the captive to Carson, "This is King Jaspeth, let us lead him to our lines," as he pulled out a rope. "Watch him while I tie his hands and arms."

The two rode alongside their prey who they positioned to walk ahead and between them.

The conflict continued for several hours before the Randar army broke and fled in total disarray.

They led Jaspeth to Erith's tent. Upon meeting his opposing number, Erith had to resist killing Jaspeth right there. He decided to consider the most opportune venue and time for Jaspeth's demise.

"So, Jaspeth, at last we meet."

He could tell his prisoner was confused and frustrated.

"You are probably wondering why none of your Druid magic has been working. We have our ways of countering Druidry. We work with a Power much greater than anything you could imagine possible."

Jaspeth, looking defiant, said nothing. Guards led him away in chains with orders he be watched by twelve men. Erith confirmed again with Percival that all of Jaspeth's powers had been neutralized. He was a little concerned about losing their prize. But he had decided they should make a show of killing him, in front of the troops and the Randar prisoners who were still being kept for future considerations. The execution would be carried out tomorrow at noon.

The next day started with the elimination of all those Randar prisoners considered expendable. Only a dozen or so of the prisoners taken in the latest battle were considered worth keeping alive for now.

At ten minutes to noon, the guards led Jaspeth out from his prison stockade. He looked like a beaten man, unusual for a king and especially one known to be proud and arrogant. Unable to exercise his Druid powers must have sucked the life and fight out of him.

The troops were assembled together with the remaining prisoners. One of the soldiers, experienced in beheading executions by sword waited on a hastily constructed scaffold.

Two soldiers led Jaspeth and two followed behind. Up the stairs they went with their charge. Erith, standing in the first row, nodded to the man who would be reading the death warrant.

"For crimes of promoting evil intentions against the people of Evansing and of the practicing of Druidry, you, King Jaspeth of Randar, are hereby to be executed by beheading."

With that, Jaspeth was led to the block. He asked if he could say something before he died. Erith said no. He placed his head on the block and with one swift blow the axe removed his head from his body.

A great cheer arose from the troops as his head fell to the scaffold. The executioner then picked up the head of the tyrant and showed it off. This resulted in more cheers.

The prisoners seemed to sag a little more at the sight of their king being so summarily executed like a common criminal. This was precisely what Erith wanted. He wanted to insult the King of Randar and his prisoner noblemen. As well he wanted to raise the spirits of his own men at seeing a major objective achieved on this campaign.

Reports were coming that the Randarian forces twenty miles down the road from them were surrendering. The two princes who were commanding them had been killed by their own men. Two messengers had been sent out to communicate to those troops that their lives would be spared if they surrendered without a fight. They included news about the impending execution of their king and also the death of the King's son. The couriers were prisoners whose lives would be spared if they delivered the message. They were warned if they didn't deliver the communication they would be tracked down. They were escorted for the first ten miles to ensure as much as possible they would fulfill their mission. Upon the receipt of the message, the two princes said no to surrender, which resulted in certain officers rising up and killing them.

The Randarian mission had started to come together rapidly as their vaunted opposition quickly melted away.

The Nerland forces had also been experiencing great success. Edwin, however, was saddened to hear his dear friend Glynn had been killed in their initial battle. Upon hearing this, Edwin excused himself and went away by himself to consider what it was all about. He spent some two hours to grieve his friend. This was all his present responsibilities would allow him. Before retiring for the night he wrote his condolences to Glynn's widow. He also shared his grief with Greer in his regular correspondence to her.

"Life goes on," as he drifted off to sleep.

The news came that the people in the tower had surrendered with none of the women and children injured. The Evansing troops destroyed the stronghold and executed or dispersed its remaining inhabitants.

They also tore down the next fortified settlement, which had been abandoned. Its building blocks were of a good quality. Several wagonloads of these blocks were carried to a nearby village in need of building materials for its homes.

Evansing's and Nerland's challenges were now becoming more of the nature of what do we do now as to the proper administration of Randar. Also focus increased on rounding up the people on their wanted lists. The will to fight seemed to have at least for most part dried up with the capture and death of their king. It was a mystery why Jaspeth would have put himself in such harm's way. His arrogance and pride became his undoing.

The remaining strongholds en route to the Randar capital were destroyed and the inhabitants dealt with as planned. The Evansing army arrived two days after the Nerland army. The new king accompanied the Nerlanders and was to be crowned the day after the Evansing army came into the capital.

In Randar's capital, Erith assigned Edwin the task of liquidating the royal family. Edwin carried out this assignment with ruthless thoroughness. There were over eighty relatives of Jaspeth identified to be removed from the Randar succession. To accomplish this objective Edwin had a troop of three hundred men combing the capital and outlying districts. They executed on the spot anyone on the list. Edwin primarily coordinated the search and oversaw the tracking of who had been killed and those still at large.

The evenings were now generally free and available for more pleasant pursuits. One of these came in the form of a young lady of nobility whose husband had been executed by Jaspeth almost two years earlier. He had been charged with conspiracy to commit treason. Due to her favor with certain key royals she and her property were spared. They had been childless as they were only married for a brief time. She sent an invitation to Edwin and some other officers to attend a supper and a musical presentation by several leading Randarian musicians. When Edwin received it he at first thought he would pass on it. However, one of his fellow senior officers chided him to take a break and have some fun. So after a few minutes of considering it he changed his mind and decided to attend it after all.

The officers showed up to enjoy a welcome break. They entered a splendid home hosted by Faro, a bubbly appealing young woman. She had dark black hair and darker features than normal. There were also several local nobles, mainly couples. These were all nobles considered safe and amenable to the new regime.

The evening progressed pleasantly enough with the officers enjoying the music and delicious food. The hostess sat across from Edwin and accorded him great attention whenever he spoke. As well she often looked directly at him when she was conversing, almost as though he were the only one there. The look in her eyes whenever she looked at him indicated she thought very highly of him. Edwin of course appreciated the attention of this fine looking young woman. In some ways she even reminded him of Greer. As the evening proceeded and the wine and mead had been flowing freely, Edwin and Faro found themselves sitting side by side. They both enjoyed relating one on one and seemed to be unaware there were other guests, not very good form for the hostess. Then one of the Evansing officers, who had noticed this growing attachment decided to intervene. He walked up to the pair and asked her if she could help him with some artwork he had noticed in the other end of the room. She looked at him, trying to not look annoyed and then realized she was the hostess. All smiles, she apologized for neglecting her guests. Then after answering some questions about the artwork, she spent twenty minutes circulating with her guests. In the meantime Edwin engaged in conversation with two couples of the local nobility. He realized he too had responsibility to connect with the other guests. After all, diplomatic relations were an important role he played in the Evansing scheme of things. Edwin listened carefully to the couples as they shared their struggles under Jaspeth and how they now looked forward to a brighter future under the new King. They knew of Chafen and had met him several times. They expected him to be a fair and just man. Edwin welcomed this news as it provided further confirmation of the rightness of their choice. The time got late and Edwin prepared to leave when Faro rejoined him at his side. She touched his arm lightly and looked up at him with a look of delight in resuming their conversation.

CHAPTER 32

In his mind Edwin is thinking, "I should get going." But in his heart he is feeling the attention from this young woman is most delightful. The other Evansing officers were about to leave and again the same officer came to rescue Edwin. This time Edwin felt a little perturbed at being interrupted. But his sense of duty to be well-rested for tomorrow and of course his loyalty to Greer, prompted him to say good evening and to thank his hostess.

Faro gave Edwin's hand a little squeeze goodbye, which seemed to linger a bit longer than would be considered proper for their relationship.

During the next day, Edwin found himself thinking about Faro. He had to shake himself out of it. He felt a bit disconcerted that he had rather friendly thoughts about her. After all he dearly loved Greer and had no intention of doing something inappropriate with another female. During their courtship and marriage, no one else ever caught Edwin's eye. He had been totally sold on Greer and intended to stay that way. Oh well he would be going back pretty soon and would probably not see Faro again. During the day he received a message from one of Faro's servants. It contained an invitation to dinner tomorrow. Edwin studied the invitation and considered his options. His first inclination was to say no. But then he considered how Faro represented someone of significant influence. He should act to ensure she and her circle of friends were on good terms with the Evansing government. And Edwin happened to be a significant part of that government. Besides there would be servants there, maybe he should ask Carson to join him. No, maybe not, being Greer's cousin he may not appreciate this was just diplomacy.

During the next day, Edwin found himself looking forward to seeing Faro again. After all she was fun. People would understand that he, a soldier away from home would look forward to spending time in the company of a lovely lady. As he prepared to leave for Faro's he realized he had missed writing Greer the day before and he hadn't written her yet today. He had been writing her everyday and now he had missed two days in row.

"Hmmm, she will understand I've been busy with my responsibilities, maybe I will do it tonight when I get home."

He stopped himself and chose to be a bit late rather than miss another day. He scrawled a hastily constructed note, his briefest yet to Greer, but at least she will know he still loves and misses her. Then he handed it off to the military courier on his way out.

When Edwin arrived at Faro's home he apologized for being late. But then again with the water clocks being the way they were, who would know for sure how late and even if he was late at all.

Faro had on her best greeting outfit, showing a little more cleavage than Edwin remembered seeing a couple of days earlier. She appeared so glad to see him again and he appreciated her enthusiasm.

They sat across from each other conversing about anything and everything. She was a very fun lady.

He felt this ache for Greer, "Oh to be back home." After awhile Edwin noticed there didn't seem to be any servants around. "Strange, where'd they go?" He passed it off and carried on in their conversation. After awhile she sat next to him. She rubbed his arm and looking increasingly appealing, in fact she looked gorgeous. He patted her hand she had on his arm. It felt very fine. Now he held her hand on his arm. He looked at her in the way he had only looked at Greer before. The brakes seemed to be coming off. The train seemed to be picking up speed as they both started to get that look. Then they were kissing.

Then they were touching and grabbing, and then…"STOP!" went off in Edwin's head. He stopped, startled. "What was that?" he thought to himself or so he thought, but he actually said it with his outside voice.

His playmate asked him, "What's what?" irritated their progress had stopped.

"A voice went off in me that said "STOP!" And I am going to stop. I should never have let this happen in the first place. You are a wonderful young lady and may you find a new husband, but it's not me." He got on his jacket and left without further ado.

When he arrived back at the home that were his quarters in Randar, he was greeted by Percival waiting for him.

"Percival, it is so good to see you. What brings you here?"

"You do."

"Oh and in what specific way?"

"An officer friend of yours and I do emphasize friend, let me know you were seeing a certain lady tonight, which he had noted seemed to be unduly interested in you."

If the light had been brighter, then Percival may have noticed Edwin blushed at the revelation of this episode with Faro.

"Ohh really, Percival," replied Edwin. He dismissed the thought of trying to discredit this as idle thoughts by the officer in question. He knew Percival would not be thrown off by deception.

"Yes, really, Edwin. You could have done serious damage to your relationship with Greer. If I hadn't yelled "STOP", who knows where your little visit would have ended up?"

Edwin stood there in silence considering what he had said.

"Yes, you are right. How did you know the most opportune time to yell 'STOP'?"

"After your officer friend informed me about his concerns, I sat quietly for a few minutes. Then I started to get a vision of you and this young lady. I waited until it looked like it was now or never."

"Whooo, your timing was impeccable for a moment later it may have been too late. Mind you if you had said it too early it may not have had sufficient impact."

"Yes, I know, timing is everything."

"So can you drop into people's private lives any time you want to?"

"No. The Divine Power, which makes it possible only does it in appropriate ways and times when it is necessary to do so. So don't worry I'm not going to drop in on you and Greer in your personal times."

"That is certainly reassuring, although I wouldn't have expected you to do that."

"What's your take on how I, who is so in love with Greer, could be foolish enough to risk wrecking our relationship and everything else I have for the sake of a little gratification?"

"I believe an enchantment aided your lady friend a slight bit and maybe a lot, which made you more amenable to her wiles than normal."

"What do you mean than normal? Are you insinuating I have it in me to be unfaithful to Greer?"

"Well you are a virile young man and therefore you do have to use your head in your interactions with attractive members of the opposite sex. You have to remember you are a Crown Prince and that raises your attractiveness score to women looking to upgrade themselves in life. Even if they thought about you losing it all if you did get involved with them, they probably would pass it off, thinking somehow it would work out. When I say normal I am also cognizant of the fact your moral upbringing or lack thereof, did not create a lot of internal framework for protecting yourself in these sorts of situations. You have been growing in your nobility, but we have not had enough time to cover everything."

"Thanks again, Percival. Eamon told you, right?"

"Yes."

"I will have to tell him thanks as well. Also I will tell him that if he sees me being a bonehead in the future he has my full permission to tell me straight out."

"Good idea. We all require people to cover us when we are in our stupid moments. For we all have them. A friend, who we can trust to tell us what we need to hear and not just what we want to hear, is valuable indeed."

Two weeks later the Evansing leadership decided to allow Erith and Edwin and a third of the Evansing troops to return home. Up to one-half of the Nerland army would pull out within ten days. The whole campaign achieved outstanding success. A lot of the unexpected positive results occurred because they had not realized how unpopular Jaspeth had been with his people. Once he died the people had little will to continue fighting. Evansing told the people of Randar they had no desire to rule them. They would have their own King and institutions. Evansing only required Randar to cooperate in the pursuit of Irish unity. Most Randar nobles considered this acceptable. Their new King Chafen had been pre-screened to ensure he favored Irish unity. He selected leaders he knew would work with that vision.

Edwin felt so impatient to get back to his little honey bunny. He felt like letting his horse just gallop ahead. This would have been poor decorum plus of course his horse would have keeled over from fatigue.

He and Carson chatted amiably on the way home. If he knew anything about Faro, he didn't indicate it.

Erith did have a conversation with Edwin which seemed to make a veiled reference to the importance of keeping ones virtue intact.

"Yes, Sire," was about all Edwin could say. Hopefully nothing would get back to Greer.

CHAPTER 33

Upon arrival at Evansing, there was his sweetheart out on her horse to greet her father and her husband. She looked pleased to see him, not a hint of anything troubling her.

That night was a night of catching up on one of their favorite games. This involved exploring. I leave it to your imagination as to what they were exploring.

Late the next morning, Edwin and Greer went to the nearby lake. Edwin had been given a couple of days off. Then Erith wanted to start strategizing what to do with Tara. For now, Edwin would give his undivided attention to Greer.

As they walked to the lake, they chatted about all manner of things. She had been contacted by both Athandra and Chandra. They both formalized their previously expressed desire that she be their Maid of Honor. She felt deeply gratified to receive such an honor from both of them. Both Kerris and Carson had already indicated to Edwin they wanted him to be their Best Man.

"So, Edwin, did you feel lonely without me while you were in Randar?"

Edwin felt a little tingly with that question being asked, especially since it sounded so innocent.

"You know it, babe. I missed you all the time. You should know from my letters. They told you how much I loved you and missed you."

"I appreciated how much you wrote me and so consistently too. Every day except one, which you followed with a quick note the next day. I guess you were rather busy and couldn't fit it in."

"Yes, I was busy in the Randar capital looking after my duties."

"I guess one of those duties was someone called Faro."

Edwin did not feel totally surprised at the question for he knew Greer well enough to know she was leading to something.

"Yes, she is a local noble woman who invited me and some officers for an evening of dining and musical entertainment. We enjoyed a welcome break from the usual routine. Plus it gave me an opportunity to put on my diplomat's hat and create bridges with the Randarian nobility."

"How far does your bridge building go? I understand you followed up your initial evening at Faro's with more personal attention a couple of nights later."

"Yes, she did invite me for dinner a couple of nights later."

"Dinner and….?"

"Conversation, we of course discussed a variety of things. I don't remember exactly what"

"Maybe because the discussion part wasn't so important after awhile."

"Okay, Greer, what's up?"

"I don't know. Maybe you should tell me. I wasn't there."

Edwin took a deep breath and told Greer everything.

"And that's everything?"

"Yes, Greer, that is everything, I swear."

She looked him straight in the eye.

"I believe you. Of course I am disappointed this happened."

"Greer, I truly am sorry it happened. You know I would never do anything deliberately to harm you or our relationship. How did you find out if I may be so bold as to ask?"

"I believe it must have been Faro herself. I think she felt the wrath of a woman scorned and decided to take it out on you and me. I received an unsigned message last week. The note did not mention the stop part. It just left what happened to the imagination. I asked Percival if he knew anything about it. He filled in the missing details. Fortunately what you told me lines up with what he told me. I am grateful you have told me the truth, which is what I expected you to do. I could love you last night because I had already forgiven you. By talking about it with you I am able to get it out in the open, so we could put it behind us."

"Greer, thank you for being you. I know I was a dolt to allow myself to get into that predicament. I have learned my lesson and I will never allow it to happen again. From now on I am never going to any engagement with a woman unattended by at least one officer."

"Percival figures you were at least partially impacted by an enchantment. That would be a hard thing to be aware of, and therefore be able to respond to rationally.

However, he believes you need a little strengthening in this area. That way even if you did have an enchantment on you, your internal resolve would be able to overcome it."

"In other words if I am totally resolved to be faithful to you no matter what, then I will have the wherewithal to resist this sort of thing if it should take place again?"

"Precisely, and given who you are I suspect it is not a matter of if but rather of when. By that I mean you being a conquering hero Crown Prince. Obviously there are women who will be attracted to you, not only because you are gorgeous," she said with a warm smile, "but also because of your position."

Her warm smile brought him great relief. "I will take whatever steps are necessary to ensure it never happens again. In fact, tomorrow I will go see Percival about this moral structuring stuff he talked about. I've already told Eamon he has total freedom to talk to me about anything he doesn't think is appropriate. He tried to save me at the initial dinner and then he told Percival about his concerns."

Greer grabbed her husband and kissed him. She held him tight. She didn't care there were twenty pairs of eyes watching them because of course they had guards escorting them outside the castle walls.

Then she looked up at him and said, "I love you Edwin. You are my sweetheart and always will be."

He mumbled sweet somethings and kissed her back.

The next morning, Percival and Edwin met to see about strengthening some of his internal moral structures.

Percival began, "Moral frameworks are strengthened by consistently making the right choices. As a consequence, no matter what the circumstances are, we continue to make the right choices. This means we must make right decisions, even in seeming little things. For if we haven't established a mindset of how to deal with what appears to be the minor areas of life, we will have no moral reserve to draw upon when major temptations come upon us."

"This talk of strengthening is a bit premature in your case, Edwin. Due to the deplorable lack of proper parental guidance, the moral structures weren't put there in the first place. You can't strengthen what isn't there. So therefore, we need to develop in you what should have been deposited in you as a child. Not a small thing. You have had no problem with being faithful to Greer, because you have been so smitten by her. And because she has always been nearby except for short absences. Then the circumstances changed, so you weren't naturally protected. Now you were on your own. Without an internal compass as to how to respond to an interested attractive woman, you were pretty much at the mercy of what your hormones and emotions wanted to do. We must establish in you such a rock solid, non-negotiable sense of loyalty to Greer. This is so no matter how justified you are feeling, or how rough your circumstances, or how appealing the woman, you will stay the course of marital fidelity."

"Okay, so how do we do this?"

With that the two men spent the rest of the morning delving into Edwin's early years. This resulted in some more snotty-nosed embarrassing weepy episodes but also greater freedom for Edwin. To top it all off, Percival proclaimed some blessings over Edwin. These were designed to create for Edwin new levels of wisdom in his relations with women.

"I'm feelin' good, real good, Percival. Once again you have been a master of personal transformation. I also feel a bit drained after all that. Thanks to you I feel a new level of peace. Yeah, that's what I'm feeling, peace. I don't have a lot of familiarity with that feeling. It feels good. I could use more of it. It has sometimes troubled me that no matter how many good things were in my life I had this sense of unsettledness. Like something still not right. It felt rather frustrating. I mean what do you do when you have everything a person can imagine being necessary for happiness, and yet you still don't feel happy. Don't get me wrong, I've been feeling up and positive most of the time. But lately I have noticed those feelings of frustration were coming more often and staying longer, sometimes even when I am around Greer. I know it bugged her. She figured I should always be happy dappy because I'm with her. I did my best to explain it had nothing to do with her. Now I have a new sense of being okay in a way which has nothing to do with stuff or other people. I feel okay about me just being me."

Later in the afternoon, Edwin and Greer were out and about walking along the castle walls, taking in the view and enjoying being together.

"Since you saw Percival I can tell there is something different. You are more content and more satisfied. I would say there is even more peace about you. Perhaps the best way to describe it is that you seem to be more comfortable in your own skin."

"That's it. That's how I feel, more comfortable in my own skin. I was looking for the right collection of words to describe it and nothing seemed to fit. Once again Greer you demonstrate your incomparable insight and wisdom of human nature, or at least Edwin nature." He looked at her with a big grin.

She batted him on the shoulder. "Now you are making fun of me."

"Yes, I guess I am, a little. But you are right how you described it. For the first time I am feeling comfortable with being who I am, comfortable in my own skin."

The next day, Erith, Percival, Edwin and several generals gathered together to consider how to best resolve the impasse with Tara. No communication had been held with Tara's King Clarendon. It seemed as though he took the tack that no communication was the best solution with Evansing. Several messages had been sent in regards to the strike force members that were captured in the failed mission in Tara. Reports had come to Evansing, which indicated at least three, and perhaps as many as five, of the force members had been captured.

Erith spoke, "As a result of being stone-walled, we have not been able to get any sense of what, if anything Tara is willing to receive in exchange for the strike force prisoners. At this point we don't even know for sure if they are still alive. The longer the silence, the less likely they are still alive.

Tara is a difficult place for us to get information. Its citizens are tightly controlled. Nothing goes in or out of its borders without the authorities knowing about it. They have a substantial military force. With our growing alliance we could overpower them, but I don't want to have war with someone if there is another way to accomplish our objectives. Today I wanted to introduce you to the Tara issue. Let's meet again in a couple days after you have had some time to mull it over and come up with ideas. The meeting is dismissed."

Outside the room, Percival and Edwin discussed how they would come up with the best solutions.

"For me, getting dreams is always the best way to come up with solving problems," said Percival.

"Yes, dreams are a great way to come up with solutions. I will try that plus I am going to ask Joan if she has some strategies that would get us the ideal outcome."

"Good idea. She's available, might as well make the most of her insights. That's why she came to you."

"Do you want to meet her? We could both talk to her."

"No, I don't think that would be a good idea. She was assigned to you and I don't believe she is meant to manifest to anyone other than you and perhaps to Greer. I don't know why I said Greer, but there may be special grace available because she is your wife. You could ask Joan about that. Ask Greer to see if she is interested in meeting Joan. She most likely is, but you never know."

That evening, Edwin asked Greer if she wanted to meet Joan.

"You mean I can see her too if I want to?"

"I don't know, but I thought I'd ask you first. If you want to I will ask Joan if she will appear to you also."

"Sure, it would certainly be different to meet someone from the future."

"I'll ask her right now. Joan, would you please come and show yourself to Greer also?"

Nothing happened. They waited for an hour and still nothing happened.

"Well I guess there's our answer. Mind you she may come later when we aren't expecting her."

Greer responded, "Well I hope she has some sense of decorum if she does show up unexpected."

"Oh I'm sure she knows how to be gracious," replied Edwin.

"I'll talk to her right now about our need for a strategy with Tara. Joan, as you may know we need to have a successful strategy for Tara. I need your help. Thanks in advance for your help."

When Edwin went to bed he asked to have a dream, which would give a solution to the Tara problem.

No dream that night and no response from Joan.

In the morning Edwin and Percival conferred as to what they had received for insight about Tara.

Percival shared how he had had a dream of a large locked door. The key hung from a tall Alder tree. That was the extent of the dream.

Edwin asked, "What does it mean?"

Percival replied, "I don't know."

"I think it means King Barris of Aldred is the key to relationship with Tara."

"Edwin, I believe you are right. By the way did you get a dream and what did Joan tell you?"

"I neither received a dream nor did Joan talk to me. I think it's because your dream tells us what we need"

"I believe you are correct. Now the next step is how does Barris play a role in this?"

"I could go visit Barris and ask him about his relationship with Tara. I know they have some degree of connection and exchange of commerce, but I don't know to what extent. I'll take Carson along for I know he is aching to see Chandra. First let's discuss this with Erith and get his input and permission about seeing Barris. He should give me a letter of greeting to take along."

Percival and Edwin shared the dream and interpretation with Erith.

"It's an interesting idea to get Barris to help with Tara. I know years ago they were fairly close as friends and as kingdoms. They have not been as close in recent years. However, he is much closer than we are. Given how you got the insight it makes sense for you to try it out. I will prepare a letter of introduction to Barris today and you and Carson can leave in the morning.

Later that day Edwin informed Greer he would be leaving for Aldred. She felt disappointed to see him leave again so soon. "Oh well, I guess you will only be gone a few days, right, Edwin?"

"I would think so, Greer. I don't know of any reason why it should take longer."

CHAPTER 34

The next morning Edwin and Carson along with one hundred and eighty soldiers left for Aldred. The trip went uneventful except for a large flock of ravens, which flew over them for several minutes. No one could recall ever seeing such a large number of ravens before. They appeared to be on their way to Aldred. Also, it seemed as though a noticeable drop in the temperature occurred while they flew overhead. The coolness stayed with them for the duration of the trip. Aldred was chilly and not just its physical temperature but in every way. The people on and along the roads seemed almost hostile to the men from Evansing. This stood in stark contrast to their last visit when almost everyone seemed cheery and friendly.

The most disconcerting part was the rather cool reception from Barris, Kerris and Chandra as well as the other Aldred notables. Something was not right. Chandra did not greet Carson like a woman meeting her future husband after a protracted absence. She seemed distracted and almost irritated about him being there. One would be hard pressed to believe Kerris had asked Edwin to be his best man at his rapidly approaching wedding. The most important person for this mission, Barris, seemed angry as if being imposed upon by Evansing in regards to Tara. This seemed strange given his previous attitude of wanting to cooperate in any way with Evansing and its Irish quest.

In their quarters that evening, Edwin, Carson and several of the higher ranking officers accompanying them were discussing this most peculiar turn of events. It almost seemed to be like a mass hypnosis of some sort had happened in Aldred. And the weather to be so unseasonably cool didn't seem right.

"Maybe those ravens are more than ravens," stated Carson. "Is it possible for a whole kingdom to be bewitched?" he added.

"That is a good point, Carson," replied Edwin. "It does look like that is what has happened. I mean what else could so drastically alter the warm connections we had with these people a short while ago?"

"We will need to get a message out to Percival. In fact he should come here and check it out first hand. There has to be some major power working over this entire kingdom. There is no other explanation. Neither Barris nor the others wanted to talk to us until tomorrow. It appears Evansing unknowingly sorely offended Aldred. It reminds me of a husband whose wife expects him to know what he did wrong and he doesn't have a clue."

The next morning at the dining hall no one showed up except the Evansing contingent. The servers were barely civil let alone respectful to the Crown Prince of Evansing and his companions. Edwin recognized some of these servers as treating him with great deference when he was crowned here not so long ago.

The servers repeatedly told them, Barris and his family would come shortly, but after two hours they still were not there.

Edwin conferred with Carson and the other officers.

"What are your thoughts? Do we insist on meeting them? Do we return to our quarters and see if they will send for us?"

One of the officers ventured that they ask to be taken to the King and see what response they get. By this time though, there weren't any servers around. The situation had become very perplexing and annoying. Edwin struggled with keeping his cool. He had to convince himself this wasn't simply people being ignorant. There had to be some reason beyond the norm.

He started to get a very uncomfortable feeling about their presence in Aldred, when they heard the sound of marching feet. The next moment the hall filled with Aldred soldiers. The lead officer came to the Evansing contingent, a group of eight men, and announced to them they were to accompany him and his men. The man acted cool and professional like he had never met them before. Yet Edwin remembered this same officer coming up to him last time to congratulate him on his promotion to Crown Prince.

If they were to be led to the King it would not require a hall full of soldiers to facilitate the ceremonial function of doing so. Edwin thought to himself, "They must be arresting us."

Sure enough, they were taken to the Royal Prison, where they were disarmed and each placed in a separate cell.

Icy silence met Edwin's request to see the King.

"So what are the charges against us?"

"You are charged with spying and plotting against the Royal Family of Aldred," replied the lead officer.

"What is the basis of these charges?"

"You will be placed on trial starting tomorrow. All the evidence for those charges will be presented to you at that time."

The next day the cell door opened up and Edwin looked up to see a bailiff with six burly guards to escort him to the trial.

The King was the only Royal Family member present. He didn't sit as the judge, but Edwin noticed the judge kept looking at the King for direction.

Barris would not talk to Edwin.

The judge told him that due to the preponderance of evidence against him, it would be a waste of time for him to have a lawyer. However, he told Edwin he could present his own defense. "A defense against what? I haven't done anything requiring a defense," he replied to the court officer assigned to liaison with Edwin.

"What about the men with me?"

"They will suffer the same fate you will."

"You talk as though the outcome has already been determined. What is the fate you talk about?"

"Death, sir. What other outcome would you expect for spying and plotting against our beloved Royal Family?"

"If it has already been decided we are guilty, why are you putting us on trial? Why don't you just kill us and get it over with?"

"Sir, we are not barbarians without any sense of justice. We do not execute people until after due process of law."

The court bailiff announced, "Silence!" As the court was about to begin.

The judge spoke to Edwin, "The defendant is to stand up as the charges are read out and enter his plea."

Edwin arose, looking at the King as he did so. The King did not look his way.

The bailiff read out the charges, "Crown Prince Edwin of Evansing you are hereby charged with spying and plotting against the lives of our beloved Royal Family. How do you plea, guilty or not guilty?"

"Strongly not guilty."

"No added comments are permitted by the defendant," intervened the judge. "Guilty or not guilty?"

"Not guilty."

"Bring the first witness," called the judge.

An officer in the Aldred army came up to the stand and swore to tell the truth and nothing but the truth. Edwin noticed he didn't swear on a Bible, but rather on some eerie looking book with strange writing on the cover.

The officer shared how two days earlier he had uncovered letters from Edwin to conspirators in Aldred. These letters gave instructions to kill the Aldred Royal Family in preparation of a takeover of the Aldred government by Evansing. It also asked for information to be provided on Aldred troop numbers and movements in and around the Aldred capital.

As Edwin listened to this he could not believe what was happening. "This is so bizarre, even ridiculous," he said to himself. He even pinched himself to make sure he was awake. He had to be dreaming this. He could feel the pain of the pinch and nothing changed. It was really happening.

The next person said they had overheard Edwin discussing the takeover of Aldred with his officers as they rode to Aldred the day before. The man appeared to be a farmer and looked vaguely familiar to Edwin. "Yes, he remembered him now. He had scowled at them as they had gone by his field several miles from the Aldred capital."

What he noted listening to these people was that they both sounded so sincere. If they were deliberately lying then they were incomparable as liars. They appeared to truly believe what they were saying.

Three more persons followed to the stand giving additional evidence against Edwin and his Evansing companions.

The court then adjourned for lunch and a squad of four guards led Edwin back to his cell.

As Edwin munched on his dry piece of bread and sipped his stale water, he considered the situation. At this point no one back in Evansing would be even aware of what had happened. There had not yet been an opportunity to send a messenger to Percival. Maybe he got a dream that told him what had occurred. What would Erith do when he discovered what had happened? Oh, he missed Greer. I hope she doesn't worry.

"Joan where are you? I need a brilliant strategy. Where are you?"

Silence. Nothing happened.

"Hmmm, where is that woman when you need her? She said she would be available to help and now she is a no show."

"What is the source of all this nonsense?"

"Randarian Druids," popped into his head.

He recalled how they had liquidated almost all the known practicing Druids in Randar, except for a band of twenty or so who had fled to the eastern hills of that kingdom.

"They must have whipped up some exceptional means of trying to get revenge. Okay relax, Edwin, there's got to be a way out of this."

Just then he heard Carson in the cell next to him.

"Edwin, can you hear me?"

"Barely. What's up?"

"This morning I received a visit from the couple whose boy I saved. They were the same as I remembered them before. For some reason they have been unaffected. They told me how everybody turned strange yesterday in a matter of hours. They had great difficulty in getting permission to visit me. But they have great influence and given the nature of their indebtedness to me, they were able to visit me for ten minutes."

"Did they have any idea why they weren't impacted like everybody else?"

"They've considered that they are the only ones of very few, that they know of, who take the Eucharist every day. Now they are taking it two times per day and are considering taking it three times per day. They said they can feel a pressure on them to change, but it's like it's been held at bay. That is why they are increasing their intake, so as to increase the protection. They've also been encouraging other devout followers to increase their partaking of the Eucharist.

"So are they going to try and help us?"

"They've been trying to win a sympathetic ear, but they have to be careful because there have already been a couple of people voicing suspicions about their loyalty."

"I guess that means no."

"Not totally, but they have to pick their spots with the right people. One person with whom they have had some success is the Bishop. He of course takes the Eucharist daily as well. The Bishop has endeavored to talk to the King and other high level Royal Family members. To date he has had little success. They all meet him with icy stares and express veiled threats that he is not beyond suspicion for disloyalty to the King. He is not a particularly brave man so this has caused him to back off."

At this point the bailiff returned with the guards to take Edwin to the afternoon session of court.

The first person on the witness stand called everything a sham what Edwin had done in his relationship building with Kerris and Chandra. It had been a way of weaseling into the confidences of the Aldred Royal Family. He also referred to how Edwin had killed Barris' nephew in cold blood. "That expressed the true Edwin and his motives towards Aldred."

CHAPTER 35

At this point, Edwin is realizing everything is being accepted at face value as being true. He has had no opportunity to question the witnesses or express any sort of defense. When the witness finished, Edwin tried to get the attention of the judge to ask him a question. The judge at first ignored him, then acknowledged him and gave him permission to stand up and speak.

"Your Honor, may I please question this witness and also the previous witnesses, who gave testimony this morning?"

The judge looked at the King; at first the King said nothing, which created an awkward silence for the judge. The King looked like he would indicate no and then his expression changed and he nodded yes.

"That was interesting," Edwin thought to himself, "What caused him to change his mind?"

Unbeknownst to Edwin and the King himself, the courtroom had become a major battleground. The dark controlling spirits over Aldred were now facing some opposition. The increased intake of the Eucharist by the noble family, and others who have responded to their encouragement to do so, had shifted the spiritual environment. Even the weather showed a slight warming over the last few hours. When the King intended to say no, a large warrior angel pushed away one of the dark spirits oppressing the King. This released sufficient light for Barris to make a just decision.

As the critical mass of virtue in more and more people in Aldred grew, the angelic forces were growing in numbers and strength. Thus they were able to more and more overcome the persuasive ridiculousness, which passed for rational behavior.

The witness returned to the stand so he could be questioned by Edwin.

"Now, sir, you made a number of very bold statements about me and my motives with members of your Royal Family. You also said I killed the King's nephew in cold blood and that expressed the true reflection of my character and attitude towards Aldred. However, I did not hear or see any evidence to indicate support for your statements. Where is your evidence, sir?"

The man looked at Edwin dumbfounded and then at the judge. He even took a quick peek at the King. All he got in return were blank stares. Finally the man said it was self- explanatory given the nature of Edwin's character.

"What is the basis for you knowing about my character?"

"You obviously had no scruples when you killed a prince of the realm in cold blood."

"What facts do you have about that battle?"

"A reliable source told me you challenged the Prince and before his sword was even out of his scabbard you had run him through."

"Sir, who is your reliable source?"

"I am not at liberty to share that information."

"Would it be because there is no source other than your fertile imagination?"

The man turned red, "How dare you call me a liar."

"Sir, that is what you are. You are a liar. And you know it."

The man looked to the judge for support and got none. The previously interfering dark spirit on the judge was now held in a head lock by an angel of light. The judge was now free to be just.

The man sputtered at the judge, "Aren't you going to make him stop, your Honor?"

The judge replied, "Are you going to give evidence and not just your opinion? Do you have the name of the reliable source? Is that person available to testify in this court?"

The man, now red with confused embarrassment said, "No, I have nothing further to share, your Honor."

The judge then said something which convinced Edwin that the case had turned.

"All of that testimony is to be stricken from the record as it is inadmissible hearsay."

Addressing the judge, Edwin asked if he could continue with cross examining the previous witnesses beginning with the first one of the trial. The judge called up the officer who had shared about discovering incriminating letters from Edwin.

Edwin stepped up to the officer in the witness stand and asked, "Sir, you referred to letters from me to local conspirators. I noticed you neither presented the actual letters nor did you give the names of the local conspirators. Why is that?"

The officer appeared rather uneasy at first and then caught himself and replied, "We have them in our possession and my word to that effect is sufficient. The names of the conspirators are known to us and their disclosure is not necessary for the proof of your guilt."

"You may not require it for your purposes, but I and this court require it for our purposes. Do you or do you not have the letters in your possession?"

"I have them in my office."

"Your Honor, I respectfully request you require the officer to go to his office and retrieve those letters within the hour."

The judge ordered the officer to bring the letters to the courtroom within the hour. The dark spirit which had been controlling the judge now had two angels on him restraining him from interference. At the same time they were creating a bigger and bigger halo of invisible brilliant light over and around the judge.

The officer looked rather distressed but left the courtroom without a word.

Now came the turn of the farmer who had testified he had heard Edwin discussing the takeover of Aldred.

"Sir, can you explain how you were able to hear so precisely this conversation, which supposedly occurred within your earshot?"

"I heard some horses coming and I got down in the grass right beside the road. I was totally hidden from anyone on the road."

"Is that your normal practice when you hear horses on the road?"

"You can't be too careful nowadays. There are all kinds of thugs out there."

"Do you have a horse?"

"No, sir, I do not."

"Really? I must say you must be a wizard then. I should press charges that you are a practicing wizard."

The man's countenance got dark with rage, "How dare you accuse me of being a wizard. What is your basis for saying such a thing?"

"I distinctly remember you standing by the road scowling at me and my men as we rode by. To be able to do what you said you did would mean you would have to be supernaturally fast to meet us twice on the road."

"You must be mistaking me for someone else. I only saw you while hidden in the grass."

"It's interesting that we saw all kinds of people on the road, no one looking like they were afraid of us. It was the same when we were here a couple of months ago. Now you are saying you had a reason to be hiding in the grass. Perhaps you have something to hide from?"

The man started to unravel and look confused. He didn't know the lying spirit feeding him those lies now laid a crumpled heap in the corner of the courtroom. Three angels had kicked the crap out of that spirit. They were now releasing truth into the farmer. He started to become unglued and confessed.

"I lied. I never did hear Edwin say anything harmful. The officer sent to get the letters asked me to lie."

The judge ordered the man be arrested for perjury. Two guards took him away.

The stories of the other people also got exposed as a bunch of unsubstantiated lies.

The officer sent to get the letters never did come back. He was later arrested for perjury and for conspiracy to commit perjury through the farmer.

When the last bit of testimony had been refuted, the Kings' countenance totally changed. At that point the dark spirits on him had been hammered into submission and no longer could impact him.

The King came over to Edwin and apologized profusely for the reprehensible way that he and his men had been treated. He gave orders for all the Evansing men to be released at once. He also ordered a banquet be immediately put together for their Evansing guests. With the King now being free, the remaining dark powers over Aldred were broken and rapidly dissipated.

Edwin, Barris, Kerris, Chandra and Carson spent the evening reestablishing relationships. All the Aldred royals were sorry for their behavior and had no explanation as to their actions. It had seemed so reasonable and now it seemed to border on lunacy. Whatever had possessed them?

The Evansing party was of course very gracious. Edwin and Carson would sometimes give each other knowing looks when another Aldred royal or noble would express amazement as to their behavior.

The next day they were able to address the purpose for their visit.

Edwin began, "Barris, we need your help with King Clarendon of Tara. We can't get anywhere with him. He totally ignores us. Since you still have fairly friendly relations with him we would like you to use whatever influence you have with him to create a bridge for Evansing with Tara. While we are able and willing to use military solutions, we prefer a peaceful resolution with Tara. Perhaps one course of action is for you to invite him to Aldred. Erith could come here as well and together they could meet with you as mediator. Would that be something you would be willing to do?"

Barris considered what had been said and then after a moment he responded, "It is true we are on friendly terms. But we have had our disagreements over the past few years and it has been awhile since we have exchanged correspondence, let alone seen each other. It's been almost a year since I saw Clarendon. I will invite him to come and dialogue about some matters which have been festering for some time. I will mention to him Erith's desire to meet him with my role as mediator. If he says yes, great, if he says no, well I tried."

"Yes, that is all we can ask," replied Edwin.

The next day the Evansing crew returned home. Due to the unexpected events they were a few days longer than originally anticipated.

In eight days time the word came from Aldred that Clarendon of Tara had accepted and would be arriving in Aldred in fourteen days. The first two days of his visit would be with Barris. He consented to meet with Erith on the third day and a willingness to spend an extra day if necessary. He also indicated he would bring his fourteen year old daughter Kendy, to connect with seventeen year old Chandra.

With the news about Kendy the thought came that this could be an appropriate time to pull out one of Evansing's secret weapons, Greer. She could connect with both and be like a big sister in relating to Kendy. The Evansing party would arrive the day after Tara arrived. They would discretely stay out of sight until the third day of Clarendon's visit when his talks with Erith would begin. The only exception would be Greer. She would start engaging Kendy and Chandra right away. Erith asked Edwin to discuss it with Greer and see if she would be okay about doing it.

"Sire, knowing Greer she will love the opportunity to travel and visit."

Later that day Edwin asked Greer about an assignment in Aldred.

"You know, Edwin, I like the idea of traveling and it will be fun to see Chandra again. There is one thing I have to work out though. How do I feel about trying to befriend Kendy because it is politically expedient to do so?"

Edwin rolled his eyes.

"What do you mean, Greer? Of course you are going to try and befriend Kendy because it is politically expedient to do so. You wouldn't have any reason to get to know her if she wasn't Clarendon's daughter."

"Yes, I know that, but it seems so crass of me to want to get to know somebody just because they're somebody's daughter."

"You are the daughter of a king, which means part of your role in life is to get to know daughters of other kings."

"You know sometimes I would like to just be a young woman called Greer, without the never ending expectation on me that comes with being a princess."

"The reality is you would like that for about twenty minutes and then you would be real glad you are a princess. Look around the next time you are outside the castle. It is a rough world out there. Most women would love to exchange places with you."

"Yes, I suppose you are right, but I can still express my frustration about those parts of being princess that aren't always so wonderful. I know

I have duties which go with the privileges. Usually I like the duties too. I guess I am being a bit philosophical about the moral rightness of befriending someone for personal or Evansing advantage."

"Yes, Greer, I acknowledge your pain about not being perfect in every motivation. However, in the real world we all make choices based on personal advantage. There is always an advantage or value accruing to us in a relationship or we wouldn't be in it. Likewise unless we bring someone a benefit or some value, they will quickly look elsewhere."

Greer looked at Edwin and smiled.

"You know of course you just broke every guideline for how a man is to respond to a lady in this situation. When she is sharing things, which are troubling her, you are supposed to listen and commiserate with her. Instead you were giving me reasons why my thoughts were invalid."

"Yes, I know, Greer, and I told myself what I was doing was not very smart. But I couldn't help myself. I got all those great responses and I didn't want them to go to waste."

"Actually it's alright, Edwin. I kinda liked your witty repartee. I know I am supposed to be in my princess mode, but it's nice sometimes to consider other alternatives. Believe me I know I am blessed. Being a princess is the life for me. I will do my duty and befriend Kendy. It will be interesting to connect with someone new, especially since she is the daughter of someone who we aren't friends with. It will make for an interesting challenge. I will try to be as genuine with her as possible."

The time came to leave for Aldred and meet Clarendon and his daughter. Erith felt excited about the prospect of meeting with Clarendon. It would be hard, but this meeting represented a tremendous opportunity to advance the Irish Quest. It represented an opportunity to exercise diplomacy which could win an important ally or at least partially defuse their opposition.

Erith and Edwin decided to stay at a secure place just outside of the Aldred capital, to do a couple of days of deer hunting. They were joined by Kerris. Greer continued on to Aldred castle to meet Kendy and Chandra.

The two days of hunting with Erith gave Edwin an opportunity to connect with his father-in-law in a fun and enjoyable activity. It permitted him to see Erith more as a regular guy instead of primarily as the King.

Greer on the other hand was challenged in connecting with Kendy. It seemed as though Kendy had been briefed to dislike Greer and not trust her.

This led to rebuffs and rudeness, which Greer would normally never experience from another human. The only ones, who could get away with this, would be another royal on equal or higher terms. Chandra, distressed by what was happening, tried to resolve the impasse. Greer responded with good humor as she recognized it wasn't about her or Kendy. It was about Evansing and Tara. To ease the pressure, she chose to spend the morning of her second day with her two ladies in waiting. They enjoyed themselves walking around the castle grounds. Greer quite liked her ladies. They were more like friends with whom she shared all kinds of secrets, and they in turn shared secrets with her. Greer spent more time with them than anybody else.

She would resume her attempts with Kendy at noon for lunch with the two princesses.

She and her two ladies were walking to the place for lunch. They were engaged in laughing and enjoying their banter with one another. They were all about the same age, just being young women enjoying one another's company. Greer allowed her ladies to be quite familiar with her when they were alone. If she had known they were being observed, she would have toned down their interactions to a more regal level.

Consequently, she was observed being very real by two men who came from their blind side. When she and her ladies realized they were not alone, they all shifted to princess and her ladies mode going for a proper royal walk. The one man who looked to be the senior of the two smiled at the sudden about face he had just witnessed. Greer thought herself it probably looked ridiculous, but she decided to pretend nothing out of the ordinary had happened.

The man who smiled, greeted Greer, "Good day, my lady, may I have the pleasure of your name."

"I am Princess Greer of Evansing."

"I thought perhaps you were. You are certainly a perky young lady."

"Perky, what insolence to call me perky," thought Greer, but said nothing.

"My associate and I were enjoying the sight of you young ladies enjoying the day together. I must say you are very relaxed with your ladies in waiting."

"Sir, I did not know we were being observed or else we would have been less relaxed. You have me at disadvantage for I do not know who I am talking to."

"I am Clarendon and I think you are a remarkably refreshing princess."

Greer and her ladies each curtsied and bowed low, "Pleasure to meet you, Sire," Greer said politely.

Greer was intrigued. Here stood the man who was the object of this trip and he actually liked her being free and easy with her ladies.

"Interesting," she thought to herself, "he seems to be rather informal himself."

"Sire, I am on my way to lunch with your daughter and Princess Chandra."

"Yes, I know and I'll bet you are not all that keen to meet Kendy again."

Greer was shocked at his frankness. Uncharacteristically, she did not know what to say.

Should she lie and say something polite like, "Oh of course I look forward to seeing your daughter again."

Before she could respond, Clarendon continued, "I told her to not to trust you and to be indifferent to your advances to her."

This amazed Greer. Clarendon was certainly different. He was being straight up with her. She liked him. To her, he too was refreshing.

"Yes, I figured as much. I knew it wasn't her and I, it was Tara and Evansing."

"May we accompany you? I would like to talk to my daughter a moment."

"It would be our pleasure."

On the ten minute walk, Clarendon and Greer enjoyed chit chatting about very ordinary things. There developed a special link between the two. They genuinely enjoyed interacting with one another. They both had qualities the other appreciated and enjoyed.

When they arrived together, so amiable with one another, the look of surprise on Kendy's face was starkly apparent. Conversely, the look on Chandra's face expressed obvious pleasure at seeing such warmth between the two.

Clarendon asked to speak with his daughter and took her away outside of the room for several minutes.

"Kendy darling, I have a new set of instructions for you regarding Greer. I have observed her in somewhat candid moments and have enjoyed her company. She in my opinion is someone you can trust. Be as friendly with her as you choose. I told her I had instructed you to be cool toward her."

This surprised and delighted Kendy at the same time.

"Father, this command gives me much more pleasure than the other one. For I could tell she was a fine and noble woman. It pained me to treat her with such indifference and disdain."

When Kendy returned she greeted Greer with a warm hug and kiss and apologized for her previous behavior. In no time the three were talking about all manner of things, and the past differences were gone as though they never happened.

The day came for Erith and Clarendon to meet. Their initial meeting felt a little awkward given the history between the two kingdoms. However, they both put their best foot forward and were civil in their opening exchanges. Then something most remarkable happened. As if Clarendon had remembered something, he completely changed from being cool and reserved to warm and ebullient.

"Erith, I have met your daughter and I am much impressed. I figure if you can have a daughter with as much class and character as she has, then you must have some qualities I can trust. My daughter, Kendy, has been much delighted in her time with Greer."

"Well, thank you, Clarendon, I must say she pleases me very much. She shared how you had come upon her unaware with her ladies and how it all turned out so well. She has also come to quite appreciate Kendy, and she's enjoying the role of being like a big sister to her."

"Kendy could use more of a big sister influence in her life. Since she is the oldest girl in our family, she has to be the big sister, but I feel sometimes she's not really up to it."

"I am confident Greer can help with that. Clarendon, I know our mission sent to kidnap your son was ill conceived and we were wrong. Would you forgive me for carrying out such an attempt?"

"Just like that, Erith, you want me to forgive you? I appreciate you are a man of great passion. However, I am not sure your idea of Irish unity is necessarily the best course of action."

"What are your concerns about Irish unity, Clarendon?"

"The nature of the Irish people is such that they are too fractious to ever be able to function as one united body of people. I believe the best you can hope to accomplish is to develop some level of cooperation with respect to trade. Other than for financial purposes why would the kingdoms scattered through Ireland want to come under a common government?"

"I'm glad you asked that question, Clarendon. I agree with you financial advantages are important. A fundamental aspect of our push for unity is to facilitate trade across Ireland. This will eliminate all the various tariffs and hindrances to free movement of goods and people. The net result will be ultimately greater prosperity for all."

Erith continued, "While at least some fiscal advantage is attainable without full unity, it is not enough. The Irish people are heart people. They don't just live for commercial advantage. Something magical will happen across this island when we have one common leader, government and purpose. The people of Ireland can and will set aside their present differences. When they do, they will all draw from one another the capacity to fulfill their destiny. Each individual will have a new level of mystical force at work in their life to possess their birthright. In turn the entire nation will possess its birthright and attain the greatness intended for Ireland. Even with a common central government, there will still be the individual kingdoms to govern the regional issues. That is the most sensible way to manage local and regional matters."

Clarendon asked, "How would life change initially if we decided to work with you?"

"Tariffs and all barriers to trade would be eliminated immediately across the board. The only exceptions would be where there are special considerations and certain sectors needing protection for a period of time.

Also you would contribute forces and supplies to the furtherance of Irish unity. Evansing will provide the central government, which regulates Irish national affairs and anything crossing kingdom boundaries. You will continue to govern your local matters unhindered by the central government unless they infringe on another kingdom. There will be consultation between us and the individual kingdoms to sort out the mechanics of administration and disputes. I am not going to run a dictatorship, but neither am I going to allow kingdoms to do as they please in national matters."

"Let me mull that over a bit. I am assuming you are also interested in knowing about your men we captured?"

"Yes, we certainly are."

"There are two members who are still alive. What will you give me for them, besides the apology?"

"We'll give you ten horses apiece from my personal herd. There are about a hundred or so to choose from except for ten or eleven, which I will set aside as unavailable. If you don't find twenty acceptable, then you can examine our army horses as well."

"Twenty horses are a reasonable payment subject to our acceptance of the horses. I will have two of my horsemen go to Evansing and receive payment. To show I trust you, they will bring the two prisoners with them."

"Good, then it's a deal," responded Erith.

"As far as your request for forgiveness, I agree to forgive you. It is surprising to me how amenable I am to come to terms with you. I don't understand it, but it feels like the right thing to do."

Due to the increased level of virtue in Aldred, which started a few weeks earlier, there existed a strong atmosphere for forgiveness and harmony.

The two kings were to meet again the next day to discuss further the potential for cooperation. Clarendon had given the Irish unity question serious thought and something started to stir up inside of him. It intrigued him to consider building a legacy bigger than simply preserving his family's role as rulers of Tara. He started to appreciate the greatness, which would accrue to all the Irish peoples.

Greer arrived with her father to present an invitation to Clarendon.

"Sire, I would be delighted in hosting Kendy for a fortnight, even to take her to Evansing when we return tomorrow."

Clarendon looked at Greer for a moment without saying anything.

Then he responded, "Young lady, you are charging ahead very quickly. I am not sure that yet would be appropriate. However, I am not saying it is out of the question. Let me consider it further. In the meantime I thank you for your offer."

"You're welcome, Sire," and then Greer excused herself and left.

"Erith, did you put her up to that so as to curry favor with me?"

"No, Clarendon, I did not. She came up with the idea herself."

"Interesting girl," replied Clarendon.

"Yes, she is my pride and joy."

"I must admit I would like some of what is on Greer to rub off on to Kendy. Perhaps for that reason it would be good to have them visit together."

"I will decide later, for now I would like to discuss further what specifics will have to be worked out for Tara to form an alliance with Evansing."

Erith was delighted at what he heard. The two kings spent the rest of the day working out details of their alliance. They also sharpened their understanding of what their vision of Irish unity would look like.

The three kings, that night celebrated the successful conclusion of their series of meetings. It was a rare moment for Clarendon. He had a history of being rather recalcitrant in relationships with other kings. Now he acted all agreeable. Something had shifted in him.

At the celebration dinner, Kendy came to Greer, looking very excited.

"My father says I may come with you to Evansing. He asked me if I wanted to come and I said yes, very much. Thank you so much for inviting me. What a change from how we first started our relationship."

Greer replied, "That's wonderful! We will force Edwin to listen to all kinds of girl talk, right Edwin?"

Edwin smiled saying nothing. He enjoyed Greer being Greer.

The next morning the two visiting kings returned home. Kendy traveled to Evansing with Greer.

After the fortnight of visiting with Greer, Kendy returned home escorted by a troop of Tara and Evansing soldiers. It represented a tangible symbol of the two kingdoms starting to work together.

A week after Kendy returned home, Greer received a message from Clarendon. He profusely thanked her for her time spent with his daughter. She had had a fabulous time and couldn't stop raving about how much she enjoyed Greer. More importantly to him, he noticed in Kendy a new level of maturity and well-being. She now played a positive role of big sister with her younger siblings.

Erith felt pleased with the warmth of the message from Clarendon. As he considered it he seemed to get an uncomfortable feeling.

"What was that all about?"

CHAPTER 36

The Games had resulted in a thawing out of relations with the Kingdom of Dagarath. The beginning of a friendship by Edwin and Greer with Prince Evo and his wife Tamara was a major basis for this. The relations with Evo's father, King Nelwyn were a bit on the murky side. While Erith's relating with Nelwyn seemed to be better than before, it was hard to tell. King Nelwyn always gave the appearance of playing his cards close to his vest. Therefore the decision to release him was not without risk. Erith decided Edwin and an Evansing troop would escort Nelwyn to Dagarath's border. At that point Dagarath soldiers would take over. Upon hearing of this decision, Evo issued an invitation to Edwin to come to Dagarath to continue the relationship building. The King of Dagarath gave his approval without any expression of enthusiasm, but he did give it.

They travelled to Dagarath without incident. However, Edwin thought he could sense a shift in the atmosphere from what existed in Evansing.

"Oh well, hopefully we are not going to have another Aldred experience," he said to himself. He hadn't seen any flocks of flying ravens. Of course the dark side had a host of ways of operating.

As they got closer and closer to the Dagarath capital the air got thicker and thicker. Not that you could tell from natural perceptions. This was Edwin's inner knowing acting up, which indicated something was percolating. When they were in sight of Dagarath castle they could see black billowing smoke. As they got closer they could hear the sounds of battle behind the walls and even see fighting going on the top of the walls and battlements.

The soldiers who were accompanying Edwin and Nelwyn did not seem concerned. This certainly was odd. When Nelwyn asked if they knew what was going on they told him it was nothing to be concerned about. Given the stark contrast between what he saw and their response this created concern for Nelwyn. When he started to get more insistent as to an explanation one of the soldiers pulled his sword and killed Nelwyn by a thrust through his heart. The soldiers drew their swords and surrounded Edwin. He surrendered his weapons. They informed him he would be unharmed as long as he didn't try to escape.

"Well here we go again. Although it is a different spin from what I've experienced before," thought Edwin.

When they arrived at Dagarath castle it was apparent fierce fighting had occurred. The General of the Army had decided to usurp the throne. He was popular with his men and had garnered wide support. He decided the return of Nelwyn was the time to strike so he could eliminate all members of the Royal Family. This is indeed what happened. The troops loyal to the throne were outnumbered two to one. Their ability to resist the rebels was broken and they were totally crushed. No quarter asked and none given. All the troops who were loyal were killed.

Edwin regretted the news of Evo and Tamara's death. They were a pleasant couple and he had looked forward to visiting with them. Who was this General Haydek? It was an unusual name for a Celt. His requests for information about Haydek were met by stony silence.

As they brought Edwin into the courtyard, the smoke started to die down and fighting had all but ceased. There under a canopy sat the newly self-proclaimed King.

"Crown Prince Edwin, what a pleasure. I apologize for not being able to better greet you in a way you are accustomed to, but Dagarath is in a state of transition."

"Sire, I respectfully ask you release me to return to Evansing immediately."

"That is not yet possible. I must first consider the strategic alternatives of what to do with you. After all, releasing you is just one of those options.

In the meantime you will experience a special suite we have available for high ranking guests."

They led Edwin to a corner of the castle near the dungeon. They opened the heavy iron door and motioned Edwin to go inside. For some reason Dagarath chose to coddle its higher ranking prisoners with a spacious two room suite. It was sparsely furnished and had bars on the window.

"This imprisonment thing is starting to bug me," he laughed. "Oh well I guess it comes with the territory. Somehow it will work out."

The next day the cell door opened and in walked Haydek.

"I hope you slept well, Edwin. You know you provide for us an interesting dilemma. I could release you right now, but I don't think there is a lot of advantage in doing so. My previous experience with Evansing has not been very positive. In fact my parents were both slaughtered in a village in the southern part of Evansing. I understand recently Erith has made some attempt at amends for that atrocity. However, it's not enough for me. I am of the suasion of blood for blood. You provide me with an opportunity for revenge; therefore I am going to take it. A major blow can be struck against the heart of Erith. In three days you are going to be burned at the stake. We could burn you tomorrow, but anticipation of something adds to the spice of life, don't you think Edwin? Therefore I decided waiting a couple of extra days would add to the experience. Enjoy the rest of your day."

"Hmm," thought Edwin, "this is different than anything I've been in before. First, stay relaxed. What do we do now? Oh, Joan, I could use a great strategy right now. Where are you?" Nothing happened. He waited an hour. Nothing happened.

Then he thought of the angel Percival had summoned. "Prospero are you available to help? I could use a little help." Silence. He waited awhile more. Still nothing.

"Okay, let's see what else can we consider?"

He checked the two room suite for any possible weakness in its design which would allow for an escape. He couldn't find anything that looked like a promising possibility. Three days were a very short time to be able to create some sort of escape route from a well secured cell.

The three days went by slowly and quickly all at the same time.

The morning of the third day arrived. A part of Edwin resigned to a cruel death. Another part was convinced an intervention was forthcoming.

Surprisingly, a priest was assigned by Haydek to hear Edwin's confession. Not being a regular church going kind of person, Edwin didn't feel comfortable with the confession process. He decided he would confess whatever came to mind and trust it would be adequate for his eternal soul.

Several guards came to the cell and led Edwin away. It all seemed surrealistic to him as they walked to the square. There he saw the post, surrounded by firewood piled high for a great bonfire. The square filled with the citizenry out for a day's entertainment at Edwin's expense. The executioner led him up the firewood to the post. There he secured him with rope. He picked up an already lit torch and looked in the direction of Haydek for the final go ahead.

Haydek nodded his head indicating to proceed.

The executioner lit the outer edge of the firewood. The dry wood caught fire and the flames started to advance toward Edwin.

CHAPTER 37

A t that instant through a portal leading from the fifteenth century into the eleventh century, Joan of Arc came on horseback with three hundred of her men. She raced straight to where Edwin was and cut him free and helped him get on her horse. In the meantime they were surrounded by Joan's troops accompanying her. The Dagarath troops and general citizenry were stunned into immobilization. From their perspective three hundred foreign troops on horseback had materialized out of thin air. There was no thought to try and battle them for how could they battle people, if indeed they were people, which appeared by such supernormal means.

Joan, Edwin and her soldiers then turned around and disappeared back through the portal to the fifteenth century. Now Edwin arrived in France some four hundred years in the future. Joan told him why. "We can move from a portal in fifteenth century France directly to your time and place in Evansing. Thus this way is much quicker to get you back home than if we were to ride you from Dagarath to Evansing. We will have to wait a few minutes to let our metabolisms adjust to the time travel."

Edwin's head is swimming. He had just been rescued from being burned to death as the flames were starting to lick at his legs. Then a moment later he was transported four hundred years into the future over to the European continent.

"What do all these soldiers think about what happened?"

"They are special forces who I can trust to go on these kinds of missions. Each one of them has a high level spiritual awareness and sensitivity."

"How come you haven't been responding to me lately when I've been asking you for help?"

"Are you healthy and well?" asked Joan.

"Yeess," Edwin replied slowly with a trace of irritation in his voice, "I am healthy and well, thanks for asking. Would you please answer my question?"

"I just did, Edwin. It would appear since you are healthy and well you didn't need my help before."

Edwin started to laugh. "Well I guess since you put it that way you're probably right. I must say though when I asked for your help I certainly thought I needed your help."

"Yes, I'm sure you did. You were just wrong in how the deliverance would come. You always got the required help. It didn't necessarily require my help."

"So why the last minute heroics today? Did you really need to wait until I felt the heat of the flames?"

"Yes, didn't it make for much more of an exciting rescue experience? Think how it will sound when you share it with the people back home?"

"There are only a few people with whom I can share what truly happened. It was not your typical rescue experience. Mind you there were thousands of witnesses to what happened in Dagarath. That is sure to get around. By the way would you be willing to reveal yourself to Greer?"

"I'm not sure. It's not entirely up to me to decide such things. It would probably be okay, but I'm only a part of your life for those very essential times."

"Well I hope it doesn't have to always entail such extreme experiences like today. Do you know already all the times I will need your help?"

"No, I am not given that knowledge in advance. I do hear your requests and I do have the right to say yes or no, but I don't know the how and the when. All of a sudden there I am charging through the portal getting my instructions as I'm going."

"Okay so your interventions are not solely dependent on you choosing to respond. You are getting your instructions from elsewhere."

"Yes, that is correct. The Divine Source gives me the orders and empowerment to do what has to be done. After all I can't go on my own to Ireland four hundred years ago."

"Yes, that is true. Please see if you can introduce yourself to Greer in an other than emergency situation."

"By the way, what happens with the people from your time and place when you disappear?"

"That is a mystery. Somehow even though it may seem we are gone a long time, it's only an instant in my time. So no one notices and it doesn't interfere with my present life."

"I can take you back now. Hop on my horse and we will go."

FLASH! BANG! There they were back in Evansing, right outside the castle walls behind some trees.

"See ya later, Joan." She disappeared without so much as a good-bye.

"Interesting lady."

When Edwin walked through the gates it caused a great commotion. Evansing had heard the news he would be executed this very morning an hour earlier. Everyone thought him already dead. Dagarath Castle was a two day ride away. Yet all of a sudden he's appearing in Evansing. People thought he was a ghost. They looked at him with fear. He said he had Divine Intervention and here he was.

Greer's eyes were swollen with tears from mourning her husband's death. When he entered their suite she at first thought it must be his ghost and he had come to say good-bye. Then he took her in his arms and held her tight. He assured her he was very much alive and told her what had happened. She kept holding him and looking in his eyes, until she was convinced he was really flesh and bone and right there with her.

"We had heard yesterday you were to die early this morning. To see you now is enough to give a person quite a start."

Erith, Edwin, Percival and the Evansing War Council met to consider what their response would be with Dagarath. It was quite unexpected given their previous hopes of building on the relationship with Prince Evo. Now it was all for naught. They originally had planned to invade Merethath. Now it would be more pressing to attack Dagarath.

CHAPTER 38

This impending invasion created an opportunity to bring together a couple of new allies. Erith would ask Aldred and Tara to supply troops and be part of the new Irish War Council. It would be important to quickly arrange a meeting of the Council. Erith had sent a messenger to King Clarendon of Tara to see if he would host the inaugural meeting of the new Council.

Other messengers were also sent out to Nerland and Aldred to give them heads up as to a prompt invasion. They were asked for their feedback as to what and when they could provide for the war effort. The invasion would count heavily on the new allies' resources, as Evansing and Nerland still had a substantial troop presence in Randar. The pacification of that kingdom had gone well. There were still some pockets of resistance, but the responsibility for their crushing had been turned over to the Randar regular army. The expectation was all allied troops would be out of Randar within a month.

The crises with Dagarath dictated a rapid response. This was required before the usurper, Haydek, could more firmly entrench his control. He had crushed the loyal army members. But there were outlying districts where the citizenry did not want the new ruler. This opposition would keep Haydek distracted and at least a bit off balance in his ability to defend against a united force.

Several days after sending the message to Tara, a response was received. The King of Tara indicated no interest in either hosting or in participating in any invasion. Not even to send supplies. What happened to Clarendon's previously expressed enthusiasm? Erith had no idea and now lacked the time to discuss it with him. The other two kingdoms said yes. A quick rescheduling had to be arranged. The inaugural meeting of the Irish War Council would now be held in Aldred. At least Aldred was fully on board. Three days later the three kings met in Aldred. Each of the kingdoms' armies were mobilized and massed along the border with Dagarath. Aldred's army had crossed over into Evansing in order to access Dagarath. It had originally expected to be able to march through Tara, but permission had been refused for them to do so. They had no concern about the element of surprise, for Haydek undoubtedly knew a response would come. Had he made a deal with Tara? For now there was no sign of Tara's troops being mobilized against the alliance.

Keltic, uncharacteristically, seemed a little recalcitrant to throw as many soldiers into it as Erith hoped for. The King of Nerland felt his commitment in the Randar conflict had been substantial. Now to again contribute a large force would create too much of a drain on his kingdom's resources. This created a new challenge for Erith as to how this alliance would work. His vision included everyone providing as required and requested. He wanted to avoid taking on the role of a demanding dictator. To be successful the Irish Quest required a strong central leadership. However, Erith needed to balance that with offsetting the individual kingdoms natural aversion to having him lord it over them. This required him having sensitivity as to when to use a firmer approach and when to use a more relaxed approach. So when Keltic raised these concerns, Erith encouraged him to share his concerns and frustrations. It came out he felt Nerland had contributed the lion's share of the forces in Randar. They had sustained significant losses in relation to Evansing. At first Erith had been geared to figure out ways of pooh poohing Keltic's reasoning, but as he listened he realized the King of Nerland had a point. To ensure a feeling of equanimity among the Kings, Erith agreed to cut back his request of Nerland by twenty per cent and increased Evansing's share. Also he asked if Aldred would increase their contribution. King Barris of Aldred said yes, he was willing. Twenty four hours later the Kings had worked out a war strategy they could all agree on. The invasion would commence in three days.

The night before the invasion, Edwin was writing his thoughts to Greer.

My dearest, loveliest Greer,

I am sitting on a log around the campfire. The men are as usual rather quiet before we go into battle tomorrow. There is the normal appreciation of the fact some of them will die and some of their comrades will die. I am expecting us to be overwhelmingly victorious. I figure since I already died a little while ago and narrowly escaped it again less than two weeks ago, I shouldn't be due for awhile. Therefore I go into this battle with an expectancy of personal success and protection. I have a deep inner knowing I will not expire before I have completed my purpose here in this life.

I love you so much my heart aches for you.

Stay in rest.

Always yours,

(signed) Edwin

That night, Edwin went to sleep as a man who knew he had a purpose for being here. He knew he had attracted Divine Interest in his life. This attraction was there for a reason.

The next morning the troops and their warhorses were up early and impatient to go to battle. This is what they trained for and their present reason for being. The point of crossing was flat and unguarded. That part of Dagarath was known to be fiercely supportive of the usurper, Haydek.

Like their entry into Randar there arose a large hill upon which sat the opposing army. This hill stood somewhat larger, width and length wise than the one in Randar. Also the terrain on the other side could be used to effectively harass the Evansing troops from a position of protection. In addition, a settlement of almost three thousand citizens sat on top of the hill. The Dagarath army there had been estimated to represent approximately twenty-five per cent of their total army. Thus for the reasons mentioned they could not simply skirt around it. Edwin and his fellow commanders of course hated the idea of fighting an uphill battle. Scouts were sent to check out the lay of the land, and see where would be the easiest place to focus the attack.

Over five hours later the first scouts returned. It would be another two hours or so before they all returned. After assimilating all the information provided by them, there seemed to be one particular route which would afford the most protection while minimizing the upward climb. It was almost two miles southeast of their present location. A ridge ran along just above the route. This ridge was almost two-thirds way up the hill. It represented both an advantage and a disadvantage. Until Evansing advanced up far enough so their arrows could reach the enemy troops, this route would be initially tougher. This was due to the protection the Dagarath troops received from the ridge. However, once the Dagarath troops were eliminated, the easier incline and the protection provided by the ridge made it preferable to other alternative routes. The uphill climb made it advisable to hold off on using horses until at least they had taken that ridge.

The Evansing army camped at the bottom of the hill. At night the main army would move to the part of the hill below the ridge. There would be campfires maintained at the original site, to give the illusion the army had not moved. A game plan had been formulated. The officers decided speed would be essential. The swiftest, fittest warriors would be sent first. They would move as quickly as possible without being loud. Then when the Dagarath sentries were aware of their presence, they would start to run up the hill to capture the ridge. The warriors had small shields to provide some protection against arrows, but otherwise they were exposed. Therefore moving under the cover of darkness provided much additional coverage.

Edwin would lead the initial wave. He felt invincible and not because he was a young man soon to be twenty-one. He had this inner conviction nothing could touch him.

Edwin gave the signal and his men started up the hill with him. It would be two hours before daylight. The men had ascended about a third of the way and still had no indication of being sighted or heard. As they got close to half way they could hear shouts of alarm coming from above. The Evansing men started to run as fast as the topography allowed. Soon arrows started flying down. Men were groaning in pain and death as volley after volley of arrows were unleashed. Fortunately the night provided protection but with many men in close quarters, it was inevitable there would be numerous casualties. The entire army now ascended up the hill. Even as the numbers of wounded and dead mounted they were unstoppable. They knew they were victorious. Edwin continued to shout encouragement and lead the charge. All the men in the front lines were also archers as well as swordsmen. As they got to about half way they started to unleash their own showers of arrows. They would stop for a moment and from a crouching position release two shots. Then they would run up another twenty or so yards and release another two shots and so on up the hill. As they progressed they could tell more and more of their arrows must have hit the mark. For the arrows coming down the hill were becoming fewer and fewer. When they were within fifty yards of the ridge, some of the Dagarath defenders were starting to come down with their swords and axes.

They had the advantage of momentum from coming down hill. They also had the disadvantage of being susceptible to being skewered. The Evansing men were bracing themselves for attack with their swords and javelins extended. This would be a grisly affair. As the light broke out it appeared the attackers had taken moderate casualties. But not as great as what would normally be expected. The juggernaut from Evansing continued its relentless upward ascent. At the ridge itself the bulk of the Dagarath army took its stand. It made the most of their physical advantage. Their biggest exposure was to the ongoing release of arrows from the Evansing archers.

Edwin found himself in a sword fight with two defenders. A parry here and a thrust there with a backhand slash, which caught one defender in the face. Now he had one to contend with. Edwin continued his upward progress while attacking the defender. He took his opponent's sword to his left and made a thrust, but the enemy soldier shifted out of the way and responded with a slash to his left side. Edwin got his sword up in time to deflect the blow. All around them the sound of battle rang out as the two armies were increasingly being fully engaged. Edwin backed up a bit which caught his opponent off guard as he had been thrusting towards Edwin. Consequently he fell forward and lost his balance. Edwin took advantage and ran his sword through the Dagarathian's throat.

Next, a man who stood at least a foot taller than Edwin came at him with an extra large battle-axe. Size wise the opponent had a decided advantage. But Edwin had been here before and he would not be intimidated. The man swung and grazed Edwin's mid-section causing Edwin to back up. He came right back at the enemy soldier with a slash at the man's exposed throat. The man moved quickly and brought his axe back to slash away Edwin's sword. The heavy weapon almost struck the sword out of Edwin's hand. The opposing soldier then followed up with a fierce run leading with his axe. Edwin deftly moved out of the way and stuck his foot out causing the Dagarathian soldier to fall. Edwin thrusted his sword between the shoulder blades of the enemy. The man swung his axe around at Edwin narrowly missing Edwin's ankle. Edwin withdrew his sword and at the same time his opponent stood up as though he hadn't even been wounded. Edwin couldn't believe the man was still alive. He must have just missed the man's heart. Edwin was a heart man, he normally never missed hearts.

"Need more practice he thought to himself." Now the soldier had a new sense of rage in his charge toward Edwin. This time Edwin ducked and thrust his sword into the man's stomach. But he still wouldn't go down. Edwin had to quickly draw out his sword to deflect another blow of the axe. They now had each other's arms wrapped around each other. Edwin managed to dig out his dagger and stabbed the man in the side. Likewise the soldier had out his dagger and flailed at Edwin. He narrowly missed catching Edwin's throat. Again Edwin dug his dagger deep, this time in his opponent's pancreas. The man struck at Edwin like a man possessed and threw Edwin off to the side. Immediately Edwin stood up and flung himself at the Dagarathian going for his jugular. He cut deep and the blood spurted all over. This finished the enemy off. By this time both were covered in blood. It would have been impossible to tell whose blood was whose, but fortunately none of it was Edwin's.

Right away another attacker arose to contend with. The man had a steely glint in his eye and flashed his sword. Edwin, still in the process of standing up, had to defend himself. He was now starting to get upset with being attacked. This time the vicious side of Edwin came out. He would make short work of this guy. The man looked very confident.

"Fool," Edwin thought to himself, "you are dead, but I'm going to play with you." As the Dagarathian came toward Edwin they thrusted, they parried, they deflected and then Edwin sliced the man's left arm off. That left him still with his sword arm. They thrusted, they parried, they deflected and then Edwin cut off his sword arm. Then Edwin cut his head off, picked it up and ran toward the Dagarath line. This startled and frightened a number of enemy soldiers who broke into retreat before the charging Edwin. He threw the head down and turned on an obliging enemy soldier and ran him through in his heart. Edwin started to warm up. The feel of blood excited him and pushed him to another level of adrenaline rush and superhuman strength. He picked up an opposing soldier's javelin and rushed two soldiers who were retreating. He struck the first one and ran over him as he continued after the second one. He threw it into the retreating soldier's back bringing him down. Now he looked around to see who else he could kill.

"Ah there is a likely candidate, looks like a lord. It would be good to kill a nobleman."

He confronted the man. The enemy raised his sword and brought it down against Edwin's sword.

"The guy has pretty good form," Edwin said to himself. Then he taunted him, "How does it feel that today you are going to die?"

The soldier replied, "You talk big for a little man."

Edwin laughed, "My sword does the talking, you are dead." The man took a run at Edwin. It caused the latter to have to back up a little. Then Edwin came right back slashing at the Dagarathian lord causing him to retreat several paces. He got up close and pulled out his dagger and started cutting his opponent's throat.

"Die! You Dog! Die!" For a good measure he also stabbed him in the heart. He took the lord's sword because it had a beautiful pearl handle and was a fine weapon.

"Too bad you weren't worthy of it," Edwin muttered to himself.

He continued onward and upward as did the rest of the Evansing army. The attack started to turn into a route. Dagarathians were being pursued and killed from behind. It appeared fear had been released into their ranks and all the fight had left them. Edwin thought of it like hunting for deer. A helpless prey, easy to kill. The Evansing onslaught came on like a wave to the top of the hill.

There sat the enemy commander on the top of his horse, an inviting target. Edwin asked an archer for his bow and an arrow. Aiming and pulling the arrow back he relished what was about to happen. He released the arrow and it hit its mark, catching the commander in his heart. The man died before he hit the ground. You may ask why he didn't take him captive. At this point Edwin had no interest in captives. He had one objective, kill as many of the enemy as possible. It had been decided before the invasion they were going to be harsh with the Dagarathians. Besides, they were all rebels against the previous king and justice was due.

Most of the Dagarathian army was in retreat. However, a fierce looking man with red hair and a bushy red beard stood his ground. When Edwin came to the top of the hill, this man attacked him. The man's sword came down hard on Edwin's upraised sword. Then he did a sort of swirl and came right back with a body slash. Edwin stepped back to avoid being struck.

"This man is a warrior," thought Edwin. Then he rushed the enemy with a ferocious set of swordplay. The opponent still carried a shield which gave him added protection. Edwin had long lost his and hadn't bothered to pick up another one. An almost reckless sense of invincibility permeated in around Edwin. He knew he couldn't lose. So once again he charged and deflected the defender's attempts until he found an opening and jumped forward to catch the man in his groin. The enemy howled in pain and went down, thus affording Edwin to finish him by slicing off his head. Edwin had become very adept at cutting off heads. He used to practice on cadavers on the battlefield after the combat ended. To cleanly cut off someone's head was an art form. It took a special snap of the wrists and you had to cut in the right place. Otherwise you would have a vicious slice with only a partially severed head, not nearly as satisfying.

Again Edwin picked up the head of a fallen foe. Once more it had a galvanizing effect on the enemy. It released fear into their midst causing more and more of them to lose heart and turn and run.

"This is fun," thought Edwin as he slashed at retreating soldiers. Sometimes he would cripple them with a well placed blow against their legs. To others he would deliver a back breaking blow against their spine. Edwin's energy levels continued to soar as the sweet taste of victory spurred him on. He realized as leader of the attack he needed to redirect his attention. He stopped his pursuit, but yelled encouragement to his soldiers to press the enemy.

"Take no prisoners." That was his credo.

As he surveyed his battle scene he could see the Dagarathian army had been decimated. The hill lay littered with their bodies. Unfortunately, Evansing had also taken substantial casualties. Edwin noticed the town in the distance. He started to gather several hundred men to approach to inspect it. If any resistance he would destroy it and its occupants. If not then he would leave it alone. As they approached the town, a crowd grew in the streets. A man who appeared to be the leader came walking boldly toward Edwin. He held a set of keys in his left hand.

"Interesting, what could this be all about?" thought Edwin.

As the man got closer he suddenly dropped to his knees and bowed his head before Edwin.

"Well, that is certainly an about face," thought Edwin. "Rise up, sir, and tell me your business."

"O Gracious One, we beg for our lives. There are no soldiers in the town. We give you the keys to our wealth," as he handed over the keys.

Edwin looked hard at him for a moment.

Then he replied, "Go in peace and take your keys," as he returned them. "Remember the grace you have been dealt. We do, however, make a request for any medical personnel you have. Plus we need bandages and other supplies for helping our wounded. As well we would appreciate food and drink."

"But of course we would be happy to supply you with whatever you require."

Edwin spent the evening and well into the night visiting with the wounded and dying. Even though he didn't concern himself with his personal safety, he did care about the welfare of those under him.

King Erith joined Edwin and the other officers in a meeting on top of the hill, right outside the town. The mood of course was jubilant as the enemy force on the hill had been vanquished. Most of the Dagarathian army on the hill had been killed, with an estimated 30% escaping down the hill and onto the plain heading west to join their compatriots. Reports had come to them indicating both Aldred's and Nerland's forces were advancing without encountering much in the way of resistance. There was, however, a large force of Dagarathian troops massing at a field ten miles east of the Dagarathian capital. This army was led by Haydek himself.

CHAPTER 39

Couriers had been sent out advising the Aldred and Nerland armies to cease their advance and await orders. Both were some ten miles west of Evansing's army and only eight or nine miles from Haydek's forces. The leading officers of both armies were coming to meet with the Evansing leaders to develop battle strategy necessary to crush Haydek.

Erith's officers briefed him about the casualties and though dismayed at the degree of their losses knew they could have been greater. He had expected them to be at least 25% higher. He had considered the great disadvantage afforded them in having to go uphill. Erith enquired why things turned out as well as they did. Several officers offered the following observation: Troops had been noted as commenting how they had been inspired to dig deeper and fight more fiercely as a result of seeing Edwin charge up the hill. They had seen him battle with such wild abandon and a seeming lack of concern for personal safety. This drove them to another level of courage and boldness.

Erith turned to Edwin with a big smile and said, "Well done, Edwin! It would appear you have demonstrated a warrior capacity above and beyond what we have seen in you before. What do you have to say for yourself?"

"Thank you, Sire, and to the rest of you for your kind comments. Something about this battle got me into a place where I considered myself invincible. It's like I could do anything and it would work out. I could take on the most overwhelming odds and still come out on top. Not to say I would run headlong into overwhelming forces just for the sake of being reckless. I would do a quick calculation of risks and weighing of the strategic importance of whatever maneuvers I engaged in. It all happened so quickly, it's like it transcended my normal thinking processes. Consequently when I moved to engage the enemy I had absolute confidence I would succeed no matter what the odds. This kind of battling on foot is what I am most used to. It enabled that extra confident part of my warrior psyche to be fully released to good advantage.

Just then the officers from the Aldred and Nerland armies arrived together. After the initial greetings they all settled down to determine what they would do with the Dagarathian force massing before them. There had been consideration of a quick strike by the Aldred and Nerland armies, but Erith did not regard it as the best timing.

Erith had a sense a delay could also work to the advantage of creating dissension in the ranks of Dagarathian troops. Reports came that many of them were farmers who had fields in critical stages of harvest. These were men who had been drafted into battle. Every day away from their fields resulted in their becoming antsier about their participation. A little longer and more and more of them may even risk desertion. They would prefer risking death by execution versus death from starvation for themselves and their families.

After a few hours the officers had hammered out an agreement, which they all felt confident would be successful. The Aldred cavalry, who were known to be swift and fierce, were going to come up from behind the Dagarathian force. The rest of their army would be coming from the right side. The Nerland troops would be coming in from the left side. Their cavalry would be charging in from the rear after their infantry had already engaged the enemy. At a predetermined signal, the infantry would part leaving a clear path for the Nerland cavalry to charge down the middle. In the meantime, the Evansing army would be coming up the middle of the three armies. On its left side the Evansing cavalry would be riding in with their swords and lances. The infantry would be coming on the left side of the Evansing army. In the middle, the Evansing archers would be releasing torrent after torrent of flaming arrows into the midst of the Dagarathian forces. Evansing scouts reported the enemy forces were situated by an abundance of dry grass. Once it caught fire it would be like another ally as it would add confusion and fear to the ranks of the Dagarathian army.

The forces would all be in place in forty-eight hours. They would then await the timing Erith and the officers felt was right. This was a bit strange from Evansing's normal battle strategy. But they felt waiting long enough may even result in a rebellion in the Dagarathian ranks. The growing dissension may also result in Haydek being forced into a premature assault.

Erith asked Edwin to come to his tent for he had some things he wanted to talk to him about. As they walked toward Erith's tent both men were silent.

Edwin thought to himself, "I wonder what Erith would like to talk about. It seemed peculiar the tone in Erith's voice. It didn't seem like he wanted to discuss battle strategy some more. It actually seemed like a connecting wanting to relate kind of tone. What sparked that? This could be interesting."

At Erith's tent, the King motioned to Edwin to sit down and then he sat down himself. At first Erith looked at Edwin not saying anything. He looked like he was about to say something not familiar for him and not easy for him to express. He appeared to be getting his thoughts in order so as to speak in a manner most appropriate. This was most unlike Erith as he had no problem expressing his thoughts in a quick forthright manner. Something you would expect from a king who has all the confidence anyone would ever want.

Finally, Erith started to speak, "You know, Edwin, I have become increasingly fond of you. Not only are you a valiant warrior and leader, but you are someone I can respect as a person in other areas of life as well. I see you as a person who is on a quest to grow and produce fruit in your life. Most of the people at court, including most of my family, are busy, but all they produce are leaves. Their hive of activity is focused on self-indulging nothings, which have an appearance of being worthwhile, but naught of substance comes from it. You and Greer are also active, but I see lasting benefit to yourselves and those around you. Somehow you enhance your environment and grow as people at the same time. Percival has been most impressed by your determination to be all you can be and put your past misfortunes behind you. I know our relationship has been rather formal, even though you are my very fine son-in-law. I would like to change that. For starters, when we are together with just the two of us or with Percival or Greer, you may call me Erith. I have decided I want to spend more time being part of a family of humans instead of always being the King. Therefore hopefully you and I will start to relate more deeply than we have in the past. So what do you have to say to that?"

Of course Edwin is listening almost with disbelief at what he is hearing. At the same time he is becoming filled with a sense of incomprehensible joy at the prospect of having a real relationship with Erith.

"Sire, I mean, Erith, a deeper relationship with you has been one of my fondest desires, ever since just before Greer and I got married. I have wanted to connect with you in a warmer more meaningful way. What caused this change of heart?"

"Edwin, one morning several days ago I awoke and started to ponder my life. I realized I was living my whole life keeping almost everyone at arm's length in order to maintain kingly protocol. This I have decided is most unsatisfying and not totally necessary; at least not to the extent I have done it so far. Therefore, I now want to be a real father-in-law to you. Someone you can confide in and look to for some of those wonderful relational fuzzies which are meant to exist in families."

"May I call you Father?" asked Edwin.

Erith looked surprised and then a little uncomfortable as he considered the request.

Then he shrugged and said, "Sure why not."

"Could I call you Dad or Daddy?" asked Edwin with a smile. He was on a roll and he was going to see far it would go.

Erith sputtered, "Dad or Daddy! Wow! Edwin, you are really stretching me. Greer hardly ever calls me Dad or Daddy. Now you want to?"

"Yes," replied Edwin, "I do, and it is interesting how you are becoming more and more a regular person even as we speak about it. You said 'Wow!' which I have never heard you say before. You showed me vulnerability when you told me you were being stretched, and you shared an intimacy about your relationship with Greer. I am seeing a transformation before my very eyes."

Erith looked back with surprise and sat speechless for a moment. Then a laughter rose from his lips and eventually it became such a rollicking hilarity he almost fell out of his chair. When he recomposed himself he had a whole new youthfulness in his appearance. Something about such unabashed humor created an alteration of sorts in the King's features. Erith looked at Edwin with a new softness in his eyes. Edwin had just witnessed something beautiful.

The King said, "I'll bet you never thought you would see me looking and acting so undignified, eh?"

"I saw you become real before my very eyes. I will never forget what I saw tonight. Tonight you and I have truly become family."

"Well don't tell anybody," replied the King. Then after a moment he continued, "You can tell Greer and Percival if you like. I may even tell them myself."

"Thank you, Erith, for I relish the prospect of sharing with them what happened.

So, can I call you Dad or Daddy when it's appropriate?"

"Sure, son, why not?" came the welcomed reply with a smile.

The next day at dawn, the Evansing army got up and ready to move on to the next battle.

CHAPTER 40

Wagons were being used to transport the wounded and dying back to Evansing. Both Erith and Edwin, along with three of the other leading officers made the rounds to comfort each of these men. Every one of these soldiers was now experiencing the painful reality of being a battle casualty.

Edwin walked up to one soldier who had had his left leg amputated. He put his hand on the man's shoulder and gave it a squeeze.

"You will be taken care of, brave warrior. What's your name?"

The man replied, "My name is Wicklow, sir." He gave a salute as he spoke.

"No need for that, Wicklow. Be at ease. You look familiar. You fought in my regiment in Randar, didn't you?"

"Yes, sir, I did."

Edwin turned to his accompanying aide and asked him to draw up a note that this man would be given a job upon his return. One copy was given to the man to present when he had recovered and one copy was kept by Edwin's aide. The soldiers knew Edwin always kept his promises.

Wicklow gratefully received the note which documented the promise. He put it into his pocket and smiled at Edwin.

"Thank you, sir, that is indeed very kind of you. Why would you pick me to give employment when there are so many wounded?"

"I saw a light above your head and heard a voice saying you were to be given an opportunity for gainful work," replied Edwin.

The man's eyes got big with wonder.

"Really? That's what inspired you to do that?"

"Yes, that is the truth. That is what happened," responded Edwin.

"Well, sir, that is most astounding. I had just not more than a few moments before you came asked God to provide for me and my family."

Edwin looked surprised but not totally.

"That is amazing. Wouldst all prayers be answered so quickly," he replied.

"Are you a regular praying man?" Edwin asked.

"I am ashamed to say I am not. I have normally considered it a waste of time," responded the soldier. "But I felt so desperate I figured I had nothing to lose by asking. I can only assume His Grace made up for my lack of virtue."

"Interesting," replied Edwin, "I wish you well," as he continued on to the next soldier.

When the wounded had all been visited, then Erith, Edwin and the three leading officers, along with their escort, left to catch up to the rest of the army.

Edwin rode alongside Erith and decided to broach the subject of Joan of Arc.

"Sire," he began looking around to make sure no one else would over-hear, "I have another source of battle strategy, which we could consider."

"Oh really? What source is that?" asked Erith.

"What would you say if I told you that French lady warrior from the early 1400s gave us strategy for Randar and rescued me from being a barbecue?"

"I would say that was pretty fantastic, let's ask her."

"Okay, Sire, I will ask her to communicate to me. She may or may not. It depends on whether she gets permission to help. Of course if we are already pursuing a winning strategy, she has no need to show up."

"Well no one can accuse you of necromancy since she's not dead yet. It would certainly give some of our priests a knotty problem to consider, as to the correctness of what you are doing," replied Erith. He continued, "Personally I believe if God gives permission to connect with a now deceased saint, then it would be alright. Its only if we try to conjure them up that it could be considered necromancy."

"Sire, that is a most interesting statement to hear from you. I don't normally hear you refer to God in that way. If what you say is true we could perhaps ask Him if we could connect with St. Patrick himself."

"Now that would be interesting. We should consider it. However, I would like to talk to Percival first about it."

"Yes, I agree with you, Sire. That would be wise."

That night after arriving at their initial battle line, Edwin asked Joan if she had any ideas about strategy, which would be better than what had been developed so far. He had no response prior to going to bed. So he thought maybe she would show up in his dreams.

As his normal custom, Edwin wrote to his beloved before going to bed.

Dearest Greer,

Here we are on the verge of another battle. We don't know yet when we will engage the enemy, but it will happen soon enough. Haydek the usurper is waiting for us. This one battle and it will all be decided. I have no doubt we will win but enough of that.

I love you, Greer, beyond life itself. Oh what I would give to hold you in my arms, to caress your soft cheek and hold your breasts tenderly. I better not go down that path too far, or I am going to go to bed frustrated.

You are beyond words, my beloved, simply beyond, beyond, beyond. I'm amazed at the way you love me. I'm amazed at the way I love you. Oh it is truly, truly beyond my comprehension. How did I ever end up being your lover? How did you ever end up being mine? Fortune has smiled on me and indeed on us. I can't imagine spending life with anyone else, but you.

With hugs and kisses,

(signed) Edwin

PS. Your father is letting me call him Dad or Daddy when it's appropriate. Only when it's just the two of us or in front of you or Percival. Isn't that way cool?

That night Joan came to Edwin in a dream. She appeared without her armor and advised Edwin a better way existed to bring down Haydek. Needless bloodshed could be avoided if Edwin would pick four excellent men to accompany him. They would approach Haydek's camp under the cover of darkness the next night. He would be given a special knowing of the route to take to avoid being detected and at the same time get them to Haydek. With the assassination of Haydek the Dagarath force would fold as they did not have a heart to fight. Only by the sheer force of his personality and the fear he had fostered kept the Dagarathians in the field. She and her troops would be available to intervene in the event things got too hot to handle. However, he and his men must be prepared to go to the wall first before they could expect assistance. In other words it may first look like certain death.

The next morning Edwin shared his dream with Erith and asked permission to undertake the mission.

"Sounds very dangerous, are you sure you can trust Joan on this one?"

"Yes, Daddy, I am," replied Edwin with a smile.

Erith winced as if taken a bit aback by this new familiar address. However, he said nothing. After all he did give permission to Edwin to do so, and they were alone.

"What are you going to tell the men you want to accompany you on what appears to be a certain suicide mission?"

"I will tell them to trust me. I am eager to get back to Greer and I am not engaging this assignment because I have a death wish. I will inform them there are special forces standing by to assist us."

"Okay, son, go to it. You are simply doing what you were made to do."

"Thanks, Dad, I will see you later today with the men I've selected."

Edwin had potentially a dozen men who would fit the requirements for such a dangerous and demanding task. He whittled it down to four based on their capacity to absolutely trust his instructions in battle, no matter how foolhardy they seemed. The other men all trusted and obeyed orders as well, but these four had a special bonding with Edwin. The extra connection facilitated the superior dimension of trust, which would be paramount for this mission. Edwin knew it wasn't just for his sake, but also because Joan and her troops would require it in order to be released to the rescue if necessary.

"If necessary?" he thought. "It was a certainty they would need Joan and her troops."

The four men were asked if they would join. They weren't commanded to. All of them readily said yes, just as Edwin had expected. Men of this ilk only knew one response to a request, no matter what the assignment. Edwin took them to the King for his personal wishes for their safe return. He expressed his appreciation at their willingness to undertake an assignment, which could avoid many casualties.

That evening as night fell; Edwin and his four men prepared by camouflaging themselves with soot on their faces and other exposed parts of their bodies. They wore black clothes.

Edwin sensed the nearest enemy soldier was at least a half mile away. Haydek was probably about a mile and a half after that. His knowing didn't give any specific directions other than to start walking. So they did.

After the party of five had gone almost that half mile they moved more and more surreptitiously. They could hear some voices ahead and detect some movement at an apparent Dagarathian checkpoint. They stopped and Edwin's knowing told him they should avoid the checkpoint by going fifty yards to the right. By this time there were undoubtedly guards patrolling all through the immediate vicinity. Unexplainably, there existed a gap in the area his internal knower had told him to go to. Edwin went back to collect his men and they crouched along as they proceeded through the gap in the enemy line. The Evansing contingent continued on the course given to them for about another half mile. At this point there were groups of four or five soldiers each, spread about twenty five yards apart. It was decision time. It would be impossible to crawl undetected only ten or twelve yards from the guards. To attack a group would be noticed by the troops only twenty five yards on either side. So Edwin said to wait until he got some sense as to what to do next.

They waited, and waited, and waited for almost an hour. Everyone sat patiently and quietly with no complaint. Then for no apparent reason the two nearest pickets of guards left in quick haste. This left a wide open hole for the five assassins to proceed with relative ease.

The next half mile proceeded without incident as surprisingly there was still a dearth of enemy soldiers even when so close to their command headquarters. Now they were only about another half mile from Haydek.

His knower kicked in again and they moved thirty yards to the left where they discovered a river small but deep enough for them to swim and submerge if necessary. It would be a challenge with their weapons, but they were all strong and they had equipped and dressed as lightly as possible. To enable their ability to swim even further they stripped anything they considered superfluous to their mission. The river's current carried them in the direction they were going. It brought them right into the center of the enemy's camp. They needed to find a place unguarded where they could land. They got to such a location only a stone's throw from a large heavily guarded tent. Edwin recognized Haydek's coat of arms on the tent. The area around the tent was well-lit with torches. There were at least thirty enemy troops standing around the tent. It would be impossible to creep up unseen.

"Well, Joan, I hope you are paying attention," Edwin said to himself.

Again they were facing an impossible situation. But this time they couldn't just sit and wait for something to happen. For the night had progressed along and it was now after midnight. As well, Haydek's guards would not leave him alone and vulnerable. Edwin sat in silence with his men considering their options. The word "CHARGE" came very clearly in his mind. To charge now would appear to invite certain death. Joan had given a strong hint this would happen. Indeed it very much seemed it was a requirement before she and her troops would, or perhaps even could, intervene.

"Okay, Joan, I'm going to commit my men and myself to your safe-keeping."

CHAPTER 41

Edwin turned to his men and said, "Draw your swords, we're going in and we will all stick together running towards the entrance of the tent. Stay silent until we are spotted, at which time start your most blood curdling yell. At the count of three we go. One, two, three." Upon the count of three all five men ran toward the eight men standing guard at the tent entrance. When they were about forty feet away the enemy spotted them and sounded the alarm. The rest of the thirty or so guards around the tent started to congregate where the Evansing troops were attacking. The five offensive troops cut down the eight men at the door, but they were speedily set upon by the other guards.

Edwin yelled, "Form a stockade." Upon the command the five men went back to back so as to provide a strong defense against the Dagarathian guards. As the uproar continued more enemy soldiers came to the attack. They were now surrounded by dozens of opposing troops. Just as it appeared they were about to be overrun, three huge grey animals appeared out of the darkness and started to run over the Dagarathian troops. They also flung some of them out of the way with what appeared to be a part of their nose. This consisted of a long relatively thin membrane they could wrap around a man. As well they had huge horns under their mouths they used to gore some of the enemy soldiers. The remaining defenders fled in terror at the sight of such terrible beasts. This left the five invading soldiers free to run inside, where they caught Haydek standing with his sword ready to defend himself. All five men charged him and thrust him through with their swords. They then ran outside declaring the traitor Haydek dead. By this time the enemy camp was in an uproar. The men of Dagarath stood in bewilderment when they saw the five Evansing troops surrounded by the three huge strange beasts. Upon hearing the news of their leader's death they started to put their arms down and walked away. Joan had predicted this would happen with Haydek's death.

Within half an hour the Dagarathian camp had been deserted. All that remained were the men from Evansing and these three strange creatures which had come to their rescue. Then a most peculiar transformation occurred. Before their eyes the strange creatures became men. These did not look like ordinary men. These men looked like holy men from long ago. The most distinguished of the three men walked up to Edwin and introduced himself.

"I am Patrick; I understand you wanted to meet me."

Edwin stared agog for a moment. Thinking to himself, "Am I going crazy or have I seen what I think I have seen?" He turned to his men and saw they too were all staring in amazement at what they had witnessed. Then realizing he had been addressed, Edwin turned back to the man who called himself Patrick.

"Pardon me, sir, for ignoring you, but I am in a state of wonderment over what has just transpired. Did you say your name is Patrick?"

"Yes, that is correct. I believe your name is Edwin?"

"Yes, I am Edwin."

"The Chief Lord of Ireland has sent me and my friends to come and rescue you in a rather unusual manner, as you have just witnessed. He indicated you had wanted to meet me, so he arranged for a two for one, a rescue and an introduction."

Edwin asked, "So you are, Patrick, from six hundred years ago who is known as St. Patrick?"

"Yes, I am the one and the same."

After a moment of letting that response sink in, Edwin replied, "Welcome, sir, and thank you for rescuing us." Turning to the other two men he thanked them as well.

Returning to look at Patrick, he asked, "Who is the Chief Lord of Ireland you referred to?"

"He is a senior angel who has been given authority over this isle. At some appropriate time I will introduce you to him. It will be in your best interest to be familiar with him so you can interact as is appropriate. It will facilitate you being in tune with the divinely ordained plans and timetable for Ireland. Of course he is accountable to the Creator of All Things, and he receives his instructions from Him.

"What do we do now, sir?" Edwin asked.

Patrick replied, "You have a power vacuum in Dagarath. The royal family has been eliminated and the tyrant Haydek is now dead. You have the responsibility to assist in establishing a new royal family."

Hearing some disturbance from his men, Edwin looked away from Patrick and noticed the two men who had accompanied Patrick were no longer there. Edwin's men said the two men had disappeared right before their eyes.

Patrick smiled, "Their mission here was done so they went back."

Edwin asked him, "How long are you going to stay with us?"

"I am supposed to meet your king so I will remain with you for awhile. We can start walking back to your army. You will find all the Dagarathian troops have melted away so you are safe to return."

As Patrick and Edwin walked back toward the Evansing line, Patrick shared with Edwin greater and greater insights about his future. He told him how he would eventually become a great king over all of Ireland. In order for him to be successful he must have a heart passionate in his pursuit of Wisdom and Understanding.

"How do I grow in wisdom and understanding?" asked Edwin.

"Learn to listen and truly hear what is being said. It is easy to think we hear, but often there are influences which affect the way we hear. For example, consider the word love. What does it mean to you when someone says they love you?"

Edwin considered the question.

"Well it depends on who says it. For Greer to say she loves me means something more fuzzy wuzzy and wonderful than if someone else were to say it. But I don't know what it would feel like to have someone else say it, because nobody besides Greer has ever said that to me. I suppose my parents said it, but I don't remember if they did."

"Expand for me what Greer's expression of love means to you."

"Hmm, it means even when I am a knot head she still wants to be my lover and friend. As I am learning from her, I don't have to be perfect or the conquering hero every moment with Greer, in order for her to respect and value me. Ahh that is something, she values me. Now that speaks to me. I never really considered before what her saying she loves me meant to me." Edwin went silent and he threatened to get emotional; his eyes were starting to mist over a bit. "Steel yourself Edwin this is not the time to get emotional," he said to himself.

Attempting to change the subject, he asked, "So what can you tell me about how to truly hear?"

Patrick continued, ignoring the attempt to divert the subject at hand, "What can you tell me about your understanding of being valued by Greer?"

"Why don't we discuss that later?"

"You mean when we are alone?"

"Yes, Patrick, when we are alone," replied Edwin, a little testiness creeping into his voice.

"Why do you want to wait until we are alone?"

At this point Edwin's agitation is starting to build. Venerated 600 year old saint or not, he is becoming rather impatient with this fellow who keeps prodding him to go deeper.

"Look, sir, I appreciate your help today and the things you have been sharing, but I don't want to go down this path right now."

Unfazed, Patrick kept on the pressure, after all what could Edwin do to him? Kill him? He was already dead.

"You selected these four men with you because you saw them as persons who totally trusted you. Do you think if you were to be emotional they would lose respect for you and quit trusting you?"

Edwin considered the question. As he did so his anger began to recede. It surprised him because if anything it should have gotten worse. He decided he wasn't going to be afraid of being real with these four men he valued greatly. He turned to them.

"Patrick here is trying to get me to be open and real about expressing my emotions with you guys. That may well include me getting teary eyed and emotional. If that happens will you still respect me as your leader?"

The out of the blue question presented to the four valiant warriors took them by surprise. At first, none of them said anything because the subject matter was not in their grid of normal thoughts and considerations. They had no framework with which to assess such a topic.

Then Edwin decided to push it to another level.

"Look if I got mushy and started bawling like a baby would you still consider me worthy to be your leader?"

One of the men spoke up, "Edwin, you could stand on your head in your underwear in Evansing Square and we would still love, respect and consider you as our leader. You have proven yourself as our courageous and wise leader so many times and in so many ways. Your worthiness as our leader is indisputable. So if you want to cry like a baby, go right ahead."

Edwin thanked him for his response and then asked, "You said you love me. How do you mean that?"

The spokesman answered with deep feeling, "We would lay our lives down for you, for you have already demonstrated a willingness to do that for us."

The response greatly touched Edwin for he had never before heard such a deeply felt expression of how his men perceived him. This represented another expression of how someone valued him. This together with what had already tweaked him on this subject finally broke the dam. Edwin lost it and started to weep and weep and weep. The men stood in silence around their leader. They all knew this to be a sacred moment. Their courageous leader who would face anything was experiencing a dramatic moment of freedom in his life. They were witnessing firsthand the birthing of a new level of courage in expression of his emotions.

When Edwin stopped crying, he refused to be embarrassed. He thanked his men for their support and carried on like nothing unusual had happened.

A comfortable silence prevailed the rest of the walk as Patrick let the emotions stirred up to be allowed to settle.

When they arrived back at their camp they went to Erith's command headquarters.

"Sire," Edwin began, "the mission has been a resounding success. The Dagarathian usurper, Haydek has been killed and his army has been disbanded. As well I would like to introduce you to someone who led the intervention which made our victory possible. Sire, it gives me great pleasure to introduce to you someone you very much wanted to meet. This distinguished looking gentleman is none other than St. Patrick himself."

Erith felt very surprised by this revelation, but being the King he had a self-imposed role to play of being unduly stirred by anything in front of his subjects. So he resisted the initial inclination to be open with his amazement. Gathering his thoughts he got up and warmly greeted the saint and shook his hand.

"Welcome, sir, this is indeed a great honor. We were just discussing the other day about whether it would be appropriate to try and meet you."

"Yes, I know," replied Patrick, "that is partly why I am here. I have a message to relate to you when we are alone."

Erith looked deep into Patrick's eyes for some indication as to what the message may be about, but he could not discern anything. He did, however, notice a brilliant light and substance in Patrick's eyes which were most entrancing.

Erith called in his council for a hurried meeting to decide what to do next. He also sent couriers to bring the leaders of their allies to come as quickly as possible and to inform them of the apparent victory. The Evansing Council decided a deeper level of investigation should be started of all the Dagarathian nobles, who had been previously short-listed as possible replacements to Haydek. The object would be to try and narrow down to a handful of families most likely to be both appropriate rulers of Dagarath, and also sympathetic to Irish unity. Any further action would await the arrival of their allies so a joint go forward decision could be made.

When everyone left, there remained only Erith and Patrick. The moment arrived which Erith had been awaiting with anticipation and trepidation. He didn't know which was appropriate so he vacillated between the two.

Patrick looked rather sober, but then he cracked a smile. "Lighten up, Erith. I've got good news for you from Him who is both your Father and my Father."

Erith felt pleasantly surprised with what he heard. His face must have betrayed that he seemed a bit troubled as to what the message may be.

Patrick continued, "The Father says: Well done my good and faithful son, for you have pleased me."

The message though brief, contained exactly what Erith needed to hear. It washed over him like a cool refreshing stream of water. Washed away once and for all were any doubts about the legitimacy of his call to unite Ireland. After the losses of the last battle, questions plagued Erith as to whether this call had been given to him to pursue. Erith fell to his knees and wept for joy and relief. After several minutes he got up and profusely thanked Patrick for the message. He also said he would like to talk to Patrick about a host of matters that were unresolved in his faith.

Then the thought dawned on him, "By the way, sir, do you know which Dagarathian family would be the best to rule in Dagarath?"

"As a matter of fact I do. The O'Connor family with its leader Jillian would be the best choice."

"The O'Connor family? I don't think they were even short-listed. In fact I know they weren't short-listed."

"It's true they weren't short-listed. Your standards for selection look at all the usual characteristics men think are important. However, Jillian has a noble heart, which none of the others can surpass. Therefore what he may lack in some skills and influential relationships he will far surpass with nobility of character. There is one other quality, which he has in spades over his counterparts. He is loved by the common people."

"Well thank you, sir. I will bring this up at our joint council meeting and will recommend Jillian as the new king of Dagarath. By the way I assume he is also friendly to our cause?"

Patrick replied, "He will require some coaxing in that area, and you will need to spend time building relationship with him. In time he will become a loyal supporter who will stand by you when others will not. A little investment upfront will produce rich dividends in the long run. Others on your list may look more promising in the immediate as supporters, but they will flag in the long run. Go with Jillian for long-term success."

That evening when Erith had finished getting his questions answered, Patrick said goodbye and vanished before Erith's eyes.

The next morning the joint council of the allies assembled to decide on the next course of action.

King Erith began the meeting with a recommendation that Jillian be appointed as the new king of Dagarath. He also spelled out the reasons why without of course mentioning St. Patrick. He decided to not stretch his credibility by forcing them to believe he communicated with a long dead saint. Even though Jillian had not previously been one of the front runners, they voted him in. The lack of resistance surprised Erith. His influence had become so great that seldom did anyone question him.

The next item consisted of how to approach the Dagarathian capital. The allies decided a low key approach would be best. The allied armies would neither come into the capital nor even be within sight of the capital. A contingent of three messengers would be dispatched forthwith to the capital. The message they carried would be addressed to the nobles of Dagarath. In it would be the invitation for them to come to the allies' camp for discussion of terms.

The messengers would be selected from each of the three allied armies. They left the next morning and arrived at the gates with a flag of truce. The gates opened up and the three men were brought to an assembly of the nobles of Dagarath.

The noble overseeing the assembly, a burly dark bearded man looked quite hostile. This was surprising given the situation of their army leaving the battlefield. The man asked to see the message. After reading it aloud he looked at the messengers and with belligerence asked, "Why should we waste our time with going out to the country? What is this about terms? What terms? What is the basis for terms?"

The messenger from Evansing, a captain, one of the five who killed Haydek, indicated he would like to respond.

"Distinguished nobles of Dagarath, we come as representatives of the allied armies of Aldred, Nerland and Evansing. As you know your army left the field of battle upon the death of Haydek. We have no desire to create hardship for your kingdom. Our only desire is to seek ways to bring reconciliation, peace and prosperity which will benefit us all."

The belligerent noble interrupted, "What do you mean benefit us all? You just mean to pick our pockets for your personal advantage."

The Evansing messenger, keeping his cool, once again motioned he would like to speak. This time several of the nobles indicated their desire to hear what he had to say.

"As I was saying, the objective is to find a solution which will benefit you and us. We have no desire for needless bloodshed or destruction of property. However, do not believe our generosity in coming to you in this manner as a sign of weakness. Rather we come in this manner as a sign of friendship and a desire to build bridges."

At this the troublesome noble once again spoke up derisively, "How do we know you have the capacity to enforce those words? How do we know you will deal with us justly?"

CHAPTER 42

The Evansing messenger responded, "Sir, you are in danger. If you continue to obstruct this overture of peace and goodwill you will be responsible for whatever folly befalls you and your family." The boldness of the reply came from the depths of a man who had already faced death on more than one occasion, and had lived to tell about it. With this, several nobles who were the man's kin, asked to have a separate council with the noble in question. After several moments of overheard heated exchange, the men returned to the assembly.

The noble, now somewhat more contrite, indicated he and several nobles would come to the meeting to discuss terms. A total of seven nobles were to return with the messengers. Jillian was not one of them.

The next day the procession of messengers and nobles proceeded to meet the allies at their camp, some ten miles east of their capital.

Upon their arrival they were cordially greeted by the three kings. Each of the seven visiting nobles were seated at a table and given a meal of rich food and drink. Initially they did not discuss anything of a serious nature as the kings wanted to create an atmosphere of warmth and trust. After two hours of socializing over food and drink the venue shifted to a tent for more serious discussions.

Erith began, "Gentlemen, as you know your former leader Haydek is now dead. He was a man of blood who had annihilated the entire former ruling family. We are now here not to subjugate Dagarath, but rather to liberate it to be all it can be as part of a new united Ireland.

There are many benefits for your kingdom to come under the umbrella of our alliance. There will be the elimination of custom duties and various other barriers to trade. This will open your products to new markets and also enable your people to receive at lower costs the products of other parts of Ireland. As well there is added security you will enjoy of being part of a union of allies, as opposed to constantly struggling out of insecurity and fear of your neighbors. And finally there is the development of passion and pride in being part of something bigger than yourselves which will create a legacy for generations to come. All we ask at this time is you not oppose us. Also we ask you to provide us with whatever supplies we will require to facilitate the ongoing quest for Irish unity. This will be a fair levy, which should be viewed as an investment in your future prosperity. We will consult with you as to what is reasonable. We will not at this time require you to provide troops to assist us. Are there any questions or comments to what I have shared so far?"

No one ventured forth a question or a comment. Even though they had been treated most civilly it appeared the Dagarathians felt intimidated. They were on the losing end of a brief war and were now in the midst of the kings and high ranking nobles of the victors.

Erith assured them they were free to express themselves and that no retribution would be forthcoming from their statements or questions.

One of the nobles from Dagarath then did ask a question. "Will our rights, privileges and holdings be unaffected by this new regime which you are proposing?"

"That is solely an internal matter for you to decide. We will not interfere with your internal governing and societal structures. The exact nature of how you will interface within a greater whole will be worked out and implemented over time."

"Any other questions or comments?"

Silence.

Erith continued, "One other matter which we do require is the appointment of Jillian as your new king."

At this the nobles expressed surprise. Not necessarily a negative, for they generally quite liked Jillian, but rather because he was not a part of the inner circle in Dagarath. One of the nobles ventured to ask how Jillian came to be considered for such a position.

Erith responded, "We considered factors other than his pecking order in your nobility. Our consideration included who would best represent both your and our long-term interests. We ask that you support Jillian and his family in their new role as the rulers of Dagarath. At this point we have not had an opportunity to communicate this to him. Can you support Jillian?"

The Dagarathian nobles asked for the opportunity to discuss among themselves the advent of having Jillian as their king. The allies granted this request. They then vacated the tent and left the Dagarathians alone.

After almost an hour the nobles from Dagarath indicated they were ready to resume the meeting. They agreed that though they were surprised at the selection of Jillian, he would be a wise choice.

A troop of one hundred soldiers were sent to inform Jillian and escort him back to the camp. As well another dozen prominent nobles were requested to come with him. In the meantime the formal part of the meeting shifted into light hearted socializing. This enjoying fun between the Dagarathians and the allies would build trust and friendship.

The Dagarathian nobles informed Jillian of his appointment. This surprised and even rather overwhelmed him at the prospect. When he shared it with his family members they too were surprised, but they were actually happier than he was at being part of the ruling family. Unlike Jillian they did not consider the responsibilities which came with such a position. They were only considering the perks and new opportunities for wealth creation. Jillian however, being a noble man concerned himself more with whether he would be the right man for the job. He went into his family chapel and contemplated the prospect of being King of Dagarath. When he came out a half hour later, he had decided yes, he would be king.

When Jillian arrived in the allied camp, they treated him with all the honor and respect of a fellow king. Erith, Keltic and Barris greeted him as a friend of theirs. They didn't overdo it though as they knew Jillian had some reservations about the quest for Irish unity. But they also knew him to be a man they could work with and trust. Differences for now were acceptable as long as they could be resolved in a reasonable time. The allies emphasized they didn't require troops from Dagarath at this time. Nevertheless, they would expect them in the not too distant future.

Jillian in his meetings with the kings handled himself with remarkable aplomb. He had decided he would act like a king. He made it clear he did not at this time unreservedly support the quest for Irish unity but may change his position in the future. However, he made it plain he would cooperate with the allies in whatever they required. This assuming it would not be punitive and harmful to Dagarath. The allied kings asked him to visit each of the allies' capitals and become more and more connected with his fellow kings and their families. This he agreed to do and seemed quite enthusiastic at doing so.

Edwin at this time was becoming quite keen to get back. Greer's arms were awaiting and he couldn't wait to enjoy her once again. Instead, Erith informed him that he had been appointed to spend six weeks in working as a liaison officer between the new Dagarath ruling family and the allies. This came as quite a shock for Edwin. He had had no advance warning that all of a sudden he had been shifted from conquering warrior mode to a civilian function. Erith convinced Edwin he was the best man for the role. He would be accompanied by the same soldier who had originally delivered the message to the nobles. That would be his dear friend Eamon and Edwin was glad to have him.

The next letter he wrote:

Dearest Greer,

I have some unfortunate news. Your father has posted me to Dagarath as a liaison officer for six weeks. So you and I will have to rely on memories to get us through the nights alone. This has been a most amazing time. One day we are facing the prospect of again taking costly casualties. The next day we are celebrating a victory over a battle we didn't have to fight. We killed Haydek and it was all over. That Joan did a reverse play on me. I figured she and her army were going to show up and instead she sends St. Patrick with two of his companions in the form of what he said were elephants. These were large gray animals, large horns called tusks coming out just below their mouths, and they had these long narrow noses. Well they made short work of the Dagarathian troops and rescued us just in the nick of time. According to him elephants are real animals which live in Africa. St. Patrick also told us who we should appoint to be the King of Dagarath and he spent time with Erith answering his questions. Then he disappeared. I hope to see him again. He's another one I would like you to meet. We are starting to create quite a collection of special friends, a 600 year old saint and a lady warrior from four hundred years into the future. The surprising thing is as I write this it all seems so normal. Go figure how such fantastic things can become so regular so soon.

I love you with all my heart and soul.

I Love, Love, Love You,

(signed) Edwin

Edwin and Eamon were riding along with the Dagarathian nobles and the new designated king, Jillian. They were accompanied by one hundred allied troops. These troops would not enter the capital but would return back to their camp. The allies were going to keep one-third each of their present strength in the camp for an indeterminate time. The rest of the troops and the kings and nobles were starting to return to their homes. Great pains were taken by the allies to make their presence and influence in Dagarath as low key as possible. Even Edwin and Eamon were to keep out of the public eye and spend time with the ruling family and other key nobles. One of their objectives involved instilling a larger view of things for the Dagarathian rulers. No longer were they their own little island. They were now part of a bigger island known as Ireland. This would require an expansion of their thoughts and vision. They would also start creating friendship ties. The final unspoken, but understood objective would be to maintain an allied overseeing presence which would help to protect their interests in Dagarath.

Upon their arrival in the Dagarath capital, the two Evansing soldiers were shown to their quarters and given time to clean up and change into new clothes. They would be brought to the dining hall for a time of getting acquainted with the nobles of Dagarath.

Edwin and Eamon were seated on either side of Jillian. Both men started to ingratiate themselves very quickly with their free and easy ways. They avoided any air of being the conquering overseers. Yet they exuded an understanding that they were not to be trifled with. Eamon had made that very clear in his confrontation with the bullying noble.

The reputation of Edwin as Crown Prince of Evansing and his renown as a warrior had also preceded him. Consequently, both men were treated with the utmost respect. As the night progressed the locals often approached Edwin and asked him what was going to happen. He reassured them that only good things were going to happen. He informed them he and Eamon were there to help in the transition and facilitate a new vision which would benefit Dagarath.

One person who wanted to meet Edwin was not so keen on him. A young noblewoman had been recently widowed in the battle on the hill. She walked up to Edwin and spit in his face and screamed insults and curses over him. Dagarathian guards took her away and out of the hall. Edwin calmly wiped the spittle off of his face and attempted to resume as though nothing unusual had happened. Jillian and others profusely expressed their apologies as to what had occurred. When Edwin became aware of her loss, he asked that she be absolved of all wrong doing and that no action be taken against her. Jillian and the nobles were quite astonished at such generosity of spirit. They were pleased this was the man they were to be dealing with. The incident, which at first looked like a great misfortune, translated into something positive and beneficial.

The noble who had originally been so recalcitrant came up to Eamon and said, "You are one of the ballsiest men I have ever met. I salute your courage. How did you know I wouldn't order you to be cut down right there?"

Eamon replied, "I didn't, but a potential adverse outcome doesn't deter me from doing what I know to be the right thing to do."

The noble offered his hand in friendship and expressed pleasure to make Eamon's acquaintance.

The official coronation for Jillian would occur in seven days. He was now known as the designated king, but not until the bishop crowned him would he be addressed as King Jillian. In the meantime he and Edwin spent a lot of time getting to know one another. In the course of riding and hunting they shared about each others lives and their hopes for the future. Whenever appropriate, Edwin would bring up the Quest and what it meant to Ireland and Dagarath. Edwin had become increasingly passionate about the Quest. It even surprised him how passionate he sounded when he talked about it. He liked to talk about it. It became more and more ingrained in him. Eamon would spend his time doing similar activities with other members of the ruling family. Being friends with the Dagarathians would facilitate ongoing success. If you swept away all the complexities of politics and the various kingdom issues, it still boiled down to the nature of relationships between real flesh and blood people. This involved persons with hurts and fears and desires for a better life for themselves and their families. The Dagarathians must be convinced their hurts would be best healed, their fears would be best allayed and their desires would be best fulfilled, in a united Ireland.

On the day of the coronation both Edwin and Eamon stayed in the background. As they were about to leave that young widow appeared again. She walked toward Edwin when a guard interfered and insisted she turn back. Something about her demeanor told Edwin she had changed since last time. He indicated to the guard to let her come.

The woman said to Edwin, "Sir, I want to apologize for my actions the last time we met. My actions were ignoble and sparked by my grief and rage at seeing possibly the man who killed my husband, or at least played a role in his death. Your generosity in dropping all charges against me was most unexpected and much appreciated. Thank you for your magnanimous gesture. Would you please forgive me?"

"Yes, madam, I do forgive you. I extend to you my condolences at your loss. May He who is Abundant Joy replace your grief with His Joy."

"Thank you, sir," she replied and walked away.

The next several weeks passed by as rapidly as could be expected for Edwin and Eamon, who were both missing their sweethearts back home. With one week to go they were starting to get antsy and excited about returning to Evansing.

The relationship building had been going remarkably well. Edwin could also tell King Jillian was starting to warm up more and more to the idea of a united Ireland. Jillian would accompany Edwin and Eamon on the return trip. King Erith and the Evansing nobles wanted to connect in a deeper way with Jillian. Also accompanying them would be several of Jillian's family members and key nobles who would be coming on the week long visit.

The two Evansing soldiers were walking down the castle corridor to their meeting with King Jillian and his nobles. Out of nowhere fear struck Edwin. It felt so tangible as though he were wearing it. Edwin felt positively craven and yet he had to pretend nothing was wrong, but how could he? Eamon noticed the terror in Edwin's eyes and asked what was wrong? Edwin could not answer; he only stared in response, unable to speak. Eamon told their escort they needed to turn around and return to their suite. This they did. Eamon told one of the guards to advise the King and the nobles that something had come up and they would join them when they could. When alone Eamon again tried to get a response from Edwin, but all he got was a terrified look. Edwin appeared to be speechless with fear. Given Edwin's normal fearlessness, this could not be a natural fear. Therefore it must be something supernatural of the evil kind. As Eamon considered the possibilities, he heard a knock on the door. It was the widow once again asking to see Edwin. Eamon tried to explain to her now would not be a good time and she should come back tomorrow or the next day. She explained that was precisely why she came. Earlier in the morning she had had an open eye vision of seeing a very large black spider landing on Edwin. She saw the word FEAR written on its back. The longer he sat on Edwin the more Edwin became paralyzed with fear. Then she saw herself pour a small pitcher of blessed water from the chapel over Edwin's head and the spider disappeared. She carried with her that pitcher of water. Eamon looked askance at her response, but he didn't have any other answers so he figured why not. The widow came over to Edwin and told him what she would do. Edwin said nothing and looked away. She poured the water over Edwin's head. As she did, a blood curdling scream came from Edwin. He started to scream obscenities and smash and throw things. Then he stopped all of a sudden, as he held a chair in mid air. He had a look of total puzzlement.

He slowly put down the chair and asked, "What happened? How did we get back here?"

Eamon explained all that had transpired. Edwin looked at him blankly.

"I don't remember anything. It is so weird. Like how could that happen to me? It seems like the work of some very strong magic, magic of the wrong kind."

Then he turned to the widow, "Thanks for your help. Do you have any idea how this spider came on me? Do you know of any witches or warlocks or Druids here in Dagarath who could be capable of such a thing?"

"I do not know, sir, who could have done this. All those types of people you referred to are prohibited in Dagarath and have been so for more than ten years."

Then he asked her, "Why do you think you got the vision?"

"I regularly get visions which tell me the future before it happens. Sometimes these include visions about what the evil side is doing or about to do to someone."

He turned to Eamon and said, "We should get to that meeting now."

He thanked the lady again for her help. She asked if she could accompany them as far as the meeting room. Edwin didn't see any harm in that and told her she could come along.

The lady put her hand on Edwin's arm part way on the trip to the meeting room. Edwin looked at her and she looked back at him with a very disarming smile. He had never acknowledged before that she was a very beautiful woman. He was momentarily dazed by this new discovery.

Eamon looking over at Edwin and the woman took Edwin by the arm and told him they were almost there. He added, "Are you okay now, Edwin?" Edwin felt a little agitated for being disturbed by his friend, but he answered in the affirmative.

Then they were at the room. Edwin turned to say good-bye to the woman and again she looked up at him with a most captivating smile. Once again Edwin was momentarily mesmerized by her beauty. And once more Eamon came to the rescue taking Edwin's arm and ushering him into the meeting room.

The meeting went extremely well with the Dagarathian rulers. They were impressed with the wisdom and grace, which Edwin and Eamon demonstrated. Part of the success appeared to be due to a further warming in their attitude toward Irish unity.

When Edwin and Eamon returned to their room there laid an invitation to them from the widow. Edwin thought this very sweet and wanted to go. Eamon did not think it would be a good idea and started to express his concern that she was making a play for him.

"Nonsense," replied Edwin, "she is just being friendly and wants to further solidify the connection."

"Precisely," responded Eamon, "that is what I am concerned about. Remember what happened in Randar?"

Edwin looked at Eamon and then a strange new awareness came upon him.

"You know, Eamon, it wouldn't surprise me if our widow friend perpetrated that fear on me. Not only that, on the walk back when I looked in her eyes I felt like I was in love with her. She may well be a witch herself."

"Well you did look bewitched when you looked in her eyes. Who knows what would have happened if I hadn't pulled on your arm. I don't think you would have made it to the meeting."

Edwin wrote a polite decline to the invitation. He stepped outside and gave it to one of the guards standing there and asked him to arrange its delivery.

Edwin told Eamon, "When I get back to Evansing I need to find out from Percival how to become immune to these sorts of attacks. It is rather disturbing to be so vulnerable. What would have happened if I hadn't had a faithful friend like you to protect me?"

CHAPTER 43

Finally they were on their way back. Edwin and Eamon were excited at the prospect of soon being reunited with their wives. The ride back was pleasant. The party contained King Jillian, his wife, his eldest two sons, aged 18 and 15, and his eldest two daughters, aged 16 and 13. As well there were half dozen nobles of Dagarath with various members of their families. In addition there were servants and two hundred escorting Dagarathian troops. They were also joined by two hundred Evansing troops when they crossed into Evansing.

Edwin and Eamon made a point of riding with Jillian's sons. They were both interested in archery and were already quite accomplished at it. Both had attended the Games as part of the Dagarath contingent. The eighteen year old had placed fifth in the competition which Edwin won. Both wanted Edwin to give them lessons. This he agreed to do. Edwin enjoyed interacting with these two youths. He also promised to introduce them to Carson the winner of the horse racing event. They were looking forward to learning something from him on the selection and training of the fastest horses. Both of them wanted to go really fast on horses.

When they were two miles from Evansing both Greer and Eamon's wife had ridden out to greet them. Greer had arranged for a lookout to be posted to let her know when the party from Dagarath got within a few miles. Both young men's faces were beaming at being greeted in this extra thoughtful manner. It made them so proud to know their ladies were at least as eager to see them as they wanted to see their ladies.

With great pleasure they introduced them to King Jillian and the others.

Greer warmly greeted the two young princesses and said they would have fun getting to know one another. She quite charmed the Dagarathians, some of whom had had at least a passing acquaintance with her at the Games. However, she also slightly shocked them. To see a Princess riding miles outside of the castle to greet Edwin was considered very bold and perhaps even unladylike. The Dagarathians' view on lady behavior was quite conservative compared to Evansing.

The two couples disappeared ahead of the entourage eager to be alone and get reconnected. They had no official duties until that evening and they wanted as much alone time together as possible.

The next morning, Edwin arranged to see Percival at 10:00 water clock time. He must resolve these susceptibilities to manipulative influences.

"Good morning, Edwin. It must be very important for you to want to tear yourself away from your good wife to come and see me."

Edwin, smiling replied, "Yes, it is very important and Greer agreed with me it was most urgent."

"So what is it?"

Edwin then proceeded to share what had happened with the widow in Dagarath.

"I believe you may well be right about her being a witch. In any event you need to be free from those things inside you which made you susceptible to those attacks. This is probably the second time you have been hit by an enchantment. I'm sure you recall your experience in Randar."

"Yes, I do. Eamon and now you have reminded of me of that. I would rather forget that experience."

"Don't berate yourself about it. We've all done things we wish we hadn't. The important thing is to learn from them and avoid repeating those mistakes. It's important to be able to forgive ourselves and let it go."

"Yes, I know and my brain agrees with you. It's just that my heart doesn't want to cooperate. I still wince when I think about that Randarian episode."

"Well, Edwin, then we will have to resolve why and get rid of the pain associated with it."

"Great, let's do it," replied Edwin.

"Okay, we will start by sitting in silence and see what comes to us."

For thirty minutes the two men sat in silence. Occasionally, Percival would make a note of something.

Percival broke the silence, "The first order of business is your susceptibility to female enchantments. What can you tell me about your parents' sexual history?"

"My parents' what? How would I know about that? Remember I was an infant when they died. Even if I had been older, how or why would I become privy to that kind of knowledge? What do you know about your parents' sexual history?"

"I grant it's not something typically discussed around the family dining table, but little tidbits tend to come up one way or the other. As far as my own parents, I used to get clues about their background, especially my father since he was a bit of a rogue with women. We may need to tap into generational memories."

Edwin responded, "Before we do that, whatever are you referring to? I do recall some stuff about my father. When we were on raids and were pillaging a village, some of the men wondered why I wouldn't join them in the raping of the women. Several times I heard men say my father would never miss an opportunity to take advantage of captive women. I remember cringing when I heard it. I told them that is not what I did, regardless of what my father did. To hear of him engaging in such behavior greatly disturbed my image of him being wonderfully perfect. I suppose because I lost him so early and had to live with my uncle, I imagined him to be better than he was."

"Yes, that would certainly be a natural response. We all want to believe our fathers are noble, barring of course personal experiences which are contrary. Do you have any information on your mother?"

"No, I haven't. I would hope she was virginal when she married my father."

"Yes, that would have been the ideal," replied Percival, "however, given the number of guys trying to deflower as many virgins as possible; it starts by simple math to reduce the odds on everybody's mother being a virgin upon marriage."

"What exactly is the point of this trying to uncover my parents' sexual history?"

"To the extent your parents or their parents were involved in unsanctioned sexual activities they created for you a proclivity to be likewise. It gets passed down to you like the color of your hair or eyes for example."

"Okay, if that is true then why did I not rape women like my father supposedly did?"

"There must be some compensating strengths. Perhaps they come from your mother or further back from your grandparents or even great-grandparents."

"So what do we do now?"

"I am going to speak to your spirit and ask it to recall any relevant generational memories which relate to your parents and earlier ancestors."

"Spirit of Edwin, I call you to start bringing to his conscious memory anything important for him to know about his ancestors' sexual history."

A few moments later Edwin started to get thoughts coming to him which did not seem like they came from his mind. It seemed to be coming from his abdomen. He felt some rather peculiar sensations in his abdomen, a tightening sort of feeling. He started to write down the revelation. Then he shared various episodes which seemed to relate to his family line.

Percival got up and laid hands on Edwin's shoulders. He began muttering in some unintelligible language. After five minutes or so he said it was done. Edwin felt a tingling come over him as Percival muttered.

"Now you should experience a much greater protection from enchantments from lonely women. However, remember you will still have to exercise wisdom and self-control. For the reasons we discussed with respect to your experience in Randar, you need to be circumspect in your relationships with women. Keep a trusted friend like Eamon with you or whatever you have to do to protect yourself. Don't think you can flirt with someone and always be able to keep it under control."

Percival continued, "Now for the attack of fear. Given the early loss of your parents and your difficult relationship with your uncle, fear got an extra big hook in you. Your years as a warrior have also exposed you to fearful situations. These experiences of fear have been deposited into your body."

Edwin interjected, "How do you explain me normally feeling fearless and willing to undertake all kinds of dangerous missions?"

"You probably have some compensating factors there as well. After all your father and uncle were also brave warriors. You most likely have a combination of inherited bravery and that which you have willed yourself to demonstrate. For indeed you have a very strong will. Your manifested bravery does not preclude you having pockets of fear in your body. It would be unrealistic to expect you would be unaffected by fear. For the witchcraft to work on you it must have had a place to land. Therefore what you need to do is progressively work from your head down to your toes, commanding fear to leave each specific part of your body. It would be best to place your hands on the part you are speaking to. There is power in touch. Also be sure to name those parts you are speaking to."

Edwin did as instructed. As he did so he could feel release and a sense of well-being. Then Percival told him to do it again, but this time to speak peace into each part of his body. This Edwin also did and could feel a growing peace throughout his body he didn't have before. Percival counseled him to do both parts of this process once or twice a day over the next seven days.

Edwin thanked Percival for his help. He couldn't wait to share with Greer what had transpired.

When Edwin made it back to their suite he was surprised and little bit irritated to find the two Dagarathian princesses still there. They were eating lunch with Greer. He knew she had invited them to come over that morning, but he had thought they would be gone by now. Breathing deeply he put on his best plastic smile and endeavored to be as charming and agreeable as possible. Greer sensing not all was well took the hint and cut things a little short with the two girls.

After they left, Greer said to Edwin, "What's the matter? Don't you realize I am supposed to develop a friendship with these princesses?"

"Oh yes, my dear, it is all starting to come back to me. I am not allowed to be a petulant impatient little boy. I must be patient at all times. Drat. I guess I zigged when I should have zagged. Please accept my heartfelt apologies for my abominable behavior."

This unexpected response took the wind out of Greer's sails. Yet she felt the situation required some further kind of angry reaction. She almost felt like she had been usurped of her rightful duty to harangue and berate Edwin. Besides, his tone didn't sound totally sincere.

"Humph!" She replied. "Do you really mean that?"

"Yes, my dear, I do or at least I would like to. I was afflicted with temporary insanity which caused me to be self-absorbed with what I wanted. Thus, when I walked through the door I just couldn't shift into a more appropriate mode. Actually I thought I had done pretty well in disguising my true feelings."

"You did well in disguising those feelings to yourself, but not to me and quite likely not to the two princesses. They are both such darlings. I love them to pieces. Besides the political concerns I like them as friends."

"Can we make up now, my sweet?" Edwin asked as he took a step closer to Greer.

She couldn't stay mad at him any longer and they both embraced, and embraced and …

Edwin spent later that afternoon at the archery range with the two Dagarathian princes. He enjoyed his role as mentor and they appreciated his instruction. After a couple of hours they were both noticing tangible improvements in their scores.

The younger prince asked Edwin seemingly out of the blue, "What is it like for you to kill someone?"

"That is an interesting question; surely you must have asked warriors in your family and circle of acquaintances."

"Yes, I have, but I want to know what it's like for you," replied the prince.

"May I ask why?"

"You strike me as a noble and even a gentle man in the qualities I have observed and heard about you. Yet you also have a reputation of being bloodthirsty as a warrior."

"Bloodthirsty? Who told you that?"

"Reports have come to us from Dagarathian soldiers who have seen you on the battlefield. They say you fight like a fiend who appears to relish killing people. Yet when that widow insulted you, you chose to let her go.

Other brave warriors I have known have a certain hardness about them. I don't notice that with you."

"Did you say you are only fifteen?" asked Edwin.

"Yes, that is right, I am only fifteen."

"You are advanced beyond your years. Such an observation and question would be most unusual for Irish men of any age, let alone someone of your youth.

"It's true when I get into battle I relish killing enemy soldiers. I know no other way to do it. If I don't throw my entire desire into doing what I am called to do as a warrior, I would potentially pull back and cost myself my own life or the lives of my comrades. The objective is to win and in war that means on the battlefield to kill as many of the enemy as possible. How does it feel for me to kill someone? Strictly speaking I don't kill people. I kill enemies or destroy objectives. I depersonalize persons into an objective or target which needs to be eliminated. It is simply what is necessary to get the job done. Therefore when I am not in warrior mode, I can shift into whatever role is appropriate for a situation."

"So does that mean you are role playing right now? In other words this isn't the real you right now?" asked the young prince.

"No, that's not what I mean. Perhaps role is not the best word to describe it. The bottom line is this: Whatever I am doing is the real me for that particular part of my life. My doing what I am doing with you now is the real me teaching you archery. When I am in battle that is the real me doing battle. We as people are not the same all the time regardless of what we are doing at a given moment. Every part of life requires us to relate to it, or perform it in a way that is appropriate for it and yet consistent with whom we are. Your values should always be constant in how you determine to relate to people. However, different settings and different persons require appropriate changes in our behavior with people."

The Dagarathian prince thoughtfully considered what he had just heard, "That sounds very wise, Edwin. Thank you for sharing."

The rest of the week long visit with the Dagarathians went better than expected. King Jillian and his accompanying nobles seemed to be warming up to the Irish Quest. After the Dagarathians had been sent off, the next order of business entailed solving the mystery of King Clarendon of Tara. Whatever had happened in such a short time to cause such a turnaround from being chummy to uncommunicative? This was given to Edwin as his next assignment. He would include Greer in this for if anyone could crack open the mysterious Clarendon it would be her. Nothing new had developed since the last communication from Tara when Clarendon rejected any involvement with the invasion of Dagarath. Sources from within Tara did not indicate anything untoward in the government there. Clarendon and his inner circle of nobles were still firmly in control. There was no indication the King of Tara had been pressured by anyone to back off in his relationship with Evansing and her allies. King Erith, Percival, Greer and several chief ministers met to consider the Tara Mystery, as it was now being known.

Erith began, "I believe the most intelligent initial approach is to propose Clarendon comes here for discussions or Edwin and Greer go there. What do you think?"

Greer asked if she could speak.

Erith replied, "Yes, of course, dear."

Greer continued, "In my brief acquaintance with King Clarendon I believe I discerned that part of his seemingly mysterious ways is due to a remarkably sensitive nature. That nature is not initially apparent for he certainly conducts himself like a typical king in many ways. Nevertheless, I believe something seemingly inconsequential has created some sort of offense for Clarendon. It is probably something he is not fully aware of, but it created a sense of no inside him when he considered furthering his involvement with us. I believe we should re-visit how we introduced Clarendon to his involvement with the Dagarathian campaign. Do we have copies of the correspondence sent?"

"Yes," replied Erith, "we always keep a copy of everything going out to other kings."

Turning to one of the attending scribes he ordered all the correspondence with Tara to be brought to them at once.

Fifteen minutes later the pertinent scrolls were brought to the meeting.

Greer asked, "Father, may I review them?"

Erith replied, "Yes, of course."

In the course of her reading the scrolls she uncovered something which tweaked her.

Greer read aloud, "We are expecting you to provide at least 4,000 troops and provisions not only for your own men but also sufficient to feed 2,000 allied troops for up to four weeks."

She continued, "I believe this may have been a little too demanding and direct for Clarendon's sensibilities. He had just come a long way from where he began and all of sudden he is expected to make a very substantial commitment."

Erith pondered what she said, "Yes, I believe you are right. I take full responsibility for the wording. Next time, my dear, I will get you to handle correspondence with Clarendon. So what do you suggest we do now?"

Greer responded, "I will write a note expressing my interest in visiting Clarendon and his family. I will express my desire to also bring along Edwin. Somehow I need to word it in a conciliatory manner which almost apologizes for the previous communication, yet without outright implying the wording offended him. This will be tricky, but I can do it." She said the final sentence with such confidence no one doubted she could do it.

She drafted the message and had it sent away three days later.

CHAPTER 44

Eight days later Greer received a reply. The favor Greer had with Clarendon must still be there for he said yes to a visit. He invited them to come in four weeks. Greer issued a prompt acceptance of the invitation. Now to plan the strategy for the visit, she and Erith decided a gift would be brought for Clarendon of one of Erith's favorite horses. Also there would be gifts for Clarendon's wife and their children. Greer relished the prospect of selecting the gifts.

The four weeks passed and the morning for the departure to Tara had arrived. Edwin and Greer were eager to fulfill this assignment. They'd had a splendid time of hanging out together around Evansing. They'd also spent a week traveling to Aldred and celebrating the wedding between Kerris and Athandra. Now they got to do something that teamed them up in an adventure of national importance. Three hundred troops escorted them, which indicated some concern for their safety by Erith.

As they got within a couple hundred yards of the gates of Tara they could see Clarendon and Kendy coming out to greet them. They looked pleased to see them. When they got right up to them it appeared as though nothing unusual had happened. They appeared to both be genuinely pleased with the opportunity to re-connect. Indeed they almost appeared to be too pleased given the recent history.

Everyone in the royal family and the nobles they met were extremely pleasant and delighted to meet Edwin and Greer. The Evansing couple found this very gratifying. After awhile Edwin and Greer noticed wherever they looked people were smiling non-stop. Even the servants and guards were smiling. The externals all looked great, but something in the couple's inner senses told them not all was what it appeared to be. It should be fantastic that everybody seemed so upbeat and happy. However, it seemed very unnatural. They had never encountered such universal merriment before.

That evening in their suite, Edwin asked Greer, "What do you think about all the good humor we've witnessed today?"

Greer replied, "I think it is most peculiar. I don't think I heard any conversation of depth all night. Everyone just engaged in continual frivolity. Do you feel different since we've arrived here?"

"Not really."

She continued, "Neither do I, but I do sense there is something not so benign at work in Tara. Maybe we should both ask for dreams to see if we can clue into what is happening."

"Great idea, Percival, I mean, Greer."

That night Greer sat on a cloud way above Tara. Below her she saw a huge blood red dragon resting over the capital of Tara and its environs. She could see right through the dragon. As she peered at the scene before her, she saw how the dragon released a green liquid onto the people below. She saw an arrow pointing to the liquid. Written on the arrow were the words "complacency with the short-term and frivolous." As the people received more and more of this green liquid, they became increasingly inclined to not only be okay with just living out their day to day activities, but they started to believe it was all there was. There seemed to be an extra zinger with it which made people inordinately happy about the frivolous and ultimately inconsequential. At first this seemed like it could even be a good thing, after all people were happy and content. But then she saw a vision showing this situation being like people having a beautiful picnic, while floating ever closer to a 1,000 foot drop over a massive waterfall.

Edwin dreamt he attended a meeting in a hall with Clarendon and his nobles. Everybody appeared agreeable and said yes, they wanted to be a part of the Irish Quest. They also agreed to supply whatever Evansing and her allies required of them in the way of supplies and troops. Then the dream fast forwarded to receiving back from Tara a response like the last one. Except this time Clarendon refused to assist in any way for the upcoming Merethath invasion. The refusal came because the complacency made Tara unwilling to risk loss and discomfort by participating in the Quest.

The next morning the two traded notes on their dreams.

"So, dear, what do you think we should do next?" asked Edwin.

"Oh you're asking me for my opinion? I like that. Are you sure you are a native Irish man, or did you drop in from some superior civilization?"

"What do you mean? You know I value your input?"

"Yes, I know that, but given the normal attitude of Irish men toward their women, it still startles me when you treat me like I have something of consequence to contribute. Especially, since you've asked my opinion in this very critical matter."

"Greer, we are a team. I see you being an equal in our negotiating new relationships and alliances. In many cases you will be the dominant player because you combine winsomeness with wisdom which almost nobody can resist. Besides that, you are very cute."

"Wow, that's really how you see me?"

"I wouldn't say it if I didn't mean it. Now what do you think we should consider doing about this Tara situation? Oh by the way I wondered how do we keep from being infected by this complacency. After all we are in the same environment"

Greer replied, "I don't think we are as vulnerable because both of us are very focused on this Irish Quest. It is a quest that is the antithesis of complacency. For it is based on not being satisfied with the status quo and the normal way life. We recognize our life purpose is something greater than us."

"Okay I agree with you, but we should keep an eye on one another for signs of change. We should also get out of here as quickly as possible. Of course we need to resolve the dragon problem. There is no point in negotiating when Tara will back out anyway. I wonder if Patrick would help us in this situation, or perhaps the angel Prospero. Yes, that's it, Prospero could help us. I don't know how Percival summoned him. I'll ask him to come. Prospero, we need your help with this dragon over Tara. Please come."

They waited and waited and waited. Nothing happened.

Edwin added, "The spiritual realm operates on its own timetable. I think he will come. Let's give him till tomorrow morning. If he doesn't come we will try something else."

One bright spot was the time Kendy and Greer spent together. There appeared to be a genuine bonding between the two. However, Greer noted a good and bad aspect to the connection. More and more Kendy emulated Greer not only in vital aspects such as values but also in ways which were contrary to Kendy's identity as a person. It seemed as though Kendy valued Greer more than herself. When this dawned on Greer she reminded Kendy she had her own inherent value and beauty. That included her being true to herself. Being a genuine Kendy was more important than being a copy of Greer.

That evening as the couple prepared to retire for the night, Prospero showed up. Both Edwin and Greer were startled with fright and then began to adjust to having this majestic being in their midst.

"Greetings, Edwin and Greer," the angel began, "you have requested my assistance."

"Yes, we have," replied Edwin. "By the way is it possible for you to give us a heads up when you are coming? Or is it standard angel procedure to scare people with your entrance?"

"Do you want me to reduce my appearances to the mundane and ordinary? Or do you want to have something you will remember, something of the mystery of the Divine?"

"Okay if you put it that way, I prefer being uncomfortable as opposed to reducing you to the ordinary. As I am sure you know there is a dragon over Tara, which has created a fortress of complacency in the people. This has created a reluctance in them to want to join us in the pursuit of Irish unity. We have two options. Kill them all and be done with it. Or get rid of the dragon. We prefer the latter option."

Prospero, being all business, continued, "The dragon is here because he has been invited by the chief warlock in Tara. This warlock has been given authority over Tara through an agreement made by Clarendon's father with the dark side. This agreement occurred when Clarendon was a young boy. He had suffered a serious injury in a fall and the doctors did not expect him to live. Since he was the only male heir of the king, this created an extra measure of desperation concerning his recovery. The chief warlock, through an intermediary, communicated the possibility of Clarendon's recovery. The King sent for the warlock and asked him to do whatever was in his power to help his son. First the warlock asked the King to agree to give him spiritual authority over Tara. This the King foolishly agreed to do. His desperation led him to not consider the implications of such an agreement. The King had limited interest or respect for the spiritual and consequently sold it cheap. His concern for self outweighed the interests of his subjects. Clarendon got healed and recovered. The dark side has an inroad in his life through this healing. Consequently, Clarendon is easily influenced by the warlock. The same warlock is still alive. He has kept himself much in the background, being surreptitious in how he uses his spiritual authority over Clarendon and Tara. The dark side is not keen to have a united Ireland. Whether it is represented by Druids or warlocks, the dark side will do whatever it can to foil Irish unity. It knows the Divine Banner of Victory desires it, and their cause will be weakened as a result. The warlock released the dragon of complacency shortly after Clarendon agreed to you coming to Tara. The warlock knew he could frustrate you with a process of having to deal with an apparently amenable and cooperative Clarendon, but one who would never deliver on his promises."

At this point the angel stopped and stood in silence. Both Greer and Edwin awaited the next words, but after several moments still nothing came. They stood there wondering whether they should say something. Then Prospero slowly disappeared from their sight and was gone.

"What?" Edwin blurted out, somewhat exasperated, "He didn't give us what we are to do next. Why would he do that?"

Greer put her hand on Edwin's arm and said soothingly, "Relax, Edwin, I'm sure there is a good reason for it. Either he will come back or somehow we'll get the next step. Maybe it is simply eliminating this warlock. We at least now know what the source of the problem is."

"So do we try to find this warlock, or do we try to get some more info from Prospero or some other source of insight? Maybe we should try to connect with Patrick for this. He certainly had a lot of success with battling Druids and probably warlocks as well."

Greer replied, "I believe you are right about asking Patrick. Let's do that. Do you think I can ask him?"

"I don't see why not. I don't think the spiritual realm considers gender as a factor. After all Joan is a woman and she is powerful."

Greer said, "St. Patrick we respectfully ask your assistance in getting rid of this warlock. Please come and help us now."

Boom! There he was. St. Patrick himself.

"Hello, Edwin. Hello, Greer," greeted Patrick.

"Wow, Patrick, that was fast."

"Yes, Prospero gave me the heads up. We decided to tag team this assignment. It adds to the fun factor. After all we are into fun. You may think we are super serious all the time, but we do have a sense of humor. Edwin, you should have seen your face when Prospero left without telling you what you wanted to know. You reacted like he left out the punch line and left you hanging. Yes, your response made it all worthwhile. Mind you it also created an opportunity for Greer to demonstrate her ability to deal wisely. Greer, you are a woman of great wisdom."

"Thank you, sir, for your kindness. It is a great pleasure to meet the patron saint of Ireland," responded Greer.

"Thank you, but don't be unduly impressed by that. Only His Grace made it possible. As far as that goes it's only His Grace that makes anything possible."

Edwin asked, "So how do we get rid of this warlock?"

Patrick looked at him a little sharply.

"Edwin, I'm not like Prospero, I'm not into just doing business. I'm also into interacting a little. Let me at least get to know your darling wife a little better."

Then turning toward Greer he said, "My how fortunate Edwin is to have a wife like you. If he ever forgets that, just let me know and I will be sure to remind him."

Greer blushed and thanked Patrick for his kind remarks. They then chatted about some light and airy matters while Edwin looked on.

Edwin didn't know whether to be annoyed or pleased at first, but then he realized he had the wrong attitude. If this divine emissary thought they had time to chit chat about unimportant matters, then who was he to question it.

Patrick had to force himself to bring his conversation with Greer to a close, for he greatly enjoyed his chat with her.

He then switched to a more on assignment demeanor and spoke, "The warlock you want to eliminate is a very slippery individual. He gives the impression of being noble and wanting only the best interests for Tara. Therefore he has many supporters. Most of these are not into witchcraft per se. However, due to the low level of true spirituality in Tara, no one has discernment about his true intentions. I share this so you will know you are on your own, as far as who you can depend on among the citizens of Tara. The warlock's name is Eldredge. He has his residence on the western outskirts of the capital."

Patrick pulled an arrow out of his cloak and handed it to Edwin.

"You must use this arrow. It is tipped with gold as you can see. The reason for that is because Eldredge has been into some very powerful magic. It has rendered him almost invincible against attack. The only vulnerability is a gold tipped arrow into his heart."

"Really? You mean if I swung my sword at his head he wouldn't die?"

"That's right. As hard as it may be to believe it, you could not kill him with a sword. Only this arrow shot to his heart will accomplish the objective."

"So do you have any potion to make me invisible?" asked Edwin. "I know no other way to get close to Eldredge with a bow and arrow undetected. He must have guards and attendants surrounding him constantly."

Patrick replied, "You will have to do it tonight. I am going to give you the power to be transformed into an owl. The bow and arrow will be reduced in size and concealed in your feathers upon your transformation. They will be returned to regular size upon you becoming a man again. Tonight is the night. I will fly with you and show you which house and where to enter. Are you ready to go now?"

"Yes, if you are ready then I am ready."

"Good, go get your bow to go with the arrow."

Edwin got his bow and also holding the arrow stood with excited anticipation.

Swoosh, in a twinkling of an eye both men were transformed into owls. For Edwin it was indeed a close encounter of the third kind. He felt extremely weird as he still thought of himself as a man, but now he had the body of an owl.

Patrick flew out the window into the darkness of the night closely followed by Edwin. They flew for several minutes until they got to a rather large sinister looking home in the west end of Tara. It had gargoyles on the walls surrounding it, and also on the iron gates, which blocked the entrance to its grounds.

They stopped on the wall. Patrick communicated with his thoughts to Edwin. He indicated the room with the top window above them was where Eldredge slept. Once Edwin entered the room, Patrick would change him back into a man to carry out the mission. Edwin landed on the window sill. As he stood there a moment, he noticed a pair of malevolent green eyes staring at him. Edwin leaped backward and out the window. A large black cat whizzed by him and grazed him with its outreached paw. The cat, in its eagerness to catch Edwin the owl, leapt with wild abandon out the window and now fell the two stories down to the ground. Whereupon landing it yelped and screamed. Patrick communicating by thoughts told Edwin to try again. Again Edwin landed on the windowsill. Eldredge had not woken up and his breathing remained steady.

Edwin hopped inside and stood on the floor. Then he started to grow and in a moment he returned back to being his young man self. He pulled out the bow and arrow and took aim, trusting that in the dark he could accurately pick out Eldredge's heart. He let it go and thud went the sound of the arrow finding its target. At that point the door to the room flung open as two guards came inside. Edwin took out his dagger, which he always carried with him. The first guard came at him with his sword upraised. Edwin deflected the blade, which pointed hard in his direction. Edwin then flung a stool at the guard catching him on the side of the head. The guard went down stunned by the blow. The other guard came with his sword and started swinging away at Edwin, who jumped back to avoid being hit. Edwin pulled down the curtains around the window and used it to grab the sword the next time it came within reach. He pulled it out of the guard's hand and picked it up. Now he had the advantage for the guard was defenseless except for his dagger. There was a general uproar and Edwin could hear other guards running up the steps.

He heard in his head, "Run to the window and jump."

CHAPTER 45

Without considering whether it was rational or not, he dove out the window and before he reached the ground he flew as an owl and swooped over the wall. Patrick quickly joined him. The two arrived back at Edwin's and Greer's quarters. There they were awaited by Greer, who wasn't going to bed until Edwin came back.

The two men changed back into their human forms. A shudder went over Greer as she witnessed this most dynamic transformation. She increasingly had become accustomed to the marvelous and astounding, but it did not leave her unaffected.

Patrick began, "Congratulations, Edwin. I have been informed your arrow hit its mark and Eldredge is now on the other side. The dragon has left and we should start to see a change in the people of Tara very soon. I am now ready to go, but keep me in mind for future missions. You and your wife are starting to grow on me. I will request I be given priority in being assigned to you."

"Thank you, sir," replied Edwin.

The saint then disappeared from view leaving them alone.

Greer looked at Edwin with relief and swung her arms around him holding tight. They then talked about what had happened. In the distance they could hear a messenger shouting Eldredge had been killed. After the couple had gone to sleep, they heard a knock on the door. There stood the

347

sheriff of Tara with several guards. In his hand he held Edwin's bow. He asked if he could come in. Edwin nodded yes.

The sheriff asked, "Is this your bow?"

Edwin took the bow and looked at it closely; he noted it had his Edwin of Evansing initials in the bottom inside part of it. He gave it back to the sheriff and went to look in the storage area just off the room they were in. He came back a moment later.

"It's not there. My bow is not where I had left it. This must be mine. It certainly looks like it and those are my initials." He picked it up and pulled the string back. "Yes, I would say this is my bow. Thank you, sir, for returning it to me. Wherever did you find it?"

"This bow is the weapon used in the murder of Eldredge, a prominent citizen of this kingdom. Do you have any idea how this bow came to be at his home?"

"No, sir, I do not. I didn't know it had gone missing until just now. I hadn't used it since I arrived in Tara."

The sheriff looked inquisitively into the eyes of Edwin and Greer. Seemingly satisfied they knew nothing of the murder, he bid them goodnight and asked to be pardoned for his late night intrusion.

After he left, Greer and Edwin sat in silence for a moment.

Greer whispered into her husband's ear, "I never knew you could be such a consummate liar. I almost believed you and I know you did it."

Edwin replied, "See what your influence has done for me. Before I met you I could never have lied like that."

She laughed at his cheeky response.

The next day at breakfast with Clarendon and his family, the tone had become rather subdued. Part of the blame undoubtedly lay with the news of the murder of Eldredge. But as well it was a bit like a drunk becoming sober. In this case the whole kingdom had been on a perpetual high from the narcotic of complacency. Now a new realization started to come upon the people of Tara; an awareness of life being more than just day by day or self-absorption. Now people started thinking again about things beyond themselves and their own little world.

Edwin and Greer looked knowingly at one another realizing the atmosphere had shifted. Soon it would return to a normal homeostasis where people could decide for themselves whether they wanted to be joyful and happy, without an external influence impacting their thoughts and emotions.

Clarendon seemed rather ambivalent toward Edwin. He must have given permission to the sheriff to question Edwin the night before. No evidence tied him to the murder, other than his bow at the scene, which had been explained away. As well, due to the darkness, the guards could not verify without doubt the identification of the intruder. One of them said it certainly seemed like it could have been Edwin. However, Tara was not about to create a major diplomatic row with Evansing over suspect evidence. Besides, Clarendon much liked Greer and the influence she had on his daughter Kendy.

An official funeral for Eldredge would be held and so everything was put on hold for a couple of days with respect to discussions between Clarendon and Edwin. Ironically, Edwin and Greer were invited to attend.

The next day at the funeral, Edwin had an opportunity to walk past the casket and see who he had killed. The corpse's face had a gross look, dark and foreboding. One got the impression he had had a lot of hitchhikers in his life. In other words, there had been numerous spirits from the dark side inhabiting this now deceased warlock.

On the day following the funeral, Clarendon seemed to be much more amenable to serious discussions about ongoing cooperation with Evansing. Indeed the change in the atmosphere became evermore apparent. Edwin asked him to give a number of troops he would be willing to commit. He indicated he would supply up to 2,000 soldiers if requested for a military campaign. As well he would be willing to provide supplies for up to 1,000 other allied troops. Edwin noted this to be exactly half what he had been asked to provide for the war with Dagarath. He would have wanted a higher commitment but decided against trying to push Clarendon. At least a commitment had been obtained. And a major obstacle in the form of Eldredge had been eliminated.

The next day Edwin and Greer said their goodbyes. Clarendon had warmed up somewhat to Edwin during the last day of the visit. It boded well for the future. Greer and Kendy had an extended good-bye and they both had tears of emotion at having to say farewell.

Upon their return to Evansing, a servant requested the couple meet with Erith about briefing him on the trip. Plus there were urgent new developments which had arisen with Merethath.

CHAPTER 46

Erith was pleased to hear Clarendon had made at least some significant commitment. He also agreed it was wise not to have pushed him for more.

"He will have to make good on his commitment sooner than he had expected," commented Erith. "We had hoped to take the initiative with Merethath, but apparently our friend King Taryn has decided the best defense is a good offense. He has sent his army over the Nerland border and has already advanced twenty miles into Nerland territory. That is the news we received today. It took two days in getting to us so who knows what the status is as we speak. The call from Nerland has been issued for us to go to arms immediately. As well we are sending out requests to Aldred and Tara. The Dagarathians are being asked to permit the Aldred army to cross through their territory."

Merethath had waited until all the foreign armies were out of Dagarath and safely back in their home territory. This meant Evansing and Aldred had significant distances to travel to get to the fighting. In Dagarath they had been right on Merethath's doorstep. The allied troops had returned home. No invasion of Merethath had been expected for another couple of months. Now their hand had been forced to undertake an earlier conflict. At first it seemed a foolish gambit by Taryn to expose himself to total devastation by the allies. His kingdom stood all alone in its battle with the allies. Perhaps he counted on swaying Tara to his cause. He may not have known of the growing connection Evansing enjoyed with that kingdom. And now Tara itself would be fighting against him. Who could understand why people did things which made no sense? Evansing's army would be ready to go in two days. Edwin would be the field commander and Erith the overall commander.

Two days later the Evansing army journeyed on their way to Nerland to come to the rescue of their closest and oldest ally. Clarendon had agreed to supply as promised and so Tara troops were expected to start marching tomorrow or the day after. Dagarath had granted permission to the Aldred army to march across its territory. Erith decided that to ask Randar to contribute would be a bit premature. Its new king, Chafen, was still consolidating his hold and that kingdom continued to recover from the war it had fought with the allies.

While en route to Nerland the news came that the capital of Nerland had already been attacked and conquered. This was shocking and unexpected. Edwin started thinking something extraordinary must be working to enable Merethath to be so victorious so soon.

"What good fortune," he said to himself, "that Athandra is now in Aldred."

Initially upon crossing into Nerland there had been no sign of conflict. There were no Nerland troops as they had all gone to the defense of their capital.

Something in Edwin said, "STOP!" He shared with Erith, who rode alongside him what he had heard. Erith agreed he should go with the voice. Edwin issued the command for the army to stop its advance. At this point he didn't know why they needed to stop, but he knew he had to listen and respond.

King Taryn of Merethath for all his evil ways had never been known to seriously engage the dark side. As Edwin contemplated what to do next he started to get a vision of what was going on. While sitting on his horse with his eyes wide open he saw a host of seemingly invincible beings riding with the Merethath army. These beings were invisible to the natural eye and were part of the dark side. Their faces were contorted with hatred and contempt. They energized the Merethath troops to a new level of intensity beyond the norm. It had made them unstoppable in their battles against Nerland. The capital of Nerland had been taken so easily because these beings had inspired traitorous actions by some of its residents. Certain key gatekeepers had opened the gates at night to allow the Merethath army to enter. Then the vision ceased.

"Well now we know about the extraordinary part," Edwin thought to himself.

The men around Edwin figured something unusual must be happening to him as they could see him deeply engaged. When the vision stopped, Edwin looked around and could see he had become the center of attention. The King, surrounding officers and men were all looking at him, some bemused by the strange look on Edwin's face. He at first felt a little self-conscious and even a little embarrassed, but he quickly threw it off.

He looked at their faces and point blank told them he had had a vision. He told them what he had seen. Some of the men readily accepted it while others looked askance at what they were hearing. This represented the first time Edwin had shared with these men one of his supernormal experiences. It was a bold move not without risk. For invariably there would always be some who would be skeptical. It could reduce his credibility in their eyes. Fortunately with these individuals, Edwin had a vast pool of past achievements which could not be disputed. They may shake their heads at what they heard, but they knew with Edwin in charge they would win. Edwin shared his experience for the benefit of others. He felt it important to expand their horizons with respect to the spiritual realm. Even if he lost points with some, it would be worth it to help others grow. One person, of course not thrown by what Edwin shared, was Erith.

As Edwin further considered what he had seen, a rider came up with news from the front.

The message read as follows:

"Gondar has usurped his father's throne. King Keltic has been imprisoned. Nerland troops have now been ordered to ally with Merethath and march against Evansing. Surprisingly there has been little resistance to this order."

Erith asked the messenger, "How close are the enemy armies?"

"Not more than twenty miles away," replied the messenger.

Edwin considered what lay before them, "This represented a large challenge. The Aldred and Tara armies would not be joining them until tomorrow. There would be precious little time to create a coordinated effort against a now vastly greater army. What had been a great confidence as to the outcome of this war, has now been changed to concern and fear of a great loss. "Oh no!" When he realized he felt fear. "This will never do," he chided himself.

King Erith ordered his officers to dismount for they were about to have an urgent meeting. He read the message out to his senior officers.

The King, Edwin and the senior officers started considering their options and possible courses of action. Edwin would have loved to have gotten away alone for awhile and see if he could draw upon supernatural assistance from someone like Joan or Patrick, but he had no opportunity. It would be unacceptable to do it now. Besides he felt a strong impression there had been a shift in the seasons. Not the normal seasons like spring and summer, but rather a shift in the seasons of life. Just like that, it seemed that where they had been in a charge and advance season, they were now in a consolidate and hold season. This could well include retreating from their present position in Nerland. He pondered this impression. It stayed there, and he knew his brain didn't all of a sudden start thinking these thoughts. It just came on him, and he knew it was true. It also sickened him as it brought with it the possible realization their goal of uniting Ireland may not be achieved.

One of the officers, a high ranking noble, placed before the group the option of a strategic retreat. The officer expressed that the dream for a united Ireland involving the whole island was commendable but may not be feasible at this time. He suggested they be satisfied with the degree of unity which had been achieved with several kingdoms. These were now all beginning to operate in a high level of integration and cooperation in key commercial, governmental and military matters. It didn't mean they had to dismiss the idea of achieving the ultimate objective but perhaps not right now. Initially, Erith responded in anger at the suggestion of retreat and being satisfied with what had been accomplished thus far. As Erith blustered his disappointment with such a consideration, Edwin wrestled within himself whether he should share what had come to him about a shift in the seasons. If he shared it in front of the others, Erith may consider it as an act of disloyalty. He decided he needed to take the King aside, and alone one on one he would share what he sensed. The meeting continued on for another hour with no clear convincing strategy coming forth. Erith, uncharacteristically, could not decide on a specific course of action. Several times he asked Edwin for his input, and Edwin feeling rather embarrassed, had to say he had no clear idea as to a best action. If everyone had felt comfortable in expressing their true feelings with their king, they would have said they were leaning toward retreat.

Edwin decided he could not wait any longer.

"Sire, may I please talk to you in private for a moment?"

Erith looked quizzically at Edwin and nodded yes. They then both stepped away from the others some distance so as to not be overheard.

"Sire, a strong impression came to me about the time you called for a meeting. This impression indicates there has been a shift in the seasons. As you know we have been very much in a charge and advance mode for sometime now to unite Ireland. We have used both military and diplomatic maneuverings to achieve that objective. There has been significant success to date. The impression I got most definitely indicated we are now in a consolidate and hold season. As unpalatable as this may seem to you, Sire, I agree with the proposal made to retreat."

"Traitor, you are an ungrateful traitor. How could you side with someone who wants to retreat?" replied Erith.

The vehemence of the response took Edwin by surprise. He had expected a strong negative reaction but not this strong. He could feel a wave come over him as Erith spoke to him. Struggling to maintain his composure, Edwin remained silent for a moment.

"So do you have anything to say for yourself, Edwin?" demanded Erith.

"Sire, this is not based on me deciding all of a sudden we should retreat." Edwin's voice got stronger and indeed firmer as he went. "This came upon me on its own. It's not an attitude I had been harboring beforehand. One moment I am flat out in charge and advance mode. And the next I am getting this strong impression the times had changed. Percival and I have had discussions about the timing of things. About how there are different seasons in life. To do what may be an excellent thing in the wrong season can be disastrous. If we are no longer in a time for us to continue the active pursuit of the uniting of Ireland, then it is time to stop. It is as simple as that. I too am much disappointed by this turn of events."

Erith had started to calm down, but he remained quite distressed as to what he heard. This dream to unite Ireland had totally possessed him. To now come to the realization it should be put on hold, even for a while, almost devastated Erith. He continued to glare at Edwin but remained silent. Edwin could tell Erith started to come to some sort of terms with what he had heard. At least Erith's glare had noticeably softened.

"Let's return to the meeting," the King said in a very disheartened tone.

The men had been waiting in silence until their leaders returned.

"Gentlemen, I realize I may have not made it easy for everyone to truly express how they felt about our options. I now want to rectify that. I promise there will be no negative ramifications, if in your considered opinion we should retreat. Who thinks we should retreat?"

Six out of eight officers put up their hands including Edwin. The other officers were much surprised at seeing Edwin's hand go up.

"Gentlemen, it pains me to agree with you in retreating, but I will abide by your decision. Let's make arrangements immediately for an orderly retreat. As well we need to advise Aldred and Tara to cease their advance and return home. We will need to engage them and Randar and Dagarath in serious diplomatic meetings to ensure what we have achieved does not unravel. Any further comments?"

Silence.

The King and his officers then spent a half hour working out the details of the retreat and the messages to be sent to their allies who were advancing to the front.

The impression Edwin had received about a shift had undoubtedly been reflected in a general malaise over the Evansing troops. It hadn't been apparent or perhaps it had been ignored by Edwin. The soldiers had lacked their usual enthusiasm to charge into battle. It became most apparent upon their return into home territory for they gave an excited cheer when they crossed their frontier.

"Interesting," thought Edwin, "how the seasonal shift impacted the moods of the men. I need to be tuned in better to their feelings. If I had we could have at least factored it in sooner with respect to our decision to march to war. Mind you neither Erith nor I and probably not many of the officers would have entertained anything different than what we did. We just weren't ready for it and the shift had not yet become apparent. Or perhaps it shifted when we were en route. The spiritual realm is a curious thing, hard to figure out, but it's imperative we try."

Defensive positions were set up at the border. The big unknown was if Merethath and Nerland now had plans to invade Evansing or one of its allies. After two days the news came that the Merethath and Nerland armies had stopped within two miles of the Evansing border. Four days later they still had not advanced. Then a courier came with a joint communiqué from King Taryn and self-proclaimed King Gondar. The message indicated they would not invade Evansing as long as Evansing agreed to not invade Nerland. Erith returned the courier with the message that they agreed not to invade Nerland. Three days later the bulk of the enemy troops left leaving a force necessary for manning the border with Evansing. As discovered later, most of the Merethath troops returned to their own kingdom. They took King Keltic with them and imprisoned him there. Merethath had stationed a sizeable contingent for the defense of Nerland. The official Nerland reason given said they were there in case of Evansing aggression. The real reason was suspected to be to prop up Gondar, whose close allegiance to Merethath was generally reviled by the people of Nerland. As subsequent intelligence reports would indicate, Gondar got his orders from King Taryn of Merethath.

Upon removal of most of the enemy troops the Evansing army did likewise with their own troops.

The last few miles into Evansing town were especially painful for Erith. The internal dialogue for Erith became pretty dark. All he could think about was that his dream was dying. Or at least that is what he felt. It seemed this quest, which had so consumed him now hung precariously over a ledge. It appeared to him all he had invested would fall off that ledge and into the abyss below. The men around Erith could not recall seeing him so glum since his wife had died. No one dared say a word to

Erith. They didn't know if he was working up to be in a rage or severe depression or both.

In contrast to the mood of Erith, the troops were feeling exuberant about their early return home. The townspeople turned out in droves to greet their returning sons and fathers.

Edwin, as well sensed a void in his soul. He felt as though his reason for being had been taken away. He didn't have the same degree of grief Erith felt, but he too grieved. The fact Edwin had gotten the impression of the shift in seasons helped to mitigate for him the impact of the retreat. The impression had at least given him some understanding of the retreat, and the likelihood of no longer pursuing the Quest, at least for now.

Greer of course was ecstatic about having her Prince Charming back in her arms. Certainly the prospect of Edwin spending more time at home pleased her. Nevertheless, she felt deeply concerned about her father and Edwin. She knew these men and some of the other men could not settle for a mundane ordinary life. These were men created to build huge. Even though she wanted the feel good aspects of marriage with Edwin, she also shared his vision for seeing a united Ireland. Yes, it involved pain and sacrifice, but for her as well, the fulfillment of destiny transcended her need for personal comfort.

Erith and Percival met together in the King's chambers. There was no one else with whom Erith could share how he felt. For him, Percival embodied an extraordinary combination of wisdom and compassion. He trusted him like no one else. The two had gone through many painful and challenging experiences together. Percival had Erith's absolute trust for maintaining confidences. Kings always struggle in finding people with whom they can be real, and who will also be willing to tell them what they need to hear.

"Percival, I am so glad I can talk to someone like you. I feel like my heart has been ripped out. Life seems like endless winter with no hope of spring. I have to give myself reasons to get out of bed in the morning. This may even feel worse than when my wife died. I feel like I have died, but I'm still walking around. My most encouraging thought is to tell myself maybe I will die today."

"Erith, you have experienced death, the death of a vision. It was as real and alive as your wife was. You need to do the grieving. When you embrace that, you will facilitate the process of letting it go. In time a new vision will come to you, or perhaps the Quest will return in a new form."

"I was so sure what I had received was Divine revelation. It has shaken my belief in my ability to know what is truth. Do I hear accurately or am I influenced by my own ambitions? Even worse, it raises questions like, is He faithful?"

"Yes, you have now unwillingly become part of a process in going deeper in your higher life relationships. Painful realities invariably create questions. If we choose to embrace our challenges as opportunities for personal growth, they can bring profit to a situation which otherwise only seems like loss."

"It may take me awhile to really believe that, Percival. At this time I only see myself as a burnt out wreck at the side of life's road. That is so extreme, given my position as king with all the attendant privileges and other marvelous aspects of my life. Yet, that is how I feel."

"That may well be how you feel, but soon you will need to combine grieving with exercising a credible presence in the kingdoms which have become directly allied or potentially sympathetic to our cause. This is required in order to keep the gains made. There will have to be salesmanship on maintaining the level of integration and cooperation already in place. Aldred should be easily convinced. King Clarendon of Tara may well wonder about the credibility of what he has just become a part of. The King of Dagarath will probably require additional coaxing to continue warming up to the idea of at least a partially united version of Ireland. Randar's king is a strong supporter and should still be willing to continue the process of a closer association. With these kingdoms I believe it would be appropriate to establish a model of what a united Ireland could look like."

Erith looked at Percival. He felt like some glimmer of light and hope had come back. If this was what was available to him, then that is what he would do.

36375946R00204

Made in the USA
Charleston, SC
01 December 2014